THISTLEDOWN

BY

SULLATOBER
DALTON

The right of Sullatober Dalton to be identified as the author if this work has been asserted by him in accordance with the Copyright, Design and Patents Act, 1988.

This is a work of fiction and any resemblance of any character to any real person or persons, living or dead, is purely coincidental

For Ann and Archie

I would like to thank Val Hughes for transforming a loose idea into a cover work of art.

THISTLEDOWN

THISTLEDOWN

CHAPTER 1

A flush of anger and frustration swept over Fergus Findlay as he turned the corner of the farmhouse at The Mearns and saw the men standing waiting. His first reaction was that whoever was following had somehow managed to get word of his coming to their friends.

Instinctively, his left hand pressed against his waist to confirm the money belt was secure and it was only with a determined effort that he kept his right hand from reaching to his shoulder for the hilt of the broadsword that hung down his back, hidden in the folds of his plaid.

Regaining control, he maintained his easy stride, his eyes sweeping over the group. He didn't stare, but his glance saw no out of place finery or sullen aggression that might presage evil intent.

As the group showed only mild interest, he told himself there were many reasons, here in the Scottish Highlands in these years after Waterloo, why men would gather together in a farmyard like The Mearns; they could be waiting to be paid, or told what to do, or told to vacate their hill farms to make way for sheep.

After a nod to the men, he followed the track further into the glen.

You're not even sure you're being followed, he told himself. He'd just been feeling uneasy ever since leaving

Glasgow on his way north to Invercauld in Dornoch and home.

His last drove had been his most profitable and maybe it was just the money belt and being on his own that made him worry. He'd sent the hired drovers away north with the garrons, sturdy highland ponies, well suited to their work of carrying goods and food on the drove. Now he was alone and on foot.

When he'd first felt suspicious of being followed, just as a precaution, he'd turned off on a side track that led into a clump of trees and watched.

He'd seen nothing.

Still wary, as he neared Loch Lomond, he'd taken a long slant down into a valley. He'd walked steadily along the valley floor for a while before increasing his pace so that anyone following would have to hurry and show themselves if they wanted to keep him in sight. He'd looked back but seen no one.

He'd run up the facing slope and over the rim before circling back to watch.

Again, he'd seen nothing.

Still concerned, instead of going directly to Kirklea to visit Fiona McRae, he'd turned abruptly on to the cart road that led to The Mearns. The road didn't stop at the farmhouse but narrowed and continued up the glen and over the hill. If he walked to the head of the glen, he'd be able to look back. From there, he could go on quickly over the hill before turning off sharply into Kirklea's own valley.

Twenty minutes after passing The Mearns, he was following the track's back and forth wanderings between tufts of brown grass and patches of gorse as it climbed the long slope.

Having had nothing but a drink from a burn and a handful of oatmeal that morning, when he reached a spot where of a patch of birch trees on the high side of the track provided a break from the chilly fingers of the autumn breeze, he stopped to rest and eat. A low bank on the top side of the track provided a seat and he spread his plaid on the tufts of tough grass to let it air, sat down beside it with his legs dangling and took the oatcakes and cheese he'd kept for a midday break from his bag.

The spread plaid's splash of colour would be seen from a long way off.

Fergus relaxed and his thoughts drifted to Fiona and his determination to offer her an alternative to the constant struggle to keep Kirklea afloat. Was she all right, he wondered. He'd already paid some of the farm's debts, nothing like all, but enough to give them meal, flour, and sugar. He'd also paid the few pence she owed the haberdasher, no more than thread and needles, no cloth, so she was patching and darning but not making something new and that worried him.

Something disturbed his reverie and his gaze dropped down to the fields and the farmhouse in the valley. The men had been joined by someone with a gun and were spread out on either side, making a line that hooked round in a shallow crescent, a beater's line, beating towards the hill.

Fergus wondered idly what they were beating for - a fox, possibly, pheasant or partridge, maybe. The slope was long and, no doubt, they would flush out whatever it was they wanted before they came near him.

What was that? Something in the background. Maybe a shadow moving across the hillside, a crow sliding across the sun.

There it was again! A dark shape angling across to the shelter of a clump of gorse low down on the slope. He realised it was a dog, and the dog had come from the field the men were beating in. The dog hadn't jumped the low dry-stone wall where it would have been seen, but had slid through the gate and must have crept along in the shadow of the wall for fifty yards before risking the half shelter of the grassy clumps that dotted the slope.

Fergus smiled as the black shape came out of the gorse at a lope but lost sight of it when it dropped into a burn. If it had been worrying sheep or cattle, Fergus would deal with it without sympathy, but for the moment, like himself, it was an outsider, and he focused on its movements.

The dog didn't show itself again until it turned into the ditch that led along the side of the track up to where Fergus watched. Even then, he'd only seen it because it was moving.

It came out of the ditch a few yards from Fergus.

It looked long and deliberately at Fergus, dark eyes staring into his, assessing each other - then Fergus touched the plaid and the dog slid under it between the grassy tufts and lay still.

When the men finally reached Fergus, the man with the gun, a big man in tweeds, who seemed to be in charge, came forward, uncocking his gun as he came. 'Have you seen a black collie pass here?' the man asked.

The florid features and blustering familiarity, reminded Fergus of Black Duncan, one of the farmers for whom he had driven cattle south, and produced the same dislike.

'Nothing has passed me,' Fergus answered truthfully.

'The black devil has been worrying my sheep,' the man added. 'If you see him, send word to me, if you please, Maitland of The Mearns.'

'We're no' certain it's the one that's doin' the worryin', Mr Maitland,' suggested one of the men.

Maitland turned on him. 'I don't care if I kill every black dog in the district; I'll stop my sheep being worried.'

'Are you for turning the place into a sheep farm then?' Fergus asked.

Maitland turned back to Fergus. 'I have already started.'

'And what of the fee farmers?' Fergus asked.

'Some already gone, some to go. What's it to you?'

'I only asked because I see Morrison there,' Fergus said, nodding his head towards the group of men waiting for further instructions. 'He bought some beasts from me the other day and paid a good price for them.'

'More fool he, he's one of the next to go,' said Maitland. He took a more intense look at Fergus then turned his look on the plaid. 'That's a nice plaid you have there, is it for sale?'

'No, it's not,' Fergus told him, mildly.

'It's a fine bit of material,' Maitland added, stepping forward and reaching out a hand to feel the tartan.

Fergus leaned forward and grabbed the outstretched hand, making Maitland's eyebrows lift in surprise. Fergus smiled as he stared into Maitland's eyes. 'It's mine,' he said quietly.

Maitland stepped back. 'No need to be so quick with your challenge,' Maitland told him. 'Mind you, you might need to be if you got a good price for your drove, there are enough thieves in this part of the world who would kill you for sixpence, never mind the decent price of a few cows. And remember, stolen money isn't like a beast, it leaves no track, or trail.'

'Oh, I can take care of myself, and who'd expect a man like me to have money?' Fergus answered, arms spread, smiling openly.

'That's true. You don't look much like a fighter. Wiry enough, I suppose, but short on weight.'

'It's not always brute strength that wins, Mr Maitland.'

'No. But it helps,' Maitland said, walking determinedly away to lead his men back down the hill.

Maitland's square back reminded Fergus even more of Black Duncan and he wondered again why Duncan had asked him to take only three of his cattle to market. He would need to sell his whole herd to stock his place with the sheep he seemed set on getting.

Fergus pushed that thought out of his mind. Maitland's last comment had touched on his main worry. He had golden guineas in the money belt round his waist, money to be divided between the others who had trusted him to sell their cattle. If Maitland felt the money was worth commenting on, others would hear of it and he must needs take care.

That was as far as he got in his musing because the dog crept out from under the plaid and nuzzled his hand. Without conscious thought of the name, Fergus said, 'Aye, Bruce, that Englishman would have had you hung and quartered like Wallace if he'd kenned you were there, but come away now, out of his road.'

＊

The dog seemed happy enough to go with Fergus. He smiled as the thought crossed his mind that, instead of being followed, daft as it seemed, he had somehow been delayed so that he could meet the dog. He grinned as the thought struck him that Old Babs at Ault-na-main would swear that was the truth of it.

Nevertheless, as he walked, he let his plaid flap in the breeze to make it easily seen. He walked over the lip of the hill at the head of The Mearns' glen but, instead of continuing on the track, he turned off to the side and made for the adjacent one in which Kirklea nestled.

He looked down the hill at the farm. It must have been a grand place in its day. The walls of the outbuildings were dry stone built, rugged under their sod roofs. The barn was timber built but black with the application of years of tarring. The yard, he knew was cobbled and the house beyond a solid stone two-story building with a slate roof. The front door was on the far side, facing further down to where the glen opened and gave a view of far hills. There had once been a driveway that swept up to that front door with half a dozen wide steps leading up to it.

That front door hadn't been opened in several years. The cobbles in the yard were half buried in moss and the sod roofs sagged and had fallen in here and there. The barn's black walls were stained brown where wind driven rain had washed the tar. In the last few times he had come, he'd felt he was visiting an aristocrat in a ragged coat. It was time he took Fiona away from this!

His father had used McRae's farm as a stopover for years. On the way south with their drove, glad to let the cattle rest and browse in the glen before the last stage to the markets. On the way back north, glad of a break before starting the climbs and dips through the western highlands before they reached the Great Glen and the road to the Moray Firth.

Fergus, now twenty-two, had first come with his father at the age of ten. They'd gone all the way to Glasgow to sell directly to customers rather than go to Crieff; his father reluctant to allow others to take the cattle south to England. On the return journey, while his and Fiona's father discussed the news Fergus's father brought from the city, Fergus and Fiona had roamed, running and laughing through the hills surrounding the valley farm every year until Fergus was sixteen and Fiona, at thirteen, though still skinny, was starting to develop into a young woman, and her mother became more protective.

Two years later, Fiona's mother had wasted away and Fiona's days had become filled with chores. Fergus helped when he was at Kirklea, hating to see Fiona lose more of her smiling infectious gaiety to tiredness with each visit.

Fergus's father had died two years ago and Fergus had taken on the droving as well as the Dornoch farm, buying up small bits of adjoining land to expand the farm with the money he earned. In two years' time, if all went well, he would be able to offer Fiona the kind of home and comfortable living she deserved.

That was the future he hoped for, but this evening, would she ask him to stay and eat? Would her father be so hungry for news that he'd get the chance to stay overnight in the barn? Her father rarely moved from the house these days and it was only a matter of time before they'd have to give up Kirklea. Would they last out the two years he needed to accumulate the money? Would Fiona wait another two years without some firm commitment on his part? At nineteen, she was getting old for marriage.

He knew of no rivals, but that didn't mean there were none; Fiona had become a striking young woman with long dark hair, brown eyes that were alternately smiling and calm. She was almost as tall as he was and he found it was disconcerting to look directly into her eyes. When he watched her move, with the wind blowing her dress against her, outlining the slim curves of her figure, he had no doubts about what he wanted to do. But then her eyes would challenge him, yet ask protection, warn him away, yet make him want to take her to a place she seemed to know of but was hidden from him.

While he hoped she would invite him to eat and sleep overnight in the barn, above all, he wanted her laughter and the lightness of her voice in his ears as he set off on the long trail to Easter Ross.

As he and the dog neared McRae's farm, with the late afternoon sun already gone behind the surrounding hills, Bruce ran ahead. The dog sniffed the air, making Fergus laugh, before it came back to Fergus' side.

'Satisfied?' Fergus grinned.

The black dog glanced up but kept moving, eyes searching, ears pricked alert as they approached the farmyard.

As they entered the yard itself, two dogs rose from the step at the back door of the farmhouse. An old grey muzzled collie and a younger one, unsure of its response. The old dog growled and Bruce let out a high-pitched bark. The older dog relaxed and lay down again. The younger one was still confused and Bruce gave him a low growl that seemed to settle things.

***

Inside the farmhouse, Fiona was angry. Her father had made all kinds of excuses for not doing things, even milking the cow. She grabbed the bucket and slammed the kitchen door open. There was someone there, another straw for the camel's back.

'Oh, it's you, Fergus Findlay. Come looking for a meal. There's no free meals around here, not any more. This is Monday and there's no more than gruel and I'll thank you if you'll milk the cow while I prepare it.'

Fiona held out the pail. Fergus took it, his features darkening into a scowl. 'I'll milk your cow for you but after that, I'll get on my way like the beggar you seem to think I am.'

Fiona hesitated. 'I'm sorry, Fergus, I've just had a disagreement with my father. You're welcome to eat …' she smiled, eyes mischievous …'after you've milked the cow but, as I say, it's Monday and washday, and I've had no time for even thinking of making food before now.'

To her surprise, Fergus, who would normally have responded to her smile, continued to scowl. 'In two years, Fiona McRae, you'll come away with me to Easter Ross, where no woman of mine will have need to work like a skivvy,' he told her as he turned and made his way to the cowshed with her pail.

Fiona stood frowning, whether Fergus had meant she should go as a kind of sister, or had hinted at something more, she was at a loss to know, but the idea that he was thinking she was worth rescuing her from the drudgery of her father's farm made her watch his determined steps thoughtfully. Rather than a beggar, Fiona had always seen Fergus as a romantic figure, someone who appeared from the mists, brought a wild gaiety into her stolid life and left her dreaming daft dreams of ball gowns and silver slippers. Despite hearing how the farm was expanding in the last few years, she'd imagined his 'farm' as a croft in a sheltered glen but he seemed to have - what?

Back in the kitchen, she took more care than she'd intended over the meal and, when Fergus brought the milk, a pot of thick broth was starting to simmer on her range and its smell was mixed with that of bread in the oven.

When Fergus returned he sniffed, and grinned, and Fiona felt her cheeks redden.

'Let me wash and make myself fit for the company of the lady of the manor,' Fergus said making a short bow.

'Get off with you, Fergus. Take this towel to dry yourself,' Fiona laughed, throwing the towel at him.

She watched as he stripped to the waist, his dark hair falling over his face as he bent to splash water. His body was lean, muscled, and creamy white and she turned hurriedly away wondering what it would be like to have his skin against hers. On trips to buy sugar and necessities, other young men had tried to come close, but this wondering, wanting to touch a particular man's skin was disturbing. Did Fergus want to touch her and, if he did, how she would react?

11

Without conscious thought, she took off her working overall and spread the neck of her dress so that a little of her shoulders were bare as she waited for Fergus to come back in.

As he gave her the pail, she saw his eyes glance at her bare shoulders, and knew suddenly that he wanted to caress her and also, how she would react.

She took the towel from him, smiling.

Fergus, still holding his end of the towel, cleared his throat. 'I'm sorry, I was abrupt just now, Fiona ...' he began, but was interrupted.

'Come away through and tell me the news from the rest of the world,' her father insisted.

Fergus seemed as reluctant as she was to release the towel. When he did, it broke some kind of connection between them, but she smiled as Fergus followed her father's stringy, slightly bent figure into the front room.

As she busied herself in the kitchen, she could hear her father cross examine Fergus on the Duke of Wellington's intentions on income tax and excise and smiled as she prepared, then called them to eat.

***

Fergus slept in the barn with Bruce and when Fiona looked out in the grey light of early morning, he was busy repairing the door of the cattle shed, his movements quick and sure.

She took the milking pail and went out.

'Thank you, Fergus, I've asked Father to get that fixed but he promises without doing anything.'

'He's getting past doing over much, Fiona. It's time he had someone to help.'

'There's no money for helpers, Fergus,' Fiona pointed out. 'We owe most of the merchants already and there's winter to come. Still, I suppose we'll manage somehow. How will you get by yourself?'

Fergus hammered a nail into the door. 'I'm on my own, Fiona. A hovel is good enough and there's deer on the hill and enough oat meal to see me through to the spring drove.'

'So you'll be coming again in the springtime?'

Under his stare, she felt nervous and ran her hands over her dress, smoothing it over her midriff, tightening it over her breast. She saw Fergus's eyes follow the movement. When he looked at her eyes again, his face flushed. 'I need two more years to stock the farm properly and start on a house, Fiona. After that, I'll stay at home.'

Fiona stood silent for a few moments. 'I had wondered if you'd maybe come here and help my father,' she said, at last.

Fergus looked round. 'My own place is ...' he seemed stuck for words and Fiona wondered why. 'Easier worked, Fiona.'

Frustrated, Fiona asked outright, 'How big is it?'

'It would be three times the size of this, maybe,' Fergus admitted.

'But why haven't you told me?'

His answer was to grin. 'I have, Fiona, but you've been more interested in hearing of Glasgow and where I've been, to take it in. The farm looks over the firth and I want to build a house with the yard facing south into the sun and the front looking over the water; something solid for the winter but bright in summer. I ... I'll,' he

13

stammered, frowned, looked down and shuffling his feet. 'I'll need a woman to … to see it's properly laid out … the kitchen and that.'

Fiona smiled at his embarrassment, then felt herself blush as he lifted his gaze and grinned, the mischief returning to his eyes.

Fiona went about her milking wondering what had changed about Fergus. He seemed to have matured, have something more dependable in his whole bearing, yet his eyes could remind her of running laughing through the birch wood. The thought of someone else helping him with his house made her uneasy.

They passed each other in the yard as she went about her chores and he did little jobs that had been neglected. To her disappointment, he spent another evening going over the latest news with her father, before coming to help her in companionable silence with late chores.

In the morning, Fiona had porridge ready by the time he had washed and made ready to leave. When he had eaten and was about to go, she was surprised when he said, 'Now, smile for me, so that I can take some sunshine on my journey.'

It made her laugh and he seemed pleased.

She waved him off and turned back to her chores and to nagging her father into activity.

***

McRae said little as he ate his breakfast, and when Fiona mentioned what Fergus had done, her father straightened in his chair. 'I think it's time you were married,' he told her. 'I think it's time you looked for a man to take care of us both, someone who can put the farm back in order.

We've borrowed as much as we can and we need someone with money to get the place right. Fergus was talking of that Maitland who has taken over The Mearns. He seems to be a man of consequence; maybe we should go and make a friendly visit.'

Fiona sat down and stared at her father.

Her father fidgeted. 'Findlay might have done what was most needed and I'm grateful for that, but there's much more that needs attended to and I'm not fit to do it any more, nag as much as you like,' her father continued.

Fiona frowned.

'You need a home,' her father pointed out. 'And so do I. Think on it, lassie.'

'I had thought to ask Fergus if he'd come and ...'

'Fergus Findlay! A drover! Here at Kirklea! Your mother would turn in her grave. I'll not have such a thing. Not have it, d'you hear!'

Fiona could only stare at the storm the idea had raised in her father, but became suddenly angry herself. 'Well, you'll not bully me the way you did my mother, Father. I'll not wed the first rich man you pass in front of my eyes to save your precious Kirklea. It's been nothing more than a drudge, first to mother, and now to me.'

With that, Fiona stamped out to her chores.

CHAPTER 2

As he walked over the brow of the hill and lost sight of Kirklea, Fergus led Bruce deliberately past small groups of sheep and cattle but the dog showed no sign of wanting to harass them, except a ram that decided to challenge him. Bruce sidestepped and left the ram looking foolish. Fergus grinned and they settled into an easy friendship, Fergus beginning to feel the dog had become an extension of his thoughts, an extra sense.

'I hope those two days haven't let anyone discover I turned off the track and been able to work out what happened and gone to Kirklea,' Fergus muttered as they climbed another slope and Maitland's comment about thieves returned to nag him.

He stopped now and then to check if he was indeed being followed. Bruce was disinterested until late afternoon on the second day when he stood alert and pricked his ears several times. When Bruce yipped and turned into a screen of young firs, Fergus followed him.

After ten minutes, Fergus made to go back to the track but Bruce headed him off. They'd been waiting for close to half an hour among the scented trees when they saw three figures hurry past the plantation as if trying to overtake someone.

'I don't like the look of the other two, but the third one is MacInnes,' Fergus told Bruce, frowning. 'I'm wondering why is he with them? He's no' likely to rob us, he has a wife and a grown daughter to think of, but we'll just go over the hill to the west and take another track.'

Turning abruptly over the hills towards the west, Fergus paused for some time, watching. He saw no one.

The nervous feeling persisted, however, and when he reached the start of the Great Glen and the normal route along the side of the lochs to Inverness he decided to take the more arduous route over the hills to the north.

As he walked, he followed the burns and hollows in the terrain, jumping the burn's brown rattling water when the burn crossed their path, always below the skyline. Bruce followed or went ahead, companionable but alert.

As they walked into a long gully with the light fading, Bruce gave a low growl and Fergus turned to see five men, some in ragged red coats, hurrying to catch up. He looked ahead and saw, near the top of the gully, two boulders, half-buried in the crest, reduced the path's width so much that only one would be able to pass through at a time. Fergus made his way to the gap, not rushing to get there breathless, but wasting no time. Once through the gap he turned and drew his broadsword and dirk and listened as the sound of footsteps came closer.

The footsteps stopped and there was a murmur of voices. Fergus gripped his sword more tightly and stepped close to the boulder on one side.

There was a slither of stealthy footstep and a burly Redcoat with a black beard covering most of his face, thrust himself, sword drawn, pistol pointing, through the gap. He saw Fergus, grinned and pointed the firearm at Fergus's breast. He was about to pull the trigger, when Bruce growled. The man's attention was momentarily distracted and Fergus swept his broadsword across, knocking the firearm aside as it exploded. The ball grazed Fergus' cheek, burning a crease. The man raised his own sword in defence and Fergus's backhanded downward slash at his wrist slid down the man's blade and took him in the neck. The man fell back without a sound, blood spurting on his companions. Bruce followed the body, low and underneath, unseen, tripping and confusing those following the attacker. From a determined group, the men became a yelling cursing rabble, fighting and stabbing at each other.

Bruce was back with Fergus before his attackers could understand and organise themselves.

Fergus moved off to the right, steps soft on moss covered ground, turned downward and made his way back the way they had come before settling in the long grass among some birches, watching the gully.

It grew dark and the chill settled as he watched.

There was a spark of light, only a spark at first, but after an hour, it grew into a fair blaze.

Fergus made his way towards it.

The men had settled under a bit of an overhang that shielded the light of the fire from the direction they assumed Fergus had taken. Fergus stood watching. The smell of the scented smoke made him feel the cold. Bruce came and sat beside him, turning his head briefly to one side before staring towards the fire.

'Some of them have red coats, Bruce; they're old soldiers and not to be taken by surprise too easily. They might even have set a guard,' Fergus muttered.

The voice startled Fergus. 'That they might. You should run while you have the chance,' it said calmly.

Fergus twisted towards the sound, stiff with cold and almost falling. It took several moments before he could distinguish the figure of a well-built man hunkered down near him. The man wore a dark coat, on the sleeve of which Fergus could just make out three stripes. The man held a gun by the barrel with the butt on the ground.

'Do you know who they are?' the newcomer asked quietly.

'Not beyond the fact that they meant me no good,' Fergus answered, whispering. 'Who are you?'

'I mean no harm to anyone, not here at home, anyway,' the man answered. He nodded to Bruce. 'The dog knew that. Have you had a disagreement?'

'I might have killed their leader.'

'Then they'll be none too pleased with you, and likely to chase you unless you do something about it. Would you kill them all?'

Fergus snorted and looked at the man. 'I've no wish to kill anyone. I'm sure I can find my way in the dark well enough to lose them.'

The man laughed softly.

'Come, then, we'll make a better plan,' the man said. 'They're probably more hungry than angry. Have you anything to eat.'

'Bannocks and cheese,' Fergus answered.

The man stood up and walked towards the fire.

'Haloo,' he called. 'It's getting chill out here and your fire looks inviting. Can we come in?'

His voice startled the men but one of them called out. 'You can come in and share the fire but we have no food to welcome you with.'

'Then we'll share whatever we have,' Fergus' companion called, walking forward into the firelight.

The four faces, white in the firelight, turned to watch the newcomers.

'You mentioned food?' one of the men queried.

Fergus unslung his deerskin bag from his shoulder, placed it on the ground, opened it and laid the bannocks and cheese on top. 'There's two bannocks each and I'll cut the cheese into six pieces, not much,' he told them.

'Enough to feed five thousand,' Fergus' companion said, grinning.

In the glimmering firelight, Fergus had a chance to see his companion's coat was dark green and braided with silver - where the braiding still held.

'A rifleman,' one of the others commented. 'And a sergeant, no less.'

'We'll not be taking orders,' the youngest of the four snarled, grabbing cheese and bannock.

'Nor would I want to give them. My name's McNeil. I'm on my way home to Wester Ross. I see you have red coats. I take it you've come from Waterloo.'

The men scowled. 'Aye, that we have, just to be discharged and short paid and thought the killing done with, but someone took our friend's life and I'll have his, if I find him,' the youngest of the four, red haired, told him.

McNeil smiled. 'Ah, well, that would be a great shame and us so near Glencoe and the memory of how the Campbells ate the McDonald's food and turned traitor to Highland custom and killed them.'

'What do you mean?' the young man demanded, standing.

'Just that you've eaten bread from the man you wanted to murder. You can hardly blame him for wanting to stay alive, can you?'

'It was *him*,' the young man shouted, grabbing for a weapon.

One of the older men drew the weapon away. 'He's right, Hamish, if that chiel hadn't got in first, Butcher would have killed him. Look at the wound on his cheek.'

'We only wanted to rob him,' Hamish protested.

'That's what Butcher said, but Butcher was a bad lot. If he was still alive, we'd have left him in the morning.'

'He killed our mate,' the youngster shouted back at his friend, pointing at Fergus.

His friend's voice took on an edge. 'And you've eaten his food, Hamish, and if you harm him, every man's hand in the Highlands will turn against you.'

'He's tricked us,' Hamish complained.

His older companion nodded. 'That he has, but maybe he's done you a service. If Butcher had lived, you and he would have felt the hangman's noose.'

Hamish glowered at Fergus but sat down.

McNeil grunted and the others turned to look at him. 'I would have killed a deer before, but what would one man do with a whole stag. If you're agreeable, I'll take...' he turned his hand towards Fergus.

'Fergus,' Fergus told him.

'... and yourself ...' pointing to the older man, '... and see if I can get us all some meat for the journey. You others can collect firewood and keep the fire going to roast the venison. But first, let us all get some sleep.'

With that, McNeil rolled over and prepared for sleep.

Fergus moved a little aside and lay down in his plaid, Bruce settled, close for warmth but where he could see the men at the fire. Fergus could hear the men muttering but ignored it.

CHAPTER 3

It was still grey dark when Fergus, and one of the older men, followed McNeil and climbed towards the top of the hill that bordered their road. McNeil drew a small telescope and searched the surrounding slopes from time to time.

It was close to midday, and Fergus had almost given up hope of a quarry, when McNeil grunted and handed the glass to him.

'It's a fine deer but there's not much cover between here and it,' Fergus commented.

McNeil patted his gun. 'It's a rifle, not a musket,' he grinned.

They were what looked to Fergus an impossible distance from the deer when McNeil settled himself and took careful aim.

McNeil drew a deep breath and held it. Fergus held his own, his eyes staring at the deer, close to two hundred paces away.

The rifle crack released Fergus' breath. The deer stood for a few seconds, then dropped.

They carried the carcass, whole, back to the camp.

Fergus slit it open and took out the liver and heart, throwing the heart to Bruce.

The roasting took the rest of the day and it was growing dark when they cut into the meat.

'Take it easy,' McNeil warned. The older soldiers nodded and chewed slowly. Hamish tore at his portion until one of the older men grabbed his arm. 'You'll be sick,' he warned. 'Eat a little to let your body get used to it. There'll be plenty tomorrow.'

Fergus ate, but with a wary eye on the one called Hamish and was surprised when McNeil turned to him. 'So, you're a drover,' McNeil commented. 'You travel light for someone who journeys half way down Scotland.'

'Like you,' Fergus answered, becoming wary.

'No, I have no choice, no horses, no one but my own self to carry what I need.'

'The horses are with the others,' Fergus explained. 'They were in a rush to get back to wives and bairns. I had other business to attend to.'

'Buying cattle for next year?' McNeil asked.

'No, that I'll do at the spring drove.'

'I ask because I'm going home to bring what I can find of my family away to Canada.'

'Canada!' Fergus exclaimed. 'I thought Canada was full of savages.'

'Aye Canada! There are groups being organised to go there, even some ministers and priests are involved. As for savages, what could be worse than some of the clan chiefs and lairds? They count their folk like pennies.'

Fergus looked more keenly at his new companion. 'I've seen a few trekking off to Canada, or Australia, even South Africa, and it seems to me the best is to go in a group. Pool your resources. There are all kinds of officials to deal with, for some you'll want a body quick with figures, for some others a body with a smooth tongue, or even a rough angry one. I hear many die on the voyage from starvation, or from lack of nursing, and a group deals better with that.'

The others sat, watching and listening, sucking the juice from strips of meat.

'You know some of the lairds stop the people from leaving,' Fergus said.

'I thought that had stopped,' McNeil commented.

'Mostly it has,' Fergus told him. 'Most lairds are glad to have the land open for sheep, but here and there, there's a laird with the old idea that his riches are in his people and they use all kinds of legal tricks to keep them tied. Despite the Union with England and all its fancy clauses, a man still owes his laird service in this Scotland. Hamish there, might still have to serve ten years.'

The youngster jumped up. 'I've served the King himself since I was twelve, six years ago. I'll not serve a damned laird who sat at his own fireside while we were chasing Froggies through Spanish mud and snow.'

'Then, the sooner you emigrate the better, laddie,' Fergus commented.

'I'm no' a laddie, Drover, as you'll see if I find you out of these highlands,' Hamish warned.

The others had watched him while he spoke but then turned their faces to look into the fire, dissociating themselves from his attitude.

'How do the people get the money for the fare, then?' Fergus asked.

McNeil leant forward. 'In letters, I've heard some are financed by a landlord wanting them off the land for sheep, some have had a bit put by, some must sell what beasts they have and trust they can get enough to last them until they can find work, or farm a crop.'

'A crop! That's near a year,' Fergus pointed out.

'Aye, no doubt some of them will starve, but they're starving here anyway. What I wanted to ask you was, what would be the best way to sell a beast or two. There'll be fares to pay and seeds to buy.'

'McNeil, if those people sell just an odd beast, just where they are, to drovers like me, they'll no' do all that well, I can assure you. Every man in these Highlands must look after himself, or starve.'

'He's cheated us already over the food last night. How do you know he'll not cheat you again, Sergeant McNeil?' Hamish sneered.

Fergus laughed. 'One crofter on his own, maybe, but myself, and maybe one other drover, to cheat a group of maybe forty odd, one of them a sergeant,' he joked. He turned to McNeil. 'Better they take their beasts, and anything they can make to sell, south with them. If you're not used to the markets, a group will watch for each other better than someone on their own.'

'Just the same, it wants thinking over,' McNeil said, undoing his bedroll and preparing for sleep.

***

In the morning, McNeil divided the deer carcass in four.

'You four take a quarter each,' he told the others. 'Fergus can get by, and I can shoot what I need. Save some for your families. They're like to need it.'

'I'd like to come a bit of the way with you,' Fergus suggested. 'I've been over the road before, but I like to check the different drove roads on the way home every time. Just to make sure.'

McNeil grinned. 'You're a canny soul, Fergus. I'll enjoy your company.'

Fergus made no reply until they had stepped out over the hills for an hour and were well ahead of the others. 'And you're a canny soul yourself, McNeil, loading the others with great lumps of meat to slow them down.'

As they walked, looking round at the hills, some capped with purple heather, some brown with autumn grass, some with dark green splashes of fir clumps or the browning leaves of other trees where burns slashed the hillside, they talked.

'So you've a mind to go to Canada?' Fergus asked.

McNeil looked round. 'I've seen enough of this Scotland, beautiful though it is, there are too many grovelling for a living on bits of ground that would be too small to support a family, even if the bits of land they have were lush along the banks of the Clyde.'

They walked further.

'Talking of your fares and selling beasts. You can sell them locally for what you get, but you'll be going south yourselves. I'd say again, your best plan would be to join a drove and sell them near Glasgow for a better price.'

'And how would we join a drove?' McNeil laughed. 'These people are farmers, Fergus; they know nothing of droving, or the drove paths, or the markets.'

'Like you said, I've been thinking on it, and maybe we could do something together.'

McNeil walked on for a space before saying, 'But you'd take commission, and we'd be no better off.'

Fergus laughed. 'Let's say I had two hundred beasts. That would mean four drovers with their bits and pieces. Five of us. I'd be mad to try to drove through the Western Highlands, full of men like our ex- soldier friends with starving families to feed, with just five of us to keep them from a decent meal. It's likely there will be fifty beasts brought to me in Easter Ross come spring. Two of us can handle that, especially if you come to meet us in one of the glens. I could buy a hundred beasts in Wester Ross and we could collect your ten families, each family with ten beasts and four bodies, say. That would make over two hundred beasts, but with forty people. If even a quarter of your people were able to look after the herd, there would be ten drovers, and as many more guards listening and watching, and little fear of being set on by reivers. Forbye, the beasts from the West are highly favoured and I'll make as much from the hundred I buy there as I would from two hundred from around Moray. Why would I want to take commission from you?'

Fergus walked on quietly, letting McNeil get used to the idea, before turning to him again. 'The first thing we have to do is to find a decent route with places we can stop for the night that are safe from reivers. They rarely take the whole drove, just a few beasts each time until they have a drove of their own.'

'But the beasts are all marked in the ear or on their hides.'

'It's not all that difficult to change a mark, McNeil, and who's going to challenge heavily armed wild men. There's not that many redcoats about, and not all of them have a well-developed sense of justice.'

McNeil laughed.

Their route took them along the shores of lochs and over hills, their craggy tops covered with heather in full bloom, softening the ruggedness. As they walked, they talked, growing closer step by step; McNeil telling of hard campaigns, Fergus explaining the pitfalls of getting cattle across swollen rivers.

By the time they parted, it had been agreed that, as soon as the passes were clear in spring, Fergus would do his local, Dornoch buying, then come to the market 'stance' in Strath Carron and buy whatever beasts he might need to complete a drove. McNeil would bring his family and any who wanted to join him. To avoid the confusion of the market, they would meet at a nearby loch.

Fergus would bring a drover with him but, hopefully, some of those who joined McNeil would be able to help on the way south. Their help would be payment for Fergus's leadership.

CHAPTER 4

Leaving McNeil to go and find his family, Fergus, thoughts of Fiona in his mind, turned up the long strath towards the Dornoch Firth.

Word about the guineas would have travelled. He was always nervous at this point. Until now, there'd always been several tracks he could take. From here on, there was only the road through the glen, or an exposed walk through heather deep enough to hide a hundred assassins.

Coming to a burn with sheltering trees on either side of a little gully, while it was still light, Fergus cut a few thin branches, leant them towards his fire and thatched them roughly with long grass to serve as a shelter from the now threatening rain. He lit a fire, cooked, and shared the rabbit Bruce had caught before spreading his plaid under the makeshift shelter.

He was about to settle into the plaid when Bruce grew uneasy. What troubled Fergus most was that Bruce didn't seem to know what the trouble was, or maybe where?

Fergus kicked dirt on the fire and, as it died, he moved into the shelter as if to sleep, wrapped his plaid round him but, once settled, slid out of the plaid and into the dark of the trees.

Bruce stayed where he was, as if settling for the night. Knowing the dog, Fergus could see the tension in its body.

When enough time had passed for Fergus to be asleep, a shadow crept into the shelter and stabbed at the plaid with something, another turned towards the dog as Bruce growled.

Fergus hit the figure under the shelter. His dirk reversed to use the hilt to stun the man.

There was no sound and he stepped around the shelter to drop the second figure in the same way.

He heard Bruce growl followed by a pistol shot and turned to see Bruce hanging from the shooters sleeve.

The shooter staggered and fell. Fergus's dirk was at his throat while he was still dropping.

'McInnes!' Fergus grunted in surprise, stopping the slicing cut that would have slit the man's throat. 'What call have you to be on this gate?'

'Dinna kill me, Fergus, I had little choice in the affair.'

'Man, if it hadn't been for the dog you'd have killed *me*,' Fergus shouted into the man's face.

The man nodded calmly. 'Aye, that we would, though it wasnae what I intended. I only meant to frighten you, but when the dog took my arm, I pulled the trigger.'

'So why should I no' cut your throat?' Fergus asked.

'It was Black Duncan's doin',' MacInnes explained. 'He said he would forget what I owe him and even give me a share of what you've got. Enough for a boat to America.'

'But some o' the money is his!'

'Aye. But no' it all, and only enough to keep him from bein' suspected.'

'But why you, McInnes?'

'The other two would have taken the money and run. He needed me to make sure it came to him. That's why he gave me the gun. He said my wife and lassie could stay on the croft until I came back with it, but then we had all to go, money or no'.'

The other two were recovering and Fergus turned to see Bruce licking one of their faces. When the man's eyes opened and looked into Bruce's black face and eyes glittering in what faint light still came from the fire, his scream was eerie with terror and he blundered off through the trees, followed by his companion.

'That dog o' yours is no' canny,' McInnes mentioned.

Fergus laughed and Bruce came, tail wagging, to lick his hand.

The break let Fergus calm and come to a decision.

'McInnes, you're a man I always thought of as honest, and I've need o' somebody to watch my ain place while I'm away on a drove. There's a bit of a house, and I expect you could find the odd rabbit to give you meat. But you'll have to do something for me, and if it works as I think, you'll have no need to worry about Black Duncan.'

'I'll listen, Fergus, but I've had enough o' black deeds.'

'All I'm asking is that you take a message to four men. Ask one of them to send word to Black Duncan, but they're not to let on they got the word from you. Tell them to meet me at the Hielan' Cow in two days' time at twelve sharp and they can get their money.'

***

At her chores at Kirklea, Fiona heard hooves in the yard and looked out from the kitchen to see a well-dressed, heavy man on horseback talking to her father. Through the open door, she heard the man say, 'I'm Maitland from the Mearns over the hill. I thought, as it's close to the season of good will, I'd make a visit to my neighbour.'

Her father gave him a toothy smile. 'Come away in, Mr Maitland. Fiona will be in just now and get us some buttermilk. You'll be ready for something after your ride over the hills.'

Maitland dismounted and her father held the door open to allow him to enter.

'Fiona, this is Mr Maitand come to visit. Maybe you could change into something nice; something more suitable to welcome a visitor, and get us some buttermilk and a bit of scone.'

Fiona stared. 'What have I got that's *nice,* father?' Fiona asked. 'And there's no scones, not for us, or for the king himself, if he was to visit.'

Maitland held out his hand. Fiona took it. He held it just longer than necessary. Fiona allowed him to do it, but let her hand go limp in his grasp and turned to her father, ignoring Maitland's smile. 'Go through to the parlour, Father, I'll get some buttermilk and bring it through.'

'Maybe you'd like a glass of something stronger, Mr Maitland?' McRae asked.

Maitland smiled again to Fiona. 'That's not necessary, Mr McRae, I'll enjoy the buttermilk.'

Fiona brought a tray with glasses and saucers.

'Is there something to go with the buttermilk?' her father asked.

'You know fine well, I've had no time to make anything, Father,' Fiona answered.

'She's a grand baker, Mr Maitland,' her father said, angering Fiona with the obsequious tone of his voice. 'And careful in the kitchen. She wastes nothing, nothing at all.'

'There's nothing to waste, Father,' Fiona interrupted.

Her father was not deterred. 'Aye it's hard, Mr Maitland,' he put in. 'But we manage, we manage.'

Maitland smiled. 'With a daughter like Fiona, I'm sure you do. A woman's touch is something to be grateful for, Mr McRae.'

'It is, it is, Mr Maitland. You'll be speaking from experience?'

'Unfortunately not, Mr McRae, I'm a bachelor. Never had the opportunity to acquire a wife. Building a business has taken all my attention, until now, that is.'

McRae looked significantly at Fiona and she felt her anger grow.

'I'll leave you to your men's talk,' Fiona said, picking up the tray and going out to the kitchen.

'She's always busy,' she heard her father say.

Maitland's voice was loud enough for Fiona to hear and his next words drew her ear.

'Would you consider selling this place, Mr McRae?' Maitland asked.

'It's my home, Mr Maitland, and Fiona's. She was born here,' her father answered.

'Oh, I'm sure we could come to some arrangement that would allow you to stay here, at least until Fiona is married and you can move in with her.'

Her father made no reply and Maitland came into the kitchen, obviously ready to leave.

'It's been good to meet you, Miss McRae,' he said, again holding her hand just longer than necessary.

Fiona waited in the kitchen until her father had said goodbye.

Her father came in smiling and rubbing his hands. 'Well,' he started. 'You've made a right good impression with Mr Maitland. Maybe we'll get ourselves out of this yet.'

Fiona stiffened. 'You mean maybe I'll get you out of this mess, Father! You'd have me marry that man, knowing nothing about him, just to make sure you're not pushed out into the cold.'

'I'm thinking of you as well, lassie.'

'No you're not, Father, or we'd have sold this place long ago and moved to somewhere I could get a job.'

'This was your mother's place, Fiona.'

'Aye, it was, and trying to make it pay, killed her in the end. It'll not kill me, Father, and I'll not wed some rich schemer to preserve it.'

'I'm not asking you to marry anyone yet, Fiona. However, don't turn the man down before you've had the chance to get to know him. That'll not hurt, will it?'

'I'll not let you down in front of a stranger, Father. But I'll not try to impress him by being what I'm not. I'm a farm girl, not some society hostess and if Fergus would come here, we'd have no need to think of ...'

Her father's face reddened. 'You'll not think of having a drover in your mother's house, Fiona, I've told you, I'll not hear of it. In fact, come spring, I'll not allow him to use the glen.'

'That would be cutting off our nose to spite our face, Father. His hard cash is the only money we can depend on.'

Her father stared at her for several minutes, then stormed out of the kitchen.

CHAPTER 5

Fergus arrived at the Highland Cow just before twelve, and found no one there. He asked for a table to be put in the inn's courtyard and sat waiting for noon.

With the promise of something unusual, a small crowd distilled from the air. When the farmers arrived, their companions, including McInnes, augmented the crowd.

At twelve sharp, when Black Duncan and the other four stood in front it, Fergus put down four cloth wrapped bundles of guineas and the pistol.

He handed out the four wrapped bundles, then turned to stare at Black Duncan across the table, before offering him the firearm.

'This is your share. It's your pistol, and you can take it and get what I owe you from the thieves you hired to steal what belonged to these others,' Fergus told him, deliberately.

Duncan's face and neck reddened in anger, 'Accuse me o' robbery would ye, I'll not need any pistols, a dirk's good enough for the likes o' you.'

Fergus shrugged and got out from behind the table, plaid over his arm and dirk drawn, evading Duncan's first rush easily.

They circled, a big solid man and the spare Fergus; now hemmed together in the ring of watchers.

Duncan rushed and although Fergus pushed the thrust aside, Duncan's blade sliced his sleeve and came away red tipped. Duncan's rush took him into the crowd.

They scattered before the dirk but reformed the ring round the two knife-wielding antagonists.

Duncan lunged again. Fergus twisted away and used the hilt of his weapon to split the skin on the big man's cheek. Enough would close the eye, but it was a wearing down tactic, no killing, an ignominious defeat. Risky.

The blaze in Duncan's eyes spoke only of a dead Fergus.

Fergus feinted to one side and Duncan lunged, almost overbalancing. Fergus hit him again but it cost him a cut in his trews and another red tip on Duncan's dirk.

Duncan recovered, rubbed his now swelling cheek, and set his balance for another strike.

The two circled warily.

Fergus was quick. He fainted left, then right, then looked as if he'd decided to back off. Duncan took a step forward but found he was within Fergus's reach and the swelling around his eye reddened as the hilt of Fergus's dirk hit it again. Duncan backed off, rubbing the eye.

A yell from the crowd brought a distraction. The crowd turned to see Bruce shepherding a rough looking character.

'For the sake o' Heaven, save me, Duncan,' the man pleaded. 'He kens you sent us to rob Fergus. Save me! That dog o' his is no' canny. He got me in the back room and was stare, starin' into ma soul wi' his black eyes. *He's no' canny, I tell ye.*'

Fergus watched Duncan, but the big man turned to glance at the newcomer.

As the man burst into the ring, now glancing wild eyed behind him at each step, as if the Devil might catch him, Fergus recognised him as one of the two who had been with McInnes. Bruce, his head low, was herding him forward.

Fergus could feel people in the crowd beginning to give Bruce room and think there was something unusual about the dog, but as they were making up their mind whether to turn on him as evil, Bruce picked up a stick someone had discarded, dropped it at the ruffian's feet and ran back, barking excitedly.

The crowd laughed. 'The dog only wants you to throw the stick for him,' someone shouted.

When they looked round, Black Duncan was gone.

As Fergus relaxed, his arm was grabbed and he turned to find Davie, the deaf fifteen-year-old he had left in charge of his house and the few sheep he kept on the hill, grinning at him. Davie had been found wandering in the hills by Fergus's father several years earlier and become almost a wee brother. Not being able to hear meant it could be dangerous among the cattle, but he seemed to have developed an understanding of sheep.

As the pair hugged, Bruce nuzzled against them and, as they drew apart, the dog made friends with Davie, making Fergus smile.

Letting them enjoy their meeting, Fergus searched among the crowd and managed to find MacInnes with his wife and grown daughter, Morag, full figured, red haired, blue eyes and three years older than Fergus.

'You'll come to Invercauld as soon as you can and settle in before the winter gets a proper grip?' Fergus asked.

'It's kind of you to invite us, Fergus,' Mrs MacInnes told him. 'We'll just have to hope Black Duncan and the snow hold off until we can build something.'

'I've no need of much for the present, Mistress MacInnes. I'll build something that's enough for Davie and me, and we can extend the place I've been using for your own use, if you like. It's nothing grand, but it was big enough for my father and mother and me while she was alive, but you have a lassie instead of just a laddie, and she'll no doubt need something better than I did,' Fergus grinned.

Morag smiled back. 'You're as cheeky as ever, Fergus Findlay, and don't be getting muddled with whisky some night and think you can sleep in your old bed. Your Fiona McRae might not be too pleased.'

'Your tongue's too sharp for me, Morag McInnes but what do you ken about Fiona?'

'You've been talking about her since you were a laddie, Fergus. Every one kens about Fiona McRae. I'd be surprised if Black Duncan didn't ken and if he wanted t get back at you, she might be the first one he'd think of.'

Fergus frowned; there was something in what Morag had said but Kirklea was out of the way and he shrugged. 'Come tomorrow with your father, and we'll see what we have to do to make my old place fit for you.'

***

The hovel Fergus and Davie needed took several days of cutting sods and stacking them into walls before they cut poles and thatching.

Morag came to check on progress and think about what she wanted at the old place. Her own door, she insisted on.

Fergus insisted on a decent fireplace – since she had no husband to keep her warm.

Fergus enjoyed the company and helped with rabbits and a few bought things. He didn't compare Morag to Fiona. They were different people, one a friend, the other, he wasn't sure of, but the thought of whom made any work easier.

CHAPTER 6

At Kirklea, Fiona was getting another talking to.

'You must think of yourself,' her father told her. 'You should be thinking of marriage and having children. A family of your own.'

Fiona listened, wondering if her destiny was to be the same as her mother's; a life devoted to scrubbing and cleaning and enduring.

'Mr Maitland would be a fine catch,' her father insisted.

Fiona thought of the man. Overbearing and as stolid as a sack of potatoes but she'd have a roof and, as far as she could see, no financial worries. She didn't really hear the rest of her father's monologue.

It was as she composed herself for sleep that it came back to her. What kind of children would she have? What kind of children would she like? Boys like Fergus Findlay, she smiled. Boys who carried the sounds and smells of spring, who lifted hearts and made you long for ... and girls, girls who would run and laugh as she had done with Fergus; girls whose marriages would be an adventure not a drudge.

A picture of her mother came to mind. A picture she wondered over, one of her mother taking care about her toilet when Fergus's father was due. She'd asked her mother once if she wished she had married Fergus's father. Her mother had grown angry and talked of duty and a woman's place but Fiona had seen the tears behind the hard words.

***

Days later, Fiona, making a rare visit to Luss, was in the haberdashery buying, or trying to buy, thread and needles. The lady serving her was polite but adamant.

'I'm sorry, Miss McRae,' she was saying, 'but the owner has given strict instructions that no more credit is to be given.'

'Surely ...' Fiona pleaded.

'What's the trouble?' Maitland's voice asked.

'I came in for thread and needles but I seem to have left my purse behind,' Fiona told him.

'I think for such a paltry amount, you can allow me to pay, Miss McRae,' Maitland said, nodding to the assistant.

As the assistant put the purchases in a paper bag, Fiona thanked Maitland.

Maitland took her hand in heavy fingers. 'For such a charming young lady, it is a privilege to be of service,' he said, lifting her hand and kissing it.

Fiona smiled weakly, took her purchase and left the shop. Fergus had cleared her minor debts from time to time and she'd accepted it without thinking, but she hated the idea of being indebted to anyone else for even a few pennies.

It was the same story in the shoe menders.

'I'm afraid you'll have to pay before I can give you the boots,' the cobbler told her. 'I have my own bills to pay, Fiona.'

'Father needs those for working in the field,' Fiona pleaded.

'More trouble, Miss McRae,' Maitland's voice sounded behind her. 'You really must remember to bring your purse. Let me pay for the repairs. It will give me an excuse to come and visit.'

Fiona hesitated. Damn the man, she thought. The price for keeping her father's feet dry would be to be indebted to this man, whom she instinctively distrusted. Was it worth it?

Before she could object, Maitland had given the cobbler money and the cobbler was handing the boots to Fiona.

***

On New Year's Day Fergus prepared to visit Old Babs, as he had done since he was old enough to walk the five miles to Ault-na-main. When Morag heard he was going, she insisted on joining him.

Her mother was discomfited and, knowing Old Babs' reputation as something of a clairvoyant, if not in fact a witch, Fergus assured her mother they'd be back before dark. But it took Morag's promise, made several times, not allow the old woman to tell her fortune to settle things.

Fergus was amused at Morag's surprise that the old witch's hovel she'd obviously expected, turned out to be remarkably clean and they were served herbal tea, laced with a fair drop of spirit, not only in cups, but saucers.

Fergus told Babs all that had happened on the drove, only glossing over his visits to Kirklea.

Babs mmmm'd as he talked but then turned to Morag. 'So you've brought a lassie at last, have you?' She looked at Morag, who smiled back. 'But not the one you'll marry,' Babs added.

Fergus was taken aback but Morag answered. 'I'm glad to hear that,' she laughed.

'Oh, you could do worse,' Babs commented. 'But you'll have your own, in good time, though not without sorrow, either. But you didn't come here to listen to the ravings of Old Babs, did you now?'

'I came because I wanted to see you for myself. Not to be told what to think, Babs,' Morag answered.

Fergus interrupted. 'We came just as friends, Babs, as my father and I have every year.'

Babs looked keenly at Fergus. 'Your father came when your mother took ill but there was nothing I could do for her. He came later for something to ease the loss, and I told him to love you. Then he started coming to see which road to take when he went on a drove. Mostly he knew himself but, sometimes, a man needs reassured.'

Fergus grinned.

'Just as you do now,' Babs continued but became serious. 'This new year will set you on a different path, Fergus Findlay, but if you're afeered, you'll risk the happiness of more than yourself. Maybe even that of this lassie who came out of curiosity.'

As they walked back to Invercauld, Morag teased. 'So you will risk my own happiness, Fergus Findlay, if you're not brave and bold. Then remember, if you let me down, I will haunt your dreams.'

'Don't take what Babs says too lightly, Morag,' Fergus warned. 'I don't think she has the second sight entirely, but she kens people.'

'At least we're not to be wed to each other, and I won't have to go stravaging all over Scotland after you.'

***

At Kirklea, Maitland was visiting. Fiona, in the kitchen, felt her anger grow as she listened to her father talk in the front room.

'I'm afraid Fiona doesn't see over many eligible men, Mr Maitland,' McRae was telling him. 'Luckily, she's not the kind to go gallivanting or wasting her time in dancing and the like.'

'I'd have thought a girl like her would have a number of suitors,' Maitland commented.

'Oh, there's one or two have looked but I've given them short shrift.'

'Quite proper, Mr McRae,' Maitland agreed.

'The last was a drover chap that came through on his way north, but the likes of him is not suitable for a girl of Fiona's accomplishments. Her mother was from a good family, of course, and she knows how to behave in good company.'

'Well, think about selling and what price you might want, McRae. You may want to talk it over with Fiona.'

'Fiona is an obedient girl, she'll do as she's told.'

'That's good to hear, Mr McRae.'

Fiona's anger turned to worry as she heard her father disclose more of their financial situation than she thought wise. Not that Maitland asked about it directly, he just seemed to lead the conversation into corners where her father was obliged to reveal details of what they owed, and to whom, or abruptly change the subject. While generally avoiding the whole truth, the information her father gave Maitland was enough for the man to draw the right conclusions or, if he questioned the merchants as deviously as he was leading her father, to fill in the missing details.

Without causing a scene and embarrassing her father, there was little Fiona could do, but she was uneasy as she went about her chores.

She was glad when the big man excused himself and got up to leave.

Maitland came into the kitchen and looked round. 'You're busy, Miss McRae. Perhaps, the next time I call, you'll join us when we talk.'

'Aye,' her father interjected, looking at Maitland. 'Maybe next time, if you let us know you're coming, we can have a meal, and Fiona can put on something more suitable for company, and join us.'

Fiona stared at her father, on the verge of rebellion, but held her tongue.

Maitland smiled and held out his hand. 'I'll look forward to that, Miss McRae,' he said.

'I'm afraid my hands are dirty, Mr Maitland. I'll just wish you a pleasant journey and not shake your hand.'

Maitland forced his smile wider and turned his outstretched hand to McRae. 'Till we meet again, Mr McRae.' he said and went outside, followed by McRae.

Fiona heard Maitland's horse leave and turned to face her father as he came back into the kitchen, all smiles. 'Well, unless he's stupid, he'll know we owe money to half the country,' she said.

'What do you mean by that?'

'Your Mr Maitland has wormed all about us out of you. What he wants to do about it, I don't know, but I don't trust the man.'

'I'll not hear you talk that way of a fine man, Fiona. He's a gentleman, not like that Findlay who comes and scrounges from us,' her father told her, and walked out of the kitchen.

CHAPTER 7

The winter eased and the snows began melting, at least on the lower slopes, allowing movement through the passes and Fergus had his hands full. Preparing for a drove was always exciting, but energetic, and now he had Morag McInnes on his back; not so much on his back as looking over his shoulder, asking questions and making remarks.

As usual, he sent word round to tell people he was preparing to leave and the local farmers brought what cattle they wanted sold to him. When he was ready, he hired a drover he could rely on for the first stage of his drove. If he needed more, there was always someone at the market stances he bought extra cattle at. He collected six garrons, not big enough to be called horses, yet bigger than ponies and ideally suited to the ups and downs of highland travel; he used two for riding now and then, or carrying someone ill or injured and the four others to carry supplies and local produce to trade on behalf of his neighbours. His final preparation was to visit old Babs at Ault-na-main.

***

Getting Babs' predictions of the price was more superstition than necessary advice, but served a useful purpose. If they heard Babs had predicted good prices, the drovers would nurse the animals under their care to get top value; if they expected low prices, they would take care none were lost in rivers or fell down cliffs while bringing them in top condition to market.

How Babs arrived at her predictions, Fergus wasn't quite sure. Whether it was based on news from travellers passing through Ault-na-main's Half Way House Inn, or intuition, he didn't know, but visiting her had been an indispensable part of his father's routine and he had carried on the tradition. He also collected what Babs wanted sold. Babs was not only the local herbalist but an accomplished weaver and Fergus used what she produced to interest the farm women at stops along the way. Some bought - some copied ideas.

Fergus signalled to Davie to come with him and the smile of delight on Davie's face made Fergus grin. Davie had originally gone to Babs with fleeces from the few sheep Fergus kept, become fascinated by the weaving, and, after a few visits, had started to make suggestions for patterns, pointing out colours that would change Babs' ordinary design. Some she adopted, some she shook her head at.

Morag insisted on joining them. The day was warm and the air clear for once. They laughed at nothings as they tramped, sometimes warm, sometimes cool in the trees, drinking hill water from streams brown with peat.

They were still laughing when they got to Babs.

'When a lad and a lassie come together, it is usually to see will they have bairns, Fergus, but Miss McInnes will have no bairns by you,' Babs greeted them as they entered her cottage.

'I'm glad to hear it,' Morag teased Fergus. 'He's too much of a rover to father any bairns.'

Babs sobered. 'Oh, but I did not say you'd not be wed,' she said.

Fergus looked at Morag's shocked face and laughed. 'She did not say you would be wed to me, only that you'd be wed. Now you can worry about which tinker may sweep you off your feet.'

'Tinker or no, he'll be a fine man,' Babs assured Morag.

They busied themselves with Babs' weavings for some time, then sat to hansel the coming drove with Babs' whisky. Babs became suddenly serious. 'Take care, Fergus, this drove is no ordinary venture. There's evil afoot.'

'There's always evil afoot,' Fergus joked.

'That kind of levity was all right when you were just yourself, Fergus, but others depend on you now.'

'Dinna worry, I'll bring your money back,' Fergus joked, but felt a stab of concern. 'Now what of the prices of the beasts?'

'You have no need to worry on that account, Fergus. The prices are better, not as good as before Waterloo, but the emigrant boats and the people going from the land to the city, and all the Irish here to dig the canals, all take meat, even if it is only a bit of bone for soup. And, now, all those new rich folk demand meat, sometimes twice a day, if you can believe it.'

Their attention turned to the woven pieces. Jean Abernethy, the daughter of Fergus's man of business in Glasgow, had been selling bits and pieces of Babs' things for several years and Davie's choice of articles and designs had proved highly saleable. Fergus let him point to what he should take down to the city shop. Once or twice, Babs disagreed with Davie's choice, but when he was adamant, Fergus respected his decisions.

When the dealing was over, Babs faced Fergus. 'You must take the laddie with you, Fergus; you'll have need of him.'

Fergus hesitated, but Babs held his gaze determinedly, and he turned to Davie. Davie looked puzzled at first as Fergus asked, by signs, if he wanted to go on the drove. Davie's answer was a broad grin.

'I suppose McInnes could look after a few sheep while we're away,' Fergus said.

On their way back, Morag was quiet at first. Fergus wondered what was wrong, but was, nevertheless, taken by surprise when she asked, 'Will you ever settle, Fergus?'

'They are building a canal here in the Great Glen, Morag, and with the new steam ships that can travel into the wind, and even without the wind, the droving will be finished in a few years and good riddance. I want to build a proper house on Invercauld, where I can watch my bairns grow up.'

Morag went quiet again. 'My father has talked of going to America to get away from this grind with never a chance of having a place you can call your own. America eats into him, Fergus, but talk is easy, it takes money to move.'

Fiona must feel the same, Fergus thought. Kirklea would not last much longer. Others depend on you now, Fergus, Babs had said. That included Fiona.

***

On her next visit to the town, Fiona discovered the extent of Maitland's intruding in their lives. The haberdasher she'd been expecting to fight with over thread, smiled and asked if there was anything else she wanted.

'I'm sorry, I don't have enough with me to pay for more than I have taken,' she apologised.

'That's all right,' the haberdasher told her. 'Any friend of Mr Maitland is a friend of ours.'

'Exactly what do you mean?' Fiona asked.

'Mr Maitland has cleared your debt,' the man smiled.

Fiona frowned, went to the grocer, found the same thing and began to worry.

She made further enquiries, and found the seed merchant, and the blacksmith, had been paid. The blacksmith sympathised with the rundown condition of Kirklea, and hoped they would soon be on their feet again.

As she stopped to rest on a rock at the head of the glen, she realised, if Maitland had bought up all their debt, then, in fact, he had become their only creditor and could call in the debt any time he wished. With the farm run down, that would mean he virtually owned the farm and, unless she had an alternative, her as well. Her head dropped into her hands, she started to weep and, without knowing why, called on Fergus's name.

***

In the north, several farmers had brought cattle to Fergus, some wanting paid, some asking him to sell on their behalf for a commission. For the first few days, when the cattle retained their homing instincts, Fergus took them through the hills. There was a drove road, but it wended southward, and he was going west and would only meet the big droves coming from that direction at Achnasheen.

Despite the devious route, they met people with a few cattle, which he was able to buy at a decent price, and was soon herding close to a hundred head.

Five days later, they were settling beside the loch at which he had arranged to meet McNeil.

In the evening, Fergus left the cattle grazing contentedly under the care of his hired drover, and took his garrons to drink from the loch's dark water. He was just musing there were plenty of lochs in the area, and hoping McNeil knew which one to come to, when he saw the man himself coming towards him. Dropping the halter, Fergus ran to McNeil and they grabbed each other in bear hugs, laughing and slapping.

Bruce was jumping excitedly and drew McNeil's attention. 'Is he good with sheep?' he asked.

'Sheep?' Fergus asked.

'Aye, some of the folk had a few sheep, and felt, if they'd get a better price for the cattle father south, then they'd best take the sheep as well.'

Fergus shook his head. 'Neil McNeil,' he laughed. 'Old Babs warned me there would be problems, but she never mentioned sheep, just that I would need Davie. He's deaf, but he kens sheep.'

Fergus waved to Davie to join them. As he came, he pointed.

Fergus turned to look and saw a procession, like the Children of Israel, coming over the brow of the hill. McNeil burst out laughing. 'Come and meet your new drove, Fergus,' he invited.

'The folk or the beasts?' Fergus asked, watching children, women, cattle and a few carts flood down towards them.

'There's only ten families,' McNeil explained.

'I was thinking there would be no one left in Wester Ross,' Fergus grinned.

Fergus looked round the hollow they stood in. 'There's enough trees for firewood, and water in the loch. Better they camp here for the night,' Fergus commented.

McNeil passed the word, and the crowd settled. Much like cattle, Fergus thought; some in groups, some on their own, but still in touch with one another. Spaced out along the shore of the loch.

The children played, splashing and laughing; their parents shouting to be careful; the women lit fires; the men talked to neighbours or searched in bundles in the back of carts for what the women needed. Some had family carts, others seemed to share one, but even those with their own carts had bundles that belonged to others. The ponies that drew the carts were released and herded, singly, and in pairs, beside the cattle and sheep.

McNeil introduced Fergus to each family. They were like a procession of names and faces, until he came to the camp of the old soldiers he'd met on his way north, including the carrot headed Hamish. The other two shook Fergus's hand openly. Hamish merely nodded recognition.

Then a family of five, called Sinclair, whom Fergus remembered for the pretty, dark haired girl, who smiled coquettishly at both Fergus and McNeil. Sinclair's wife was flouncing in bad temper as she clashed her pots and glared at her daughter, but smiled with brittle brightness for both her visitors.

The last visit was to a family where the man broke out coughing, bringing a worried frown to McNeil's face. 'I'm better, I'm a bit better,' the man told McNeil as McNeil introduced him as Stewart. Stewart's wife was busy with preparations for supper but kept a blank face in answer to Fergus's enquiring glance.

'You'll eat with us?' the woman asked, Fergus looked at McNeil and found him smiling acceptance.

As they sat down, McNeil asked, 'What do you think?'

Fergus shook his head. 'I'd thought maybe ten men and some women, Neil. Not a gathering of the clans. We'll need to organise. Are their beasts all marked? If they get lost will they know them?'

'They have their ears marked,' McNeil told him.

Fergus thought for a moment before starting to speak with authority. 'The cattle we'll make into one herd to make them easier to manage. The children and their mothers, I'll leave to you, McNeil. What we need first is a tally of the cattle. There's no telling which ones, or whose, might break a leg and the fairest way is to have shares and just divide the money we get according to that.'

McNeil frowned. 'There's some that think their beasts are worth a lot more than the others, Fergus.'

Fergus's reply was sharp. 'Then they've more to lose if they fall into a gully. During the drove, some will fatten, Neil, and some will lose weight. At this stage, there's no way of knowing which will be which. Believe me, the fairest way is to have shares. Let anyone who disagrees look after their own,' he told McNeil in ultimatum.

McNeil nodded.

'And the children, can they be kept out of the way?' Fergus asked. 'If I buy fifty more beasts, as I intended, there'll be over two hundred in the drove and that's no place for bairns to be running about.'

'I'll speak to the women,' McNeil told him.

'We'll need to organise some of the men as drovers as well,' Fergus pointed out. 'Your people's beasts will have to settle in and learn the drove. One or two experience drovers might handle the lot, but I think we'd be better to have five of the men as well as yourself. Not men their families depend on, nor men who can't chase after a cow, but people like your old soldier friends who know about discipline. I must admit I'm surprised to see them here.'

'Aye,' McNeil said frowning slightly. 'I was surprised to see them myself, but they came to me in the glen, angry and upset at the way their families were scratching a living on bits of land hardly big enough for a woman on her own, never mind a family. They've seen foreign places and English farms where the people live in comfort, remember, and I couldn't refuse them. They've fought for this country and deserve a chance of something better.'

'Including Hamish?'

'Including Hamish! His mother is a fine woman and she's determined his young brother and two sisters will not have to grovel to the laird.'

'There's none of your own kin,' Fergus remarked.

'They were all gone.'

'Dead?'

'No, just gone, and no one knew where. When I told them why I was looking, this lot came asking for help. What could I do?'

'I just didn't expect so many,' Fergus commented.

'Beasts or folk?' McNeil asked.

'Both,' Fergus answered, grinning.

CHAPTER 8

Wakened by a piper, which had Fergus shaking his head, they spent the next morning organising. Neil brought six men to help with droving, including Hamish. Fergus hesitated, almost sending him back, but shrugged, and let him stay.

First, they split the cattle from the other animals and herded the newcomers to join Fergus's drove despite protests and tears over some beasts that had become more pets than farm animals. It raised the total to over two hundred.

They separated the sheep and let Davie and Bruce look after them.

The men and women sorted themselves into groups around carts.

By midday, Fergus was talking to his six helpers. 'For the first few days the beasts will straggle but they'll soon settle. The object for those few days is to get them used to travelling in a crowd, so we'll not make many miles.'

At that point, the hired drover, whom Fergus had left keeping a general eye on the cattle, came towards the group and stood waiting. Fergus went to talk to him but was soon back. 'He doesn't like being with so many people,' Fergus told McNeil, looking after the figure of the drover now disappearing up the hillside. 'Old Babs was right,' he muttered.

They barely made enough distance to be out of sight of their first camp before Fergus called a halt, to the great relief of his assistants who spent their time chasing errant cows back into the herd.

They made three miles the second day, tired chasing cows out of trees. The day after, another three, before turning the drove into a little glen for the night.

Being confined together seemed to settle the herd, and by the time they joined the main drove road, the leaders among the beasts had established their authority, and they were making their ten miles a day. Not without complaint from some of the people about sore muscles and feet, but at least with acceptance.

The coughing man, whom Fergus now knew as Gordon Stewart, was coughing more but insisted on keeping up. Mary, the man's wife, smiled through her worried frown and stayed determinedly cheerful. Her two boys, six and eight, wandered about and were a trial to her and others. Neil suggested they help with the droving. Fergus looked at them and, reminded of his own childhood following his father, agreed.

Sheila Sinclair was more of a trial.

Fergus was busy with his garrons one evening when she came past with her bucket on the way to fetch water. 'It's really heavy,' she told Fergus, putting the bucket down. 'I'm not as strong as the others and I've no brother to help. Could you please carry it, or even take one side and we could carry it together,' she simpered.

Fergus grinned back. 'I'm sure you'll manage. Just take your time.'

'You won't help a maiden in distress, Mr Findlay?'

Fergus turned back to his garron. 'No, I won't, but I'm sure Hamish will be delighted,' he said, nodding towards the hovering carrot head.

In the morning, the Stewart boys were overjoyed to 'help' for the best part of an hour. After that, McNeil and

Fergus kept them busy until the smaller one was almost dropping. Fergus lifted him on to one of the garrons for a break but insisted he walk again after an hour. The older boy struggled on but fell asleep as he ate in the evening.

The country was wild and, while the carts with their high unstable loads could face the gentler slopes directly, they had to detour round much of the rising ground to avoid overturning. Despite that, there was an occasional spill. In the Sinclair case, it happened just before they stopped for evening and Fergus was suspicious Sheila had arranged it to have the younger men around her.

As they moved on, the wind blew hair out on ridges and swirled in gusts in the valleys. Recent rain had left the lower ground soft and the cattle turned it to mud. In the occasional dry patch, they churned up clouds of dust.

So far, despite clouds gathering and hanging over the hills and screening the bens, the rain had held off.

As the going became easier, instead of trying to make up for lost time, Fergus insisted they take it easy to give the cattle time to graze as they walked.

It was then that the storm that had been threatening broke.

They'd been travelling for an hour, with clouds glowering darker with every step, crowding round like a blanket. People and beasts started to crowd together for comfort and become unnaturally quiet. The clop and swish of moving beasts and the bump and squeal of cartwheels seem to fill the air. The change came with a flash and a solid thunderclap that released sheets of rain. The rain streamed down faces, flattened hair on cheeks, dribbled down necks, wetting from the inside any patches of clothing the rain didn't reach from the outside.

It didn't stop until mid-afternoon, when the cloud broke and the sun chased the clouds high and bleached them into white fluffy balls.

The cattle steamed, the horses steamed, the people steamed and were glad when Fergus called a halt beside a gurgling brown stream.

Fergus was again rubbing down his garrons when Sheila Sinclair came.

Sheila took off her coat and stood warming her hands at the fire Fergus had built a little apart from the crowd.

'What's wrong with the Sinclair fire?' Fergus asked.

'They're all crowded round it and there's no room and I hoped you'd be prepared to help a maiden in distress.'

The light was darkening into gloaming and the fire cast a glow on Sheila's figure as she turned her front and then her back to the heat.

'How much longer will you be?' Sheila called. I need someone to talk to, maybe you could hold my hand, it's cold,' she answered.

Fergus finished his grooming and walked to the fire. 'It's growing dark, Sheila, and it's time you went back to your mother and family. It's not seemly for you to be here with just me,' he told her.

Sheila looked up at Fergus, her eyes wide and insolent. 'I won't go Fergus Findlay. Not until I'm dry and you apologise for ignoring me all day.'

'Ignoring you?' Fergus asked in surprise.

'You haven't even spoken two words to me.'

Fergus looked at her. 'I had no need to speak to you, Sheila Sinclair, now, come, I'll take you back to your father,' Fergus insisted, taking her arm.

'Take your filthy hands off her,' Hamish shouted, rushing forward.

Frustrated, wet, tired and sick of Hamish watching him all the time, Fergus hit him.

Hamish sat down.

'Get up, get up,' Sheila screamed at him. 'If you want to fight for me, you can't do it sitting on your backside.'

Fergus gaped at her. Hamish struggled to his feet and glared at Fergus.

'Get on back to your father, Sheila Sinclair,' McNeil's sergeant's voice ordered. 'And you, Hamish, go with her.'

Hamish hesitated. '*Go now,*' McNeil ordered.

'Yes, sir,' Hamish answered automatically and followed Sheila.

'What was that?' McNeil asked.

'I don't know,' Fergus told him. 'I was rubbing down my horses when she came to dry off at the fire. I took her arm to conduct her back to her people when Hamish came rushing at me.'

McNeil burst out laughing.

Fergus frowned. 'She's trouble, McNeil, and she's your responsibility. Keep her away from me.'

'I can hardly order her not to speak to you, Fergus,' Neil argued. 'I'd have to be with one of you all the time.'

'I don't care what you ...' Fergus started but turned as he saw McNeil was staring past him.

Coming into the firelight with a stick in his hand was Sinclair, followed by his wife and Sheila.

Before Fergus could work out what was happening, McNeil stepped forward. 'And what do you think you're about?' he challenged Sinclair.

'I'm going to beat the man who tried to take advantage of my daughter,' Sinclair spat out. 'Stand aside.'

'Your daughter's nothing but a slut, Sinclair,' McNeil told him.

'A slut you say?' Sinclair demanded angrily, raising his stick.

'That's right, or will be if you don't stop her playing up to men and boys. I don't care if you beat her, but keep her under your eye, Sinclair, or I'll beat her for you.'

'Hamish told me ...' Sinclair shouted.

'Hamish is loopy with love, or lust, the way your daughter encourages him. Why do you think he was fighting that other lad the other night?'

'Beat him,' Sinclair's wife shouted. 'I want you to beat the blackguard.'

'Get back to your pots, woman. I've had enough of your complaints already,' McNeil ordered.

Sinclair hesitated, glaring at Fergus. 'If you lay a hand on her again, I'll kill you,' he warned.

'Then keep her away from me, or her rump will be raw from a switch, Sinclair,' Fergus told him. 'If you can't control her, I will.'

'He can't speak to you like that,' Sinclair's wife shouted.

Fergus advanced until he was staring into Sinclair's eyes. 'And if you don't keep your woman under control, you can take your cattle and go back to where you came from.'

Fergus's anger was now a physical thing, like a wall. It brought a look of fear to Sinclair's eyes.

Sinclair backed off.

***

Next morning, leaving the final preparations to the others, including a wary Hamish, Fergus went to talk to Sinclair. Sinclair's wife stepped forward.

'What do you want?' she demanded.

'To talk to the head of the house,' Fergus told her.

The woman hesitated, but stepped back as Sinclair himself came forward. 'What is it, Findlay?' he asked.

'I meant what I said last night, Sinclair. If Sheila comes bothering me again, I'll skelp her arse.'

'Over my dead body,' Sinclair's wife interrupted.

Fergus turned to her. 'And if you interfere, woman, I'll skelp yours as well,' Fergus promised.

'You hear that! *You hear that, Sinclair*!' the woman screamed.

Sinclair's face twisted as if in pain as he turned on her. 'Shut up, woman,' he rapped out. 'It's you and your talk that's given Sheila the idea that every man is chasing her.' He nodded apology to Fergus, whether for speaking so roughly to a woman, or for speaking to her in front Fergus, Fergus wasn't sure, but SInclair then turned back to his wife. 'Now, get ready to move,' he ordered.

'I'll not be spoken to like that,' the woman said, her mouth tight, angry tears coming to her eyes. 'If I'd married McLay, I'd have lived like a lady.'

'Not spoken to like that,' Sinclair smiled ruefully. His voice was sad and defeated as he spoke again. 'Then take your plaid and your brat of a girl, and the cart too, if you want, and go back and see if *Mister* McLay will have you. She's his lassie anyway.' He stood staring at her for some moments and when he spoke his voice was firm. 'Now, make up your mind. I'm going with Findlay, and if I hear another complaint out of you, he won't need to do the skelping, I'll do it myself.'

With that, Sinclair took Fergus's arm and walked him away.

'You'll be sorry,' the woman called after him. Sinclair actually grinned.

As the two men walked to the herd, they were joined by McNeil. 'I've been round the camp, Fergus. Everything is fine except for Mary Stewart's man. This rain has made his cough a bit worse.' McNeil said, hunching his shoulders and wiggling his arms for warmth.

The cattle had settled themselves quietly near the river, chewing the cud, ignoring the rain. When Fergus looked round, Hamish was one of the guards. Fergus nodded recognition. Hamish glared at him, at McNeil, at Sinclair.

Fergus roused the drove and set them moving, with Sinclair, but without his wife, or Sheila.

Late in the afternoon, with the rain still falling, now heavy, now almost stopping, now filling the world with damp, the herd stopped and stood, waiting patiently. Fergus moved forward to see why they had stopped and found the river Garry wide, brown, and boiling with flood.

'And now,' McNeil asked.

Fergus smiled. 'Sufficient unto the day is the evil thereof. We'll deal with it in the morning.'

During the night, Sheila Sinclair walked back into the camp, wet, limping and crying. Sinclair took her to Mary Stewart, where she was given soup and warmth at the fire but, otherwise, left snivelling.

CHAPTER 9

Fiona washed some clothes and went to hang them out. The washing basket was heavy and she was perspiring and it was only when she was half way across the yard that she noticed the dark unpleasant looking man coming towards her. 'What do you want?' she demanded, hefting the basket on to her hip, irritated at the interruption.

'This is Kirklea?' he asked.

'Yes.'

'And you'll be Fiona McRae.'

'Yes. What do you want?'

'Just some of what Fergus Findlay enjoys.'

'You know Fergus?' Fiona asked.

'He kens me as Black Duncan, and you can tell him when you next see him, I got my money's worth.'

Sensing what was to come, Fiona dropped the basket and turned to run to the barn to get a pitchfork to defend herself. Black Duncan was too quick, in three strides he had grabbed the shoulder of her dress. The dress ripped and Fiona knew from the cold air on her damp skin, her left breast was exposed. She grabbed at the dress and tripped.

Her father rushed from the house, but Duncan hit him hard. Fiona saw him fall back and lie still.

She struggled to rise but a hand turned her over and she saw Black Duncan's face leering down as his hand took her throat and his knees pushed her legs apart. She was aware of his other hand fumbling with his trews and could smell his sweat and raw breath. She raised her hands to scratch at the fleshy features but, before she could reach them, the features were dashed aside.

'Are you all right?' a voice asked, but Fiona rushed to where her father was groggily beginning to rise. She helped him up and steadied him as he stood.

'Where is the blackguard?' McRae asked.

'I have him here,' the voice said and Fiona turned to find Maitland holding Black Duncan. 'He'll not get away.'

Fiona turned to look at Maitland, about to thank him, but realised from the direction of his gaze and the brutish look on his face, that her torn dress was exposing her body, and she released her hold on her father's arm to hold the flapping shoulder of her garment closer. He's just another of the same ilk, she thought.

'Come inside,' she told her father.

'What about him?' her father asked, nodding at Duncan.

'I'll take care of him,' Maitland assured him. 'I'll tie him up and take him to the proper authority. Can you give me some twine or rope to tie him up?' he asked, turning the still dazed Duncan over and pulling his arms back and his hands together.

Fiona went to the cowshed. Proper authority, she muttered to herself. If I'd got to that hayfork, the proper authority would have been the grave digger.

Holding her dress together, she took some short pieces of thick cord from a hook.

When she got back to Maitland, her father was smiling at him like a schoolboy with his school captain, simpering, she thought, as he turned the same foolish smile in her direction.

'You haven't thanked Mr Maitland properly,' McRae chastised. 'Sort your dress and we'll welcome him as we should.'

Fiona gave Maitland the twine and went inside, feeling mean. Up in her room, she sat on her bed, her head in her hands, willing herself not to weep.

She sat up, changed her dress and went downstairs, where her father was pouring whisky for Maitland and himself.

'If you can entertain Mr Maitland for half an hour, Father,' she said, 'I'll make some scones as soon as I've dealt with the chores I was busy with.' She turned, now smiling, to Maitland. 'I thank you for your most timely intervention, Mr Maitland, but I must see to my washing, if you'll excuse me I'll leave you in my father's care for the moment.'

Maitland returned her smile. 'There's no need for thanks, Miss McRae, I'm sorry I didn't come earlier and in time to prevent the whole incident.'

'I suspect if you had, he'd have returned later, after you'd gone, so, your intervention was most timely.'

Outside, she gathered her scattered, muddy washing, glared at her late assailant, now tied up firmly. She resisted the temptation to kick him where he squatted, and took her washing back inside.

She was back in the kitchen with a pail of clean water, preparing to wash her hands when her father came through. 'I've asked Mr Maitland to stay and eat,' her father told her.

'Eat? Eat what? We've nothing for entertaining! I can manage a scone and cheese but that's it!'

'Maybe you can make some soup,' her father suggested, turning and going back to the front room and his guest.

Fiona washed her hands and arms, dashed water on her face and found her hands shaking in delayed shock. Her throat thickened with tears but she held on, pushing them back and began cutting savagely at kale and carrots before sliding the choppings from her board into a pot of simmering water and adding the remains of the skin of a ham long eaten.

She could hear her father answer Maitland's questions by calling the seed merchant a blackguard and a cheat – they still owed him for last year's seeds – as she finished setting the kitchen table to eat.

She went into the front room, forced a smile, and was met by a sweeping glance from Maitland that took in her hair, her neck, hesitated on her breasts, her waist, hips and dropped to her feet.

'Have you had any more trouble with the haberdasher, Miss McRae?' Maitland asked as Fiona served him with soup.

'What's that,' her father asked. 'Has that old witch been uncivil?'

'No,' Fiona told him, keeping the smile on her lips. 'I didn't have my purse with me and Mr Maitland kindly paid for me.'

'Damned pinchpenny,' her father muttered, slurping his soup.

'So what kind of farming will you be doing at The Mearns?' Fiona asked.

'Some sheep and a bit of this and that,' Maitland explained.

'No crops?' Fiona persisted.

'We'll see,' Maitland answered. 'How did your own crops do, McRae?'

Not giving much away and asking all about this place, Fiona thought, as she collected plates.

'The weather was too wet and then the market took a down turn,' McRae explained. 'And then those drovers come through demanding grazing.'

'Do they bother you a lot, Mr McRae?'

'No, they don't,' Fiona butted in. 'I don't know what Father is going on about. The Findlays have been coming here and bringing Father news for as long as I can remember.'

Maitland scratched his chin. 'Findlay, I think I've met him. Shortish, well, average height, not the bear like men most of them are.'

'That's him,' McRae said. 'Torments Fiona when he comes, but I'll put a stop to that.'

'Charge him for the grazing,' Maitland suggested. 'I understand many of the farmers and places they stop at have resorted to that.'

'We've never charged the Findlays,' Fiona intervened.

'Not in the past, lassie. But there's always a first time. Oh, aye, always a first time,' her father told her, smirking in satisfaction.

Fiona glared at her father and noticed Maitland was smiling to himself. 'One of the reasons I came today, was to see if you'd come to my own place some time, you and your daughter, Mr McRae.'

Fiona thought her father would burst with delighted surprise.

'I have a woman who *does* for me,' Maitland explained, 'but I can't offer the kind of meal a visit from a young lady like Fiona deserves, but perhaps you'd come for tea some afternoon.'

'Delighted, we'd be delighted,' McRae told him, almost dancing in excitement.

As Maitland was leaving, he bent forward as if to kiss Fiona's cheek, her father smiling approval, but Fiona backed off and held out her hand. Maitland smiled, took her hand and raised it to his lips.

As Fiona watched, Maitland untied Duncan's feet, then tied the cords together, knotted one end round Duncan's neck and the other end to his stirrup, before saluting the McRaes and urging his horse forward.

As they moved off, seeing them together, it struck Fiona that Maitland's intervention had been so precisely timed it could have been arranged. Her musing was interrupted by her father.

'He's a thorough gentleman, Fiona. You could do much worse than marry him,' McRae commented as he watched Maitland ride away.

Fiona shuddered. 'He's a lecher, Father, as much as the man he's taken away to the proper authority. He strips me every time he looks at me.'

'You're a well formed lassie, Fiona. Men will look at you.'

Fiona stared at her father. 'A gentleman? He makes me feel a slut. I'm no great beauty, but Fergus Findlay makes me feel like one when he looks at me.'

'That tramp! I'll not hear a word about him and you, d'ye hear, Fiona?'

'Then you'd better get someone else to clean your house and feed your hens,' Fiona flung back as she went inside and up to her room to prepare for bed.

In bed, Fiona's thoughts turned to Fergus — what would he have done if he'd found someone molesting me, she wondered. Beaten him to death, or slit his throat; she'd seen Fergus violent, passionate, but his passion was directed differently to what she'd seen in Maitland's eyes; a proper gentleman, she smiled to herself.

CHAPTER 10

Fergus didn't rush the morning. As people took their porridge, he called McNeil and walked along the bloated surging river until he came to the head of Loch Garry itself. The loch was wider but the water calm. Fergus didn't stop but carried on until he came to a spot where the loch was at least fifty yards wide.

'We'll cross here,' he told McNeil. 'The current in the river is too strong and would sweep the beasts away. The pull of it stretches into the loch for a bit, the animals feel it, and panic. Here, the water's deeper, but calm.'

'What about the people?' McNeil asked.

'What would you have done in the army?' Fergus asked him.

'Float them over on rafts.'

'There's plenty of timber about,' Fergus pointed out. 'And I expect your old soldiers know how to make a raft.'

Two boatmen came, Fergus spoke to them and they nodded agreement.

Fergus and the others drove the cattle to the loch's edge, where they drank and stood staring, but showed no inclination to plunge in. Fergus let them stand as he sorted three-foot lengths of thick cord from his packhorse. McNeil and the other men involved in droving watched. Fergus chose one of the beasts he had seen regularly at the front and tied one of the cords to its tail. He pulled a second beast forward, forced its mouth open and tied the free end of the string round its bottom jaw.

'The tie has to be under the beast's tongue or it will drown and drag the others with it. Remember that!' Fergus told the men.

McNeil took another of the leaders and did the same with its tail and the jaw of a second beast.

Once he had eight beasts tied together, Fergus checked what McNeil had done and nodded, then told each of the two watching Stewart boys to get into a boat.

Fergus led the first of the eight beasts into the water until it was knee deep behind one of the boats and tied a cord round its bottom jaw and the other end of the cord to the stern of the boat before jumping into the boat himself and grinned at McNeil as the boatman leant back on his oars. The lead cow bellowed in surprise at the new pull on its jaw and hesitated before starting to follow the boat. As the water grew deeper, the leader started to swim and the rest followed.

McNeil laughed and repeated the process with the second boat.

On the other side, Fergus untied the beasts with the help of the two boys and had himself rowed back to the main herd.

On the third trip, Hamish led a string of eight forward to the boat Fergus was in. Fergus noticed the smirk, but took it to for a grin of triumph at getting the cows sorted.

'Ready,' the boatman called and Fergus leapt into the boat.

The cattle had just started swimming and Fergus was looking ahead when the boatman stopped rowing and pointed behind.

The lead beast had started to gag and flounder. Fergus leapt on to its back, drawing his dirk as he went.

He felt the beast's body sink under his weight but managed to retain his balance and slashed at the cord that tied its tail to the second in line. As he fell, he could see the cow's horns threatening to impale him. He twisted his body and felt the horns brush him as he dropped into the water. He sank until his feet touched bottom and he kicked himself to the surface, grabbing what was left of the cut cord.

By this time, the boatman was yelling and pointing at the gasping threshing lead cow tied to the back of the boat. 'Cut it loose,' Fergus shouted. 'Let it drown.'

At the sound of Fergus's voice, the boatman gathered himself, grab his knife and cut the floundering beast loose.

The boatman threw a line to Fergus who tied it to the now leading beast and struggled back into the boat.

When they reached the shore, leaving the surviving beasts in the care of the Stewart boys, Fergus went back to the main herd. Hot anger keeping him warm despite his dunking.

As he got out of the boat, Fergus saw Sinclair was holding Hamish by the scruff of the neck. 'He was checking the ties just before you left,' Sinclair said.

Fergus hit Hamish in blind anger, then felt arms imprison him. He struggled but couldn't get free. He stopped struggling and was released and tried to grab Hamish's throat but was again restrained.

Hamish's mother came and took his arm to lead him away but he shook her off. Her look of dismay did nothing to relieve Fergus.

'Calm down, calm down,' Fergus heard McNeil tell him and turned to face him.

'All eight would have drowned, *all eight*,' Fergus shouted.

'I know, I know, but even eight beasts are not worth a man's life, nor a hanging for taking it,' McNeil insisted.

Fergus was not calmed. 'My good name would have gone with them, McNeil. I don't lose beasts. I'll kill him yet.'

'No you won't. He's too stupid to understand why, and we've lost a beast or two before.'

'Three,' Fergus pointed out before turning to the gape mouthed others to explain. 'I divide what price I get evenly between what beasts I've bought myself and those the farmers have trusted me with. Every drove loses a few beasts. It comes off the price of the farmer's beasts as well as the drover's. If I lose too many, the best farmers will lose confidence and I'll just have to take what I can get. My good name is something I protect with my life, if I have to.'

The men nodded understanding.

Calmer now, Fergus turned to McNeil, 'Keep that Hamish away from me. Let him look after Sheila, it's all he's good for!' Then, taking a deep breath, Fergus grinned at McNeil. 'Let's get on with the drove,' he said, squeezing some of the water from his trews.

By now, even McNeil could see the cattle on the one shore were staring across at their friends on the other side of the loch, bellows from there calling them to come over.

The towing boats, crawling like beetles back and forth across the loch with their trailing strings of cattle, had made only a few more journeys, when it became clear the rest of the cattle were ready to cross by themselves.

'You and you,' Fergus called to Sinclair and three other men, 'take a garron and swim with them, two of you with me and the others with McNeil,' he ordered, mounting one of the garrons. 'Keep the beasts heads forward or they'll wallow about and drown in the end. Keep the herd tight so that the ones in the middle can't turn round.'

They yip, yip, yipped across the loch, waving sticks and prodding cows that threatened to turn out of the lines.

The other men got into the boats and were ready to manage the dripping beasts as they waded out of the loch.

It was now Fergus's turn to help McNeil deal with the rafts.

Among the people gathered on the shore, they found Mary Stewart trying to restrain a trembling Stewart from being involved in the work. 'Getting wet in the storm didn't do him any good,' Mary confided.

The old soldiers had scrounged old timbers, dead trees and had chopped what extra they needed to make two rafts, wide and long enough to take a cart, then used the ponies to drag the rafts into the shallows. They tied one of the rafts to a boat with a rope. The boatmen got into the boat with an oar each side as the women and the younger children were ushered on to the raft. The boatmen lay back on their oars and the raft wobbled its way across to shrieks from the children. On the other side the children gathered excitedly. Bboys pushing and telling how frightened the girls had been and how unconcernedly they themselves took the adventure.

Again, the third trip almost proved a disaster. The raft was loaded with people. For the older boys, who had helped push and load, it had become old hat and they became boisterous. First one, then another, ran from side to side of the raft, making it rock, first to one side, then the other, to the screams of the girls. One mother took a swipe at her son. The boy dodged and fell over.

'He can't swim,' the mother wailed.

The rowers stopped. The crowd on the raft moved to see what was happening and the raft tilted dangerously. Women cuffed children back and the raft righted itself with a splash.

The boy in the water was wallowing, gasping, sinking. Fergus had already turned his swimming garron towards him when Hamish jumped in and grabbed the boy. The boy grabbed the swimming Hamish round the neck and they both sank. By then both Fergus and McNeil had reached the spot and took hold of one body each, pulling them to shore.

Hamish grabbed a stick and advanced on the retching lad. Fergus stepped in his way. 'He's a boy, Hamish, let his mother and father deal with him, you're too angry.'

Hamish glared at him, but turned away to the fire, shivering, as he picked up the coat and jacket he'd discarded to swim.

McNeil organised the loading of the first cart on to the raft. It meant pulling the raft close to the shingle beach, pushing the cart on to it, then heaving the raft forward until it floated in the deepening water.

By the time Fergus could relax, he noticed Sheila Sinclair was feeding Hamish hot soup and was glad to join McNeil and take some from Mary Stewart.

'How is Stewart?' Fergus asked.

'Bad, Fergus. I don't know if he can travel.'

'We won't go far. I just want to walk the beasts to warm them a wee bit,' Fergus told her. 'Stay here, the fire is good and see how he is in the morning. McNeil can stay with you, I'm sure.'

McNeil nodded.

Late next morning, resting in company with several other droves, Fergus could tell by the way Mary had her arms round the two boys' shoulders that the news was bad.

McNeil came later. 'I've buried him,' was all McNeil said.

The death brought sadness to what had promised to become gaiety after the adventure of the loch. Fergus could see Sheila was by now driving Hamish mad as she talked and smiled with other lads from other droves, and had a foreboding of more trouble from that direction.

Next day they were on the move. They splashed over the one river, round the rising ground of a hillside and over a second river to the more level stretch leading to the easy walk to Fort William.

With the easier going, Fergus's thoughts turned to Fiona. He'd noticed she looked tired that last time. Maybe his idea of two more years was too long. Should he suggest she come away with him on his way north again? Would her father come?

CHAPTER 11

Two days later, from the kitchen window, Fiona watched Maitland dismount.

Her father rushed out to meet Maitland and shake his hand.

'How is Fiona?' she heard Maitland ask.

'Come away in and take some refreshment,' McRae invited. 'Fiona will soon have a scone made. She's a fine worker in the kitchen, not to mention her other work with the milking and her hens.'

'So, she's recovered, has she?'

'Oh, aye, a thing like that she can take in her stride, Mr Maitland. In her stride, just, aye. But come on in, Fiona will see to the horse, don't you worry about it. FIONA,' he shouted.

Fiona ignored the shout and continued to watch.

'She must be busy, Mr Maitland. Let me put the horse away but go you right in, go right in,' McRae encouraged, taking the horse's reins and leading it towards one of the sheds.

Maitland stood looking around, stretched to his full height, looked round again and pulled his waistcoat straight over his rounded belly with both hands.

'You're still out here,' McRae commented. 'Let's get out of this wind,' he suggested, ushering Maitland in through the door without noticing Fiona.

Moments later, leaving Maitland in the front room, her father came back to the kitchen.

'Fiona, it's Mr Maitland. I'll get him a dram while you butter a scone for us, there's a good lass.'

Maitland had followed McRae back to the kitchen and nodded and smiled to Fiona, who could do little but smile back.

'That's better,' her father said, agitation making his own smile look daft. 'I'll leave you to chat, while I get the whisky,' he added, rubbing his hands together as he went back to the front room.

'You look much more composed,' Maitland said. 'Fresher,' he corrected. 'I hope the incident the other day has not upset you too much.'

'No,' Fiona answered. 'I am quite recovered, and I must thank you once again for your intervention, Mr Maitland.'

Her father came back, smiling his idiotic smile, irritating Fiona. Her irritation increased as her father continued, almost simpering. 'Fiona's a dab hand at baking, Mr Maitland. If there's no scone or bannock left, she'll soon have one in the oven. You'll see to that Fiona?'

'Yes, Father, go through and talk, I'll bring oatcakes as soon as they're ready.'

The men went back to the front room, but Fiona could hear their talking through the open door.

'I was sorry to learn from the seed merchant that you owe him money from some time back,' Maitland said, and Fiona paid more attention as she went about her preparations.

'Nothing we can't pay once the harvest is in, Mr Maitland.'

She heard Maitland snort. 'What harvest? All I've seen, other than Fiona's kitchen garden, is a few patches of kale and corn, and a field of hay that's gone wild. And it's not just the seed merchant, is it, McRae? There are other debts. In fact, my guess is that you are on the verge of bankruptcy. I believe that selling the farm is your only real way out. It's run down and it will cost money to bring it back, but I might be prepared to offer you a fair price.'

Fiona felt anger and despair tighten her throat.

'This is our home, Mr Maitland. We have nowhere else to go,' McRae bleated.

'I'm not suggesting you leave McRae, but you must see you can't go on like this or you'll have to sell out for a beggar's price.'

'Maybe someone will marry Fiona and take over the place,' he father said, in what she recognised as his "I know better than you" voice.

'Has she someone in mind?' Maitland asked.

'Not seriously,' McRae admitted. 'But she has talked of Fergus Findlay coming here.'

'The drover?' Maitland laughed. 'Those men never settle.'

At that, Fiona went in.

Maitland smiled at her, then turned to her father. 'Drovers are by nature nomadic, wanderers. It's because of that that they have no real regard for other people's property and they thieve and rob whenever they can.'

'That's not been our experience, Mr Maitland,' Fiona interjected. 'The Findlays may be drovers, but they treat other people with respect. Is that not so, Father?'

Her father frowned. Maitland looked at her father as if curious to see if McRae would support his previous talk of Fergus coming to Kirklea.

'I put up with the father,' McRae said at last. 'But I'll not put up with the son.'

'How can you say such a thing?' Fiona demanded. 'It was Fergus who fixed the roof for us, and on his last visit, he worked on the cow shed.'

Her father stared at her.

'Well, didn't he?' Fiona demanded.

'He gets his grazing for nothing, I'm entitled to expect something in return,' her father answered.

Fiona stumped back to the kitchen.

'She seems quite defensive about Findlay,' she heard Maitland say.

'They were friends when they were bairns, that's all,' her father answered.

'I was taking that fellow who upset Fiona to the authorities when he told me his story. It seems Findlay stole from him. Sold some cattle for the man, then refused to pay. The poor fellow had to sell his herd for what he could get to pay his rent and was on his way to emigrate, as so many are doing, when he stumbled on Kirklea. Tired and hungry, he tripped as he tried to ask Fiona for a crust of bread and tore her dress.'

The lie was so blatant, Fiona was struck dumb. Memories of the man kneeling beside her flooded back, but before she could get back to answer the accusations, Maitland continued. 'I've arranged for the fellow to have some employment so that he can earn a few pennies to tide him over in Canada, or America, wherever he chooses to go.'

'So that's the truth of it, Findlay ruined the man,' Fiona heard her father say.

Fiona rushed into the room. 'Father ...' Fiona began.

Her father, red in the face, turned on her. 'Get back in the kitchen, Fiona, and watch your tongue,' he ordered.

Fiona gasped, but shock made her do as she was told.

***

Later, her blood still rushing in her head, as they watched Maitland ride away, her father turned to her. 'How could you, lassie? The man's rich and a neighbour. You more or less accused him of being a liar. I'll ask you to treat guests in this house with more respect.'

Fiona turned to face him, hands on hips, arms akimbo. 'He, or the man who came here, *is* a liar. If it is the other man, then Maitland is too eager to listen to the words of a vagabond instead of honest folk. In either case, the best that can be said of him is that he's dishonest. Now I want to know what other lies he's been filling your head with?'

'Enough, Fiona, I'm your father and I'll not be spoken to like that.'

Fiona stuck her face closer. 'People earn respect, Father. Earn it, not sitting dreaming, or listening to ghost stories about people who go out of their way to help.'

McRae slumped. 'I'm only trying to look after you, lassie. You need a decent husband. One that can provide for you. Give you a proper house to look after.'

'And slave in and be misused. I'll rather walk the hills with Fergus,' she said.

CHAPTER 12

Fergus roused everyone early and led them through the glens with the mist still clinging to the side of the bens, which seemed to tower over and enclose them. Even the most boisterous of the boys were subdued, glancing round nervously.

As they broke out on to moorland, the spirits of the crowd revived, and even Mary Stewart smiled under McNeil's teasing.

In late afternoon, Fergus turned the drove into a side glen and called a halt, but there was no rest. In the gloaming, two men, a father and son by their appearance, made their way to Fergus.

'This is not a stopping place for droves,' the older man told him. 'If you want to stay, you'll have to pay.'

Fergus stared. 'Pay? I've never paid in this part.'

'Maybe no',' the man agreed. 'But from now on, it will cost you five shillings for the drove to stop, and, if there is a crowd of people like this, it will be ten shillings.'

Fergus glared at the farmer. 'Ten shillings!'

'Well, this time it will only be the five,' the farmer conceded.

'I have no money with me,' Fergus told them.

'You're Fergus Findlay, are you no'?'

'Just that,' Fergus answered, concerned that the younger man's glance had noticed Sheila Sinclair teasing Hamish on the edge of the crowd. 'But I still have no money. All I can give you is a note and that will only fall due in three months' time,' Fergus added.

'Your note will be good enough for me,' the farmer told him.

Fergus wrote the note and gave it to the farmer. 'You'll join us for a dram and a bite to eat?' he asked.

The young man looked pleadingly at his father, who nodded assent.

Fergus led them to Mary Stewart's fire, where he found both McNeil and Sinclair.

'Mary,' Fergus said. 'I have everything you'll need, could you make us some food while McNeil and I entertain our guests.'

Mary smiled her acceptance and the farmer and his son sat down on a log and started to chat.

'You'll be for emigrating?' the farmer asked. 'There have been others, even one or two on their way back again.'

'On their way back?' McNeil queried, looking at Fergus.

'Aye, just that! Refused emigration by their laird,' the farmer said.

McNeil sat forward. 'I thought they were glad to see the people go and make room for sheep. Even burned their houses over them, and chased them away with dogs, if they refused to leave.'

'Mostly, you're right, but here and there is a laird that still counts his wealth in his people and the number of rents he's owed, even if his people are so poor they can never pay the rents.'

McNeil frowned. 'Are there any like that among our people?' he asked Sinclair.

'None that I ken of, but some of the young men may still owe the laird a year or two's work, not to mention those soldiers, who were away and never worked out their terms. That red haired lad, Hamish, for example,' Sinclair said, nodding to where Sheila was talking to Hamish, but glancing from time to time in the young farmer's direction.

Mary joined them, smiling to Fergus, McNeil, Sinclair and both the farmers in turn. 'It's good to see families staying together,' the farmer mentioned, looking from Mary to McNeil and Sinclair.

Mary smiled. 'We're not family, my husband died of the consumption on the way down here,' she explained.

'And you are going on?' the farmer asked.

'There's nothing to keep me anymore, and I've grown to think of all those here as family. You'll both stay and eat,' she asked McNeil and Sinclair.

'Sheila …' Sinclair began.

'Can come and eat. I'm sure this young man,' she smiled towards the farmer's son, 'will enjoy a young girl's company, and Sheila needs to meet more than Hamish.'

Sinclair rose to call Sheila. She wasn't far off, having manoeuvred Hamish to a point just inside the farmer's son's field of vision, where she was running round carts and fires with squeals of delight as Hamish chased her.

Fergus tried to ignore Sheila, but couldn't with her oohs' and ah's at the farmer's son's comments, and the way she would touch his arm from time to time, then turn and ignore the lad, as if listening to the adults. All this, with Hamish's gloomy presence in the background, niggled at the corners of his attention.

Not that he needed to say much, Mary and Sinclair talked easily to the farmer about crops and the weather, until the farmer thanked them and rose to go. 'I'll thank you for the food and I'm sorry for the charge, Findlay, but times are hard, as I've no doubt you ken yourself,' he said. 'And I wish you God speed, Mrs Stewart,' he added. 'Come, laddie,' he told his son. 'You've dallied enough with the lassie; if we stay any longer her faither will insist you get wed.'

The lad's face reddened, but he managed to nod to Sheila as he followed his father.

Fergus rose to go on his last rounds, looking at McNeil to see if he would join him, but McNeil was too busy talking to Mary and Sinclair. As he watched, however, Mary rose and walked determinedly to where Sheila was looking round for Hamish. The slap took Sheila, and Fergus, by surprise. As Sheila raised her hand to her cheek, Mary spoke. 'Don't you ever dare to behave like that while I'm the hostess, or you'll get more than a slap, young lady. Now, you'll help by washing the plates and pots.'

Sheila looked at her father. 'Do as you're told,' Sinclair told her.

'I'll marry a rich man, wait and see,' Sheila shouted back.

'Not behaving like his whore, you won't,' Mary told her. 'If you want him to marry you, you'll have to behave like his wife, otherwise he'll get you in the family way and dump you to get on with grovelling to keep yourself, and the bairn as well.'

Fergus left. Bruce joined him.

***

At Kirklea, Fiona gave up resisting her father's constant nagging to visit The Mearns. Her agreement had him smiling and laughing as they prepared for the walk up the glen and over the hill.

Fiona's mood lightened as they walked in the sunshine, but she drew into herself as they started down the track towards The Mearns big house. Beside it, they could see a carriage standing.

'A carriage,' McRae commented, smiling to Fiona.

The house was solid and square, built of grey stone, without adornment. Like an insane asylum, Fiona thought.

The housekeeper, who opened the door, was arthritic and abrupt, and left them standing in a hallway with several heavy panelled doors on either side and disappeared through one. Fiona could see that, at its end, the hallway led to the kitchen, from which an appetising stew smell drifted out, making the saliva gather in her mouth.

The housekeeper reappeared and closed the door of that room behind her.

'He'll see you,' the housekeeper snapped as she opened another door, nodding for them to go through. Inside the room, the heavy drapes were almost closed and it was only just possible to see the vague outlines of the furniture. As Fiona's eyes became accustomed to the gloom, she noticed the place was well, if garishly, furnished.

'Let me take your shawl,' Maitland said as he entered.

'No, thank you,' Fiona answered. At her father's insistence she'd dressed as for church, in a dark dress, high collared and severe. The dress did little for her, except emphasise the flatness of her trunk, from below her breasts down to her hips, where the dress flared into pleats. She'd put the shawl over her shoulders to reduce how it emphasised her bust, but Maitland's eyes told her she hadn't succeeded.

As Maitland continued to hold out his hand, Fiona had little option, short of being rude, but to take off the shawl and submit to Maitland's searching glance.

As Maitland pulled the drapes back to let in some light, highlighting the clashing of materials and colours in the room, a smiling McRae opened the conversation. 'It's a fine house you have here, Mr Maitland. But you could maybe do with someone younger who would be happy to let in the light.'

'Mrs Lafferty suits me well enough, McRae,' Maitland told him. 'I'm out a good deal of the time and she's an adequate cook.'

'Adequate is hardly good enough for a fine house like this, Mr Maitland. Is it Fiona?' McRae asked.

Fiona's kept her face devoid of expression as she answered. 'Mr Maitland's arrangements are none of our concern, Father.'

The housekeeper looked round the door. 'D'ye want tea?' she demanded.

Maitland glanced at Fiona. Caught between tasting tea for the first time and making the visit as short as possible, Fiona hesitated, then smiled to Mrs Lafferty. 'There's no need to bother,' Fiona said. 'I must be getting back for my own chores.'

'Please yersel',' Mrs Lafferty commented and turned to go.

'Of course we want tea, and bring some of that fruit cake, if you please,' Maitland ordered.

Mrs Lafferty straightened. 'There's no' much of it left,' she reminded.

'Bring it anyway,' Maitland insisted. 'If you please.'

Mrs Lafferty brought a rattling tray with cups and saucers and a plate with slices of fruitcake, which she dumped on a side table near the window and turned to pull the drapes closer.

'Leave them as they are,' Maitland ordered.

'As you please,' Mrs Lafferty answered. 'It's your own furniture to have bleached by the sun.'

Mrs Lafferty limped stiffly out again.

'I'm sure a younger body would be more accommodating,' McRae commented.

Mrs Lafferty came back with the teapot. 'Will I pour, or will you manage yoursel'?' she asked.

'I'm sure Fiona will do the honours,' Maitland told her.

They made general conversation as they drank from the cups. Fiona was surprised to find the tea had a delicate flavour, not sweet, yet far from bitter. The cake was delicious and, when they had finished, Fiona insisted on taking the tray back to the kitchen for Mrs Lafferty.

The kitchen proved to be bright and spotless, copper pans gleaming on the walls.

'You didnae need to bother, lassie,' Mrs Lafferty said.

'I wanted to thank you for your cake. I don't get the chance to bake over much, and I do appreciate it when I taste something as nice as your fruit cake.'

'Your mother surely showed you how to bake?' Mrs Lafferty asked.

'My mother's been dead these last few years, and I have the house and the farm to look after. As you'd see, my father isn't strong. While he does what he can, I have to do most of the heavy work.'

Mrs Lafferty seemed to be deciding about something so Fiona talked about kitchen things for a time.

Mrs Lafferty seemed to make up her mind. 'I'm not one to talk behind my employer's back,' she began. 'But be careful, lassie. Maitland's only real interest is in gathering gear, money for preference, but farms and anything that comes to hand as well. That's nothing strange, but he sometimes brings lassies,' she turned up her nose in disgust, 'that can be described as nothing but tarts, especially if that man Duncan is about. I'll thank you not to repeat what I've said, but you seem a decent lassie and I've noticed the way he looks at you.'

Fiona smiled. 'You have no need to worry about what you said being repeated. Would this Duncan be a red faced, heavy built man from the far north?'

'Aye, it sounds like him. Have you met?'

'You might say that, Mrs Lafferty,' Fiona told her, smiling. 'It's been nice to chat, but I have chores, and we must get back to Kirklea.'

As she came to the door of the room where her father was talking to Maitland, Fiona heard her father say, '... I'll think on it, Mr Maitland.'

She paused, wondering what was being discussed.

'Till the Spring, McRae,' Maitland said firmly.

Fiona pushed the door open. 'I'm sorry Father; I have chores and must be on my way.'

'I'm sorry you can't stay longer, Miss McRae,' Maitland said, rising and holding out his hand to Fiona. Fiona held hers out. Maitland took it and lifted it to his fat lips, smiling, showing brown stained teeth. Fiona struggled to keep the revulsion from her expression.

***

As they walked over the hill, Fiona let her father struggle to keep up with her angry stride. 'He's not such a bad man, Fiona,' he managed to gasp.

'Not such a bad fellow is he?' Fiona answered, stopping and facing her father. 'He's a lecher, Father. The kind that indulges himself with prostitutes.'

Her father drew back. 'You'll not use words like that. Your mother would never have done it.'

Fiona stopped and looked directly at him. 'Why are you defending him, Father?'

'Because he's got money, and would make us comfortable, if you would just marry the man, Fiona.'

Fiona stared at him in disgust for several moments. 'What has he been saying to you? What is it you have to think about before Spring?'

'He just wants to bring sheep to the farm.'

'And wants to put them on Lochlea as well? Is that it?'

Her father just stared, his mouth tight , refusing to answer.

'You know he's been buying up our debts and if he insists on payment, we'll have to sell the farm and leave.'

Her father's eyes widened and his mouth slackened.

Fiona nodded. 'Is that it? He'll make you bankrupt; send you to debtor's prison unless he gets the farm. And you hope, if I marry him, you can stay on? Do you really think a man like that will keep you on if you don't work? You'll have a far better chance with Fergus.'

Her father sneered. 'How could a drover help anybody? He's no better than a tinker.'

Fiona stared at him in disgust for several moments, before walking on.

***

As she lay in bed, Fiona's mind replayed the day. Did she want to be the lady of a place like The Mearns? Fine clothes and fine china didn't change the chores. A big house, with its decorum and gentility covering misery and loneliness, could be as much a prison as a home. There would be time enough for that. What she wanted was a break from this constant work and worry, to feel the wind in her hair and the rain in her face. With that, her thoughts turned to Fergus. Where was he? He'd hinted at taking her to Dornoch. Why didn't he just do that?

CHAPTER 13

Fergus pushed the drove on, making for Tyndrum. They were getting close to Kirklea, and he was thinking of Fiona, when McNeil asked if he would object to some of the people taking some time in the town.

In fact, Fergus had been debating whether to push on past Tyndrum, or stop short of it. Two other drove roads converged in Tyndrum and, from time to time, herds got mixed and there had been accusations of stealing each other's cattle that ended with blood spilt. He decided to stop at a place convenient enough for the people to go into Tyndrum, but clear of contamination with other herds.

'We'll need guards, McNeil,' he pointed out. 'It's too easy for a beast to disappear and, as you've seen, there are hungry mouths on their way to Glasgow to look for work that will not scruple at taking one beast from those that have many, like ourselves.'

'The old soldiers?' McNeil asked.

Fergus looked sceptical.

'They've had their days of getting drunk and into fights, and are glad enough to stay with their families,' McNeil explained.

Guards posted, Fergus and McNeil drifted to Mary Stewart's, where McNeil joked and talked with the boys. An hour later, they decided to make their rounds, taking the boys with them in the balmy, late evening light. McNeil talked to the boys, sometimes ruffling the younger one's hair. They tossed a piece of stick between them and

Fergus joined in a game of tag, laughing as McNeil tripped and fell to let the younger lad catch him.

Their attention was distracted when the older boy pointed and shouted. 'Look at Hamish. He's all bloody.'

Fergus turned to look. Hamish was trailing behind Sinclair and Sheila. Sheila, crying and protesting, was being dragged along by Sinclair. More trouble, Fergus thought.

They all made their way to Mary's fire.

'What happened?' Mary asked.

'Sheila asked if she could go and I said, no,' Sinclair told her. 'Then she started tormenting Hamish and I got so tired of it that I said she could go for an hour. In the end, I went to look for her and found her in the middle of a fight, trying to save this worthless clown, Hamish.'

Hamish's features stiffened. 'Sheila was only playing, like she always does, when three of them from another drove started to push her about.'

'And you jumped to her defence?' Fergus asked.

'What else could I do?' Hamish demanded.

'When I got there,' Sinclair put in, 'they were giving Hamish a beating.'

Hamish laughed. 'He knocked two of their heads together, and just slapped the other one out of the way.'

'Stop your sniffling,' Mary told Sheila.

'They didn't have any respect,' Sheila complained.

'I told you what would happen if you behave like a slut,' Mary responded. 'Now, go and wash and tidy yourself.'

Mary turned to the men. 'And you lot go and stay out of our way for a while, I want to talk to this young woman. Take the boys with you.'

Sinclair took Hamish away, leaving Fergus and McNeil with the boys.

'Can we clean your rifle, Mr McNeil?' the older boy asked.

'No, I don't want to take it out with all these people about. A gun makes people want to fight,' McNeil explained.

'Tell us about Spain,' the boys asked.

'And the senoritas,' Fergus suggested.

'They're fat and ugly,' McNeil said, winking at Fergus, before turning back to the boys. 'It's hot and cold, like Canada. Hot in the plains in the summer, and freezing cold in the winter ...'

Fergus listened, grinning at the way the boys sat open mouthed as McNeil talked.

In the end, the younger boy started to doze, and McNeil took both of them back to Mary.

As McNeil joined Fergus for a last look round, he was smiling.

'You like Mary?' Fergus said.

'Aye, I do. I've enjoyed being with her boys. It's not that I've had no female company. In the years I was in the army, I had enough women, some I might have settled with, but we didn't always get paid and, when the money ran out, they left. You can't blame them for that.'

He paused. Fergus wondered if he was remembering some particular woman, but McNeil continued, 'And, again, we were always on the move. I've never had a chance to have a family, boys of my own, and it's now I'm beginning to realise what I've missed. Don't let it happen to you,' he added.

Fergus's thoughts turned to Fiona and Old Bab's warning.

* * *

To ensure the young men in the company didn't carry on the spree they'd started in Tyndrum, Fergus pushed the drive through valleys, over hills and down the side of Loch Lomond for the next two days, and only eased up when they were in Kirklea's glen.

It was late, but still light, with the moon rising pale over the hills, when they had all settled and the remains of the Tyndrum whisky made its appearance. The fumes of it drew the piper, adding to the gaiety.

Despite his impatience, Fergus resisted the urge to go calling on Fiona at such a late hour, but couldn't resist going to look at the farmhouse.

Even in the dim light, it looked as it always did, needing attention.

* * *

Following their visit to The Mearns, Fiona was despondent, and made more depressed by her father's attempts at encouraging her to think well of Maitland. He started by admiring Maitland. Fiona only sniffed. He tried to denigrate Fergus, when Fiona grew angry, he resorted to wheedling.

Tired and depressed at Fergus's continued non-appearance, and feeling her resistance was beginning to be weakened by her father's constant badgering, Fiona went about her chores, finding it difficult to cling to the belief that Fergus would come back before she was somehow forced into marrying Maitland, and spending her life providing children on demand in a prison like The Mearns.

After dark, as she lay tired in her bed, her bedroom window open to the warm night, she heard the strains of a bagpipe and felt her pulse quicken as the wild notes brought thoughts of Fergus.

At first, unsure if it was her imagination, she lay listening. Convinced it was from just further up the glen, she dressed again, combed her hair and slipped quietly downstairs. She waited, listening for some sign that her father was awake. Hearing nothing but heavy breathing, she slipped out into the bright moonlight.

As she got closer to the camp, Fiona could see they had started a reel and were turning in circles, their laughter and shouts of enjoyment mingling with the piper's dancing notes.

She'd been watching for a few moments when she noticed a group of three, a woman and two men, clapping time to the music, and smiled as she recognised Fergus. He got up and walked towards Kirklea and Fiona sank into the heather. As he passed, she stepped round behind him and tapped his shoulder.

Fergus turned, looking irate at the interruption.

Before she could react, his arms were tight around her, lifting her from the ground and swinging her round and making her laugh. When he put her down, his great smile and arms around her, made her feel she was floating.

'Come and meet the others,' he told her, and they walked, arms round each other, to where the other man and woman were sitting.

'Who's this?' the woman asked.

Fiona looked at Fergus. His grin was wide. 'This is Fiona McRae,' he told them, then turned back to Fiona. 'Fiona, this is Mary Stewart and Neil McNeil.'

Mary held out her hand to shake. 'I'm pleased to meet you, Fiona McRae. If you are half as good as Fergus told us, you'll be a princess.'

McNeil stepped forward, smiling, 'He only said you were beautiful, but then he's not all that good with words.'

Fiona laughed.

'Perhaps, you'd like to dance?' McNeil asked her, crooking his arm for Fiona to take.

Fiona looked at Fergus. Seeing him smile, she took McNeil's arm. As they moved Mary spoke. 'Here's me been dying to dance and being ignored, and at the first sign of a young woman, you've become all gallant, McNeil. Well, I'll dance with Fergus,'

The piper started to play a strathspey, The graceful steps suited Fiona and she had time to glance at Fergus and Mary. Fergus smiled back over his shoulder to her.

The dance finished and they came together at the edge of the crowd.

The piper had another drink and as his pipes started wheezing, Fergus turned to Fiona, but was interrupted by a carroty head. 'I claim this dance,' Hamish informed them.

Fiona looked confused, as much by the anger she could see in Fergus's eyes as the sudden interruption, but Hamish was dragging her hand and drew her into the dance.

Fiona recovered some of her gaiety as the music started, but felt dismayed when the dance stopped and

Hamish followed her in a trance of devotion to where Fergus stood.

McNeil joined them, introducing Sheila, holding one arm as Mary held the other.

'You haven't danced with me at all,' Sheila accused Hamish.

'You're so hoity toity now that you're no fun, not like ...' he turned to look at Fiona, frowning, not knowing her name.

'Then I'll dance with you, Sheila,' McNeil intervened. 'If you'll be gracious enough to allow me?'

Sheila grinned and took McNeil's arm.

Fergus took Fiona's elbow and they moved to follow. Another man came to hold out his hand to Mary, leaving Hamish standing alone.

'Let's walk off a bit,' Fergus suggested to Fiona as the pipes squawked to silence, taking her arm and walking her out of the firelight.

'That's the first time you've done more than shake my hand since we were bairns, Fergus,' Fiona said, laughing.

'When you were skinny, I was afraid to in case you might break, and then you seemed so ... I don't know, I didn't want to spoil the look of you, mostly.'

'I'm a farm girl, Fergus,' Fiona pointed out.

'Farm girl you may be, but I fall asleep with your voice and your laughter in my head, like a lullaby,' Fergus told her.

Fiona laughed, but came close and Fergus put his hands on her shoulders, drawing her closer.

Fiona could smell the smoke of fir trees and heather, the smell of freedom, yet mixed with Fergus's own smell.

The smells of rolling down hills together, or maybe from a shared bed in the days when she was no more than eight, and her mother had smiled as she said goodnight. The smells of childhood and home, Fiona thought.

Fergus kissed her brow and she lifted her face to be kissed properly.

She nestled close, warming together, content until her body became aware of their closeness. Knowing she was becoming vulnerable, she drew away, smiling and happy. She looked into Fergus's face, pale in the moonlight and in a rush of deep emotion, kissed him fiercely before drawing away again.

'I must be getting back; I have chores in the morning. Let me just say goodnight to your friends.'

Fiona had shaken hands with both McNeil and Mary, and had turned to join Fergus, when Hamish intervened. 'I'll see you get home safely, Miss McRae,' he insisted.

'I'll be quite safe with Fergus,' Fiona told him.

'You'll need a chaperone, Miss McRae, drovers are not known for their chivalry.'

Fiona put her hand on Fergus's arm in time to stop any fighting and led him away. Hamish followed and Fergus could do nothing but accept his chaperoning.

At the farmyard, Fiona faced them both. 'Go back safely,' she said, then turned directly to Hamish. 'Fergus is an old friend, and I want you to take care of him.'

Hamish looked at Fergus.

Fiona ignored the sneer on Hamish's face. 'There are many dangers between here and Glasgow, Hamish, as well as in that town. Promise me!' she insisted.

Hamish looked from Fiona to Fergus, but nodded his head.

Fiona kissed him on the cheek, then kissed Fergus and ran into the house.

The two men stood glaring at each other. 'I swore to kill you for what you did to Butcher, but I'll honour that promise I made to Fiona, until I get to Glasgow.'

CHAPTER 14

In the morning, with the sun higher than he would have wished, Fergus washed and put on fresh clothing. He was just talking to McNeil about the cattle before leaving, when Davie came with a paper.

Fergus took it and looked at what Davie had drawn. There could be no mistaking it was Fiona, smiling as she danced. The trouble was, the back of the man she was smiling to, looked remarkably like McNeil.

Fergus showed McNeil the paper. 'He had to draw her with the best dancer, Fergus, you must see that,' McNeil said. 'Take it to her.'

Fergus grinned and turned to set off for Kirklea.

Hamish was waiting.

'I have business to talk to McRae about, Hamish. This is not an amorous expedition.'

Hamish just stood.

'Hamish, Hamish, I need your help,' Fergus heard Sheila call. They turned to see her running towards them. 'Father has fallen and can't get up. I need you to help me,' Sheila pleaded.

Hamish still hesitated.

'I've told you, I have business with McRae and I neither want, nor need your attendance, Hamish,' Fergus told him.

'Come, Hamish, please. I don't know what's wrong,' Sheila insisted.

Hamish turned to look at Fergus, but Fergus was looking at Sheila, a worried frown on his face. Sheila made a small gesture of pushing.

'Do you want me to come?' Fergus asked. 'Will it need two?'

'I'll go with Hamish,' McNeil interrupted, taking Hamish by the arm and leading him away.

***

McRae was inside, as Fergus expected; Fiona somewhere about her chores.

'So you've parked yourself and a gang of thieves up in the glen. By whose permission, may I ask?' McRae demanded.

Fergus bristled, despite himself. 'Highlanders they may be, Mr McRae, but they're decent people.'

'As like as not, like that one that Mr Maitland caught trying to have his way with Fiona,' McRae retorted.

'When was that?' Fergus asked.

'A few weeks back, but Mr Maitland dealt with him and it seems it was you that made the man desperate, Findlay.'

'Me?' Fergus uttered in disbelief.

'Aye, you, not paying the man for the cattle you sold.'

Fergus stared in disbelief. 'Black Duncan,' he muttered.

'Aye, Duncan, anyway.'

'He tried to have me killed and robbed, McRae. What was he doing here?'

'The poor man was trying to get to America to start a new life.'

'Poor man,' Fergus laughed. 'He gambled his rents away and then ran off leaving debts.'

'Aye, aye, so you say, Findlay, so you say.'

Fergus's face darkened at the implied insult, but he kept control despite the blood thumping in his temples.

'What is that you want, anyway, Findlay?'

Fergus forced himself to speak normally. 'I have families with me. Honest folk,' he emphasised. 'I'd like them to rest for a day in the glen, with your permission.'

'They'll have to pay.'

'Mr McRae, these are people who have left their homes to start new lives in Canada, some of them have fought against Napoleon. They don't have much beyond their passage money.'

'They'll pay or leave. Ten pounds!'

'Ten pounds! Ten pounds would feed a family for close to a year, McRae.'

'Ten pounds or I'll get the sheriff to them.'

Fergus glared at the older man. 'All right, McRae, but they stay until tomorrow. I have no hard cash with me but I'll give you a note for the amount.'

'A note? A note from you? It's hard currency I want, Findlay, and none of your paper money either, good gold coins.'

'That I can't do, but there's forty odd sheep I can leave as security.'

McRae's face twisted in a sneer.

'Do it, father! Or I'll leave with Fergus, right now.' Fiona interrupted.

Fergus could see the battle on McRae's face and, despite Fiona's angry interruption, put it down to plain greed.

McRae eventually turned, eyes narrowed, to Fergus. 'Leave the sheep, but be back here in ten days, or I'll sell them,' he hissed. 'Now, get out of my house.'

Fergus smiled to Fiona and left.

'Where do you think you're going,' Fergus heard McRae shout.

'To see Fergus leaves your yard, Father,' he heard Fiona shout back and found her at his side.

Out of sight of the house, Fiona stopped. Fergus smiled at her worried face.

'Come back, Fergus. Please,' she pleaded.

Fergus reached out, putting his hands on Fiona's shoulders. 'I'll be back within ten days,' he promised.

'Just come back soon,' Fiona said clasping her arms round him.

Fergus comforted, then found she was sobbing and frowned.

A sudden pain in his back shocked him and he arched away from Fiona.

'Keep your filthy hands off her,' McRae shouted.

Fergus turned, bending, his hand reaching for his dirk. Fiona's hand and voice stopped him. 'No, Fergus, he's a miserable old man, who deserves the workhouse. Just come back,' she insisted.

Fergus breathed deeply, several times, the tension leaving his body and he turned away.

'Filthy ...' he heard McRae begin but the tirade was cut short by the sound of a slap. 'Come, Father. Enough!' Fergus heard Fiona order.

Back at the gathering, Hamish confronted Fergus. 'You went to see her,' Hamish accused.

Fergus grabbed him by the front, lifting Hamish off the ground. 'I'm in no mood to play with boys,' he thundered into Hamish's face.

Fergus felt his arm dragged away and dropped Hamish. He turned to find McNeil beside him. 'What's got into you, Fergus?' McNeil demanded.

'Come and get a bite to eat,' Mary Stewart insisted.

With a last glare at Hamish, Fergus followed, to sit on a log at Mary's fire. 'Black Duncan was at McRae's,' Fergus began.

'Who's Black Duncan?' Mary asked.

As he worked through the explanation, Fergus's anger seeped away and he smiled as he heard one of Mary's boys whisper, 'Lifted him up like a bag of flour.'

Fergus was glad to find the company had no inclination to repeat the previous night's celebrations as they settled at night. He considered going to see Fiona, but decided it would only cause trouble for her, and rolled into his plaid and tried to sleep. Sleep must have come because he woke in the faded light sometime around midnight. It took him some moments to recognise Fiona shaking him gently.

Fergus unwrapped and took her awkwardly in his arms, before releasing her and rising to take her hand to walk away from the sleeping families.

They followed a rabbit run until it split. Bruce stood in one fork. Fergus smiled and took the other fork until they were out of earshot. 'Hamish,' Fergus whispered, grinning.

They sat down behind a boulder and talked in low voices for some time, snuggling close.

'I had to come to say God speed, Fergus. You will come back?'

Feeling inadequate at having to meet her in this way, Fergus held her close. 'I'll come, Fiona,' he whispered in her ear. 'I'll come and we'll not be separated.'

They parted near the farmhouse, and Fergus turned determinedly up the glen.

CHAPTER 15

Relieved that Fiona was now aware of his commitment to take her away from the drudgery of Kirklea, Fergus turned his attention to preparations for getting the drove moving. He explained by signs to Davie that he and Bruce were to look after the sheep and help Fiona as much as possible until he came back, then turned his attention to getting the drove, and the now excited emigrants, on their way down Loch Lomond side to Dumbarton and on to Glasgow.

By the end of the second day, they were on the outskirts of Dumbarton and Fergus took McNeil with him as he looked into inns and other gathering places for buyers. Several agreed to look over the drove in the morning and Fergus was delighted when one asked if he had sheep.

Two days later, Fergus had arranged the sale of everything and left to take the promissory notes he'd been given to Glasgow, hoping to exchange enough through Abernethy to pay the outstanding amounts to the families. What cash he had been given, he gave to McNeil, who, rather than allow the families to squander it on the temptations of the city, insisted on placing it in the care of Mary, guarded by Sinclair and himself.

It took Fergus the best part of the morning to say goodbye to the people. With a weeping kiss from Mary, he and McNeil at last set off with the packhorses for Glasgow and Abernethy.

Abernethy lived in a solid sandstone house in a steeply sloping road appropriately known as Hill Street, in the West End of Glasgow. Glasgow's wealth was growing and the city was busy extending in that direction. Fergus's progress was impeded by carriages, carts and street sellers calling their wares, in what he often felt was a foreign language.

'Come away in,' Abernethy's son, Tom, four years Fergus's senior, but fresh faced and looking the same age, welcomed, as he opened the door for Fergus. 'Father is not in, but we can chat after you've had a bite to eat, and something to wet your whistle.'

Tom's sister, Jean, ages with Fergus, short, rounded and dimple cheeked, bubbled in. 'As handsome as ever, I see, Fergus,' she greeted.

Fergus grinned in answer. 'And your own beauty now talked of from here to Inverness,' he bantered.

'Only as far as Inverness?' Jean asked, the sparkle in her eyes destroying her attempts to look haughty.

'Oh, once McNeil, here, gets to Canada, it will be across the globe,' Fergus pointed out.

'So, you will spread my fame across the oceans?' Jean laughed, holding her hand out to McNeil. 'Welcome to our modest home, Mr McNeil.'

To Fergus's surprise, McNeil looked uncomfortable among the plush dark red furnishings. He talked stiffly at first, but soon relaxed under Jean's easy company. He was even smiling as he talked of Spain, when Tom nodded for Fergus to follow him and they slipped into Tom's office to discuss the costs and expenses of the drove.

'It's hardly been worth your while, Fergus,' Tom commented.

'I suspected as much,' Fergus told him. 'But I'm glad I could help those people get the chance of a new life in Canada.'

'Will you carry on?' Tom asked.

'With this new canal they're building, and the steam ships I see on the Clyde, I doubt if they'll need drovers much longer. I need to look to what I've invested with your father, and to the farm itself, for the future.'

Tom's next comment surprised Fergus. 'Then I suppose, if I want to find out what the life of a drover is like, I'll have to come with you soon.'

'You'd better come this time, Tom, for I have other things that need attending to, and it could be my last.'

They re-joined Jean and McNeil, to find them laughing over some shared joke.

Whatever it was, Jean's voice was bright as she spoke to Fergus. 'And what of the fair Fiona? She was my rival for his affections when we were mere children, McNeil, but who can compete with a nymph in a wood?' Jean asked McNeil.

'Oh, she's a mysterious nymph no more, I have a drawing of her,' Fergus told her. 'It's in my bags with the stuff I brought from Babs,'

'You brought stuff from Babs and haven't shown it to me? Get it, get it now,' Jean ordered, standing.

Fergus went out to the yard and, helped by McNeil, brought in four bundles his pack animals had been carrying.

As he unrolled the packs, Jean clapped her hands. 'You're a genius, Fergus. I'll get the word out about these things. The people like them, especially the American businessmen father insists on bringing here. Real tartan plaids and rugs, they drool over. They all have a granny who came from Auchterarder.'

'This is the best bit,' Fergus said as he took Davie's drawing out and gave it to Jean.

'She's stunning,' Jean exclaimed but became suddenly serious. 'If you want her, Fergus, don't wait too long,' she said, bringing a worried frown to Fergus's face as she handed the picture to Tom.

'Handsome rather than pretty,' Tom said. Seeing Jean's stare, he added, 'but stunningly handsome.'

'But who is the handsome chap, she's dancing with?' Jean asked.

'McNeil, damn his eyes,' Fergus joked.

'Why, so it is,' Jean laughed. 'If you were not rushing off to Canada, Mr McNeil, I'd be obliged to ask you to accompany me to the first ball next winter,' Jean teased.

Fergus and the others turned as the door crashed open and Abernethy himself barged in. 'What's this aboot balls?' he grunted as he came in, taking off his coat. 'All that's in your heads is balls and sails doon the Clyde. Is there nothing to drink in this hoose, Tom, that visitors have to sit listenin' to women's blethers without the consolation of a dram? See to it, laddie, while I deal with young Findlay.'

Back in the office, Fergus arranged for the amount he owed McNeil to be exchanged for cash, before talking over his investments with Abernethy.

'You'll not think of investing in shipping, Fergus? There's money to be made in it.'

'If it was investing tens of thousands, I would, Abernethy, but ships sink and I'll rather take a modest profit on what's already landed than risk what I've got in the hope of a fortune.'

'Just what I've been telling Tom, but he's young and wants to speculate.'

'He has a mind to come on a drove, but, looking at the costs and returns, I don't see myself making more than one more drove, and that only because I have other things that need doing.'

'Like Fiona McRae, eh?'

Fergus smiled. 'Aye, like Fiona McRae.'

'Dinna wait ower long, Fergus,' Abernethy told him. 'My own wife was still a young woman when she died. None of us ken how long we have with those we cherish.'

Having heard the same advice twice within an hour, Fergus smile turned to a frown.

They re-joined the others. Fergus held out his hand to give McNeil the balance of the cash due to the emigrants, forcing McNeil to get up.

'You're not leaving?' Jean asked.

'I have people waiting, Miss Abernethy ...'

'Damn the Miss Abernethy, I'm Jean to my friends, McNeil,' Jean interrupted.

'And I've been called Neil, now and then, Jean,' McNeil told her. 'But I've still got people waiting.'

Fergus shook McNeil's offered hand. McNeil turned to shake Jean's, but her glance was on his clothes. 'I'm sure you're proud of that green jacket,' she said. 'But I can't let you go without offering you a better coat than that old uniform,' Jean told him.

McNeil's grin was twisted ruefully. 'I'll be better in this, Jean. Who'd expect someone like me to be worth robbing?'

Fergus agreed with the sentiment, but Jean was biting her lip. 'Neil McNeil, you'll bundle it up and carry it. I couldn't sleep thinking of you in that cold Canada with just an old army jacket. There must be something we can give him, Tom?'

McNeil was looking about for support, when Abernethy intervened. 'You'd better agree, laddie, or her ghost'll haunt you as you shiver in the snow. Her ghost'll talk all night and you'll no' get a wink o' sleep.'

Fergus grinned as Tom went off and came back with a bundled up tweed coat and they all stood watching as McNeil stuffed it into his knapsack, red with embarrassment.

Fergus prepared to leave with McNeil.

'There's no need for you to go rushin' off, Fergus. You look tired out, man, you need a good meal and a night's rest before you go traipsin' away to your Highlands,' Abernethy pointed out.

'He wants to get back to Fiona,' Jean pointed out.

Fergus laughed. 'No, I have sheep to deliver, but I want to see McNeil safe out of the town.'

'Then you'll come back and eat,' Jean insisted.

'We might fit in a trip to the theatre,' Tom suggested.

'No, Tom, as McNeil will tell you, I've had enough drama with drowned beasts and daft emigrants, especially lassies,' Fergus laughed.

'Drama with lassies! What have you been up to? You're definitely staying to tell me all,' Jean insisted.

Fergus was glad of Tom's company as they made their way back.

'You mentioned you had sheep to deliver, are they close? Could I come with you?' Tom asked.

'They're up Loch Lomond way. The garrons need a rest, so I'll go on foot. It's two days walk, or one day from early till moonrise, to get to them, then two days to drove them to Dumbarton, and another day back to Glasgow.'

'We could ride,' Tom suggested. 'Not on your garrons, but take two of our horses.'

Fergus grinned in agreement.

***

At Kirklea, Bruce came running as Fergus and Tom breasted the last hill before dropping into the glen.

'He's got some sixth sense,' Fergus explained to Tom as he ruffled Bruce's hair.

They found Davie shaving at a stick, which he dropped to come and 'mmm' his welcome.

After checking the flock and taking a brief respite, Fergus and Tom made their way to Kirklea.

They saw McRae was standing talking to Maitland as they rode into the yard and dismounted.

McRae studied Tom's coat, polished boots and clean shaven face before turning to Fergus. 'What do you want, and who's your fancy friend?'

Fergus ignored the sneer in the question. 'I've come for the sheep, McRae.'

'I hope you've brought the money to pay,' McRae told him, leaning forward aggressively.

Like an angry goose, Fergus thought, but kept his voice civil. 'No I have not, the emigrant people needed all the coinage but, like I said, I'll give you a note for the ten pounds.'

'A note, a note!' McRae exclaimed. 'I told you before …'

'Take his note,' Maitland suggested. 'If it's good, you'll get your ten pounds, if not, he'll be exposed as a rogue for all to see.'

They all looked round at the sound of the kitchen door opening and Fergus smiled as he saw Fiona, but turned his attention back to watch McRae struggle with his decision.

McRae glanced at Fiona again, before turning back to Fergus with a sly smile. 'I'll take your note, Findlay, but if there's any trouble, I'll have the sheriff after you.'

Fergus made out the note and gave it to McRae. 'I'd like a few words with Fiona, if you've no objections, Mr McRae?' Fergus asked.

'You'll get off my property, Findlay, and you'll never speak to my daughter again.'

Fergus felt the colour rise in his face.

'You heard what the man said,' Maitland told him. 'Take your sheep and go.'

Fergus looked at Fiona. She looked close to tears. Rather than upset her more, he nodded and turned away.

'Who was that other man?' Tom asked as they rode back to the sheep.

'Name's Maitland, he's new in these parts.'

'I think we should ask Father to make a few enquiries about Mr Maitland. There's something about the man,' Tom said, frowning.

***

Fiona found her father grinning.

'You're very pleased with yourself, Father. Is it something you want to share?' Fiona asked.

'Aye, I'll share it all right. I got five pounds for that note of Findlay's.'

'Five pounds. It was for ten!'

'It was, but Maitland gave me five sovereigns for it.'

'You obstinate fool!' Fiona spat out. 'If you'd taken the trouble to take it to the bank, they'd have given you ten, can't you understand that!'

'No they wouldn't. Notes from that tinker are not worth the paper they're written on.'

'Then why does Maitland want it, pray?'

'He'll take Findlay to court when it is proved false, that's what!'

'He'll get ten pounds for it. Can't you understand that man has swindled us out of five pounds?'

'We'll see, we'll see,' McRae told her.

***

Fergus and Tom followed Davie as he and Bruce herded the sheep on their way to Dumbarton. They were almost there when they saw the familiar figure of McNeil, his rifle slung over his back, waiting for them by the side of the drove road.

'I hoped I'd catch you on the way, Fergus, and I'm glad Tom is with you. I have a problem that I don't know how to solve,' McNeil told them. 'When we wanted to buy tickets, the redcoats turned us away. Some magistrate issued papers on the authority of one of the lairds, stopping the people leaving. The others decided if they couldn't all go, none of them would. Some were sick, so I took them out of the city to the Kilpatrick hills and came looking for yourself. I know it's not your problem, but at least you know your way around.'

'I think we'd better talk to my father,' Tom said.

CHAPTER 16

'You look as if the end of the world was about to fall,' Jean said as she opened Abernethy's door for them. 'I thought soldiers like yourself, Neil, never admitted defeat?'

Fergus, amused, looked at McNeil.

'If I know the enemy, Jean. But this time, I'm on the moon,' McNeil answered.

'Well, we'll see if the moon will provide us with something to cheer your hearts,' Jean said. She turned to Fergus. 'You haven't introduced me to this other friend.'

Fergus put a hand on Davie's shoulder. 'This is Davie; he's deaf and can't speak.'

'No, but he can draw, if I remember correctly,' Jean said. 'And this will be Bruce, I suppose,' she said, as she ruffling the hair on his head. 'Let's see if we can't find a bone for him.'

Fergus, noticing Davie was uncomfortable, told her, 'Davie will prefer to stay with Bruce, especially if you give him some paper and a pencil that he can draw with. It's his way of communicating.'

They all turned as the door burst open to let Abernethy in. 'Whit's the stramash out here, then?' he demanded. 'And what did you need the musket for, McNeil?'

'It's a rifle, Mr Abernethy, and it's been with me since Waterloo. I just didn't want to lose it. It'll come in handy in Canada, if I ever get there.'

'And why would ye no',' Abernethy asked.

'They were stopped,' Fergus told him. 'Some magistrate issued a paper on behalf of some laird.'

'Dear God, are there still some that would keep their tenants in poverty? Who was the magistrate?'

'Smith,' McNeil answered.

'I might have kenned, I'll no' even take off my coat, but you lot go away in and Jeanie'll fix you with somethin' to keep ye busy. Tom, see that my carriage is harnessed up, if you will.'

As they waited for Abernethy's return, Fergus was glad Jean kept McNeil's attention with questions about Spain, and amused at McNeil's struggles over what the ladies wore.

Half an hour later, the discussion was ended by Abernethy stomping in with his usual bluster. He was followed by Bruce and a hesitant Davie. 'I found these two in the yard,' he said to Jean. 'You canna leave a fine dog like that out in the yard.'

Fergus looked at Jean but she was not in the least put out. 'What about the people, Father?' she responded.

Abernethy turned to McNeil. 'It'll cost you money, but they'll turn a blind eye. Have you got five pounds, or can you lay your hands on a sum like that?'

'The money's not all mine,' McNeil answered.

Fergus intervened. 'I'll see to the money, McNeil, if Abernethy will accept my note and arrange for the cash.'

'Done, Fergus,' Abernethy said. 'Go and get your people together and be ready to leave before someone changes their mind, or the word gets back to this damned laird.'

'I'm grateful for what you're trying to do, Fergus, but I can't just accept it without trying to pay something back. If you'll allow me, I'll come droving for a while.'

'Fine,' Fergus agreed. 'I'll do one more, at least. Maybe there are some more crofters who want to try a new life in Canada.'

McNeil smiled his relief. 'Maybe there is.'

'What about Mary Stewart and the boys?' Fergus asked and noticed Jean stiffen.

McNeil smiled. 'Sinclair is a fine man,' he said.

'But I thought he was married!' Jean interrupted.

McNeil smiled. 'They're not going to a hunt ball, Miss Abernethy. They're going into the wilderness; Mary has two young boys to look after and will need someone to build a cabin; Sinclair has a daughter that needs a mother, and he will need someone to cook and wash while he builds and clears some land for ploughing. He's a farmer, I'm a soldier. Mary has no need of me.'

Fergus hid a smile as he noticed Jean relax.

'Settled then,' Abernethy said, slapping his thigh. 'Now, Jeannie, a bone for the dog.' He turned to Davie, 'And for you, my lad?' he asked.

'He can't speak, Father,' Jean explained.

'Aye, but he can,' Abernethy grinned, holding out a paper. 'He's told me he came with the sheep,' he said triumphantly, waving the paper and laughing.

Fergus could feel McNeil's agitation, and wasn't surprised when he interrupted. 'I need to get back to my people and see they get away all right, if you don't mind, Miss Abernethy.'

Jean smiled acquiescence and McNeil left.

***

The gap after McNeil's departure gave Tom an opportunity to turn the conversation to himself. 'I was thinking, Father, instead of making a grand tour through Europe, I might go along with Fergus and see a bit of Scotland, including the new canal that Telford is building through the Great Glen.'

'That's a grand idea,' Abernethy agreed. 'There's as many rogues in Scotland as there is in Italy, for a young man's education.'

Jean laughed. 'It's to broaden their minds, see the Greek temples and such like, that young men go on the tour, Father.'

'Nothin' but old ruins, and there's plenty o' them in Glasgow, if you care to look round. There's me for a start, eh, Fergus?'

'Talking of rogues, have you heard of a chap called Maitland?' Fergus asked.

'Maitland? No' that I recall, but I'll make enquiries. What's he done?'

'Nothing we ken of, Abernethy,' Fergus explained. 'It's just that he's been telling lies about one of those rogues you mentioned.'

'He's flyin' wi' the crows, is he?' Abernethy asked.

'I can't say he is, but it looks that way. Tom and I wondered if maybe you'd heard something.'

Jean interrupted. 'Has this anything to do with Fiona?'

'More with her father,' Fergus answered.

'I've told you not to wait too long, Fergus,' Jean told him. 'If it has to do with her father, it'll likely involve Fiona as well. If I was you, I'd let Father take care of the emigration and go to Fiona.'

The ongoing mention of the need to make haste over Fiona kept Fergus's sleep restless and he was glad when it was light enough to get away.

***

The following morning found them nearing Kirklea.

Fiona was about her chores, and smiled a welcome as Fergus came into the yard.

'I need to speak to your father,' he told Fiona.

'He's taken to his bed, Fergus. I'm not sure what's wrong with him, if anything, but he tells me his heart is beating like a drum if he tries to do over much.'

'I want you to come away with me Fiona. Now!'

'And my father? I can't leave him in his sick bed, Fergus. Surely it can wait until you're back again.'

'I'm not sure what it is, Fiona, I just feel we need to go now, or something will come between us. Babs mentioned it, and so has Jean Abernethy.'

'Old wives tales, Fergus,' Fiona laughed. 'Nothing is going to come between us,' she told him, hugging him, and smiling at his concern. 'Now, will you help me with my chores, or have you just come to talk?'

Fergus relaxed, took her pail and followed her into the kitchen, where Fiona set about making porridge.

Tom's head drooped.

'Have you slept at all?' Fiona asked.

'An hour maybe,' Fergus answered.

'Then go to the barn and get your head down and, by afternoon, maybe you'll feel taking me away is not so urgent.'

Fergus looked at Tom, unsure if he'd want to sleep in a barn, but Tom looked as if he didn't care, as long as he could get his head down.

'I think Tom will be glad of that, but going with me is urgent, Fiona. I don't want to spend another day wanting you.'

Fiona smiled and let her hand touch his face, but withdrew it when there was a thump from overhead. 'What does he want now?' she muttered, leaving Fergus to take Tom to the barn.

***

'He's no better,' Fiona told Fergus in the morning.

Fergus and Davie, helped by Tom, busied themselves with chores all morning. As they sat eating at midday, Fergus tried again to get Fiona to come with him, but without hope, knowing she wouldn't leave her bed-ridden father on his own. He insisted on leaving Davie. He would be an extra mouth to feed but with McRae in bed, Fiona would be glad of the help.

'I'll be back in six weeks, a month if things go well, Fiona. Think about what I said.'

Fiona's features hardened. 'Do you think I want to stay struggling in this place one minute longer than I have to, Fergus? I have no idea what your Dornoch is like, but we'll be together. Now, go and be back. Whatever you do, come back,' she said, pushing him away.

CHAPTER 17

A day later, they met up with McNeil.

'All well?' Fergus asked.

'Red haired Hamish refused to go in the end,' McNeil told him. 'Well, sneaked off, anyway. It gave his mother a bit extra, so some good came of it.'

'And Sheila?'

'More interested in one of the officers and behaving more like a young lady under Mary's eye.'

'And Mary?'

'Sinclair's a fine man, as I told you before.'

'So, where has Hamish gone? He knows nobody about here. Apart from people in the company, the last person I saw him speak to was Fiona.'

McNeil shrugged. 'Who knows, he's still got a bit of the drummer boy in him. Maybe he's enlisted.'

They split at the Fort William, McNeil making for Wester Ross to investigate possible emigrants, Fergus leading Tom up the Great Glen to look over the new canal works, before branching off north into Cromarty.

***

McInnes and his family made them welcome. As he listened to her father telling the latest news, Fergus was amused to see from the corner of his eye, as Morag returned Tom's smile openly, she ran her hands over her dress to straighten it and make a good impression.

'You might have sent warning you were bringing company,' McInnes's wife chastised Fergus, as she shook Tom's hand.

'He'll be going back to Ault-na-main and a decent bed,' Fergus told her.

McInnes interrupted. 'He'll be taking a bite to eat and a dram for the journey.'

Fergus looked at Tom, who smiled, 'I came to see the highlands, Fergus, not to bring Glasgow up here. I've slept in the open with you on the way up. I can sleep in a bothy with you just as well.'

Fergus shrugged, grinned and, after eating, they moved into the hovel, leaving the McInnes family in the larger house. Bruce squeezing between them as they rolled into their blanket and plaid ready for sleep.

Morag came as they struggled out into the morning air, stretching and grinning to each other as they went to wash themselves awake in burn water.

'Mother will not have you go hungry,' she shouted at them as they splashed water over their half-naked bodies.

They dressed and made their way to eat with the family.

After mornings, including a dram of McInnis's whisky, Fergus looked over what cattle had been brought for droving, and made a start to things he had been planning; a small diversion to bring the burn water splashing past the house, firewood for winter, simple tasks that were made light by Tom's company.

They went to eat and, as Fergus talked to McInnes, Morag quizzed Tom about life in Glasgow and Tom responded with anecdotes and descriptions.

On the third day, as they chopped wood, Fergus saw McNeil coming. Morag came with water, whether she'd been coming anyway, or her curiosity drew her out, Fergus couldn't be sure. McNeil looked at Morag. Morag returned his gaze and stiffened to her full height, still a head shorter than McNeil's six foot.

'And who's this?' she demanded from Fergus. 'And why does he need to be carrying a gun to visit honest folk?'

Fergus let McNeil answer. 'It's not a gun. It's a rifle, Miss,' McNeil told her. 'And it's all I have in the world. If I'm among honest people, perhaps I can leave it in your keeping,' he told Morag as he took the rifle from his shoulder and held it out to her.

Morag hesitated, looked him up and down, from his dark hair and level eyes to his old green uniform coat, before blushing slightly under his now smiling gaze.

As Morag took the firearm Tom asked, 'Where's the coat Jeannie gave you, Neil?'

'I've been so long a soldier, I feel uncomfortable out of uniform, decrepit though it is.'

While Fergus could understand McNeil's pride in his uniform, he cautioned, 'You'll have to start wearing it, McNeil. That old jacket might be warm enough here, but in Canada, you'll need something better.'

'Canada?' Morag asked.

Fergus noted a harder note creeping into McNeil's voice as he answered, 'Aye, Canada. Where a man with a gun is a hunter, not a criminal.'

It made Morag look at the rifle in her hands with more interest.

'I'd be grateful if you'd put it somewhere out of sight,' McNeil suggested. 'Somewhere I can get it if there's a deer or a rabbit, or maybe a bird we can use for the pot.'

Morag took the rifle inside.

'Are you ready to move?' McNeil asked, although Fergus noticed his eyes following Morag as she made her way to the house, before coming back to Tom and himself.

'What's the news?' Fergus asked.

'Are you ready?' McNeil countered.

'I was waiting for you,' Fergus told him. 'But before we go, I must first visit Babs and find out if there is to be good prices, or trouble.'

***

At Ault-na-main, Fergus grinned as Babs looked the others over, nodding and smiling to each of them, before turning to McNeil. 'Hmph,' she said. 'At least he's no' a Redcoat. Since you're with Fergus Findlay, welcome,' she added.

Over the usual dram, Fergus asked about prices, and was told not to worry by a Babs who kept glancing at McNeil, and then at Morag.

Fergus was about to ask why, when Bab's looked directly at Morag and said, 'Your bairns will look like their father.'

Morag looked startled, but laughed. 'Well, we ken it's not yourself, Fergus. At least that's what Babs told us the last time we were here. So who is this I'm to wed and have bairns by?' she asked Babs.

Fergus glanced first at Tom and then at McNeil, who looked at each other in mild concern.

'Oh, the two are not always the same, but he'll be a fine man,' Babs told Morag, leaving Morag to wonder who was to be the fine man. Before she could ask, Babs continued, 'The worst of it is, there'll death and blood in the heather before it all works out.'

'There's always blood in the heather, Babs,' Fergus pointed out, making light of her prediction. 'Have you heard anything at all about Black Duncan?'

'Not a thing since he went away south. And good riddance. Dark deeds hang round his neck,' she warned.

Fergus looked over what Babs wanted to send to Jean, Tom looked over his shoulder and became involved, finally buying a fine shawl. To Fergus's surprise, he gave it to Morag. Morag at first refused, despite the sparkle in her eyes as she looked at the gift.

'You've looked after us so well, Morag, please take it,' Tom pleaded.

'What will folk say, me taking gifts from a gentleman?' Morag asked.

To Fergus's amusement, McNeil answered. 'They'll say you have fine taste, Miss McInnes.'

'It has nothing to do with you, McNeil,' Morag retorted. 'Thank you very much, Tom,' she smiled.

Fergus felt his jacket tugged and turned to face Babs. 'And you and that Fiona lassie you mentioned, Fergus Findlay?' she asked.

Fergus nodded. 'Aye, when we're ready, Babs, when we're ready.'

'Dinna wait ower long. Women are feckle things, and whiles don't have the final word in what happens to them.'

The same thing had been on Fergus's mind, and he frowned.

'That's what my sister told him, Babs,' Tom laughed.

Fergus's answering laugh was without mirth and accompanied with a frown.

***

On the way back, Fergus could feel Morag's curiosity growing, until she could contain it no longer. 'So what is this Canada like, McNeil?' she asked.

McNeil looked at her for a moment. 'Cold,' he said, not taking his gaze from Morag.

Fergus saw Morag's face grow redder, either with anger or embarrassment, until McNeil went on, 'Or so I'm told. Much colder than Spain, with snow as deep as a man is tall,' he went on. 'And I believe, like Spain, it's warm in the summer. They tell me it's wild like these highlands, not just the place, but the people; Mohicans and others that love long hair like yours Miss McInnes, especially when they cut it off your head and hang it inside their tents.'

Fergus burst out laughing, but cut it short as Morag stopped and stood staring after McNeil, who kept walking a few paces. Fergus could see from her expression, she was unsure if McNeil was telling her the truth, or playing with her.

McNeil turned back to face them. 'I'm sorry, Miss McInnes,' he grinned. 'That was impolite.'

Morag stared at him. 'Why do you keep calling me Miss McInnes, when the others just call me Morag?'

'Because he's overwhelmed by your beauty, Morag,' Fergus told her.

Morag slapped him on the arm, and turned back to the grinning McNeil.

'Because you never invited me to call you by your more familiar name, and I respected that,' McNeil told her.

Morag looked at him. 'You respected that?'

'What else did you think?' McNeil asked, sobering.

Fergus saw Morag stiffen. 'If you're playing the fool with me, I'll get my father to take a stick to your back,' she told McNeil.

McNeil shook his head and turned to go, but turned back, grinning again. 'Then I must call you Morag,' he said.

Fergus interrupted the exchange. 'Well, now that you've been properly introduced, maybe Tom and I can get on back to Invercauld, and yourself off to gather your emigrants, McNeil,' he commented.

McNeil bowed to Morag, before nodding to Fergus and Tom, and walking away over the hill.

***

Next morning, as he loaded his garrons, Fergus asked McInnes about Duncan.

'He's not been seen around hereabouts,' McInnes told him. 'But if he comes, he'll get a warm welcome.'

'Take care, McInnes, he's devilish cunning at times,' Fergus warned.

Having collected the fifty odd beasts people had brought, Fergus and Tom set off.

'Is this all you'll have?' Tom asked Fergus.

'I'll buy some more at Strathcarron; West Country black cattle fetch a better price and take to the drove better as well. You and I, and Bruce, can manage this lot. McNeil can go on in front and get his people together.'

On their way west, as they slid through greening glens, between the grey crags and heather covered hills, Tom was too overawed by the grandeur to be of much help to Fergus.

Fergus and Bruce let him enjoy their majesty.

128

CHAPTER 18

Fergus could only shake his head as he watched the new group of emigrants dribble like thistledown over the hill after McNeil. Their motley appearance brought a peel of laughter from Tom.

'It's no wonder we lost to the Redcoats,' Fergus muttered, but had managed to calm himself and Tom, by the time McNeil was shaking their hands. 'At least there's no sheep,' Fergus commented.

'They traded any sheep they had for cattle,' McNeil explained.

As they travelled, Fergus noticed Tom talking among the people, learning their stories and becoming more and more sympathetic to their plight and their plans.

Having crossed the river Garry, this time without incident, Fergus let everyone rest for a day. Maybe the rest made the guards lax; maybe they just weren't the old soldiers. For whatever reason, in the morning, feeling uneasy, Fergus started counting the beasts.

'We're ten light,' he announced. At Tom's startled expression, he explained. 'The reivers take just a few from each drove, not enough to be worth chasing after, hide them in some glen until they have a hundred or so, and drive them to market.'

'So what are you going to do?' Tom asked. 'We can't let them get away with it. These people don't have much to begin with. Whoever steals from them needs to be brought to justice.'

Babs' warnings about Fiona had been nagging at Fergus and he was reluctant to delay, but his reputation for not losing beasts was a real concern.

'The men can take the drove on, Fergus,' McNeil commented. 'Even if they only make five miles instead of the usual ten, it will keep them moving.'

Fergus bit his lip.

'Could you look after them, Tom?' Fergus asked.

'Me?' Tom asked, in astonishment. 'The other men are far more used to cattle than I am, Fergus.'

'What have you in mind, Fergus?' McNeil asked.

'Taking two days to look for them and if we don't find them, coming back. This is Tuesday, we'll not get far look, looking, in the glens about here, and we should be back with the others on Friday morning.'

'Where do we start looking?' McNeil asked. 'There's tracks all over.'

'Follow Bruce,' Fergus said, pointing to where the black dog was sniffing at the ground. 'He might not know they've been stolen, but he knows they're missing. Bring your rifle.'

McNeil went off to make the arrangements for the drove and collect his rifle as Bruce set off, his head weaving from side to side as he sniffed his way forward.

Mounted, Fergus, joined by McNeil and Tom, followed.

They followed for the rest of the day and into the moonlight, when Fergus was obliged to tie a white rag round Bruce's neck so that they could see him. It was past midnight when Bruce lifted his head to sniff at the air.

'Close,' Fergus said.

After another mile, they could smell the cattle themselves, and dismounted. By now, the moon was obscured. Not knowing how many reivers they faced, Fergus, with McNeil's pleased approval, decided to wait for daylight.

As the east greyed, Fergus shook the others. They crept to where they could look into the next glen, and found themselves looking down into a defile, rather than a glen. It was closed at its far end, wide in the middle but narrowed to a bottleneck at the entrance. A low steep sided hillock sat before the entrance, hiding it from anyone passing. The valley ran north – south and the access split around the little hillock they were on, making two entrances, one from the east and the other from the west. It might have been made for hiding stolen cattle.

From the hillock's elevation, Fergus guessed there was upwards of a hundred beasts, possibly a hundred and fifty.

In the growing morning light, they watched one man walk to the grey ash of a fire, kick at it, throw a few kindlings on it, and stretch in a vast yawn.

'How many men do you think there are?' Tom asked.

'I can only see another two, Tom. There may be more, or there may be others on their way back from thieving. Who knows?'

'There's one way to find out,' McNeil said, hefting his rifle to his shoulder. 'They'll all jump up when they hear the shot.'

As McNeil began sighting his rifle, Fergus warned Tom. 'Justice is a bit more violent here than in Glasgow, Thomas.'

'You're not for killing them here?' Tom asked, in horror.

'Not unless I make a mistake,' McNeil muttered, settling again.

The shot woke the valley, ricocheting and echoing round it like a volley.

The man at the fire slumped. Two others rushed and shook him. They seemed to get no reaction. They glanced round, then began to run, presumably for guns and horses, Fergus thought.

'They'll escape. We have to catch them,' Tom shouted, rushing to mount his own horse.

Fergus turned in amazement, and made after Tom. 'Stop, Tom, they'll kill you,' he shouted, but Tom was already mounting.

Fergus ran to his own garron as Tom turned down the hillside towards the valley entrance.

Fergus vaulted into the saddle of his own pony and sent it after Tom, his head low and forward, urging the beast into a gallop. Bruce came barking beside the pony.

McNeil fired again, the single shot sounding like a fusillade as the sound reverberated in the enclosed space.

As he raced after Tom, Fergus heard the alarmed bellows of the cattle and wondered how long it would be before panic set a stampede flowing out of the valley.

He was ten yards behind Tom as they reached the western entrance and he saw one of the reivers lashing his pony towards them. He watched in horror as Tom raised his hands to signal the man to stop. The reiver drew a sword from the side of his saddle.

Tom had slowed and Fergus put his pony at the back of Tom's. Fergus's pony shied just before impact, as

Fergus had expected, but its momentum took it into the hindquarter of Tom's. Tom was thrown aside and the reiver's slash passed over his falling body.

Fergus dismounted to attend to Tom, but looked up to find the reiver swinging round in the exit, sword drawn and raised for a downward slash. Seeing them both afoot, the reiver turned the point forward and dug his heels into his pony. Fergus drew his own weapon and prepared to try to parry the thrust, knowing it would come with the full weight of both rider and horse and set his face grimly against death. A black shape barking and growling launched itself forward and the reiver's pony shied. The rider jerked upright, swayed wildly, almost lost his seat, but managed to pull away.

Fergus got one look at the man's face, but it held in his mind's eye with the clarity of a portrait. 'Duncan,' he yelled after the fleeing figure.

As he turned to Tom, Fergus could hear the growing moans and bellows of the now frightened cattle inside the defile. He dragged Tom to one side, then looked round for some way to prevent the herd coming their way. He grabbed a tuft of untrampled grass from the corner of the entrance, scrabbled for flint and tinder, praying he had time, and the tinder would catch first time. He blew the tiny flame and tipped the burning tinder into the handful of dry grass. As it took fire, he dragged it down the side of the hillock, across the floor and as high as he could reach on the other side. The grass on the floor burned, that on the sides caught and smoked as the first of the cattle came out of the glen.

The leading cattle saw the flicker of the flame, smelled the smoke, and their agitation grew. They began to mill about, uncertain what to do. Fergus began jumping and waving, Bruce joined in barked furiously as the cattle began to move. To Fergus's relief, the herd turned into the eastern gap. Fergus let them go.

Tom got shakily to his feet as McNeil came to them.

'What did you think you were doing?' Fergus asked.

'Trying to arrest them,' Tom said simply.

Fergus and McNeil burst out laughing. 'Justice has a deal less regulation to it among the hills on this side of the Great Glen,' Fergus told Tom. 'On the other side, there's more and better roads and people are law abiding. Here, cold steel and a hillside burial are what's kept the peace till now. Speaking of which, there's another of those rogues in the valley.'

They made a wary way through the entrance and found the first man lying groaning near the fire site.

He tried to talk but coughed and a dribble of blood ran from the corner of his mouth.

'Was that Black Duncan?' Fergus asked.

The man nodded and coughed again, more vigorously, before falling back.

'Where has he gone?'

The man shook his head and spat.

An hour later, they buried him on top of the hillock and set about collecting the loose cattle. The herd, having been penned together for days, had formed a bond and were not difficult to manoeuvre into a group.

With the new herd, they made their way back to the drove, which they found had sensibly stopped on the shores of a loch.

With the drove now swelled to nearly four hundred, it stretched for over a mile along the trail.

***

At the next collection of houses, Fergus let it be known he had recovered some stolen cattle. There, and as they progressed, drovers on their way back from market recognised a few and Fergus gave a note to those who were prepared to sell and mixed the new acquisitions with his drove. Those who didn't sell, Fergus insisted they donate something to McNeil's emigrant's funds.

***

At the Mearns, Maitland laughed at Duncan, then offered him whisky.

'It's been suggested that this Findlay might join McRae. It's time he was stopped,' Maitland said. 'Will he bring another drove south?'

'That's what he does,' Duncan answered.

'Do you know what route he'll take?'

'He doesna have just one. It depends on the weather, the rivers and the like, but I can find out where he's going easy enough. A herd of cows being driven across Scotland is not something folk don't see.'

'The trouble is, there are people about when he's droving,' Maitland pointed out. 'The best plan would be to catch him somewhere in the north on his way back, somewhere he'll just vanish. Even if he has somebody with him, you'll be able to handle just two or three, if you catch them by surprise, that is. Can you set up an ambush someplace?'

'Aye, close to Dornoch, where there's not so many roads he can take, but I want a firearm. He's good with a broadsword and a dirk but a musket doesna respect that.'

'I'll get you one in a day or so,' Maitland told him. 'All I have here are pistols and shotguns.'

***

Next day, Maitland was surprised to see a new red haired man with the delivery wagon and helped him unload.

'You're new and from the north by your accent,' Maitland commented. 'What brings you to this area?'

'I came to get work.'

'There's surely more work in Glasgow than out here in the country.'

The lad hesitated, the blurted out, 'I came to be near Kirklea and Fiona McRae.'

'So what's your name?'

'Hamish.'

'Well, Hamish, isn't Fiona McRae a bit grand for yourself?'

'I ken she is, but I just want to be near her.'

'Well, she's a friend of mine. I'll tell her you're about, in case she needs help.'

Hamish gaped in astonishment. 'Would you really? I'm determined that Fergus Findlay won't get her.'

'Then you and I have her best future at heart, lad. Maybe we can work together. I only want to make sure she doesn't get put out of her home. Findlay will only make her a tinker, wandering about like a lost soul.'

'As long as I draw breath, I'll not let that happen,' Hamish promised.

'That's a man after my own heart,' Maitland said, clapping Hamish on the shoulder.

CHAPTER 19

A few days after his talk with Hamish, Maitland rode over to Kirklea. Fiona was nowhere in sight but McRae came rushing out to welcome Maitland and follow him inside.

'Have you thought about my offer, McRae? I'm growing impatient for an answer,' Maitland asked. 'Although, according to my lawyer, it's Fiona I should be speaking to.'

'Fiona?'

'Yes, Fiona. I understand her mother left her the farm, not you.'

'Maybe so,' McRae countered. 'But Fiona is an obedient lassie and will do as I tell her.'

'That's not what I've observed, McRae.'

'She'll come round, don't you worry.'

'Of course, the debts go with the farm, and if anyone was to go to prison it would be Fiona, and you'd be left on your own.'

Maitland could see McRae struggle with that, but then he gave a thin eyed smile. 'She could sell the farm and you'd get your money back.'

'The debts are already half its run down value, McRae. I'd get it half price at an auction.'

'Aye but it would cost you more money, Mr Maitland. It would be better to marry Fiona and get the farm for what you've paid.'

'I'd thought of that, but she didn't seem too keen. You'd have to persuade her, McRae, and not be long about it, either.'

'Give me a week or two, Mr Maitland. You can surely wait a week or two?'

'I want the sheep on the hill while the grass is still green. Three weeks, McRae. And you'd better make sure Findlay doesn't run off with her.'

McRae stiffened. 'I'll no' allow that. It would be over my dead body.'

***

As Maitland was mounting his horse to leave, Fiona came out of one of the outbuildings.

'Ah, Miss McRae, I'm rather disappointed you haven't found time to visit again,' Maitland said, smiling.

'I am busy, Mr Maitland, as you can see, and have not much time to visit even my own bedroom these days. You were leaving, no doubt you have affairs of your own to attend to, don't let me detain you.'

Maitland frowned, but forced a smile. 'Talking to you is never a detention, Miss McRae, being neighbours, we should see more of each other.'

'My father is the one who welcomes visitors such as yourself, Mr Maitland. There's no need for you to bother yourself with me.'

Maitland smiled again. 'I'm worried that with no young woman to talk to I will become a crotchety bachelor, so, you see, you will be saving a soul, as it were.'

'I'm sorry, Mr Maitland, I have other chores to attend to, so, if you'll excuse me, I'll get about them,' Fiona said, picking up her pail and walking past Maitland into the house.

Maitland's mouth tightened and he lashed his horse as he rode off.

***

Inside, her father glared at Fiona, 'Mr Maitland was here and asking after you, Fiona.'

Fiona sat down. 'I met him, Father, and instead of sitting blethering, I'd be grateful if you'd help with some of the work.'

'You have that Davie that Findlay left to help, though I don't see what a deaf mute can do to help. You're tiring yourself out. If you married Maitland, there would be no need to work, Fiona. Can't you see that?'

Fiona pushed herself wearily to her feet. 'Oh, I can see that all right, but what would I do when he brings his whores to visit, tell me that, Father dear.'

'I've told you already, that was just the talk of a frustrated old bitch trying to keep her job.'

'It was none of Mrs Lafferty's gossip. I hear it every time I go into the town.'

'Well, so you say, but you can get someone more agreeable when you settle in.'

'When I settle in? So, you have me married to that brute already, have you? I'd rather live in a sod house and scrape for a living, than marry that lecher. Not that I'm doing much else but scrape a living now.'

'We canna go on like this, Fiona. There's no money left and we owe all round. Can you not see that you must take a husband, and not just any husband, one with a bit o' siller, lassie,' her father wheedled.

'I see that well enough, but I can get work, Father, and we'll manage. Besides Fergus might ...'

'*Fergus Findlay*! I'll thank you not to mention his name in this house,' her father shouted.

'Then maybe I'll leave this house and you can sell it to your Mr Maitland and pay off your debts.'

'I'll not move from the house your mother and I came to when we were married. You were born here, lassie, and your dear mother is buried on the hill yonder, where she can see the glen at its best.'

'See what wrought her to death, you mean,' Fiona answered.

In her room, Fiona collapsed on her bed and wept. 'Fergus, where are you,' she pleaded to her pillow.

***

As if in answer to her plea, Fergus came next day.

Fiona was late getting up and only managed that with an effort of will, her body sore and stiff and shivery.

She was dragging herself across the yard when she heard Fergus's voice. She didn't turn at first, thinking it was in her imagination.

'Fiona McRae,' Fergus repeated.

Fiona dropped her pail and ran to Fergus.

'What's wrong, Fiona? What's wrong?' Fergus asked, holding her away from him to look into her eyes. 'You look dead beat, where's Davie?'

'Davie has been a grand help with fixing the roof and other things that needed seeing to, but things are so behind, it's more than he can manage.'

Fiona took Fergus's hand and turned to go about her chores.

'So, you're back, Findlay, and what do you want?' she heard her father demand.

'A place for the people who are with me to rest for the day, McRae,' Fergus answered.

'I'll get the sheriff to deal with them,' her father shouted and slammed the door as he retreated inside.

Fergus made to follow, but Fiona held his hand. 'Don't start a fight, please, Fergus?' she asked.

'I'll pay what he asks, Fiona, whatever it is, if it gives me the chance to see you,' he told her, smiling.

Fiona's returning smile was watery. 'He sold the last note you gave him to Maitland for five pounds, Fergus.'

'We'll see what he thinks of gold coins,' Fergus said, and dropped her hand to go in to talk to her father.

Fiona shuffled into the kitchen to listen.

'I let you off with ten pounds the last time, it'll be twelve now,' she heard her father insist, and went to the door where she could stare at him.

Her father glowered at her.

'Twelve you say,' Fergus said. 'Well there's two of them,' he added, putting the coins on the table between them. He paused, watching her father. 'And that's three,' he said, adding another to the pile.

'I'll not take your filthy gold' her father spat.

'Then I'll put it back in my sporran,' Fergus said, putting his fingers on the three coins. He hesitated, then drew the coins slowly towards himself. Her father's eyes followed the coins. Fergus stopped, his fingers still on the coins. He pushed them back towards her father. 'You're certain?' Fergus asked, pushing the coins forward again.

She saw her father lick his lips, and felt revulsion at his greed.

'Well, if you're sure,' Fergus said, drawing the coins quickly towards himself, before taking his fingers away, leaving the coins on the table.

'All right,' her father said, grabbing the coins. He sat up smiling in satisfaction. 'But you'll have to leave after tomorrow,' he insisted. 'I don't want this place turned into a camp for gypsies.'

***

Next day, with the sun shining, feeling more energetic, Fiona walked to the camp. Fergus looked relieved to see her. 'I had decided to come later, when you had finished your chores,' he told her.

Fiona's' shake of her head was insistent. 'Father has been going on and on about you, Fergus, please don't come.'

Fergus put his arms round her and she hung there.

'He's been at me to marry Maitland again, Fergus. You've always said you would take me to Dornoch, but what will become of him?'

'We'll take him with us, Fiona,' Fergus smiled, then grinned. 'If he doesn't want to come, we'll tie him up and carry him off.'

Fiona smiled wanly at the idea and leaned into Fergus.

'I'll be back in about ten days, Fiona. Can you keep going till then? Let Davie help as much as possible, and try to rest, please, my love.'

Fiona smiled again at the tenderness. 'Promise?' she asked.

'Promise,' Fergus told her, smiling, but became serious and held her at arm's length. 'But then you must be ready to come away. We can be married in Tain. Morag McInnes can act as bridesmaid. I wanted to have the place made fit for you, but you are wasting away at

Kirklea. Leave it to your father, surely he can sell it and get a wee place and have enough to live on.'

'We've debt all about, Fergus. I don't know what would be left.'

'Then you and I can drove together for another year to give him enough.'

'I'd love that, Fergus. Just to walk through the hills and feel the wind blow, to see the sun rising and know there would be no hens, or milking.'

'There's that and more, Fiona. There's the wonder of the high bens and the lochs, and the floating eagles for company. And when the winter comes, it's back to the warmth and smell of the peat fire, while the wind blows over the roof and drives the snow in drifts, and makes the land clean again. Be ready, Fiona, be ready when I come back.'

Fiona smiled her agreement, and reached up to kiss him.

***

Remembering her kiss, the next day, Monday, confident that Fiona would marry him soon, Fergus set the drove moving early.

CHAPTER 20

At Invercauld, Morag saw Black Duncan, and two friends, coming, and flew inside the house, slamming the door behind her.

She heard him laughing as he battered on the door. The battering had no effect, and her fear eased. Then she thought of her father. It was about time for him to return. In fact, her mother had been pocking the fire in anticipation, when she came in.

The blows became heavier. The door itself was solid enough, but the frame and wall around it weren't meant to withstand heavy shocks, and the whole thing caved in after several minutes of heavy blows. Duncan stood facing her. She felt her mother take her arm.

Duncan grinned. 'So, what did Findlay leave you?' he demanded. 'He'd not leave you bare handed. Maybe if you give it to me, I'll leave you alone.'

Morag's mother turned away but Morag grabbed her arm. 'No, Mother, he'll do what he intends anyway,' she said, with more courage than she felt.

Duncan slapped her. She licked her swelling lips and could taste blood.

Duncan pushed his grinning face close, making her think of a wolf looking at a lamb. She just stared. Unable to move.

'I'll have what I came for, but it might go easier for you, if you gave me whatever gold Findlay left,' he shouted.

Morag backed off, stunned.

Her mother took a leather bag purse from under the straw mattress on the rough bed.

Duncan opened the bag and tipped out some silver coins. 'No gold?' he demanded.

'That's all there is,' Morag's mother told him, her eyes wide and fearful.

Morag felt her will return. 'Fergus will kill you for this. You ken that?'

Duncan sneered. 'He's already tried twice. Maybe the next time it'll be his own funeral,' he answered. His hand grabbed Morag's dress and his push sent her sprawling onto the bed.

'No, no, we gave you the money,' she heard her mother scream.

Duncan slapped her mother, hard. Morag saw her stumble and fall in a corner. Duncan turned back to herself, struggling to rise, and shoved her back on to the low bed and began fumbling with his trews.

They all turned at the sound of McInnis's foot on the flattened door.

McInnes dived at Duncan. Duncan only had time to draw his dirk before McInnes floored him. Duncan struggled clear. McInnes lay still.

Morag looked in shock as a red stain began to spread at her father's breast.

'*Murderer! Murderer*!,' Morag's mother yelled as she threw herself at Duncan, a wildcat, scratching and clawing. It broke Morag's fascination with the growing blood stain. She grabbed her mother's poker from the fire and attacked Duncan's two supporters. One man raised his hand in defence but screamed as the hot poker scorched his wrist. He stepped back into his companion and the pair bolted.

Morag's anger became cold. She took deliberate aim at Duncan's side and rammed the poker hard. There was a puff of smoke as it burned through the outer garments and a scream as it touched his side. Morag withdrew it and started to belabour him. Her mother had never stopped scratching and their combined attack forced Duncan to run.

Morag stood weeping, the poker hanging from loose arms.

Inside, her mother wailed and keened over the body of her husband.

***

Next day, Morag arranged for her father's burial, only stopping her mother jumping into the grave cavity by holding her tightly while she wept herself.

Babs came to the burial and gave Morag a bottle. 'Gi'e her six drops in some water, now and then, when she needs it,' Babs told her. 'He'll no' be the last to die,' she added, shaking her head.

'Who else will die, Babs, who else? And for what?'

'Who can tell, lassie?' was all Babs would say, but Morag grabbed her arm demanding more.

'I just wish Fergus Findlay was back,' Babs told Morag, before shaking herself free and hobbling away.

***

The morning after Fergus left, Fiona rose and went about her early tasks without energy. In the end, by a variety of hand signals, she gave Davie instructions to carry on and went back to bed.

She was roused by the sound of yelling from outside and dragged herself to the window to see what it was about. She saw her father talking, shouting at Davie and felt her body slump at the thought of another problem to solve, but she began to grow angry as her father gesticulated, took the shovel from Davie's hand and threw it to one side. Davie looked confused but pointed to the house.

Her father, after what she assumed were a few hard words, walked back to the house and she heard the kitchen door slam.

Fiona went back to sit on her bed to gather her energy to go downstairs when there was a timid knock on the door.

'Fiona?' her father's voice whispered.

'I'll be up in a minute or two, Father,' Fiona answered.

The sound of hooves in the yard brought her to the window again. It was Maitland. He looked none too pleased, and his raised voice was clearly audible.

'I understand Findlay was here,' Maitland said and Fiona stood closer to the window to hear her father's reply.

'Aye, he was, but I sent him packing.'

'Maybe you did, and maybe you didn't, McRae, but this has to stop. One morning you'll waken up and Fiona will be gone and you'll be in the workhouse quicker than you can wink. D'you understand! I'm not a man to be diverted by excuses, or denied what I want, because it will cause suffering.'

McRae tried to be conciliatory, 'I ken that well enough Mr Maitland, but things will turn out as we agreed, never worry.'

'It's you that has to worry, McRae,' Maitland pointed out. 'I want a word with your daughter. Where is she?'

'She's taken to her bed,' McRae told him, his voice pleading. 'It's nothing serious, she's a fine healthy girl, Mr Maitland, just women's troubles, I expect,' he added.

'Then get her down here. Women are often more easily convinced of what they should do when they are weak.'

'I couldna get her out of her bed when she's no' at her best, Mr Maitland, she'd not like that at all, and she'd not be properly dressed and ready to do her proper duty to entertain yourself.'

'Get her down, McRae. Do it now. You've shilly-shallied enough about this whole thing. If she's to marry me, I want it sooner, not later.'

Fiona felt her stomach grow heavy with despair and wished Fergus hadn't left.

Her father's wheedling voice continued. 'Mr Maitland, her mother died of a decline, you'd not want Fiona to slip away like that?'

'As long as she's married to me before she does, I don't really care, McRae. She's a cold fish and it would suit me well enough if she was to expire the minute the vicar declared us man and wife.'

Her father was trying to stay positive, but Fiona could feel the hopelessness of it. 'I ken you're joking, Mr Maitland, she'll be a good wife to you and mother to your bairns for many years, depend on that.'

'Then get her out of bed where I can talk to her, McRae,' Maitland ordered.

Fiona struggled into her clothes and combed her hair as best she could, but felt rumpled and untidy as she came downstairs.

'You look charming,' Maitland said.

Fiona smiled weakly.

'I just wanted to talk to you, Fiona. Your father has kindly given his blessing to our being wed, lass, and I wanted you to be the first to know.'

Fiona looked at her father, but he was smiling at Maitland. She felt betrayed, alone, a void where her stomach should be, and a heaviness about her head.

'I expect you'll want to see The Mearns again. You can get rid of Mrs Lafferty if that suits you. It will save a penny or two anyway.'

'I … I need to think about this, Mr Maitland.' Fiona managed. 'I'm not at my best, and this is a big decision. If you'll excuse me, I'll get back to my bed and give you an answer when I'm feeling better.'

'There's no need to delay, Fiona,' her father encouraged. 'We've talked about it before, and you said yourself there was some sense in marrying a man of Mr Maitland's position.'

'I'm just not … not feeling … ready,' Fiona explained.

Maitland stepped forward. 'No young lady ever is, lass. You'll see the advantages when you're feeling better, but I need to make arrangements. You'll need new dresses, and maybe a bit of jewellery suitable to your position.'

Fiona sat down. She looked from one to the other, as first her father's wheedling voice talked, and then

Maitland's red features and bad teeth demanded her attention, until they seemed to join each other in a roar of sound, and all she wanted was to go to bed.

At that moment, they put a paper in front of her and told her to sign. 'What is it?' she managed to ask.

'It's confirming our agreement,' Maitland said.

Fiona frowned, trying to gather her thoughts, realising this was important but not certain why.

'What agreement?' she asked.

'Our pledge to each other, Fiona,' Maitland's big head told her.

It doesn't matter, Fiona thought jubilantly, Fergus will be here in ten days. No, less. And there is no time in between for banns in the church, and, with a surge of relief, signed whatever it was and watched as the two conspirators stood back smiling.

She didn't even bother to say goodbye. She just went upstairs and fell into bed.

CHAPTER 21

Next day, Maitland rode into Luss and spoke to Hamish's employer. Hamish was out on deliveries. Maitland ordered a bag of meal and asked for it to be delivered the following day, Wednesday.

When Hamish came, Maitland took him inside.

'You wanted to stop Fergus Findlay from marrying Fiona,' Maitland began. 'She's agreed to marry me, but I'm worried Findlay will come and make her change her mind.'

Hamish frowned.

Maitland continued. 'I'll make sure you get the running of Kirklea, then you can be near her, watch over her, and help when she needs it, rather than that stupid deaf mute Findlay left.'

'What can I do about it, Mr Maitland?'

'Findlay has gone to Glasgow and will most likely come back in a week's time from now. I need him delayed until next Thursday. You need to trap him somewhere, Hamish. I'm not saying you need to kill him, a good bump on the head, or a wound that needs doctoring, would be enough'

'He'll have gone to that house I followed him to before. I could get him as he leaves.'

'He might have somebody with him Hamish; you want to get him on his own. Get him to come to you somewhere, somewhere dark when there's nobody about, and you can get away once you've dealt with the rascal.'

'Like a graveyard,' Hamish said.

'That's the idea, Hamish, among the dead,' Maitland encouraged. 'Not that I'm suggesting you kill him, mind you. I don't know the city, but there must be a big cemetery somewhere in Glasgow.'

'There is. It's called the Necropolis. I was there in the army. It's next to the Cathedral, but away from anything. It's massive.'

'How's he going to find you in the dark among all the gravestones? Or, more important, how are you going to see *him*?' Maitland asked.

'If I remember right, there's a big house opposite the cathedral, it's called Provand's Lordship, where I could hide in the doorway.'

'A house! What if someone hears and comes to see what's happening?'

'It's isolated, Mr Maitland. No lights but the moon, if there is one. Even if somebody hears and comes, I'll be able to slip away. But how will I get him to come?' Hamish asked.

'I'll give you a note in what looks close enough to Fiona's handwriting to convince him it's from her. Give it to a girl, to give to someone to take to the house Findlay visits. That way, when they ask, whoever delivers the note, they'll say a female gave it to them.'

'He has friends there, Mr Maitland. They might come with him.'

'I'll make sure the note tells him to come by himself. He'll likely look the place over while it's daylight. Don't worry about that, Hamish. You've been in the army and no doubt, been involved in ambuscades, eh!'

'I have that, Mr Maitland, one time Butcher and us ...'

'There you are, you'll be fine, but just in case he tries some trick, take a pistol. I'm not saying you'll need it, but you can always threaten him with it, then tie him up, or something.'

Hamish took the pistol and hefted it in his hand. 'Aye, I can threaten him with it, then tie him up,' he agreed, smiling. 'It'll take me two days to get there, Mr Maitland. This is Wednesday. You say Fergus left Kirklea on Monday. He'll be ready to leave to come back on Sunday, maybe. I'd better get on my way.'

Maitland watched Hamish drive off. 'If you kill him, so much the better. If he kills you, I'll see he hangs for it,' Maitland muttered, smiling to himself.

**

Fergus sold his own, the emigrants, and the seventy unclaimed cattle in Dumbarton, his enthusiasm creating an atmosphere that guaranteed top prices. When he divided the extra from the recovered beasts with the emigrants, he was showered with kisses from the women, and handshakes from the men.

The general mood made the walk to Glasgow to see the emigrants off, a holiday - added to, by seeing great sailing ships being towed along the newly deepened channel, right to the city itself, by puffing paddle steamers.

The three friends, Fergus, McNeil and Tom saw the new emigrants safely past the officials, through all the preliminaries of tickets, and left them, an anxious but excited group, waiting for their ship.

**

At Abernethy's, Jean greeted them, 'Come in, come in,' her dimples brightening an already beaming smile, that

153

Fergus realised was more for McNeil than himself. 'I see you've decided to leave the army, Neil McNeil,' she added, looking approvingly at his coat.

'My old jacket became too disreputable, even for me, Miss Abernethy,' McNeil smiled in answer.

'But you've still got that gun,' Jean pointed out.

Fergus interrupted. 'Keeps us in venison.'

'Who's that, Jeannie,' Abernethy's gruff voice shouted.

'It's Tom and your favourite Highlander, Father,' Jean called back over her shoulder, as she took coats.

'Tom! Man it's good to see ye, come away in and let me hear all aboot your trip. A dram, lassie, a dram for welcome,' he told Jean.

'It's in the decanter, Father,' Jean told him.

'Aye, so it is, so it is, I just forgot in my excitement.'

'We killed a man, Father,' Tom confessed.

Fergus looked at Abernethy, whose glance demanded explanation. 'A reiver, Abernethy. We buried him on the hill,' Fergus explained.

'A reiver! I thought they'd been stamped out, Fergus?'

'There's always one among the hills and glens, Abernethy,' Fergus explained. 'I doubt if it will ever stop.'

'So you saved the court the cost of a hanging, Tom. Well done, well done!'

Tom was standing open mouthed, and Abernethy sobered. 'Look, Tom, we'll never lift Scotland above poverty as long as it has a reputation for lawlessness. Would you yersel' invest in that new canal in the Great Glen, wi' the chance that every boat that passed along it would be taken by pirates in kilts? Think yersel' man!'

Tom didn't look convinced and sipped at his whisky.

Fergus took a sip and found Abernethy looking at him. 'That man you asked aboot,' Abernethy began.

'Maitland?'

'Aye, Maitland. He's been busy buyin' up debts and the interestin' thing is, the debts are in the name of yon Kirklea that belongs to a McRae. Is that no' the name of that farm where the lassie you're sweet on bides?'

Fergus nodded. 'How did you hear about it?' Fergus asked.

'Hear what?' Abernethy asked. 'About the debts, or about the lassie?'

'About the debts, Mr Abernethy. I ken about the lassie myself.'

'We're no' all as daft as we're cabbage lookin' Fergus. It's from a good source, never you mind. I would imagine he wants to put McRae in his debt for some reason. Maybe you'll ken more about that than me.'

'He wants the farm, Mr Abernethy. It's of little interest to me, but it's next door to Maitland.'

'Aye, well, that explains it. But there's another odd thing, he seems to have a wife and bairns in Northumberland somewhere, so what does he want with land in the Highlands?'

'It's cheaper, Father,' Tom explained.

'That I ken. Nevertheless, it seems odd to me, more like a man wantin' to hide himsel' away in a corner. So what's he hiding away from?'

'Maybe just a wife that talks too much,' McNeil put in. 'A bit like Sinclair's, maybe, Fergus?'

McNeil's comment led to explanations and other tales and it was late when they went to bed.

Next day, Saturday, as McNeil made his farewells and left for the north, Fergus smiled at Jean's obvious disappointment. Fergus was unsure if he was going to Wester Ross to help organise another emigration, or going to Easter Ross to talk to McInnes about Canada and wait for Fergus.

***

Fergus, ignoring Abernethy's warnings that women were feckle beings and likely to change their minds, had decided to get a wedding present for Fiona. Jean gave him all kinds of advice, dragging him round the town but, when Fergus saw the chestnut horse, he ignored all her pleas and entreaties, and bought the animal.

They were back at the house, and Fergus was making preparations to leave, when the note came. "Come to the Provand's Lordship near the Necropolis at 11p.m. Sunday. Come alone and be careful," it said in a scrawl. It was signed in what looked like Fiona's hand, or at least Fiona's hand if she were worried and tense.

'Why would she have come to Glasgow?' Jean asked.

'I don't know,' Fergus told her. 'But I can't ignore it, can I?'

'I suppose not, but you should have Tom and some others with you, Fergus. This is most unusual. There may be a gang of thugs waiting for you.'

'She says it would be dangerous to bring others, Jean. I don't know why, but anywhere in that part of Glasgow, at that time of night, is dangerous.'

'Is it just to delay you, do you think?'

'I promised Fiona I'd be back in ten days. That was last Sunday. I've time enough to get back, even if I leave on Tuesday morning. There's something curious about the note but I have to look into it. There's always the chance it's genuine. Don't worry,' he said, smiling at her frown, 'I'll be careful. Do you know where this place is, Tom?' he asked.

'It's on the other side of town. I'll take you there in the morning.'

Provand's Lordship stood opposite the cathedral. A solid building, grey and unprepossessing in comparison to the busy cathedral across the road.

Fergus was surprised to see the size of the graveyard Tom had referred to as the Necropolis.

Still unsure if the note was from Fiona, Fergus walked round the building several times, staying well back, looking for something that might indicate why it had been chosen by the note writer. In the end, he decided it could only be because it was isolated and, close to midnight, dark.

***

As the evening darkened and Fergus prepared to go, Abernethy insisted on sending Tom and several others with him, but eventually agreed to let Fergus go alone, five minutes ahead of the others.

'At least take a pistol,' Abernethy insisted. Unused to firearms, Fergus was reluctant to agree, but after some instructions from Tom, tucked one into his belt where it dug into his flesh.

'Just watch it doesnae go off in there,' Abernethy grinned.

Fergus dismounted, to walk the last hundred yards to Provand's Lordship. He tried to walk silently, but in the dark, his foot kicked the odd stone, which tumbled loud in the silence. Each time, he stopped, listening. The nearer he got to it, the more morbid and threatening the big stone building looked.

Bruce nuzzled his hand. Fergus patted his head, then urged him forward.

**

In the dark, Hamish, his eyes now adjusted to what little light came from the star shine, lay in front of the door of Provand's Lordship, watching for the shadow of someone against the grey walls of the cathedral opposite. He was still unsure if he'd shoot Fergus, or just threaten and tie him up. He'd thought the front door of the house was recessed and he'd be able to stand out of sight in the deep shadow. The door had turned out to be like any house door, and he'd decided the best plan was to lie quiet some yards in front of it with the pistol held out, ready to aim when Fergus appeared.

The cold from the earth seeped through his clothes, but he'd waited in the cold before. The dark shadow of the graveyard behind him was another matter; he tried to tell himself he wasn't concerned about the black hill rising against the stars, but fear of some dark thing creeping up on him grew, and he turned to look. There was nothing there.

He told himself not to panic, and settled to watch, but the fear crept up his back again. He could feel something pressing on his feet, then moving up his legs.

He felt the something touch his leg, and turned fearfully. There was a nebulous darkening against the hill of the dead and a vague panting shadow snuffled first at his leg, now at his side.

Hamish jumped terrified and ran, felt himself grabbed in a bear hug, something holding him tight. He yelled in terror and jerked the trigger of the pistol.

The flash was behind his attacker and shone on his own face.

'Hamish!' a voice said.

Hearing his name mentioned by this unseen phantom that was trying to drag him off to the hill of the dead, Hamish struggled and wrestled with his tormentor. He managed to half free himself and turned to run.

***

Fergus drew the pistol at his belt and hit the vague outline of his assassin's head with the butt - hard.

The assassin dropped.

Someone called. Fergus lifted the body, shaking his head as he confirmed it was Hamish. He found Tom and several others waiting at his horse.

'It's a lad who was with us on the first drove. He's young, and daft in love with Fiona. I've given him a knock on the head. Maybe I've hit him harder than I meant. We'd best take him to your place Tom. I've a question or two to ask, when he wakes up.'

***

When Fergus checked on him next morning, Hamish wasn't awake, and it was only in the early hours of Tuesday that he moaned and opened his eyes.

Fergus saw him try to rise, but Jean pressed her hand on his chest and he looked round, smiled quickly, and lay back down with a groan.

His eyes focussed on Fergus.

'What day is it?' he asked.

'Friday,' Fergus lied.

Hamish smiled. 'Then you're too late, Findlay. Fiona was married to Mr Maitland on Wednesday,' he whispered.

'Was she now,' Fergus said. 'And how does he manage that with a wife in Northumberland.'

Hamish tried to rise. 'You're a liar!' he yelled, groaned and lay back.

'If you weren't in bed, Hamish, I'd not take that, but you've been led astray by Maitland, just as you were led astray by Butcher. Now, rest easy, this is Tuesday, and I must rush off to save Fiona from a bigamist.'

CHAPTER 22

The morning after signing the marriage agreement, from long habit, Fiona got out of bed as the grey light filled her room - the bright curtains she and her mother had made having long been discarded, leaving the window bare and peeling. Her movements were slow and tired, her mind blank to all but the need to work.

She smiled briefly at the thought that Fergus would be there in five days - or was it four? - and she'd leave this drudge behind. At least it would be a change.

She went downstairs and cleaned the fireplace – her father hadn't done it in years – and coaxed it back to life, before sitting down. What was wrong with her? This tiredness never seemed to give up.

She forced herself up again, and made porridge for her father, Davie and herself; there was none for the dogs any more.

Waving Davie inside reminded her of Fergus, and she smiled as he took his plate. Davie's smile in return was half frown, and Fiona's smile broadened at his concern.

She turned back into the kitchen and found her father taking his mornings with a dour face. 'We don't need to feed that idiot of Findlay's, Fiona. Findlay should have left money for his board,' McRae muttered.

'It's your work he's doing. He's entitled to share your food.' Fiona told him.

Her father stared hard at her. 'When Mr Maitland and you are married we'll …' Fiona lost interest in what her father was saying, and started to prepare for ironing '… and I'll be glad to see it.'

'If I live that long, Father. I feel the way mother looked before she passed away.'

'You canna die on us, Fiona!'

'Why, Father? Why?'

McRae looked startled. 'You … you just canna that's all. I need you, lassie.'

'If I go away with Fergus, you'll not have me,' Fiona told him, not realising she was speaking aloud.

'You're promised to Mr Maitland, lassie, you canna deny that. It's a promise on paper!'

'And worth as much as any promise Maitland ever made. You imagine he's going to take care of you after we're married!' Fiona laughed - more of a cackle, she thought. A witch's cackle to foil Maitland, and did it again.

Her day drifted on. She worked through chores by habit, scarcely aware of when one finished and the next began.

***

Just after noon on Tuesday, Mrs Lafferty answered the door at The Mearns. She found a thin ferret faced man standing there. He wore clothes that badly needed pressing, but with a diamond pin in a cravat, looking like a well-dressed lady in a crowd of beggars.

'What do you want?' Mrs Lafferty asked.

'I've come to see Mr Maitland,' the individual smiled, thin lipped.

'I doubt if he'll see the likes of you, whoever you …'

'Who is it, Mrs Lafferty?' Maitland asked.

'A wee thief, unless I miss my guess,' Mrs Lafferty answered.

Maitland came and looked at the man. 'Come in. I hope you have good news?'

'The best,' the man said, following Maitland past Mrs Lafferty.

Mrs Lafferty watched them go into Maitland's study, and went to listen at the door.

'Half now, half when I have confirmation,' she heard Maitland say.

'He's dead, Maitland. I saw them carry him away.'

'So you say. Take ten guineas, or leave with nothing,' Maitland insisted.

Mrs Lafferty heard the jingling of coins and walked away.

***

Mrs Lafferty was waiting at the door when the man was leaving.

'I have a watch here that might be of interest to you,' she said. 'I've been offered twelve guineas for it, but you can have it for six.'

The man looked at the watch. 'Four!'

Mrs Lafferty laughed and put the watch away. 'Five,' the man said.

'Done,' Mrs Lafferty agreed.

***

An hour later, as Maitland was dressed to go out, Mrs Lafferty heard him call her. 'I can't find my gold watch, have you seen it?'

'It was in your office this morning, Mr Maitland, before than mannie came.'

'Damn the man,' Maitland swore. 'He'll get no more money from me.'

***

Some time later, Fiona became aware of Maitland being at the door. Her father rushed to let him in.

'I've just had word that Fergus Findlay has been killed in a fight in Glasgow,' Maitland announced.

Fiona looked dully at him and carried on working.

'Fergus Findlay?' her father asked.

'Fergus Findlay?' Fiona heard herself repeat.

'And good riddance to him,' her father added.

'It seems he got involved in a knife brawl and was knifed or shot,' Maitland explained.

The buzzing in Fiona's ears grew loud and her body slackened. She knew she was falling, but it didn't seem to matter.

'Drink this,' she heard her father say from far away. 'Just a sip, you'll feel better.'

***

Fergus was on his way. He'd loaded four of the garrons, added a spare and Fiona's chestnut to the string, and made his way out of Glasgow.

He'd passed Dumbarton when another pony joined them from a field with an open gate.

Fergus assumed it would follow for a short space before returning home. He had just nodded to a man working in a field when a youngish girl waved her hands. 'That's our pony,' she shouted. 'Take it back, you thief!'

Fergus turned to see the pony was still with them and was caught in the dilemma of turning back with the pony, or carrying on. He had plenty of time to get to Fiona before tomorrow, but it would be better to be early than a minute late.

The girl screeched at him and Fergus turned his string and went back to the open gate.

'Next time, don't leave the gate open,' he told the girl.

164

'My mother will want to thank you,' the girl said, suddenly smiling.

'Just keep the gate closed,' Fergus told her.

'But my mother will want to thank you,' the girl persisted. 'We haven't any money but she has ways of thanking nice men,' the girl said.

Fergus had heard of this. He'd go to the house and, while he was being passionate, the pockets of his trews would be emptied. He'd even heard of the girl rushing in to say her father was coming while her mother was 'thanking' the nice man.

Fergus got down and drew his broadsword. The girl cringed away but Fergus turned the sword and slapped her on the thigh with the flat. The girl turned to run and Fergus gave her two more slaps.

The man in the field grinned and waved to him.

It hadn't been a long delay, but small delays could fritter time away just as effectively as a long one, and Fergus hurried on.

It was sheep next. Someone with a flock had stopped by the roadside in the late afternoon. Unfortunately, they'd stopped where the road was narrow. The sheep had strayed into the road, filling it. Fergus's impatience to reach Fiona was the main cause of the delay. If he had worked his way slowly through, things would have been fine, but he tried to force his way forward and the sheep packed tight.

It was Bruce who solved the problem for him by slipping into the field next to the road and going past the sheep before driving them back past Fergus. Four dogs appeared and stood snarling. Bruce faced one. The others slunk forward, growled menacingly, then stopped to let their leader do the fighting. Bruce stood, head lowered, legs slightly splayed and stared. The other dog returned the stare for a few moments, then looked away. Bruce barked once and the other dogs turned and left.

At the sound of barking someone shouted. Fergus heard a shot, but had no idea if the shot was meant to warn, or harm, and urged his riding horse forward, dragging the others behind.

Clouds began to gather and, in the short dark hours, it became impossible to see, and he was forced to stop. He lay down in his plaid and fretted about Fiona. She would know he was coming, but would not be expecting him until Friday. She was a clever girl, but she had looked more than just tired, and if both Maitland and her father were harassing her, he doubted if she would be able to resist, or find some way of delaying things.

CHAPTER 23

Fiona woke into grey light, with the shadowy dream shapes of her mother and Fergus lingering like wisps of mist in her mind. She felt weary, but happy. They'd said they would come for her, soon, and she smiled.

She dressed, made her way downstairs, started to clean the fireplace and make ready for another day.

She was surprised to see her father come into the kitchen. 'What are you doing, Fiona?' he asked. 'Get yourself washed and do up your hair, and put on something brighter. This is your wedding day, lassie.'

'Wedding day?' Fiona asked.

'Aye, your wedding day.'

'But Fergus is dead,' she said. 'He's dead, Father, don't you realise that?' she asked, sitting down and letting the tears dribble down her cheek.

'Not Fergus, Fiona, Mr Maitland.'

'Mr Maitland?'

'You're being married to him today.'

'Today?'

'Aye, today. I'll set the fire for you and get some hot water so that you can bathe and wash your hair. You'll feel better after that.'

Fiona sat watching without expression as her father brought in the bath and poured in hot water. This isn't washing day, she thought, I've got ironing to do, and rose to prepare. Her father stopped her.

'Now bathe, Fiona. I'll leave you alone. There's water heating for your hair,' McRae told her and left.

Fiona undressed and stepped into the warm water and sat. She noticed the soap beside the bath. Fergus would want her body to be clean when he came for her, she thought, and washed carefully. How long had he been dead? She wondered. Two days, maybe three, he might come at the darkening, she thought, smiling gently as she soaped her body.

She was drying her hair when her father came back in.

'That's better, lassie. Now your smartest dress while I make some porridge, and we'll be ready for Mr Maitland.'

Maitland? Of course, she must go through with this pretend marriage until Fergus came and they could be together, spirit joined, without drudgery or pain.

Maitland came. 'With a coach, Fiona,' her father encouraged.

Her old dog growled and Maitland kicked it, twice. The old dog lay still. Maitland waved to Davie to help. Davie didn't understand, and got kicked for that. It didn't help, and Maitland lashed him with his crop, drawing blood on his face.

Fiona climbed into the coach.

'Can it no' be delayed for a day or two, Mr Maitland, 'till she's feeling better?' she heard her father ask — as if it mattered. 'The excitement might be the death of her,' she heard her father plead.

'Alive or dead, McRae, as long as she's my wife,' she heard Maitland answer. 'I just can't marry her in those rags she wears.'

Fiona looked down at her best dress and noticed the places where she'd mended seams and patches. Fergus wouldn't mind, she thought.

Her father came in beside her, Maitland waved the coachman away, and the coach lurched forward.

'He killed the dog,' Fiona said to her father.

'Oh, he's just nervous. It's his wedding day as well, remember,' he told her.

She slipped out of her body and began dreaming of Fergus.

***

With the light, a heavy drizzle started, and Fergus was soon wet through and cold, but had no time to waste on fires and comfort. The horses were rested, but far from fresh, and Fergus walked them until they were warmed, steam rising from their backs, before increasing the pace.

In the grey misty air, the time passed and Fergus was tempted to raise the pace again, but some of the pack animals were tiring, and he kept to his steady jog.

The cloud lifted as he turned into The Mearns' glen and watched for activity as he approached the house. Had there been a coach there before? He couldn't remember precisely.

An old woman, carrying a wash basket, came out and started to hang clothes on a washing-line.

As Fergus approached, she turned, startled, to look up at him. 'And who are you, sneaking up on decent women like that?' she demanded.

'Findlay, Fergus Findlay. And you'll be Mrs Maitland.'

The old woman cackled. 'In his dreams! I married a decent Irishman called Lafferty. But where are you from? No' from aboot here by the look of ye.'

'I'm from Dornoch, Mrs Lafferty.'

'I have a sister that way. Her name is Babs.'

Fergus smiled. 'I know your sister well. She has the second sight, they say.'

'That'll be Babs. She has no more the second sight than you or me, but she was always a shrewd biddie.'

Mrs Lafferty took a hard look at Fergus before commenting, 'You'll not be that Fergus Findlay I've heard Maitland talk of?'

'I am indeed, Mrs Lafferty,' Fergus told her

'So, you're no' dead. Well that's good news.'

'Dead, what gave you that idea?'

'A weasel faced mannie from Glasgow,' Mrs Lafferty informed him.

'I met one on the way here. He had a gold watch he told me was worth fifty guineas, but I could have it for ten,' Fergus added.

'The blackguard! It's Maitland's watch anyway, but if you're on your way to see Fiona McRae, you'd better hurry, for Maitland has been gone these last two hours on his way to marry her.'

Fergus felt cold. Maitland had already left to marry Fiona! Fiona herself thought him dead! Two hours! Dear God, maybe he was too late.

'Where is the wedding?' Fergus asked as he mounted.

'That I canna tell you. I'm sorry, but maybe she's still at Kirklea.'

Fergus turned and put the horses at the hill at the top of the glen. Would Fiona believe him dead, he wondered. The animals gasped and panted but he kept them at it until they were over the top and into Kirklea glen. What torment was she going through? The slower ponies dragged at his riding horse as he rode down to the farmhouse. He scanned the farmyard for life. The first thing he saw was the dead dog. Bruce ran to sniff at his old friend and lay down looking at the body.

Davie came out of the barn.

'Fiona?' Fergus yelled, forgetting Davie couldn't hear.

He might not have heard, but Davie understood. He pointed down the cart track that led out of the glen. It was only then that Fergus noticed Davie's face was puffed and bruised, and he was holding one side as he grimaced in pain.

Fergus calmed. To go rushing about was of no use to Fiona, what he needed to know was where Maitland had taken her. He motioned down the cart road, then swung his hand east, before repeating the gesture to the west.

Davie shook his head, but pointed to the spare horse and motioned to climb on its back before pointing to his eyes then down the track.

Fergus let him mount.

They rode down the road until it branched, and Davie turned his mount down the turning to the road to Luss.

CHAPTER 24

In Luss itself, Fiona sat apart from the body she used for living, watching with mild interest as a woman fussed round the body. Fiona felt tied to it, but no longer lived inside its skin. The woman was as tall as Fiona and, although her hair was darker and there were crow's feet round the dark circles of her eyes, seen from one side, they could have been sisters. The other side of the woman's face, half hidden by draped hair, was badly marked.

Fiona watched as the woman pulled at the dress and prodded at the body.

'You don't know how lucky you are to be marrying a rich man,' the woman was complaining. 'It should have been me. He took me to arrange the banns and all, but what do I get? A few measly guineas while you go to live in that big house. Straighten up, girl!' the woman ordered as she punched the body.

The woman started to button the dress at the back. It was pale blue Fiona noted, and made the body's breasts bulge over the low straight neckline. 'He likes a bit of breast,' the woman said. 'And he likes a struggle. If you want to please him, fight like a wildcat.'

'He's violent?' Fiona asked, without real interest.

The woman stood back looking at Fiona in pity. 'All men are violent,' she said matter-of-factly. 'Now, let me see ... some colour on the cheeks ...' she mused. 'I'll not waste rouge on you,' the woman said, slapping Fiona on each cheek bringing Fiona back into the body.

The dress was tight and Fiona was sure her breasts would burst out. It was tight down over her hips, like snakeskin.

'Pinch your cheeks like this,' the woman instructed and grabbed both of Fiona's cheeks and squeezed hard and then stood back.

In a sudden flush of energy and emotion, Fiona slapped her. They want me to fight, she thought, I can fight all right. Maitland might have his way with me, but some night I'll stick a knife in his thick throat and be a rich widow.

The outburst of emotion was too much, and Fiona slumped into a chair and left the body again.

She let her father lead her to a coach. The woman got in beside them.

Her father looked encouragingly at her as the coach moved. The coach stopped and she could see a small gate in front of a church lawn. Her father got out and helped the woman to step down. He led the woman half way up the path, before turning back for Fiona.

Fiona looked at the church door and a shudder of fear ran through her. This was a holy commitment, before God. Would a promise made in there mean Fergus couldn't come for her? Would she be tied to that red-faced beast for ever? At the thought, she cowered back into the seat.

'Come on, lass,' her father coaxed.

Fiona could see the church door, and the coach driver off to one side smoking a pipe. She could see the little clouds of smoke as he puffed. In a flush of clear thinking, Fiona wondered if she could just get out, climb into the driver's seat and drive off. Did she have the courage, the energy? Where would she go?

'Come on, lassie, they're waiting,' her father, standing at the open coach door, insisted, holding out his hand.

Fiona rose, bent over in the coach's interior, still undecided if she could push her father aside, get to the driver's seat and grab the reins before she was stopped, when she was thrown violently back into the seat.

She heard her father shout. The coach moved and gathered speed, wheels rattling over stones. The warm breeze through the open door lifted her spirits and she settled herself on the seat; there was nothing else she could do. She smiled.

The coach rumbled out of the town and drew to one side. Fiona rose and fell out of the coach into Fergus's arms. She looked into his eyes once, smiling her welcome, before shutting her eyes and floating off like thistledown on a summer day.

Her next awareness was Mrs Lafferty's voice asking, 'What's this?'

'I'm no thief,' Fergus answered. 'Here's the coach, and if you'll allow her to change in the house, I have clothes for Fiona to put on and leave that whore's dress she's wearing where it will be some use.'

'Give me the clothes,' Fiona asked, suddenly determined. 'I'll change here in this coach rather than go into that house!'

Fergus took a bundle from a garron and handed it in through the window. 'It's all I've got, Fiona,' he apologised.

Fiona laughed, and in what seemed seconds, was dressed in trews and a rough shirt. She had to hold on to the coach side to stop from falling, but managed to hand the dress to Mrs Lafferty.

'God bless you both,' Mrs Lafferty said. 'I don't know what he'll say or do, when he finds I didn't shoot you dead, but this is no place for a decent woman. Take her far away, Fergus Findlay.'

Fiona could do little but hang on as Fergus helped her to mount a horse and, once seated, she sat swaying. She was glad when he mounted his own riding horse and moved close to give her support as he waved goodbye to Mrs Lafferty.

They rode into the hills. Fiona raised her head to breathe in the warm smell of the heather and moved her face from side to side, her eyes closed, enjoying the feel of the breeze on her cheek.

Davie found them a cave and, as she watched, Fergus and he made a bed of gorse on which he laid a plaid before helping her to lie down.

***

Now that he had time to look at her, Fergus was shocked at her lantern jaws, her eyes were sunken, but seemed calmly resigned, even content. Fergus felt a rush of alarm as the thought struck him that she looked happy to die. Her mouth smiled very gently, her thin lips were dry and Fergus let her sip some water.

After arranging things in the cave, Fergus left Fiona sleeping quietly and rode to Tarbet, reaching it late. He bought several things, making a fuss over paying. He had a dram in a backstreet inn before leaving, going out on to the road north. After four miles he turned off the road, doubled back and was in the cave when Fiona turned and woke at dawn.

'Where's Bruce?' Fiona asked.

'Sometimes he takes things into his own hand, Fiona, but rest assured, it will be to our benefit.'

**

When Maitland had collected his horse, which Davie had released and chased away, and McRae had persuaded someone to hire him a nag, the pair set off after the runaways.

'She'll go home for her things,' McRae insisted.

They'd been seen going out of town to the north anyway, Maitland thought.

At The Mearns turn off, Maitland hesitated. He had no time to waste, but this might take several days and he had nothing but the clothes he wore. He turned into the glen to get something fit for rough travelling - and a firearm.

'When were they here?' Maitland demanded from Mrs Lafferty as he took the dress from her.

'Oh, they're half way to Tarbet by now,' Mrs Lafferty told him.

'I see she left the dress. She's never been a thief, Mr Maitland. She'd go home for her own things,' McRae pointed out.

'Whit things?' Mrs Lafferty asked. 'It's weel kenned there's no' a stitch worth losin' time for at Kirklea.'

'She had bits o' things in her room,' McRae insisted.

'You mean there's something of her mother's you've no' pawned, McRae?' Mrs Lafferty asked.

Maitland laughed as McRae glared at Mrs Lafferty.

'Which way did they go?' Maitland demanded.

'They went off up yon brae,' Mrs Lafferty told them, pointing. 'No' through to Kirklea.'

'How do you know they were going to Tarbet?' Maitland asked.

'Where else would they be going?' Mrs Lafferty asked. 'He's a highland tinker. And besides, I heard him mention the place.'

Maitland was not entirely sure if she was telling the truth, but Findlay would go north in the end.

***

Maitland had followed the escapees as far as Tarbet without any signs or reports of them being seen and resigned himself to a long hunt. He decided to stop over for the night in the best inn in the place, leaving McRae to find a stable, or whatever he could, for lodging.

In the morning, Maitland bought what he expected to need, made what enquiries he could and, following the replies, pushed on north out of the town.

McRae became suddenly excited. 'That's his dog, Mr Maitland. That black collie yonder on the hill,' McRae pointed. 'All we have to do is follow it.'

'You'd better be right, McRae, I've had enough of your stupidity,' Maitland told him.

Bruce turned and walked away north disappearing into a patch of timber.

'They're in there, I'm sure of it,' McRae insisted. 'If we hurry we might catch them.'

They were through the stand of timber and out again when they next caught sight of Bruce, seemingly chasing thrown sticks on the edge of another group of trees on the other side of the valley to the north, and hurried after him.

CHAPTER 25

Fiona woke to see Fergus and Davie grooming the horses, the chestnut's coat gleaming in the early sun.

Fergus took a tin mug, dipped it into a pot beside the fire, and came beside her.

Fiona smiled gently.

'Drink some of this,' Fergus said.

Fiona drank the liquid, tasting the tangy saltiness of meat, which made her take several more mouthfuls until the saltiness became overpowering. Fergus fetched a cup of water and Fiona lay down again, smiling her thanks.

In what seemed minutes, she was awake again, and took more of the beef tea from Fergus but what she remembered as she dropped off to sleep, was the taste of a few berries Davie gave her, their sharp sweetness drawing saliva into her mouth.

When she awoke again, Fergus gave her the cup and a piece of bread to dunk in the cup and, instead of lying back, Fiona got up. Fergus took her hand and she walked out on to the hillside, looking away west across the Lomond hills and sat down.

Fergus sat beside her, the scent from the warm heather drifting over them, his arm cuddling her warmly to his side as they watched the sun drop lower and turn the thin clouds yellow against the pale blue of the sky, then glorious pink and, finally, deep red.

Next morning, Fiona awoke, hearing a blackbird sing its boundaries and, as the sun warmed, a lark spin it's song as it climbed into the morning sky.

Davie rose and smiled at her as Fergus struggled out of his plaid and came to smile good morning. Fiona watched as they busied themselves making some kind of concoction of Davie's herbs with oatcake and cheese. When they brought it, Fiona found it hard to eat, but did her best, smiling to try to ease Fergus's frown.

'You're starved, Fiona,' Fergus told her.

Of companionship, of friends, of love, Fiona thought.

'The same happens to sailors without fresh vegetable or fruit, but Davie knows his herbs as well as old Babs. Could you manage to walk a bit today?'

Fiona managed to rise and stand, shakily at first, but then with more assurance. 'Could I wash first?' she asked.

'The waters *cold*, Fiona,' Fergus laughed.

'I know, and I want to feel it on my skin, Fergus. To know I'm alive.'

Fergus laughed. 'We'll bank up the fire. Don't be long and dress quickly.'

The water was indeed *cold*, but it set Fiona tingling and she was laughing as she dried and dressed by the fire's warmth.

She called Fergus. 'I can ride,' she told him, shaking her hair.

They drifted through the hills in the warm sun, Fiona overjoyed to hear the cock, cock, of a pheasant, the dreary wailing of a curlew as it drifted away through the hills, and to watch the bullet straight flight of grouse, upset at being disturbed at their feeding.

***

Fergus allowed her another day to gather herself among the Lomond Hills, then turned to come back to Loch Lomondside, where a few fishermen's boats lay in the shallows. Fergus talked with some of the fishermen and Fiona looked delighted when Fergus ushered her into one of the boats. The fishermen tried to load the horses but, in the end, made them swim. Their voyage across the loch passed close to islands, where the horses found their feet and Fergus guessed from Fiona's expression she would like to have stopped on one but one of the fishermen sensed her longing and glowered, closing Fiona's expression.

At Balmaha, on the loch's eastern shore, they mounted and rode out of town. There were drovers there but Fergus ignored them and chose a campsite in a little grove hidden from the others.

In the morning, Fergus left Bruce and Davie in charge of the horses and took Fiona into Balmaha; a hat slouched over her eyes, her hands in her pockets and a stone in one shoe to give her a limp. Fergus watched her walk, it would deceive a blind man in a hurry, he thought, but smiled away his concern.

They limped past a dress shop several times but Fiona was reluctant to go in. She'd never had a dress made for her by anyone but her mother, or herself, and she wasn't sure what to say.

They stood across the road talking, looking now and then at the shop. When a girl of roughly Fiona's build went into the shop, Fergus pressed Fiona's arm, telling her to stay, and walked across the street.

'Could you possibly help me?' Fergus asked the girl as she came out.

'Of course!'

'I have a sister about your size and I want to get a dress, not one as fashionable as yours with all the petticoats, but something she can walk over the hills with. She loves walking,' Fergus explained.

'Is that your sister over there watching us?'

Fergus's startled expression gave him away.

'Is it an elopement?' the girl asked, her eyes bright as she brought her hands together at her breast.

Fergus looked around before answering. 'Yes.'

'How exciting! But she'll need more than one dress, and she'll need other things, ladies things,' she explained to Fergus's frown.

In half an hour, Fergus, burdened with packages, walked out of town, followed discretely by Fiona, whom he could see was suppressing giggles.

'Keep those dresses for later, Fergus,' Fiona told him. 'Trews and a shirt are ideal for travelling.'

***

For the next three days, they drifted north through the picturesque wooded valleys, clear streams and bold hills of the Trosachs. The varied diet, including herbs that Davie collected, brought colour to Fiona's cheeks, with her smile beginning to show flashes of brightness again and her walk recovering its grace as she relaxed.

Fergus grew more tetchy, annoyed with himself for it, but not able to understand why.

A shower of rain, a few spots only, solved the problem, at least temporarily. They were sleeping beside some silver birch, when the rain pattered on the leaves, and Fiona moved close to Fergus in her sleep, much as she had done in the early frightened days after their escape. Barely aware of what he was doing, Fergus responded and put his arm round Fiona, who nuzzled closer with a satisfied sigh.

In their sleep, small movements, even breathing, became a caress and they were suddenly awake and aware. Their first violent coupling was a blur, and it was only when Fergus eased himself on to one elbow and they could see each other's faces, touch, and caress, that tenderness and love became part of their mating.

In the morning, they washed, laughing, in a waterfall and, as they dried, Fiona found the early signs of returning womanhood and was grateful for the unknown girl's thoughtfulness over 'ladies necessities'.

***

For several days, Fiona's replies were tetchy and Fergus looked for some way to leave her alone.

'I want to go into Tyndrum and listen, Fiona.'

'Listen for what?'

'To see if there is any news of Maitland and your father.'

'But you didn't want to go into Crianlaroch because they might catch you and you'd be jailed for kidnap or something,' Fiona wailed. 'That's what you said, Fergus.' She was almost shouting, close to tears.

'I know, I know, Fiona, but that was still close to Luss. I want to see if they've given up. I won't be long,' he comforted.

'Be careful, that's all. Don't leave me out here on my own.'

'If anything ever happens to me, go to Dornoch, Fiona, to Invercauld. McNeil's there.'

Fiona's frown deepened and Fergus smiled. 'I'll be fine, Fiona, back in two hours, before it's dark,' he told her, turning away from her pleading.

***

There were two droves in Tyndrum. Recognising one of the drovers, Fergus went to talk to him as he worked at his campfire.

'Hey, Fergus,' the young man greeted, 'someone was paying money for news of you.'

'Here?'

'I don't know about here. I heard about it at Fort William.'

'As far north as that?'

'As far north as that!' the youngster confirmed. 'Where are you anyway?'

'Down west at that wee lochan on the other side of town,' Fergus lied.

Leaving the fire, Fergus pulled his hat low over his head and walked along the little street with the reins of his garron in his hand. He walked past the few buildings that made up the village, and carried on west, unable to get rid of the feeling he was being followed, and wishing he had brought Bruce. The trouble was, the dog was distinctive, and had a reputation for being 'no' canny', and people pointed him out to others, drawing the attention of passers-by.

Fergus kept walking, hurrying short stretches and turning off to try to trap a follower, even stopping to give one of the bent, skin and bone beggars suffering from mine poisoning a coin, but he saw nothing. He was about to take to the hill, to bypass Tyndrum and go back to Fiona, when he came to the lochan. It was long, but narrow. If he went straight across the narrow middle, anyone trying to follow would have to swim and become visible, or make a detour of about a mile to get to the other side and, by the time they reached where he was, he'd be gone. He looked about for a boat, but there was none. He bundled his outer clothes and tied them to the garron's neck before leading the animal into the water. It was bone-chilling cold, but Fergus forced himself to swim steadily across.

On the other side, he put on his, almost dry, outer garments, and strode off until he was hidden by the folds of the ground before starting a fire. He added wet leaves that sent smoke rising through the trees like a signal, and turned back to watch.

For some time nothing happened. As the sun dropped behind the bens, he was about to abandon his watch, when a figure came to the lochan's edge, looked for some time at Fergus's smoke signal, before turning and making its way back towards Tyndrum and Fergus hurried into the hills and made his circuitous way back to Fiona.

CHAPTER 26

He found Fiona wild eyed. 'Where have you been? I thought you'd been taken and I'd never see you again, Fergus. Don't ever leave me again! Not ever!'

He took her in his arms, where sobs raked her body for a long time. She held his hand as he groomed the garron and sat close when they ate.

That night, she clung to Fergus until the heat of his body calmed her and she fell into a troubled sleep.

Fergus said nothing of being followed, or of the news that someone, presumably Maitland, was making determined efforts to find them. No doubt, that would peter out as they moved farther north.

Swinging through the hills past Tyndrum again, Fergus watched Fiona, trying not to let her see she was under observation as she walked and rode, sometimes smiling, sometimes grave.

'You've never given that horse a name, Fiona,' he commented.

'What's wrong with Chestnut?' Fiona asked. 'And stop making me feel I'm being watched all the time. I'm fine as long as things don't change, Fergus. I'm loving this journey; being able to just look at the trees, or the hills, or the crags on the bens, or watch a curlew, or a butterfly. I suppose it's so peaceful, that when any of it changes, even a small thing, it's like a disaster.'

'I'll tell you what's wrong with Chestnut, he needs a new shoe and I'd like to go into the next bit of a village and have it done. The blacksmith is on the edge of the village and I don't need to show myself anywhere else.'

'I'm coming with you, Fergus. If you get caught and put in jail, I want to be with you. At least I can explain I came with you of my own free will.'

Fergus looked doubtful.

Fiona smiled. 'Besides, I'd like to get some flour or a loaf from a baker and my mouth is watering at the thought of rhubarb tart.'

Fergus laughed. 'Right, let's make a plan. I'll go to the blacksmith, if you put on one of those dresses and go to the bakers. Take Davie and Bruce if you like. I'll stay where I can see you, but not so close anyone thinks of us as together.'

'Two strangers in a small place and not together, Fergus?'

'We won't be long Fiona. Just make sure the baker knows you're on your way to Fort William.'

***

The blacksmith looked up from his anvil. 'Fergus Findlay, what a sight for sore eyes. You ken there's a price on your head. Well, not on your head, for information leading to your arrest,' the blacksmith told him. 'Where's the young woman you abducted?'

'Gone to the baker's for tarts.'

'That wasn't too wise, Fergus. The baker's not to be trusted when there's money to be made. Go and bring her back here. You can have some buttermilk in the house until I've finished.'

Before Fergus could go to her, Fiona came hurrying.

'The baker sent a boy off for something. It seemed innocent enough, but Bruce came and licked my hand, so I told the baker I was in a hurry as someone was waiting to take me to Fort William,' she told Fergus.

186

***

The blacksmith's wife welcomed them, poured buttermilk and started chatting to Fiona. Fergus went out to the smithy just in time to see two rough looking characters go striding purposefully on to the Fort William track.

'I don't know either of them, Fergus, but they're up to no good. Best be on your way.'

It wasn't that easy. Fiona had been starved of female company, not just for the time she'd been with Fergus, but since her mother's death, and it was only after scones, and more buttermilk, that he managed to split the two women.

Fergus ignored the road to Fort William and turned up towards the heather covered rolling peat wilderness of Rannoch Moor.

As they moved across the moor, Fiona started to hum a tune she'd learned from her mother, a lonely song, haunting and eerie, but in tune with the gentle breeze that carried the smell of the peat, and stirred small bushes and grasses like the passing of fairies.

They camped by a stream, brown from the peat, in a sheltered hollow.

'Make love to me, Fergus,' Fiona asked as they rolled into their plaids. 'This place has a magic about it.'

Taken by surprise, Fergus was nervous, but at Fiona's touch, all hesitation vanished.

In the morning, Fiona tended to the fire and made their porridge, while Fergus and Davie groomed the animals and made ready for moving.

They crossed the moor and reached the line of bens beyond. Among their massive rocky strength, they could see the wind chase the patches of cloud over the peaks, but only felt it as they climbed through the gaps between them.

Fergus relaxed as Fiona took over the grooming and caring for Chestnut. She seemed to draw strength from the mountains, smiling as she walked, riding off to look at something that took her interest, sometimes returning full of questions, which Fergus tried to answer.

Fergus was again in a dilemma. He could prolong this gay tour by carrying on north to Inverness, but there were workmen on the canal and, in any case, it would limit the number of routes he might take. He chose to turn off towards Fort Augustus at the Loch Ness's southern end.

**

In the north, Morag's mother had at last died. The day of the funeral was wet and windy. A miserable day for a miserable event. McNeil put an arm round Morag's shoulders as the coffin was lowered into the ground and felt the sobs shake her body.

Later, as was expected, Morag had provided refreshments; in Fergus's absence, paid for from McNeil's meagre funds. As the people took turns at consoling Morag, McNeil was standing alone for a moment when an older man came to stand beside him. 'Terrible business,' the older man said. 'And that Duncan, who killed her father, still walking about free. I believe he was recruiting some of his own kind to try to take revenge on Fergus Findlay for exposing him as a thief.'

'Recruiting who?' McNeil asked.

'Men who don't care much what they do for a guinea; rob or murder, it's all the same to them.'

'So what will Duncan do?'

'Oh, he'll set up an ambush for Fergus on his way home from the south. It won't be far from here. He'll wait until Fergus is past Dingwall. There are too many roads for him to take before that, but when he gets into Easter Ross, maybe he'll feel he's almost home and safe, and he'll surely take that road past Ault-na-main.'

***

McNeil fretted, in a dither between giving Morag support and doing something to warn Fergus.

Later, as they sat outside the house at Invercauld, McNeil broached the subject.

'What can you do Neil?' Morag asked.

'I can't do nothing, Morag. He's over two weeks late, anything could have happened. He went out of his way to help us over the emigration and now I must try to repay the favour.'

'You say he'll most likely come over by Ault-na-main. Go and speak to Babs before you do anything daft.'

'What will Babs know?' McNeil asked.

'I don't know, but she hears things. Not just her own ramblings about the future, but tinkers and salesmen's talk.'

CHAPTER 27

Fergus and Fiona reached Dingwall without going into any of the villages or towns, buying what they needed from crofters.

'Can we go into Dingwall?' Fiona asked. 'I have a few woman's things I'd like to get.'

'I'd rather not, Fiona,' Fergus said. 'It's not a big place and I don't want any news that we are on this last stretch to alert anyone. There are not all that many roads we can take from here and it would be easy to guess I'd be likely to go by Ault-na-main to pay Babs.'

After several miles in persistent rain, Fergus decided to turn off the track. 'I know some of the fishermen about here. Maybe we can get bit of shelter and maybe a bite in one of the cottages,' he said, in answer to Fiona's raised eyebrow.

The cottages looked forlorn in the grey weather but even the ponies seemed glad to see some sort of shelter and huddled near the wall as Fergus knocked on the door.

'Fergus Findlay! What brings you on such a night?' the fisherman asked. 'Come out of this rain, there's an empty bothy next door. Let me light a fire to warm you. When you're a bit dryer, come through and have a bite to eat.'

Having replaced shirt and undergarments with dry ones from the packs, Fergus and Fiona, followed by Davie, joined the fisherman and his family.

'So, this is the lassie that all the fuss is about, is it?' the fisherman asked.

Fergus laughed. 'It is that, but I was not aware there was a fuss over her.'

'There's a fuss all right,' the fisherman's wife assured them as she bustled with platters. 'Some English gentleman is raising Cain to find the two of you.'

'A big, red faced man?' Fergus asked.

'I wouldna ken,' the fisherman answered. 'But I hear he wanted the sheriff to send the redcoats after you. Then there's Black Duncan swearing he'll have your life, and him wanted for the murder of McInnes himself.'

'McInnes is dead?'

'Aye, and his wife like to join him, from what we hear.'

The talk stopped while they ate, then went on to more mundane affairs of catches and the price of fish, before Fergus felt they could leave without giving offence.

As Fergus's mind digested what the fisherman had said, he talked out his thoughts to Fiona. 'This is strange, Fiona. This hounding of Maitland's has more to it than the loss of a bride, but I'm at a loss to think what it could be.'

'It's not the bride, Fergus,' Fiona assured him. 'He said himself that it was no matter whether I was dead or alive, as long as I was his wife.'

'What had he to gain from that?' Fergus wondered. 'What good would a dead wife be to anyone?'

Fiona looked at him and shrugged. 'There are those that might have been left jewellery or a dowry, but my mother's things are gone long ago and what I had, I left behind, because it wasn't worth sending to the poorhouse.'

'You're wrong Fiona. Whether you realise it or not you've inherited something of value to Maitland, and not a few pounds either. Could it be the farm?'

'How would he think that? When they married, my father sold his shop to pay the debts on the farm and had it changed into his name. It had been left to Mother by her parents but it was pretty run down by then. It's one of his favourite stories; I've heard it so many times I could tell it in my sleep. I think he imagined himself being a gentleman farmer, but there's never been enough money for that.'

'You've never really told me how your mother died, Fiona.'

'There was nothing to tell. She just sort of faded away. It took quite a while.'

Fergus remembered the miners at Tyndrum, the slow poisoning of their bodies by something in the lead mine. Was it possible Fiona's mother had contracted the miner's disease? How would that happen? From the water? From the cow's eating poisoned grass and the poison getting into the milk? No, McRae would have been affected. Was that what had caused Fiona's sickening? Had someone poisoned her mother, then tried to poison Fiona? No, Fiona's recovery had been too rapid, more like the sailors' disease. When her mother was alive, there had only been the three of them on the farm, so who would have done it? Many people died of consumption and that kind of thing.

'It's something to think on, Fiona,' Fergus said at last. 'If Maitland is this determined over making you his wife, it would be better to find out why, and what we can do about it. I'm sorry, Fiona, if I'd thought it would go this far, we'd have been wed already. Let me get to Tain and see if we can still arrange something, but first, we must get you to somewhere safe.'

***

McNeil walked to Ault-na-main through the driving rain and found Babs at the back of her dwelling, busy with her still.

'Aye, I've not only heard of Duncan and his friends, McNeil, I've seen the useless devils,' Babs told him. 'You tell me they want to wait for Fergus. If that's their plan, there'll be blood in the heather, mark my words.'

'Whose blood, Babs?'

'How would I ken? Maybe when I've had some of this usquebaugh, I'll see a bit more.'

'You'll not drink it from the still, Babs?' McNeil asked, shocked.

Babs cackled. 'Whiles, in the cold weather, it's all that's left, and you'll be glad of it yourself, but right now, I have some a wee bit more mature.'

McNeil didn't ask how much more mature.

'What will they plan, do you think?' McNeil asked.

'An ambush where the road turns along the shore between Dingwall and Alness, I expect. The best plan would be to go and warn Fergus at Dingwall, or as near as you can get. There are three of them, and only one of Fergus, but if he's warned, he's worth all three. There's something about Fergus Findlay that makes him dangerous, McNeil. Mind you, don't get on the wrong side of him by upsetting Morag.'

McNeil laughed, but was in a quandary; whether to go back for his rifle or press on and hope to meet Fergus before he was too far beyond Dingwall.

'There'll be blood on the heather,' Babs reminded him.

***

Back at Invercauld, as Morag watched, McNeil took down his rifle and cleaned it carefully.

'Blood leads to blood hereabouts, Neil,' Morag warned. 'Fergus never carries a firearm himself.'

'I can't fight three of them, Morag, and this lets me do something from a long way off. Mostly they don't see a rifleman, other than a wee puff of smoke when it's too late.'

'I canna stop you, Neil, but I'm asking you for both our sakes, and maybe even Fergus as well, not to go killing.'

'I can take all three to the sheriff, Morag, if I can force them. I'm not good with a knife, or a sword, but few men will disobey with a loaded rifle pointed at their belly.'

Morag's shoulders slumped in resignation. 'Just remember, according to Babs, you're to be the father of my bairns, McNeil,' she said.

It was just light when McNeil left. He waved back to Morag but saw only her head and shoulders in the drifting mist before it enveloped her completely.

How he'd find Fergus, without bumping into him, he didn't know, but unable to think of an alternative, kept going.

CHAPTER 28

Fergus waited until the sun had a chance to burn the mist away but, when it didn't, decided the mist hid them from those who might lie in wait as effectively as it hid any trap, and prepared for leaving.

'You said this was the most dangerous part, Fergus. Shouldn't we wait?' Fiona asked him.

Fergus straightened and looked about him. 'This could last for days, Fiona. It comes off the sea.'

He paid the fisherman's wife, despite her protests, tied his garrons in a loose line, gave Davie the halter, tried to get Fiona to mount, but she came to take his hand and he smiled and led the way back to the track.

The mist swirled about them. Sometimes they could see a few paces ahead, sometimes hardly one, and Fergus grew uneasy. Something darkened in the mist and Fergus's hand went to his broadsword.

The shape didn't move.

'It's just a cow,' Fiona said, laughing.

Fergus managed to grin. 'It's better not to talk, the noise carries a long way in this,' he warned.

Other noises came and went, their direction uncertain; now the waves on the shore; now someone coughing; all hanging in the air.

The track turned up the side of a hill, making Fergus hope it would climb into clear air. It turned down again and he could only see the track and its heather edge.

They'd been moving for about an hour when Bruce, leading the way, stood stock still.

Fergus held his hand up to stop Davie, then hissed to tell Bruce to go ahead and was surprised when Davie squeezed past with the garrons and followed the dog. Davie could be like Bruce and sense things, so Fergus let him go. The garrons trotted along the trail, the sound of their unshod hooves soft and ghostly.

***

McNeil was soon sweating as he marched in the clammy atmosphere and stopped often, as much to cool himself as to listen. Now and then, he thought of calling to warn Fergus there was mischief afoot, but it would also warn anyone lying in wait that someone was coming to Fergus's help. He didn't want the man who had killed Morag's father to know someone was about; didn't want him to escape - but there was nothing but the pale damp grey clinging moisture.

He stopped to listen, heard something moving, people or hooves, he couldn't tell. It was just as hard to tell where the noise came from, but he assumed it was somewhere ahead.

He only had time to jump clear as a dog, a man and several ponies cantered out of the swirl. He fell among the heather and was surprised to find Bruce and Davie staring at him as he recovered.

Bruce seemed satisfied and turned away.

The next thing McNeil heard was a wolf-like howl that sounded all round him.

It was followed by a voice. 'It's that black devil of a dog,' it whispered. 'It's no' canny, no' canny at all.'

So someone was waiting for Fergus. Duncan seemed the most likely.

There was a yell. 'He's after me, I could feel his fangs on my leg.'

Another voice muttered. 'It's only the heather catching your trews.'

'I heard its hooves. It's no' a dog. It's Auld Nick himsel'.'

There was the sound of movement in the heather. Two figures flitted past and vanished into the vapour, come and gone before McNeil could react.

Things were out of hand.

Fergus was somewhere ahead, but so was Duncan, and from what Davie was signalling, so was a female – Fiona?

McNeil cocked and fired his rifle in the air. It would warn Duncan, but it would also let Fergus know help was at hand. 'Spread out, spread out,' he shouted, as if directing a group, waving his arms automatically.

Davie seemed to take it as an order and led the garrons into the heather. They made little more than a loud whisper, but they sounded like a line of beaters and McNeil grinned.

***

Fergus heard the shot and Bruce's howl. Had someone killed Davie? If they had, then Fiona was in imminent danger; but he had to do something for Davie.

Bruce appeared, looked at him and turned back. It was either safe, or Davie needed help badly. He pushed Fiona into the Chestnut's saddle, drew his broadsword, took the reins, and ran forward, with Fiona hanging on to Chestnut's mane.

Someone stood in the way, trying to aim a pistol, dodged the sword but was knocked flat by the running Chestnut, and fell into the heather.

Fergus had a glimpse of McNeil and tried to wave, but Chestnut dragged him on. He managed to stop the horse and was grinning when McNeil caught up.

'I think it's your Black Duncan, but whoever it is, is still about somewhere,' McNeil mentioned.

'He's behind us, but all he has to do is keep still. The heather's wet and Bruce will not be able to follow the scent too well to give us warning. He'll hear us if we start searching. We canna see him, but he canna see us, either. Best we stop talking, go on, and get clear,' Fergus told him.

Fergus rubbed Bruce's neck and raised his head. Bruce yowled a warning into the mirk.

CHAPTER 29

Fiona was beginning to enjoy the warming sun, when Fergus warned, 'Babs's is not a great place, Fiona, but it's clean. Babs is honest and you'll be safe with her until I can have a word with the sheriff about being wed. I'm sorry it'll not be the kirk, but there'd be banns and delays and if we can get things sorted before Maitland finds out we're here, then it will be all the better.'

Fiona took his arm. 'That's the tenth time you've told me not to expect too much of Babs' accommodation, Fergus. I'm a farm girl, and you know what Kirklea had become. I'll not be critical,' she answered as she dismounted stiffly and turned to see a grey haired, roughly dressed woman of indefinite age.

'So this is Fiona McRae,' Babs commented, looking her over. 'We've waited a long time for this.'

Fiona laughed. 'And I've heard a lot of yourself, Babs,' she replied, holding out a hand for Babs to shake.

Babs took the hand. 'Well, come away in, whatever,' she said. 'You'll not know your father is at the inn.'

Fiona frowned. 'Father?'

'Aye, your father, just. Yon Englishman dumped him there. Told Meg, that's the landlady, he'd not pay for the old man, he'd have to earn his keep, and so, your father has been sweeping and carrying things for her.'

'He's actually doing things?' Fiona asked.

'If he wants to eat. Meg's not one for charity,' Bab's told her.

Fiona thought for a moment. 'He had a shop before he married my mother, maybe he feels more at home than on the farm.'

'Yon thin wee mannie was a farmer?' Bab's exclaimed.

Fiona laughed again. 'No, he lived on the farm. When I was small and mother was alive, he did bits and pieces. After mother died, I could hardly get him to do anything.'

'Aye, most farms are run by the womenfolk, no matter what Fergus Findlay thinks. No, nor you either, McNeil, standing there grinning. The sooner you get that Morag to a minister the better. You've been to one, Fergus?'

'We didn't have time, Babs. I must go to see if the sheriff can do something without the need for banns.'

Babs looked at Fiona. 'You know you're with child, lassie.'

Fiona's eyebrows shot up. 'I haven't had time to find out. How can you tell?'

'Never mind how. I can tell,' Babs told her. 'I thought you had more consideration, Fergus Findlay. Well, never mind, come here, lassie, and you too, Findlay.'

Babs took their hands in hers and started to recite a long sermon like thing, in what Fiona took to be Gaelic. She finally realised it was some kind of marriage service. At last, Babs clapped her hands on theirs. 'There now, that's done,' she said. 'The kirk might not be pleased, and the sheriff might not recognise it, but in the old days, my people had the power to marry, aye, and divorce too, if that was fit. It'll do to give the bairn a name and you the responsibility to care for Fiona, Findlay. With your life, if needs be, mind. Remember it well, for the spirits of the old dead will not forgive you if you don't.'

Fiona realised she was serious about the ancestors when Fergus's grin died at her words.

***

In the late evening, Fergus knocked on the sheriff's door.

The sheriff opened the door, saw Fergus, looked up and down the road to make sure there were no onlookers, pulled Fergus inside and shut the door.

The sheriff's face, with its heavy cheeks, was grimmer than usual. 'My God, what do you think you're doing, Findlay? I have a motion before me to take you into custody. Yon Maitland has laid a charge of abduction at your door, and another for alienation of the affection of a Miss McRae - not to mention a charge of breach of promise against the same young woman. If it wasn't for your father, rest his soul, I'd clap you in irons this minute.'

'I came to ask if it was possible for you to marry Miss McRae and me without the need for banns and notices.'

The sheriff, shaking his head in disbelief, straightened to his full, dignified height. 'No, it's no'. If you'd come before these charges were laid, I might have managed something, but now that this Englishman ...' the sheriff leaned forward to tap Fergus on the breast bone ...'d'ye ken he wants to call out the redcoats to haul you in, laddie?'

'I'm just back from the last drove,' Fergus pointed out.

'And with a lassie in trouble by the sound o' it! Dalmighty, Findlay, you've stirred a hornet's nest and tied my hands into the bargain,' the sheriff shouted. 'Now get out of here before I do my duty and put you in a cell.'

CHAPTER 30

The fact that her father was 'doing things' at the inn, worked on Fiona. Fergus was busy and, despite the interest of having someone to talk to, and watching Babs at her loom, a growing curiosity developed in Fiona to see this phenomenon for herself.

She groomed Chestnut and went walking. With her bonnet shielding her face, and keeping the horse between herself and anyone looking out from the inn, she walked along the road past the building. In that way, she was able to glance over Chestnut's shoulder at the building. She saw no sign of her father, and returned to Babs' to fret.

She managed to keep herself busy with washing and odd chores to help Babs but, in the end, curiosity overcame caution. Nevertheless, in mid-morning, she made a detour round the inn to approach it from the opposite direction, and knocked on the door. A matronly woman wearing an apron, her hands white with flour, opened the door.

'Can I help?' the woman, whom Fiona assumed to be Meg, asked.

Fiona was unprepared for the question and hesitated. 'I wondered if you had any need of someone to clean?' Fiona asked eventually.

'If you'd come a week ago, I could have given you work but, as you can see, I have taken on someone.'

Fiona could see past the woman into the parlour, where her father was polishing woodwork. The woman followed her gaze. 'He's not the best, but as long as I sit on him, he manages,' the woman told her.

'Thank you for speaking to me,' Fiona said, and turned quickly and left.

***

An hour later, when Fiona answered the door for Babs, she found the matronly woman standing there. 'I wondered if it was you. I'm Meg,' she said to Fiona. 'You're Fergus's wife, I take it?'

The designation confused Fiona at first. 'Yes, yes,' she admitted eagerly.

'And that's your father?'

'Yes.'

'He's not a bad man, just needs guidance. How did he get involved with that brute of an Englishman?'

'Money,' Fiona explained.

'Well, your father picked the wrong one there, that Maitland has no charity in him, none whatever,' Meg said emphatically. 'Anyway, you wanted to see him?'

'To see him doing things,' Fiona admitted.

'Not to talk to?'

Fiona thought carefully. 'I suppose I should try to explain …'

Meg interrupted. 'Talk to Fergus, and Babs, before you let your father know you're about. The Englishman dumped him there and hasn't come back, but it's not to say he won't.'

***

Later, after talking it over with Babs, and worrying at it for several hours, she went to the Inn.

'Fiona!' her father gasped.

'Yes.'

'Are you all right? What did that Findlay do to you?'

'Nothing I didn't want him to do, Father.'

'Well, you're safe now and we can let Mr Maitland know you're here.'

'No, you won't, Father. If I never see Maitland again, it will be too soon. Can't you see he's using you?'

'That Findlay has turned your head, lassie. Remember you signed a paper that you'd marry Mr Maitland, and he's insisting you keep that promise.'

'That paper was signed on a lie, Father. He told me Fergus was dead. I've no need to honour it. Why are you so determined that I marry that brute? And what have you got against Fergus?'

'He's nothing but a drover.'

'That's not good enough, Father. You entertained his father often enough when Mother was alive. I want the truth!'

'The truth is he's a wastrel, like all the Highlanders.'

'I'm leaving,' Fiona told him.

'You canna leave, we need to let Mr Maitland know you're here so that you can be married.'

'Then tell me what went wrong with the Findlays. Was it Mother?'

'He wrecked our marriage.'

'Don't exaggerate, Father. You wrecked it with your own laziness and lack of sympathy.'

'We were fine till that Findlay came. He was devious, came with news and made himself welcome, then started to tell your mother about the Highlands and his travels, raging torrents to cross, and blinding snowstorms to get through, until she was fair bamboozled and could talk of nothing else.'

Fiona's cheeks reddened. 'And you just gave up. It never struck you that all she wanted was for you to take an interest in the farm and in her, especially. Now you want me to marry a man I loathe because you owe him money, or is there something else, Father? Why is Maitland so determined to marry me, dead or alive?'

McRae's frown darkened, but Fiona leant forward and stamped her hand on the table in front of him.

'Because he wants the farm,' her father muttered.

'But the farm's yours, Father.'

'Aye, but if he knew that, all he'd have to do is foreclose and where would we be?'

'With Fergus, Father.'

'Can you not see we'd be better off back where we belong, not here among these damned Highlanders that nobody can trust.'

'So, who does he think the farm belongs to?' Fiona's eyes widened. 'You told him it was mine. And that's why he wants to marry me.'

'What else could I do?' her father pleaded.

Fiona felt her anger rise. 'We could have walked out, Father. I could have found work. What do you think?'

'I couldna ask you to be a skivvy, Fiona, that wouldna be proper.'

'*You* let me, and my mother, skivvy for *you*! Now all *your* trickery has landed Fergus and me in court.'

'I tried to save you from that blackguard, can you not see that?'

'He's the best thing that has happened to me, Father, and with any luck I'll give him a son.'

'He has you with child?'

'No, but I want his bairn inside me, Father. I want it more than anything, can't you understand that?'

'What will Mr Maitland say? You're not to tell him till after the wedding,' McRae told her.

Fiona slammed the door behind her.

***

Fiona was still angry when Fergus returned and it was some minutes before he managed to tell her he'd been unsuccessful. 'Are you all right here?' he asked.

'I'm fine as long as you're about, Fergus,' Fiona smiled.

'What I mean is, will you be all right if I go to Invercauld in the morning?'

'You want to go on your own? Leave me here?'

'I'd not put it like that. I want to know you're safe. Anything might happen on the way there, or back.'

'Then it will happen to us both, Fergus. I'll not sit here waiting, like that day you went off to Tyndrum.'

CHAPTER 31

Despite a weeping rain, to avoid being seen by the normal traffic near Ault-na-main, they started early. Fergus, riding one of the garrons, looking undersized beside Chestnut, tried to keep ahead of Fiona but the horse was having none of it, and insisted on keeping alongside. The drizzle was drifting in banks across the hills so that they could sometimes see several hundred yards, sometimes only ten. They were sometimes hidden, and sometimes exposed. Fergus, worried about Fiona, was wary.

Unable to see too far, he grew more agitated the closer they got to Invercauld. He turned off the recognised track and paused every time they were coming out of a dip or a clump of trees and waited, staring round before getting on to the skyline, or open ground. In the end, it was Bruce's stiffening and pricking his ears that made him turn their ponies abruptly uphill, off the vague track, and swing wide to come to Invercauld from another direction. His caution paid off. The rain cleared for an instant and they looked back and down from the shelter of some trees to see a small group of Redcoats clustered round a smoking fire. Two, further back, obviously the sentries, walked back and forth, beating their arms around them to keep warm in the drifting rain.

Ten minutes later, as they came out of a small copse, Fergus turned to Fiona and pointed. 'Invercauld is just over the brow of that hill,' he informed her.

At that moment, the rain lifted and Fiona gasped. 'It's beautiful, Fergus,' she whispered. Fergus turned to look at the view; it stretched over the firth to the hills on the far shore where the dark rain clouds were lit by a brilliant rainbow. Three sailing boats, their dark sails silhouetted against the blue reflection of the clearing sky to the north east, added a picturesque quality to the drama of the scene.

'How could you bear to be away from it most of the time?' Fiona asked.

'Like glimpses of you, with your hair blowing, and your eyes dancing, I carried the memory in my head, Fiona. I never leave it really, nor am I away from you. Don't think the house is as good as the view, though. It's stone built and keeps out the winter well enough, but I want something more … more … stylish for yourself.'

'I'm a farm girl, Fergus, a farm house is good enough for me,' Fiona told him.

'For a farm girl maybe, but not for Fiona, the princess who flits through my dreams, who makes me think I can be as good as …' Fergus, at a loss for the right word, waved his hand around to encompass the whole world.

Fiona laughed. 'Come, let me see this house that's not good enough,' she said, starting Chestnut up the slope and over the crest of the rise.

As they grew closer to the house, it was Fergus's turn to be amazed. 'Who are all these,' he asked of no one. 'Squatters!' he muttered, and he forced his garron forward. 'There must be close to fifty families here,' he said. 'Look at them, spread all over the place. Where have they come from? What's McNeil been up to?'

Following the sweep of his pointing arm, Fiona could see small groups, all with animals close by, an odd one with a cart, scattered over the gently sloping hillside with the smoke of fires rising into the low cloud. Some had even managed crude sod shelters. As she watched, she could see children among the family groups.

'Are they always here?' Fiona asked.

'No, they're not. When I left, there was only McInnes and his women. I can't think where they've come from.'

As Fergus led the way down to the stone built house, people in the groups watched, the children stopping to stare, the more bold answering Fiona's smile, younger ones clinging to their mother's skirts.

McNeil was busy chopping logs into firewood when they reached the house.

'Where have all these come from?' Fergus asked, his hand sweeping round.

'When they evicted them from their crofts, the Redcoats herded them here,' McNeil explained.

The mention of Redcoats reminded Fergus. 'You know you've got Redcoats watching the road, McNeil?'

'They've been here looking for you and Fiona, but I don't really know if they're sitting waiting for you, or if they're there to stop the crofters leaving.'

'Why would they want to do that?' Fergus asked.

'I'm not sure, Fergus. I think it's some kind of devilish plan of their captain's to get this place for himself.'

'What makes you think he'd be interested, an English man with a farm in the north of Scotland?'

'The army are paying off, Fergus, and maybe he wants somewhere to stay.'

'That I can understand, but how would dumping these crofters on Invercauld get me off?'

'The crofters are angry, Fergus. Not just angry, ready to do desperate things. If you were to order them off, or get the sheriff to do it for you, there's no saying what they'd do. They might even cut your throat. If, on the other hand, the Redcoats shot you, they could blame the crofters. The crofters would most likely just agree with whatever story the captain wanted to tell. Of course, once the place was without an owner, he'd be able to chase the crofters off, even if he had to shoot one or two, and just take the place over for himself.'

'It sounds a bit far-fetched, McNeil.'

'It does, but my guess is that yon Maitland you mentioned is involved some way or another. He'll maybe be hoping you've made a will and left it to Fiona, so that, when he marries her, or has her for breach of promise, he'll get his hands on your farm. It's only a guess, Fergus, but these crofters are only tools for a plan of some kind. That captain has no love for them.'

Morag came out of the house. 'Visitors, and you not asking them inside, McNeil? What kind of a host are you? Oh it's you, Fergus Findlay, and you'll be Fiona,' she smiled as she looked Fiona over. 'Welcome to Invercauld.'

'We'll not stay Morag,' Fergus told her. 'The Redcoats are watching for us. We'd only put yourselves in danger.'

McNeil raised his eyebrows and nodded. 'Like I said, Fergus, their captain wants this place for himself, and he'll go to any lengths to get it.'

'You could go with McNeil to the hovel and Fiona could be here with me, surely,' Morag suggested.

McNeil shook his head. 'No, this officer is likely to try to take advantage of any woman on her own, even both of you, Morag.'

'Aye, it would be better if McNeil slept here with you ...' Fergus began. He saw Morag's outraged expression, '... or was, at least, nearby.'

'I'll be fine, Fergus Findlay, without you arranging men for me to sleep with,' Morag told him. 'Just you take care of Fiona.'

Fergus laughed at Morag's rejoinder, but looked round at the scattering of family units. 'What are we going to do with this lot, McNeil?' he asked.

'It needs thinking on. I've already had one family, the Banes, complain they want the Gilfillans moved to the bottom of the farm, where they'll not foul the water before the Banes get the use of it.'

'Surely all they have to do is fill their pail on the top side of the camp?' Fergus asked.

'Mrs Bane is not used to carrying water over far,' McNeil explained. 'Then there's an old man that wants his son to leave him on the shore, where the tide will drown him when it comes in.'

'That would be murder!'

'The man's old and done, Fergus, and I'm not sure but what it would be a kindness. It's not the first time I've shot a dying man to ease his pain. But that's not the end of it. There's a woman badly ill, she was bad when she came, but she's just slipping away. She wants her son to go off to Canada, but he'll not leave her, or his father won't hear of it.'

'As you said, it needs thinking on. And what about the beasts?'

'You're the drover, Fergus. Maybe you can drove them, but you'd better do it quick. That Redcoat will be back and requisition more of the crofter's cows and sheep to grace his table. He's been twice and, as I said, the people are getting upset. If it goes on, they'll have nothing left and have no option other than squat here.'

There were shouts and pointing among the squatters. 'Come inside, Fiona,' Morag pressed. 'That's the Redcoats coming again. They're not a bad lot, if the sergeant's with them, but that captain's too forward for my liking.'

Fiona looked round and hurried inside after Morag.

'Go in out of the way yourself, Fergus,' McNeil ordered.

'He's never set eyes on me and I look like a tramp from all this travelling, let me stand back and watch what happens,' Fergus said, moving away, far enough not to be associated with McNeil, yet close enough to see what was happening.

Hearing was easy because the captain, looking down from his seat on his charger, used his parade ground voice as the crofters started to gather round McNeil.

'I have come for another cow and two sheep. See to it, McNeil,' he shouted.

'I've told you before, Captain. I'll not be party to the requisitioning of peoples only means of survival. They need the cows for milk and the sheep for winter wool and meat.'

'Then we'll not deprive the poorer natives. Corporal, take one of Mr Bane's cows and the nearest sheep.'

Fergus saw a thin individual step forward. 'Captain, this is the second time you've taken one of my beasts, surely you could take someone else's for a change.'

'That's the trouble when you have the tenderest of the beef, Mr Bane. Surely, you'll not deny His Majesty's troops a decent meal? Or should I confiscate the lot for your Jacobite leanings, what?'

'No, I'm just pointing out that the honour of supplying your men's needs should be spread evenly over us all.'

'Good to hear you're a loyal subject, Bane,' the captain said, turning his mount.

It was then that he noticed Fergus and shouted in his direction, 'Come to join the throng, have you? Well, you couldn't have picked a better time. We'll soon catch this drover fellow and, when we do, we'll hang him from the nearest tree. If you're here when that happens, you'll be able to stay for as long as you like, what?'

'That would suit me very well,' Fergus answered. 'For I have nowhere else to live.'

CHAPTER 32

Half an hour later, the squatter men stood in a half circle staring expectantly at Fergus.

Fergus looked at them, not knowing what to say. He scratched his eyebrow. He looked at the ground, looked round the collected men again and cleared his throat.

A big red bearded man at the front of the crowd looked round at the others.

'We didna come here of our own accord, Findlay. We were herded here like beasts and our houses burnt. There wasna much we could do against muskets and redcoats.'

Fergus nodded.

The red bearded man continued, 'We managed to save a few things, and a beast or two, but we had to leave our harvest and we need time to settle in our minds what to do next, and we'd be glad if you could see your way letting us bide here for at least a day or two.'

Fergus straightened. 'I'll not throw you off, but according to McNeil, that captain will be back for another cow and a few sheep ...'

'He comes twice a week,' McNeil interrupted.

'Well, that gives us a day or two to get the cattle and sheep out of his sight. I ken a place, a mile or so from here, where they can hide, but he'll find them sooner or later, so hiding them is no more than a temporary reprieve. You need to think longer than that.'

The men nodded, some whispering to a neighbour.

Fergus let them talk among themselves for a while, before looking directly at each of them in turn. 'Can you not see staying here, or hereabouts, only puts you back where you started? The redcoats will herd others like you on to Invercauld, and it will get overcrowded and overgrazed, and your bairns will starve at the first bad crop. Look about you,' he ordered them, waving an arm round. 'There's nothing planted here, no barley, no corn, no potatoes to last through the winter, and you'll have to kill every beast you have, or at least the ones the Redcoats don't find, to get through the winter.'

The red bearded man spoke again. 'We ken all that, Findlay. We're just at a loss to ken what to do, or where to go.'

Fergus's shoulders dropped and McNeil stepped forward. 'Fergus and I have taken two groups of people to Glasgow on their way to Canada. Maybe if you pool your resources, some of you could go there, get settled and send for the others,' he suggested.

There were murmurs among the men. Fergus could see Bane tight lipped and frowning dissent.

'For them that stay, there's work on that canal Telford's digging, and work in Glasgow for any that can weave,' Fergus pointed out.

It was received in silence.

Fergus tried again. 'I can help you hide the beasts for now, but the Redcoats will find them eventually. Even if you don't agree with McNeil, you'd be better taking them to a tryst and get some hard cash in your pockets for them. A few guineas are a lot easier to hide from the Redcoats.'

The red bearded man spoke again. 'We'll need to think on this, Findlay, but I'll be fine pleased if you can find some place to hide the cattle and sheep, even if it is just for a day or so.'

The men began drifting away, arguing and talking, some heads nodding in agreement, fingers stabbing in emphasis.

Fergus watched them go. He felt McNeil's hand on his shoulder, and smiled ruefully. 'It's a start, Fergus, it's a start,' Neil encouraged.

Fergus shook his head and went into the house.

'What's wrong, Fergus?' Fiona asked.

Fergus's face was flushed but the fire in it died as he looked at Fiona, then scratched at his eyebrow. 'I don't know what to do, Fiona. On a drove, it's easy; everybody knows what they have to do. We all have the same objective, maybe different ways of getting it done, but the same objective. These people all seem to have different priorities.' He shook his head. 'McNeil is better at this than me. My father taught me to fight to win, but to walk away from a fight I could only lose, no matter how humiliating it was. Well, I can't win this one, but I can't walk away either. As long as they're on Invercauld, I'll feel responsible.'

McNeil came in.

'That Bane wants to speak to you, Fergus.'

'Can you not deal with him, McNeil?'

'He refuses to even talk.'

Fergus went outside and found Bane standing with a short woman, her dress tight around her middle, making her look like a tube with a head.

Bane spoke. 'If you're going to drive the cattle somewhere, eight of them are mine - ours,' Bane corrected, his hand indicating the woman. 'We'd like them driven separately.'

Fergus looked at Bane, ignoring the woman.

Bane waved a hand to indicate a man standing to one side. 'We can hire Gilfillan here to help. He has no animals, other than chickens, so he's free to help.'

Fergus licked his lips. 'I'll have no servants, or hired hands, in the drove. I've heard too much about people joining droves so that they could let the reivers know how, and when, to steal a few animals. When we drove, every man involved will have at least one beast in the herd. That way, I'll know nobody's sneaking off to tell the Redcoats where we're going. Forbye, it's hard enough to drive raw cattle without making it more difficult by having beasts separated, yours will either join the rest, or stay here for the Redcoats, make up your mind!'

'Mr Findlay, my husband is not accustomed to being spoken to like that,' the woman said.

'Then he can leave, Mrs Bane. You've no need to hang about here. Take and sell your cattle and get yourselves away from these Highlands.'

The man tried to look tall. 'We were born and bred here, Findlay, and I don't see why we should be forced to leave.'

'Please yourself, but you're squatters, you and Mrs Bane. Squatters! I'll have no tenants that come to argue about rent on this farm.'

Fergus turned to the man who had been standing waiting, a burly, dark haired man, his face hidden in a black beard.

'You'll be Gilfillan, likely,' Fergus said.

'Aye, I'm Gilfillan, Findlay. I've got no cows, nor sheep either. Nothing but a few hens and a wife that's getting near her time. You were talking of folk moving on, but I'm here to stay, for I've nowhere else to go.'

Fergus looked at Gilfillan until Gilfillan straightened and returned Fergus's stare.

'So,' Fergus began. 'You want me to keep you alive, is that it?' he asked. Before Gilfillan could answer, Fergus, his features grim, carried on, 'Me, and my father before me, have worked at droving to build up this place. We were both of us away when my mother died. But you, you've frittered your life away growing stones on a hillside and depending on your laird to get you through when times were bad. Now the laird has got rid of you, you want me to feed you.'

Gilfillan stiffened, his eyes narrowing. 'I'm a Highlander, Findlay, maybe not one of your own, but one that's lived by the old loyalties, just like my father. It may be that you feel that was a mistake, that you look down on me for it, but I am what I am, and I'll not put my wife in danger.'

'His wife's due about now, Fergus,' Morag said behind Fergus.

'I'm not responsible for that, Morag,' Fergus said. 'I'll not throw her off the farm, but I'll not say the same for him,' he warned. Snorting suddenly, he turned, shaking his head and smiling lopsidedly to Morag. 'Ach, but then who's to know what tomorrow will do to us, or who we might be glad to have about us. They can stay for a while, until we can think of what's best.' He turned to Gilfillan, 'Get back to your wife and see that she's looked after. I have no wish to see any of you buried here on Invercauld.'

***

They had eaten and the four of them, Fergus, Fiona, McNeil and Morag, went outside to sit and talk quietly in the gloaming. As the light faded so that only shapes were distinguishable, Morag gasped, her hand to her mouth and Fergus turned to see a figure approaching. The figure was hooded so that where its face should be was a dark hole.

'Now what?' Fergus muttered. 'What would a priest be wanting here?'

He heard Morag gasp and turned to see what was wrong.

'You thought it was ...' Fiona said, and she and Morag began to giggle.

'I thought it was a spectre come to announce a death,' Morag explained.

The priest drew his hood from his head, revealing a smiling face. 'It's not often I'm greeted with laughter, but it's good to hear in these days,' he said, rubbing his hand over his weather beaten, lined face.

'You'll want to wash, Father,' Fergus suggested. 'There's a pump at the back of the house.'

'Let me rest for a minute, I've been walking for most of the day, you've been hard to find.'

'You've been looking for Invercauld?' Fergus asked.

'For the people who were herded here. I'm from a group that is emigrating, but they need more people to make a community.'

'A community, Father?'

'Just that! It's all very well to go off to Canada, but when you get there, you need to fit in, if you see what I mean. There is no use going off into the wilderness on your own, you must have support in case you are ill, or if you are set upon by wild beasts, or wild men. Our group is small and I was hoping some of your people would be willing to join us. A community needs all kinds, shoe makers as well as farmers, if you see what I mean, and I'd be glad of the chance to talk to the members of your group.'

'They're not my group, Father,' Fergus told him. 'And I'll be glad if you'll try to talk some sense into them. But first, let me get you something to drink while Fiona and Morag see to something to eat for you.'

Half an hour later, refreshed with soup and a dram of whisky, which released his Irish accent, the priest sat forward. 'What I'd like to do is to take a walk round and meet the people,' he said.

'Wouldn't it be easier to get them to come here?' Fergus asked.

'It probably would, but what I'd like to do is meet them one at a time, so that they can talk to me as individuals. If I talk to them in a group first, they react as a group, but if they've talked to me, even for a few minutes, as themselves, they think for themselves,' the priest explained.

'Well, it'll have to be McNeil who introduces you, Father, because I don't really know them and, in any case, I just get angry that they won't see sense, or stick together.'

The priest smiled. 'You have to give them time, Fergus. I'll talk to the men after our tour. When they've heard what I have to say, they can go back to their wives, have a chat and sleep on what I've said, before we get together in the morning.'

Fergus tagged behind as McNeil led the priest round. Some were overwhelmed and reserved, some, not being Roman Catholic, were forward, even abrupt. Mrs Bane dropped a curtsey, but stood determinedly in front of the priest so that he was forced to stand and talk. Fergus watched as the priest nodded understanding of what the Banes were saying, before straightening to look Bane in the face. 'A community needs leaders as well, you know. Not just leaders who tell them what to do, but leaders who show them how to behave, by example.'

Fergus smiled at the priest's ability to deal smoothly with something he'd have blown up and shouted about.

When they came to the ill woman, Fergus's attention was drawn away to where Davie was gesticulating to a thin, wrinkled, aged man. Somehow, Davie and the old man had established a relationship. With his hands, Davie made pictures. Fergus followed some of it, because it showed several people walking together but exactly what they were doing, Fergus couldn't tell.

In reply, the old man smiled softly and shook his head. Davie tried again. The old man laughed, and waved what Davie was saying away with a flap of his hand.

Fergus was distracted from the exchange by McNeil's grip on his arm. 'She's told the father that she wants last rights.'

'Who has?' Fergus asked.

'That poor sick woman,' McNeil explained. 'She feels she's keeping her son from going on. If she was dead he'd have no reason to stay.'

'What about his father?'

'It's his father that insists the son has a duty to wait.'

'She might get better,' Fergus pointed out.

'Exactly,' McNeil agreed. 'If she does, her son will never be able to leave. She wants him to go while he can still afford it.'

'What'll you do?' Fergus asked the priest.

'Try to talk the father round so that the woman can think of getting well, instead of feeding her depression over the boy,' the priest answered. 'I can't force them to listen, but there's a tragedy in the making if they don't.'

By now, they were back near the house and, without waiting for morning, the men began to gather, talking quietly about their impressions of the priest.

When it seemed no more would come, the priest spoke up.

'What I want you to think over is the idea of joining a group that I'm taking to Canada. There are about twenty families, but that is not enough to set up a community. You will understand a community isn't just a number of people; it needs some who have special skills, like thatching or doctoring animals, building houses from logs, or hunting for food, as well as farmers. We have enough money for any of you who want to join us, but I want you to think it over.'

There were unanswered questions, but Fergus could see that the priest's walk round had given the people confidence, and while some looked doubtful, as they straggled away, others were encouraging them to give the idea some thought.

***

In the early morning, sitting in front of the house, Fergus and Fiona talked in low tones. 'Oh, I expect he'll manage to talk them all round,' Fergus said. 'All except Gilfillan, anyway.'

'You've taken a dislike to that man without really getting to know him, Fergus,' Fiona pointed out.

'I don't know him, but I know others like him; so wrapped up in today that they can't see tomorrow coming.'

'His priorities are different from yours, Fergus,' Fiona laughed. 'He'd no more think of leaving his wife to go off droving than you would of trying to fly.'

'You mean I should have been with my mother when she died?' Fergus asked.

Fiona gasped and looked as if she'd been slapped, but composed herself. 'No ... and yes ... you feel guilty about not being there, so, yes, but you didn't know she was going to die, and your work was elsewhere, so, no. We make what decisions seem right to us at the time, Fergus. There's no going back, so we have to live with them. I just hope you can live with rescuing me,' she said, her eyes mischievous.

Fergus laughed and hugged her.

As they separated, Fiona looked down at her hands. 'You see Gilfillan as a problem, Fergus, but maybe he's not.'

Fergus looked at her.

'Just think,' Fiona carried on. 'If Maitland hadn't tried to force me into marriage, would you have come for me, or would I have become worn out and died waiting?'

Fergus opened his mouth to explain, but Fiona raised her hand to silence him. 'If Hamish hadn't tried to kill you, would you have found out about Maitland in time? Look on Gilfillan as an opportunity, Fergus, an opportunity to beat Maitland. I don't know how it will work, but be prepared to take advantage of it when whatever happens.'

'Here they come,' Fergus called into the house, standing to meet the collecting crowd.

The priest came out and stood waiting.

The red bearded man stood forward. 'We've thought about what you said, Father. Most of us agree it would be a way out, but we have one or two questions, and we need a wee bit more time to think it through. Some are worried they'll be outsiders and always at the cow's tail.'

There were murmurs from the group.

The priest stepped forward. 'The others you'll be joining feel just the same,' he explained. 'But since they've agreed to your joining them, they must be prepared to take the chance you'll be able to put up with them. It is usually the leaders who jostle for position, the ordinary folk just mix because their needs are the same. What you need is for yourself,' - he addressed the red bearded man specifically – 'and Mr Bane, say, to be prepared to take the lead, or follow the lead, depending on what's best for everyone.'

'I'm no' a leader, Father,' the red bearded man protested. 'It's just that I've got a louder voice.'

'As long as it doesn't shout others down,' the priest pointed out.

The man nodded. 'Well, we can deal with that and the other questions later on but, right now, we'd like to take Findlay up on his offer to hide our beasts and sheep.'

Fergus stepped forward. 'This will only be for a day or two, maybe a week, nobody can hide a herd of cattle and a flock of sheep for long, before talk spreads. I'll do what I can, but keep in mind you have to make up your minds what to do for the long term. For now, separate the cows and sheep. I'll be with the cows, Davie here, deaf as he is, will look after the sheep, if you'll all help.'

The men went to collect the animals

***

When they had gathered, McNeil directed the cattle to one side and the sheep to the other, while Fergus talked to Davie in hand signals, giving him directions before turning his attention to the cattle.

'How many men will you need?' McNeil asked.

'I want to let the cattle go ahead for a bit, then split them off, one and two at a time, so that the tracks of those leaving won't be noticed. That will need a man with every pair that split off, so we need everyone. They must keep going west, but keep spread out. When they're all clear, Davie and I will take the sheep in a flock off to one side and into the hills, to keep the trail going. I want the men to keep the cattle moving in ones and twos for a bit more until you come to a patch of trees. Take the cattle into them, then out the other side. There should be a bit of a glen there, where you can collect the cattle together again.'

'And you?' McNeil asked.

'I'll take the sheep on for about half a mile then scatter them so that the track vanishes all over the place. Davie and Bruce will get them together again and herd them round behind you.'

Fergus looked up at the darkening sky. 'Now, let's get moving before this storm breaks. Maybe you'll say a prayer to keep it away, Father?' Fergus joked.

The priest laughed. 'I'll do my best. I'd come with you, but that woman is fading fast. One never knows, of course, but I doubt if she'll see tomorrow.'

'Then you'd best go to her,' Fergus told him.

The cows had split off and Fergus was about to start with the sheep when he saw a bare outcrop of dark rock in the distance, and smiled. He signed to Davie, and, with Bruce keeping them close, they herded the sheep onto the rocks dark surface. Davie and Fergus then chased them, one at a time, in all directions. When the sheep were gone, the grass on the perimeter was partially flattened but after a yard or two there was only a few depressions to mark where a sheep had left the outcrop.

Fergus sent Bruce to collect them half a mile away, from where they took them to join the cattle in the glen.

CHAPTER 33

Fergus, McNeil, and the men, were hardly out of sight, when a boy came running to the house. 'The Redcoats have come,' he shouted.

Fiona watched the troop march to the house, the women gathered round it.

'Halt,' the captain ordered and the soldiers sagged to a weary halt. 'I need two cows and three sheep,' the captain shouted at the women.

No one answered.

'I said, I need two cows and three sheep,' the captain called again.

'The men have taken them away, Captain,' Morag shouted back.

'Then we'll have to take you until they come back,' the captain laughed and moved forward towards her.

The women closed ranks in front of him.

'Get out of the damn way,' the captain shouted, lashing with his crop. The women took the blows on their stout arms. 'Get out of the damn way, or I'll shoot,' he shouted.

Fiona gasped in concern, but the women's faces were grim and determined.

No one moved.

'Sergeant, fire a warning shot over their heads.'

'They're women, sir,' the sergeant protested.

'Do as you're damn well told,' the captain ordered.

Fiona was about to step forward but a hand restrained her.

The sergeant took a musket from one of the soldiers, then held out his hand for a cartridge. The soldier scrabbled in his pouch for one and gave it to the sergeant.

Fiona could see the captain growing impatient.

'Get a move on, Sergeant. We haven't got all day.'

The sergeant bit the ball from the cartridge and poured powder into the musket's muzzle. He looked directly at the women.

The women stared back, but didn't move.

The sergeant spat the ball into the muzzle, and looked at the women.

The women stared back.

'Get on with it,' raged the captain.

The women turned their stares on him and he fidgeted in his saddle.

The sergeant crumpled the cartridge paper into a ball and pushed it into the muzzle. He took the ramrod and pushed the pad down the barrel. The sergeant looked at the women.

The women stood impassive.

The sergeant raised the musket, and fired over the women's heads.

The shot seemed to enrage the women. They rushed at the Redcoats, who hesitated and looked at the captain. Fiona saw the captain's charger start to jitter. The women started to screech. The charger finally shied away, despite the captain sawing on the reins. As the horse bolted, the soldiers ran after it.

'I'll be back, I'll be back,' the captain called over his shoulder. 'I'll have that McInnes bitch, if it's the last thing I do.'

Fiona turned to Morag, but she was calmly watching him go. 'You can stay here for the night, Fiona, but I doubt if you'll be safe staying any longer.'

Fiona nodded. 'I think that applies to you as well, Morag. Maybe we should both go to Ault-na-main.'

Gilfillan himself came forward. 'I think you'd best find Findlay, Miss McRae,' he suggested. 'That Redcoat is like to come back.'

'We were thinking of going to Ault-na-main. Would you tell Fergus?' Fiona asked.

'I'll do that,' Gilfillan replied.

'And your own wife. How is she?' Fiona asked.

'Almost due and wanting it over,' Gilfillan smiled.

***

It was growing dark and the storm clouds were clearing by the time the cattle and the sheep were settled. Fergus kept half the men and let the rest go back to Invercauld.

At first light, Fergus left the men dealing with the animals and went back to where he could watch the way they had come.

The sun had warmed the atmosphere long enough to make the air hang muggy and listless under a sky in which fluffy white clouds were slowly multiplying, before Fergus caught sight of the column of redcoats following the trail the sheep had left. They hesitated once or twice when the trail swung on to the hillside, but started off again as they noticed the trail had turned back downhill. Someone in the group was being careful. It wasn't the person on horseback, whom Fergus took to be the captain, who, between taking his shako off and wiping his brow, was waving his arms and urging the soldiers on.

As the Redcoats grew closer, Fergus could see they were being led by a man in a plaid. There was something familiar about him, Fergus wasn't certain what.

McNeil joined him, taking his rifle from his shoulder. Fergus looked quizzical at the firearm.

McNeil shook his head. 'Not yet, but it's ready,' he said.

By now, the sun had gone and the white puffs of summer cloud had grown into dark lowering masses that swirled and tumbled within themselves, like a pack of dogs waiting to be unleashed. The man with the plaid glanced up at the darkening clouds from time to time, but his main attention was on the ground.

'Gilfillan,' Fergus muttered.

The troop reached the bare circular hump of the outcrop of black rock that the flock tracks entered, then vanished, like magic. The Redcoats hesitated short of the black patch.

'Now we'll see if Gilfillan is the Highlander he told us he is,' Fergus commented.

Gilfillan, his arms waving, tried to explain something to the captain, but the captain shouted and struck Gilfillan with his crop.

As if the captain had triggered it by hitting Gilfillan, the long withheld storm broke like a vision of Hell; an eye searing flash of lightening gave lurid light to the darkening scene, the thunder crackled and boomed and rebounded from the hills.

When their eyes had recovered from the dazzle of the lightening flash, Fergus and McNeil, had time to see a puff of smoke rising from the outcrop before the rain, wrapped in flashes and booming crashes, dropped in roaring sheets.

Fergus and McNeil waited for it to ease. When it did, the captain was lashing Gilfillan with his riding crop and waving his arm round.

Fergus laughed. 'Gilfillan, is a Highlander all right, and most likely believes that rock is the door to some kind of spirit channel we slipped through with the beasts, and the devil has sent the lightning to warn them off,' Fergus said, grinning at McNeil. 'The captain's not a Highlander, however, and it looks as if he doesn't believe Gilfillan that the lightning also sealed the magic channel we escaped through,' Fergus added. 'Not that it matters, that rain will have flattened the grass and done away with any tracks we might have left.'

As they watched, the Redcoats turned away.

'They've gone to Ault-na-main,' Fergus said, rising and making his way to where the animals were hidden.

CHAPTER 34

The sun was just breaking through as Fiona and Morag reached Ault-na-main and Babs.

'You're soaked, the pair of you,' Babs fussed. 'What's that Fergus thinking of?'

'He's gone with some crofters who've been put off their lands,' Fiona told her.

Babs stood back looking at her. 'Trying to save the whole country, instead of looking after you, is he?'

'He couldn't just leave them, Babs,' Fiona interrupted.

'And why not?' Babs demanded. 'What will they do next? Where will they go? What good is saving them from poverty here, so that they can die of disease and worse in Glasgow?'

'Maybe they can go to America,' Fiona suggested.

'And who'll pay for that?' Babs asked. 'And where will they stay when they get there? There's that many going to that America it will be as full as here by Christmas.'

When they had changed into dry things, Fiona stood thinking for some time before saying, 'I'm going to talk to my father. He needs to understand I'll not be forced into marrying Maitland against my will, cost what it might.'

She walked determinedly along the road to the inn and found her father washing drinking tankards.

'I've been thinking about what we can do, Fiona ...' McRae began.

'And so have I, Father,' Fiona interrupted. 'I will not marry Maitland, whatever you say, so start thinking of some way to pay your debts, even if you have to borrow from Fergus.'

'Me! Borrow from a drover? Are you daft lassie? Where would a drover get money enough to pay his own debts, never mind …'

They both turned as the door opened and the Redcoat officer Fiona had seen at Invercauld, his face reddened by much wine, came through. 'What ho!'He exclaimed. 'Entertaining doxy are we, McRae.'

'It's my daughter,' McRae told him.

Fiona felt his gaze turn to her, looking her over.

'So this is Maitland's wench, is it,' the officer said, slapping Fiona's shoulder. 'I fancy we can have a bit of fun before we deliver you to your rightful owner, eh, what?' he grinned, showing a mouthful of discoloured teeth with gaps.

Meg came in. 'Would you like something to drink, Captain,' she asked.

'What about you?' the captain asked Fiona.

'I must be going,' Fiona told him.

'Oh, no, you don't,' he insisted, grabbing Fiona's arm. Fiona tried to shy away, but the captain held her firmly. 'You are coming with me to Maitland. Well, eventually to Maitland, we may dally a bit on the way, what?'

The captain pulled Fiona towards him, shaping his lips to kiss her.

'Mr Maitland will no' be pleased when I tell him about this,' McRae interrupted.

It didn't seem to worry the officer. 'Tell him if you like, McRae. All he wants is a ring on her finger to prove she's his wench, then he'll turn her over to the best bidder as a whore.'

'You lie,' McRae shouted. 'Mr Maitland is a gentleman and will treat Fiona with respect.'

'He'll not respect a wench who has been whoring through the highlands with that drover Findlay. But never mind, Findlay will get his comeuppance when we next visit that place of his. We'll burn him out like all the other squatters, hopefully with him inside.'

Fiona, shocked, reacted. 'You can't burn it down, it's his own place,' she told him.

The captain laughed. 'Scum like him have no rights, my dear. Once he's dead it won't matter, eh?'

'You can't kill him without a trial,' Fiona insisted.

'If one of my boys catches him in their sights ...'

Meg opened the door. 'Someone's just taken your horse, Captain,' she announced.

'The devil you say,' the captain shouted, releasing Fiona and rushing to the door to investigate.

Meg turned to McRae. 'Go and help him. It's a lad with a dog. The dog will keep the captain busy while the laddie takes the horse if you dinna help. Hurry man,' she urged, dragging McRae by the arm.

McRae frowned and muttered, but followed the soldier.

Meg grabbed Fiona's arm and dragged her through to the back. Before Fiona could even protest, she was shoved into a cupboard, the door shut, blocking out the light, followed by the snick of the lock.

'Where's the wench?' Fiona heard the captain shouting.

'She ran out after you. She must have got away while you were busy with the horse,' Meg said.

'Damn this place, I'd hang every one of these damned Highlanders if I had my way.'

'Then you'd be out of a job, I expect, Captain,' Meg told him.

***

Fergus left a few boys and younger men to look after the animals and took the men not needed back to Invercauld

Fergus and McNeil had only reached the house and were wondering what had become of Fiona and Morag, when the priest came with the red bearded man.

It was the priest who spoke. 'I'd like to thank you for helping these people. I hope you didn't mind me taking over.'

Fergus laughed. 'They're not my people, Father. They were hounded from their homes, and chased here by the redcoats. I'll be glad if you can take them somewhere else, for they'll starve in the end, if they just squat here.'

The bearded man spoke up. 'We've talked over between ourselves, Findlay, and decided to go with the Father, at least as far as Glasgow. While we appreciate the Father's offer to pay our passage, it is not our way, and some of us might try to find work, some want to emigrate and send for their families later, but first we need to go to Glasgow. The father knows where to meet the others, but not where there's water and a place to rest on the way. Can you guide us there?'

'I have a court case hanging over my head,' Fergus explained. 'But maybe McNeil could take you. Are you all going?'

'Except Gilfillan,' the sandy haired man said.

Fergus lowered his head and shook it. 'Except Gilfillan,' he muttered.

'He's not Roman Catholic,' the man explained.

'What of your sick woman, Father?' Fergus asked.

The priest was about to answer, when someone came running. 'You'd better come, Findlay,' they shouted. 'That deaf mute of yours has drowned an old man.'

'Where is he?' Fergus demanded.

'Bane has him tied to the wheel of his cart until the Redcoats come back.'

'Take me there,' Fergus shouted, starting to run.

Davie was sitting on the ground beside the cart with his hands tied behind him, but managed to smile as Fergus got near. Bane was close and turned from what he was doing to meet Fergus.

'What do you think you're doing,' Fergus demanded.

'Don't start interfering, Findlay,' Bane told him, coming to stand between Fergus and Davie. 'He drowned an old man and now he'll have to face the consequences.'

'Drowned an old man! Davie!'

Mrs Bane came forward to stand beside Bane, her arms crossed on her bosom. 'And he was daft enough to bring him back here,' she said.

'Davie's deaf but he's far from daft, Mrs Bane,' Fergus told her. 'How did he come to bring the old man back?'

'He took one of your garrons and went and took him and drowned him,' Bane answered.

Another man approached. Fergus recognised him as the son of the old man Davie had been 'talking' to.

'What happened,' Fergus asked him.

'That deaf lad of yours took my father down to the shore and drowned him.'

'How do you know it was Davie?'

'He brought him back.'

'When had you seen your father before that?'

'He was fine when we went to bed last night.'

'And this morning?'

'He often goes off to do his usuals in the morning, but when he didn't come later, we went looking for him. We even went down to the shore but he wasn't there. We were starting to organise a search when your lad came with father's body on the garron. He'd been drowned; there was still water in his lungs.'

Fergus walked forward and cut Davies bonds. As Davie grimaced and started rubbing his hands, Bane stepped forward and pulled Fergus to face him. Fergus faced Bane, eyes locked. Bane stepped back. 'You'll not interfere, Findlay. We'll not accept a murderer in our midst,' Bane said.

'Have you asked Davie what happened?'

'How can you ask him? He just gives that daft smile and says nothing.'

Fergus's eyes hardened. 'He can read some words on your lips and you can make signs. What will you do when you meet a red man in Canada?'

Bane frowned.

Fergus stepped closer. 'Well, what will you do?' he demanded.

Bane made no reply.

'You'd try to communicate with a red man in the wilderness but *here* … in your *own* country …. you canna even make the effort to talk to a deaf laddie. A laddie that helped hide your sheep,' Fergus shouted, taking half a step towards Bane. 'Now, get out of my way and let me talk to Davie.'

Fergus glared round at Mrs Bane and the old man's son, and back to Bane himself, before turning back to Davie.

'Tell me,' Fergus said clearly.

Davie made his fingers walk, then pointed to the shore.

'You?' Fergus asked, pointing at Davie.

Davie shook his head, looked round and pointed to the old man's son, but stooping like the old man walking with his stick.

'Where did he go?' Fergus signed.

Davie pointed to the shore.

'How did you know he was there?' Fergus asked, pointing to Davie, tapping his head and then pointing to the shore.

Davie made a mouth with his thumb and forefinger, flicked them like someone talking, and then pointed to himself.

'He told you?' Fergus asked, miming speaking, then pointing to Davie.

Davie nodded.

'He drowned him,' the man's son shouted.

Fergus grabbed the man by the shoulders. 'When did you say you last see him?' Fergus demanded.

'When we went to bed, last night.'

'And this morning?'

'We looked all over for him, even down at the shore, like I said, but couldn't find him,' the man blurted out, sobbing between the words.

Fergus calmed. 'It was high tide earlier. It's low tide now. Your father had plenty of time to walk down to the shore when the tide was low during the night.'

'He couldn't walk without a stick. Where's his stick?'

'He had all night to get there and his stick would float away,' Fergus pointed out.

The man's wife, attracted by the shouting, came forward and put her arm round the man's shoulders.

'Think yourself,' Fergus told the man. 'Your father didn't want to be a burden. Didn't want to keep you from bettering yourself. Davie was the only one who understood. He even he tried to talk your father out of drowning himself. I watched them arguing, but didn't know what it was about - not then. When he saw the old man wasn't here and you were looking all over for him, he went and brought his body back for you to give him a decent burial. He was trying to help, but you tied him up and accused him of murder! What kind of people are you?' Fergus asked, looking round. 'You're no better than the Redcoats,' he shouted.

At that moment, the priest appeared and Fergus watched as he took charge of the grieving son.

Fergus nodded understanding to the priest and turned to go. 'Where are Fiona and Morag?' he asked.

'They were talking of going to Ault-na-main,' the man who had come to warn Fergus about Davie told him.

Fergus and McNeil looked at each other, aghast.

Fergus recovered first. 'Get these people in some kind of order, McNeil, and take them so that they only find the road south on the other side of Ault-na-main, beyond the Redcoats. Do it in the dark if you can. The beasts are difficult at night, mind. Just the same, they're nearly at the road, the first hour of daylight would be enough to get them away. I doubt if that captain is an early riser, anyway. From what I've heard, he's over fond of the bottle for that, but start at first glimmer of light and give the place a wide berth. I'll go and see to the girls at Ault-na-main. And I'll take Davie with me.'

CHAPTER 35

The stuffiness in the cupboard began to make Fiona drowsy and she shook her head to keep herself awake. Time and darkness blended. She could hear pans clashing in the kitchen after a while. Unable to more than flex her muscles, she was starting to feel cramps, when the cupboard door opened and she was blinded by the light. Unable to see, she staggered forward and strong hands took her arms. Smelling the comforting odour of heather and pine smoke and Fergus, she gasped and then fell into his arms.

'I think it's time we made our own home, Fiona,' Fergus told her. 'I'll take you to Invercauld in the morning.'

Fiona pushed him away. 'That Redcoat said they'd kill you on sight,' she told him.

'They'll have to see me to do that, and see me where there are no witnesses.'

'He said they'd burn Invercauld, Fergus.'

'Let them, I wanted to build a new house for us anyway, something of our own, to our own liking.'

'What about Morag's things?' Fiona asked.

Fergus sighed deeply. 'Then I suppose we'd best send word to someone to get her things out. McNeil is there,' Fergus answered. 'But first, can you use a dirk?'

Fiona laughed. 'You'll remember we sometimes played with sticks when we were young, Fergus. I was never as skilled as you, but I think I could still manage to defend myself, especially if someone wasn't expecting me to try.'

'Then take this, Fiona, I don't want to be farther away from you than a call, but things rarely turn out as you want.'

Fiona reached out for the leather sheath that Fergus offered. 'Take care, Fiona, it has an edge like a razor, don't unsheathe it unless you need to, but when you do, use it. Don't threaten first, a cut will heal, being ill-used will be with you forever.'

Despite Morag's presence, Fergus was unhappy about leaving Fiona at Ault-na-main and considered sending Davie to warn Invercauld. It was the difficulty of making sure Davie understood, and then that the people at Invercauld would understand from Davie, that made him decide to go himself, leaving Bruce and Davie with Fiona.

The sun was down behind the hills by the time he got to Invercauld and found preparations for the night move well advanced.

'Take your own things and whatever you can manage of Morag's on the garrons,' Fergus told McNeil.

'This is getting to be a bit of a war here, Fergus, with retreats and ambuscades and riots. Maybe we should get some help.'

'Any outsiders would stand out like sore thumbs, McNeil, but I'd be glad if Abernethy was here to give us some advice. Maybe you should go on to Glasgow and let him know what's what. He might know of someone in Inverness that knows something about breach of promise and alienation of affection lawsuits. I'll have to deal with that in the end. What about Morag's things?'

'We'll load them up as best we can, Fergus. No matter what we do, it'll be wrong, so we'll not worry over much, and I'll take it across to her at Ault-na-main.'

'Are the people ready?' Fergus asked.

'Near enough,' McNeil told him. 'We'll be away as soon as the moon's up.'

'All except Gilfillan,' Fergus commented.

McNeil laughed. 'Aye, all except Gilfillan.'

They both turned as a figure approached their firelight. 'I've come to say God bless, Findlay,' the man, whom Fergus recognised in his mind as 'the sick woman's husband'.

'And your wife?' Fergus asked.

'Dead and buried. I think she willed herself to death so that our son could get away.'

'And yourself?'

'It's been in my mind that this God they worship with all their foppery is not for me. I need someone who's with me when I'm at the plough, or when I'm at the milking, or shovelling shite in the byre. I want to go looking to see if maybe He's with the navigators at the canal, or down a mine. In any case, I'll thank you for letting me bury Mary on your ground. At least I'll ken where to find her.'

The man turned to go, but hesitated and turned to Fergus, frowning. 'I wasna listening to what was said, but I did hear you mention Gilfillan.'

Fergus stiffened.

'I ken he's got a cow that wasna there before, but, after the women had chased the redcoats away, their captain and his corporal came sneakin' back and threatened Gilfillan's wife. He's no' a bad man, Findlay.

He's just no' the kind that takes on the world at every turn like yoursel'.'

They watched the man disappear beyond the firelight.

Fergus waited until the moon rose and the crowd moved off before turning to roll himself in his plaid in a dark corner away from the fire.

***

At Ault-na-main, the girls had chattered, then grown quiet, busy with their own thoughts. Fiona had asked Babs about her father, to be told that Meg was feeding him too well and he was growing sleek and fat, like a trout. They had discussed that and were finally thinking of bed, when Fiona realised she hadn't seen Chestnut for some time and rose to investigate.

'He'll be out in the field somewhere,' Morag assured her.

'You're probably right, Morag, but it's not like him not to come for a bit of sugar, or an apple, or even a bit of bread in the gloaming. I wonder if Babs has seen him.'

She found Babs, oil lamps turned up bright, still busy at her loom.

Without even hesitating in her weaving, Babs answered. 'What would I be stopping for to feed a horse, Fiona McRae? This is not a stable. Go and look for yourself, for I've not laid eyes on him since this morning.'

With mounting concern, Fiona took her coat and went out, calling Chestnut's name. An hour later, without any result, she went back to Babs, who wasn't too pleased at the interruption. 'Yon Fergus is always bragging about that dog of his, let him do a bit of sniffing about for you,' Babs suggested, turning back to her weaving.

Fiona found Chestnut's saddle rug and let Bruce smell it. Bruce sniffed twice, barked and ran into the field. Fiona watched him sniffing here and there, taking a run in one direction only to turn back and sniff about.

Morag joined her, and Fiona clutched Morag's hand. She gave a gasp of relief as Bruce barked and set off across the field. Despite the growing dark, the two girls followed.

At first, the trail wandered about, but then seemed to make up its mind, and turned in the direction of Tain. An hour later, in the dying light, they came to an abandoned house. Beside it, in the glow from a fire, they could see a Redcoat busy cooking.

Fiona gasped and pointed to the vague outline of a horse tethered at the edge of the camp. They had difficulty seeing Bruce's black coat and jumped with fright when he barked softly, just in front of them.

Having got their attention, Bruce turned back towards the camp, looking over his shoulder as if checking to make sure they were following. Fiona would have followed close behind but Morag's cautionary arm held her back.

Bruce stopped, waiting. Fiona looked at Morag, trying to decide whether to follow Bruce, or take a more devious route.

'Can I help you in some way?' the voice asked.

Fiona grabbed Morag. Morag grabbed Fiona. They turned to look behind them and backed off at the sight of a Redcoat.

'I'm sorry, I was making my rounds when I noticed you. I didn't mean to frighten you, but this is a military camp.'

'We … we were looking for my horse,' Fiona managed.

'And thought it might be here?' the Redcoat asked.

'The dog followed a trail that led us here, Sergeant,' Morag said, seeing the three stripes on the redcoat's arm.

'Come into the light where I can see you, and don't have to wonder if someone is going to come at me out of the dark with a dirk.'

'Just as you didn't mean to frighten us, Sergeant, we had no intention of frightening you,' Fiona added.

The sergeant laughed. 'Nevertheless, it would be better to talk where we can see each other,' the sergeant insisted, waving them towards the fire.

The trio walked towards the firelight. Bruce was nowhere to be seen.

'That's one of them,' the corporal shouted.

'One of whom?' the sergeant asked.

'One of them that chased us away,' the corporal told him.

'And?' the sergeant asked.

'We should arrest her,' the corporal shouted. 'She was one of them that was going to kill us.'

'One of a group of unarmed women who were going to kill armed soldiers, Corporal?'

'Well, they were going to do us a mischief of some kind.'

'There'll be no arresting of women here, Corporal. These women tell me they came looking for their horse.'

'It's not theirs. I found it wandering about in a field.'

'That's what horses do,' the sergeant pointed out. 'Can you prove it's yours,' he asked Fiona.

'Chestnut,' Fiona called and the horse whinnied.

The sergeant nodded.

'It's not hers, I found it, Sergeant. The captain said I could keep it,' the corporal insisted.

Fiona could see the sergeant's face flush and intervened. 'I have a bill of sale, if you need to see it,' Fiona told him.

'There's no need, Miss, the horse at least seems to know you, so, if it's not yours, please take it to its owner. Now let me bid you good night.'

'The captain will have your insides for this,' the corporal shouted as the sergeant led them out of the firelight.

'Will you get into trouble?' Morag asked.

'It would find me anyway, but I'll not make war on women. I wouldn't do it in Spain, and I'll certainly not do it to my own, lass,' the sergeant told her.

As Morag and the sergeant talked, Fiona walked on, leading Chestnut.

CHAPTER 36

'I'm sorry if the corporal's doings have caused any anxiety, Miss …' the sergeant said.

'McInnes,' Morag told him, glad there was not enough light to show her blushes. She looked after Fiona, now almost lost in the darkening beyond the final flickers of the firelight.

The sergeant smiled. 'I would be glad to escort you, but I do have my duties here. Perhaps another time?'

'Perhaps,' Morag answered, before stepping out to catch up with Fiona.

There was a muffled scream, a bark from Bruce and sounds of hoof beats. Morag started to run in the direction Fiona had been walking, calling her name. Fresh from the firelight, Morag could see nothing.

'Sentry,' she heard the sergeant call. 'Did you see anything?'

A voice spoke out of the darkness. 'The woman came with the horse and then there was a scuffle and then they were gone, Sergeant.'

'Which direction?'

'Down the Tain road, Sergeant.'

Morag just ran.

She ran towards Invercauld, running until she was stumbling and weeping, her dress flapping between her legs. She had fallen several times before the moon rose and she could see grassy clumps and stones. She was breathless by the time she got to Invercauld. 'Neil, Neil,' she called, trying to shout, but her throat was dry and all that came out was a squawk.

'What' is it Morag?' she heard Fergus ask.

'Fiona … Fiona's been taken to Tain … in the dark … we went to get Chestnut and someone took her,' Morag gasped out.

'Where's Bruce?'

'Didn't you hear me,' Morag sobbed. 'Fiona's been taken.'

Fergus took her shoulders and shook her. 'And the only hope I have of finding her is if Bruce can follow her.'

Morag's shoulders went slack in Fergus's hands. 'I don't know where he is, he went after her, I think,' Morag managed.

'Towards Tain,'

'That's what the sentry said.'

'The sentry?'

Morag took hold of Fergus, shaking him. 'Go after her, Fergus. Go after her. Something terrible might happen.'

'Where's Davie?' Fergus asked.

'I don't know Fergus. Just go after Fiona. Please,' Morag sobbed.

'I will, I will, Morag, but where were you when she was taken?'

'I was talking to the sergeant …' Morag began.

'Where about, Morag?' Fergus asked as he shook her again. 'Where about?'

Morag forced herself to talk. 'We'd followed Chestnut to an old house where the Redcoats were camped and, after we got Chestnut, I was talking to the sergeant, and Fiona was walking away talking to Chestnut, when there was a scream and she was gone.'

'All right, whoever has taken her will get in touch with Maitland. I know where he's lodging. All I have to do is watch for them sending word.'

'But what about Fiona?' Morag pleaded.

'Whoever has taken her, won't want her really harmed, won't want her disfigured, or bones broken,' Fergus pointed out.

Fergus smiled. 'He'll not want her raped either, Morag,' he added. 'If you see Davie, send him to me. Can you do that?'

'I'll try,' Morag promised.

'Now, get up on one of these garrons and go back to Ault-na-main. And stay there!' Fergus ordered.

***

Fergus made his way to Tain. It was growing light by the time he reached the outskirts and settled himself in a corner of a building, from where he could watch Maitland's lodgings, and fell asleep.

He was shaken awake and thinking he had been discovered and was being arrested, his first reaction was to draw his dirk. Whoever had been shaking stepped away and Fergus saw it was Davie.

Davie sat down beside him, smiling welcome. It was not yet near noon, and Fergus was dozing again, when Davie nudged him awake.

The man in the street was furtive. After watching him, Fergus recognised one of the thugs that had been with McInnes.

The man walked past Maitland's lodgings, looking at the windows, then walked back again looking at the windows, before coming a third time to walk up the short path and knock on the door.

A woman appeared. They spoke briefly and she turned and called inside. Maitland himself appeared and began a short discussion. Maitland seemed to be insisting on something. The man was apologising but shaking his head and, eventually, Maitland went inside and reappeared with a coat on. The pair then started walking out of town.

It wasn't difficult for Fergus to follow as the man led Maitland along a well-established track. After half an hour, they stopped and the man gave a loud whistle twice, then repeated the signal.

It took several minutes, during which time Maitland paced impatiently, before Duncan appeared. Maitland began shouting and while Fergus wasn't close enough to hear what was being said, he could see Duncan was giving as good as he got.

As they argued, Fergus scanned the immediate geography in his mind, then smiled. If Fergus was right, Duncan had been careful, there was a cave not far from where Davie and he stood and he signalled Davie to follow.

They had only gone a few hundred yards when they came to a clump of trees and, passing through, they came to a grove in which a small stream fell over a waterfall. On the opposite slope, a man sat gazing into a fire outside a cave.

Fergus grabbed Davie, pulling him back into the trees and almost fell over Bruce.

'I wondered where you'd got to,' Fergus said to Bruce, scratching his ears.

Fergus waved Bruce downstream and took Davie with him round the waterfall to approach the cave from the top side. Fergus paused and took a cautious look through the trees. The guard was standing, looking downstream. Fergus picked up a stone and threw it over the waterfall into the stream. The man turned to look and Fergus had a glimpse of Bruce moving up the slope.

From his new position, Bruce had apparently growled, for the man picked up a stick and turned to face where Fergus had last seen Bruce. Fergus took another stone and threw it into the trees they had come through initially.

The man, now growing nervous, turned that way.

Bruce came out of the shelter of the trees and stood looking at the man. The man yelled at Bruce and shook a stick, undecided what to do. Bruce rushed at him, but stopped short, and turned tail. The man stepped back at Bruce's charge. Took sudden courage at Bruce's retreat, and rushed after him.

As the man moved, Fergus stumbled down the slope and rushed into the cave. Fiona was sitting, her legs tied at the ankle and her hands behind her back. A scrap of material tied as a gag round her head. Fergus grunted as he lifted her, slung her over his shoulder, and carried her out of the cave.

As Fergus came out into the open, he found Davie dragging the ex-watchman back to the fire, where he propped the man into a rough sitting position with a thick stick, presumably the one that Davie had hit him with.

The sight of the guard still there, might give them precious seconds to escape, Fergus realised. He hurried, gasping, up the slope away from the cave. He saw Bruce waiting and followed him to find Chestnut standing cropping grass.

Fergus threw Fiona over the horse's back and grabbed the reins to lead the horse away over the hill and on for about half a mile before turning to attend to Fiona.

'This is going to hurt,' he warned, before undoing the gag.

'What...' was as far as Fiona managed as Fergus cut the cords on her arms and the pain of the returning circulation made her groan.

Fergus let it subside before releasing her ankles. This time tears came to Fiona's eyes and Fergus put his arm round her until she relaxed.

'I think it's time we gave ourselves up,' Fergus said.

'But they might put you in jail, Fergus,' Fiona objected.

'They might, but at least if we're open about things, they won't be able to do this to you again.'

***

When they reached Tain, Fergus made straight for the Sheriff's office. 'So, you've decided to do the sensible thing, have you?' the sheriff asked.

'Black Duncan tried to kidnap her and I thought she'd be safer with you, sir,' Fergus explained. 'Maitland was behind it.'

'Can you prove that?'

'No, I can't.'

'Then, dinna make accusations, young Findlay, dinna make accusations. But what am I to do wi' the two of ye? I can accommodate yourself in a cell, but a lassie's a different thing altogether. If she was just a drunk man, I'd put him in with yersel' but this needs thinkin' on.'

'Could she not stay at the inn at Ault-na-main?' Fergus asked.

'No, no, but maybe house arrest in town here. I think I ken just the place.'

'Fiona could do with a drink and a bite to eat,' Fergus suggested.

'I'll see to that as soon as you're safely behind bars, where nobody can complain I'm not doing my duty, Fergus Findlay. If you'll wait here, Miss McRae,' the sheriff said, as he led Fergus away.

The cell was small and was really a room divided in two by an iron grill with a door in it. Behind the grill, there was a straw mattress on the stone floor, close to the back wall. Above the mattress was an open window space with bars in it to prevent escape. Fergus lay down on the mattress and went to sleep as the sheriff locked the cell door.

When Fergus woke, there was a man sitting in a chair in the other half of the room, nodding in a doze.

Over the next two days, the man changed twice a day and talked to Fergus about the weather and other mundane things. Fergus answered as required, and paced the cell, five steps back and forth to be active.

***

Late on the third day, the corporal came to gloat, took off his shako so that his dank hair flopped down the side of his head. 'You'll hang, Findlay, hang. And I'll watch as you dance on the rope and laugh,' he shouted through the bars. 'Me and the guard here will laugh,' he said, turning to the guard. 'We're going to celebrate right now, we are, aren't we, mister guard,' the corporal said, and held out a black bottle. The guard took a drink from the bottle, screwed his face as the raw spirit hit his throat, but smiled and offered the bottle back to the corporal. 'No, that one's for you,' the corporal told him, produced another, showed it to the guard and went out again.

'Well, that was kind o' him, but the dram has a bitter taste,' the guard told Fergus. 'Not that I'd be allowed to let you taste it,' he smiled and sat back more comfortably.

Fergus watched with concern as the man's head nodded more and more deeply and finally lay still as he began to snore.

Some time later, as the light faded, the door opened and the corporal came in. He looked at the guard's sleeping figure and nodded.

Fergus noticed the corporal now had a sword, and a pistol, in his belt, and prepared himself for what must be a serious wound and probably death, but was surprised when the corporal picked up the cell keys and drew his sword.

Fergus was standing, his hands holding the bars of the door as the corporal advanced and prodded with the sword to force Fergus away from the door. Fergus stood back and the corporal unlocked the door.

'Let's have some fun,' the corporal smirked. 'If I'm going to kill you escaping, I must have had to fight you off as you tried to get out. A few cuts here and there maybe,' he said.

There was nowhere Fergus could go but back. He backed slowly, keeping the sword just pressed against his chest. As the corporal took another step, Fergus apparently tripped and fell back. The start of a sneer on the corporal's face changed as Fergus's falling figure kicked up on his sword arm. Had the arm been free, the corporal might have shrugged it off, but the weight of the sword held his hand down and as Fergus kicked up and he could hear the ligaments tear in the corporal's elbow.

The corporal yelled out and dropped the sword. Fergus rolled to one side, on to his hands and knees, over and up. As he rose, he grabbed the sword by the hilt and backhanded the corporal on the chin. The corporal dropped like a stone.

Fergus looked at the guard but he was still snoring, doped, Fergus guessed, and stood rubbing his chin in thought. This was deeper than the corporal having fun.

Fergus took the sword, found a piece of cord and tied the sword to one of the bars of the cell window before dropping it outside. He then dragged the corporal into the middle of the 'office' space outside the cell and took the corporal's pistol from his belt. He looked round, saw the bottle the corporal had given the guard, took it and poured it over the corporal. The stink of whisky filled the space.

Fergus took the keys from the cell door and put them beside the still sleeping guard, before pointing the pistol into the cell and pulling the trigger. The noise woke the guard but he struggled to clear his head, shaking it and blinking. Fergus put the firearm in the corporal's hand and walked into the cell, pulling the door closed behind him before sitting down on the mattress to wait.

It took several minutes before anyone came and the corporal was just rising from the floor as the captain entered. The captain looked round, saw Fergus rising from the mattress, stared at the guard, who still blinking but able to see.

'What happened,' the guard asked.

The captain's face grew red with anger and he slashed at the corporal with his crop. 'You incompetent fool,' he shouted.

Maitland came in, almost dragging the sheriff by the arm.

'Trying to escape, I expect,' Maitland was saying.

'Well, he's still here,' the sheriff pointed out. 'And what's that drunken corporal doing in here?' the sheriff asked, sniffing loudly.

'He came in and took a shot at me,' Fergus explained. 'But he was that drunk he couldn't aim straight.'

Maitland looked at the captain. The captain shrugged.

'He was trying to escape,' the corporal shouted.

Fergus got up and pulled the unlocked door open.

The sheriff drew himself up to his modest height. 'Michty me, the bliddy door's no even locked, and you're tryin' to tell me the man was tryin' to escape. Lock that door, Rorie,' he told the guard. He turned to the corporal, 'It's lucky for you there's no harm done, or it would be attempted murder.' He turned to the others, 'Now, the rest of ye get about your business. I was at supper when you hustled me down to this farce, Maitland. I'll thank ye not to interfere in the due process of law again.'

He waved his hands, flushing the jail clean. 'Off with ye, off with ye,' he ordered.

When the little room was clear, the sheriff turned to Fergus. 'Now what happened?' he asked.

'I think they drugged Rorie, luckily they'd put too much in the bottle and it spoiled the taste, so Rorie only had one drink.'

'And then?'

'The corporal came in and things got interesting. Nothing too difficult.'

'What are they after, Fergus?'

'I think the captain wants Invercauld, and Maitland wants Kirklea, and maybe Invercauld as well, for all I, or even the captain, would know. The corporal is just a pawn.'

'They're no' likely to try anything here again, Fergus, but I'm not so sure about your Fiona. If the captain gets to thinkin' about revenge, he might just get ideas about her.'

'Deaf Davie and Bruce will be watching,' Fergus told him. 'And she's a farm lassie and can take care of herself, provided she's not caught in the dark.'

'I'll keep an eye open just the same,' the sheriff said.

Despite his brave talk, as he bedded down, Fergus worried about Fiona.

CHAPTER 37

Fiona felt safe. She was settled in a boarding house with several other people, travellers and people working in the town temporarily. Not being able to go out, she felt restricted, however, and was delighted when Morag came with some of her clothes.

'Have you heard what happened at the jail?' Fiona asked.

'No,' Morag answered. 'Isn't Fergus there?'

'Yes, and someone said something about a shooting, but they didn't know if anyone was hurt or anything. Maybe one of the guests knows something.'

Fiona was gone only a few minutes. 'All I could find out was that no one was hurt and Fergus is still in the cell,' she reported.

Morag seemed to have something more on her mind, so Fiona waited.

Morag talked. 'I met that sergeant, he's a fine man. A bit like McNeil in ways. I suppose it's him being a sergeant.'

'He's a fine man, is he?' Fiona repeated. 'Didn't you tell me Babs had said the father of your bairns would be a fine man, or did she mention McNeil in particular?'

'That's the trouble, Fiona, that old woman was so, so … vague, that I don't know what to think.'

Fiona laughed. 'Maybe she just didn't want you to throw yourself away on some idle nobody, Morag.'

'You think so?'

'She's shrewd, Morag. I don't know if she's got the second sight, or she just gives people advice that keeps them out of trouble.'

'Well, anyway, the sergeant is a fine man, to my way of thinking.'

'Aye, but which sergeant, Morag?' Fiona laughed.

'I wish we were together,' Morag said. 'I've never really had a close friend since I left the school, what with working on the croft and all.'

'Then come and stay here,' Fiona suggested. 'Fergus gave me enough money for both of us.'

Morag hugged Fiona. 'I must just get some things from Ault-na-main,' she said, rushing out.

***

Morag had just gone when Maitland and her father came to Fiona.

'Mr Maitland wanted to see you were all right,' McRae told Fiona. 'Why do you not just do the right thing and get married to him, lassie.'

'Because I don't even like the man,' she said, turning her gaze to Maitland.

Maitland came to stand beside her. He put his arm over her shoulder and looked into her eyes. 'We might get to love each other, my dear. Stranger things have happened.'

Fiona's hand in the pocket of her dress felt the little leather sheath Fergus had given her and her fingers closed on the dirk handle.

Maitland smiled.

Fiona could feel his breath, smelling of whisky or brandy.

Maitland moved closer, 'Surely you could give it a try, for your father's sake?'

Fiona put her hand to Maitland's chest and Maitland, feeling the point of the blade at his heart, stepped back, surprised. He frowned. 'Come now,' he said, reaching out. Fiona's hand just seemed to pass close to Maitland's, waving it away, but the blood started to drip as he drew it back.

He stared first at his bleeding hand, then at Fiona, but she was smiling. 'If we were married, Mr Maitland, how would you sleep on a dark night?' she asked.

'You bitch,' Maitland shouted, and pulled his hand back to slap Fiona. Fiona didn't draw away but instead moved close to Maitland and her hand went to his chest again.

Maitland's eyes widened as Fiona pushed the dirk point against his ribs. 'You were saying, Maitland?' she whispered, her face now close. 'Maybe Kirklea isn't such a bargain after all.'

'I'll have you arrested,' Maitland shouted. 'You signed an agreement.'

Fiona laughed. 'I'm already arrested,' she pointed out. She turned to McRae. 'I thought you had a job, Father? Or is Mr Maitland paying you to come and talk to me?'

'I've no need to be paid to come and talk to my own daughter,' McRae said.

Fiona nodded her head. 'Ah, I didn't think your generous gentleman would dip into his pocket to keep you alive, but you seem to think that if I were married to him, the leopard would change his spots and grant you an allowance. Would you do that, Mr Maitland? Will you sign a paper guaranteeing my father a thousand pounds a year for life?'

Maitland's eyebrows shot up.

'Ah, I thought not,' Fiona said. 'Not even pounds Scots?' she queried.

Maitland snorted. 'You'll be sorry for all this. I'm not a man to be thwarted, especially by drovers' whores,' he told Fiona, turning and walking out.

'Now look what you've done,' McRae grumbled.

'I've made you walk all the way back to Ault-na-main, Father.'

'What did he mean by drover's whore?'

'He means I'm married to Fergus Findlay according to the ancient laws of Scotland, but not in the eyes of the law we Scots accepted from those that make their money from making laws.'

McRae gaped. 'You've sold yourself to that blackguard Findlay, and tossed away a future of ease, for a plaid in the heather.'

'No, Father, on the contrary,' Fiona told him, her voice rising. 'I've stopped a devious villain from making a fool of you, but you'd better go before you lose your job.'

McRae stared in disbelief.

'Go, Father, you've spent all we had. Now you'll have to work, or starve. I only wish I could make you see how lucky you are to have somewhere to stay, and food in your belly.'

McRae left and Fiona plumped down in a chair, put her head in her hands and wept. For all her bombast, Fergus was in jail and from what she'd heard of the gossip at table, had almost been shot and she, herself, was shut in this house unable to help.

262

CHAPTER 38

Like Morag, Fiona had had few chances to keep in touch with friends and she hugged Morag close when she came into the room.

Morag held Fiona away, looking into her eyes.

'Maitland and my father were here,' Fiona explained.

'You're not …'

'No. But it wasn't easy.'

'Good for you.'

Fiona's hands fidgeted. 'I just wish all this was over and I could talk to Fergus,' she said.

'Fergus is fine. The redcoat corporal got drunk and made a fool of himself, that's all.'

'Someone said Fergus was shot.'

'Shot at, but not hurt, according to Sergeant Longstreet. He said the sheriff has made sure it won't happen again,' Morag added. 'In any case, Babs said it would be all right. Her sister, Mrs Lafferty, was there and said she was glad you'd got away.'

'Mrs Lafferty! What's she doing here?'

'Maitland didn't leave any money when he left. She had no food, so she came away north to her sister, Babs.'

By the time Fiona had explained about Mrs Lafferty, it was late and time for evening meal, after which they had the dinner conversation to discuss and laugh over.

As she fell asleep, Fiona remembered Morag had mentioned the redcoat sergeant. Longstreet, was it? She should have asked about that. Did it mean Morag was losing interest in McNeil, she wondered.

As if in answer to Fiona's thoughts, McNeil, with his rifle on his shoulder, came to the boarding house in the morning. He brought another man, smart, slim but worried looking, whom he introduced as Tom; a girl, plump and bubbly, whom he introduced as Jean; and, behind them, Hamish.

'I need to do a bit of searching and talking, but I hope I can get you out of here in a day or two,' Tom told her.

'And Fergus?'

'Not so easy, but I'll see what I can do,' Tom said.

Fiona searched his face for doubt, found none, and smiled.

'You're far too good looking for that Fergus,' Tom laughed.

Fiona could hear Hamish's muttered agreement in the background but ignored it.

'My one real worry is Invercauld,' Tom said, his face taking on the frown again. 'I'm not sure what Fergus wants done about the squatters.'

'Fergus isn't sure himself,' Fiona pointed out. 'But I doubt if he wants them evicted by the sheriff.'

'I'm not sure there's another way,' Tom commented, turning to McNeil.

'He can let them stay,' McNeil said.

'But they can't pay rent,' Tom pointed out.

'Fergus kens that,' McNeil told him.

Tom shrugged. 'It's something we can deal with later. The first priority is to get him out of jail and you allowed to walk about, Fiona.'

***

Fergus could not have agreed more. He had recovered the corporal's sword and hidden it in the mattress but he

264

could think of too many ways a determined assassin could kill him - or get him killed. When he heard Tom's voice, he was on his feet holding the bars of the cell door before the front door was properly opened.

'I've heard of Habeas Corpus, laddie,' the sheriff was answering Tom as he came in. 'This is no' Mars.' Fergus heard him add in exasperation. 'Findlay came and offered to be incarcerated until the hearing. And just as well, I'm thinkin', or he might have been waylaid among the heather instead of bein' used for target practice by a drunken corporal. But, if you think he'll be safe enough, you can take him away. My own wife is spending more time on his meals and things than on anything else. I've got to get down on my knees to get a clean shirt.'

The sheriff drew a breath but, before anyone could interrupt, he addressed the guard. 'Let him oot, Rorie, and get away to your family.'

'How's Fiona?' Fergus asked.

'Outside,' Tom answered, and was just able to get out of the way as Fergus rushed out to take Fiona in his arms. Fiona clung to him, laughing tears as Fergus whispered his love in her ear.

Local women, unused to displays of affection, smiled behind handkerchiefs as they passed; men frowned to hide their grins; bairns who pointed, had their ears smacked.

***

Two hours later, they were all on their way to Ault-na-main. The first person Fergus saw was McRae. Some of the creases had started to ease on his face and he even looked straighter; suits him, Fergus thought, and looked to see how Fiona would react.

She looked reserved. 'Hello, Father,' she greeted.

Before McRae could reply, Meg appeared and looked round the group. 'I've only got two rooms free,' she told them.

Fergus nodded. 'That's fine, Meg, Tom and Jean can stay here, McNeil and I can go to Invercauld and Morag and Fiona can stay with Babs,' he explained.

'And Hamish?' Jean asked.

Fergus looked at him, then back to Jean. 'There's a place at Invercauld for him as well,' he told her.

It was Tom who answered. 'Surely we can all eat together?' he asked. 'A kind of celebration. Have you got something more than beer or whisky, barman?' he asked McRae.

Fergus smiled, wondering how McRae would answer.

'He's my father,' Fiona whispered.

Fergus could see from Tom's eyes he was thinking that over; wondering why McRae was here, rather than at Kirklea, possibly.

Turning his attention to McRae, Fergus grinned as the older man tried to look down his nose at Tom. He was too short and the impression was comic, rather than haughty. 'I'm afraid we're too far from anywhere to have wine,' McRae told Tom.

'Nonsense,' Meg interrupted. 'There's that claret you served the captain.'

McRae's expression hardened and Fergus thought he was about to object.

'Get it!' Meg ordered.

McRae went off, Meg shook her head at Fiona, who smiled, eyes twinkling, in return.

'You brought Hamish,' Fergus said to Jean.

'He just came with us,' Jean explained. 'I'm not sure if it was my fatal attraction, or your Fiona's smile he wanted to see again. McNeil was suspicious at first, but they became quite pally on the way.'

'I think he misses being told what to do in the army,' Fergus suggested, and turned to McNeil. 'The priest got away all right then?' he asked.

'We met up with his others two days from here. They seemed to know their way. It wasn't hard to find anyway, so I went on to Glasgow and Jeanie,' McNeil said, winking at Jeanie.

Fergus's glance at Morag was quick enough to catch her frown of annoyance, before she turned to say something to Hamish that made him blush and rub his ginger hair.

'No trouble with Redcoats?' Fergus asked.

'None ...' McNeil began, but Tom interrupted. 'It seems your ladies were not the only ones to chase Redcoats away. One Munro ...' Tom started to say.

'Munro of Culrain?' Fergus asked.

'Munro, anyway,' Tom continued. 'Gave notice to five hundred crofters. Somehow the sheriff and the Redcoats got involved, but when they tried to enforce the eviction orders, the women beat them with sticks, and they all ran the four miles to Argay where they barricaded themselves in the inn.'

'You ... you don't ken what it's like to face an angry crowd, T ... Tom,' Hamish put in, drawing everyone's attention to him. 'Especially women, you ... you canna just shoot them and you canna push their ... their ...' he tapped his chest, '... fronts, so you just have to back off,' he added, by now deep red in the face.

'Well, said,' Jean commented. 'At least there's one gentleman in the company,' making Hamish's face flush even deeper. 'Tell us something about your days as a soldier,' she pleaded.

Fergus was intrigued to hear the reply. Hamish's eyebrows shot up, his eyes wide with astonishment. 'I … I was mostly a drummer,' Hamish managed. 'It was … men like Sergeant McNeil that … that … did the fighting.'

Once they had eaten and exchanged news, Fergus nodded to McNeil and they were making ready for leaving, Tom joined them. 'You know you're still in danger?' he warned. 'These attempts on your life are not going to go away until what's at the root of it all is settled. I hope you know what that is.'

Fergus frowned and scratched his eyebrow in thought. 'That's the trouble, Tom. If it was just Fiona's breach of promise and my own alienation of her, I doubt if it would be worth killing for. There's something deeper in this and, since it all started with Kirklea and McRae, I'm not sure what to think. Invercauld is a different thing. McNeil is sure the Redcoat captain wants the farm, and is not over worried about how he gets it, but I've a feeling Maitland is behind that somehow.'

Tom nodded. 'My father has his ear to the ground, but so far, he's heard nothing. I wonder if old McRae knows?'

They looked round and noticed McRae, with his back to them was talking to Hamish, who glanced quickly in their direction. Tom indicated McRae and beckoned. Hamish drew McRae's attention. McRae glowered but came to stand belligerently before Tom.

Fergus let Tom carry on. Tom wasted no time. 'Why does Maitland want Fergus dead?' he asked.

'Because he took Fiona,' McRae answered.

'No, that won't do, McRae. You don't go trying to kill people because they've stolen your fiancé. Not even here in the Highlands.'

'Who says he's tried to kill Findlay?' McRae demanded. 'That's another of his damned lies.'

Remembering the attempt in Glasgow, Fergus glanced quickly at Hamish but Hamish was trying to ignore the conversation and talk to Jean.

'Why don't you do it yourself?' Tom asked McRae.

Fergus saw McRae's scrawny neck swell as he stared at Tom. 'I'll not swing on a rope for a damned drover,' he almost shouted.

'No, but you'd let someone else swing to get it done,' Tom challenged.

'McRae!' Meg called. 'There's dishes to wash.'

McRae turned to go - turned back - turned to go - turned to face Tom and Fergus - 'Bah!' he shouted and went to deal with the dishes.

'I'll thank you not to upset my staff, Mr Abernethy,' Meg told Tom.

Tom apologised. 'I'm sorry, Meg. I got carried away ...'

Jean intervened. 'Tom's been impossible at times since he was a wee boy, Meg. Father used to try to beat it out of him with a slipper, but it's made no impression.'

The two women smiled understanding and Fergus relaxed. 'Are you coming with us, Hamish?' he asked.

Jean waved her arms. 'Nobody's leaving, Fergus, we're all going to visit Babs,' she announced. 'I want to talk to her about things for the shop and I want you all to come and complement her so that she gives me what I want.'

Fergus wasn't sure how Babs would react to a deputation, but it would be interesting.

CHAPTER 39

'What all this?' Babs asked. 'Is it a wedding party, or what?'

'Jean here wanted to visit,' Fergus introduced, and looked on as Babs looked Jean over.

'So you're Jean, are you? I'd fancied a more business like body, but everything about Fergus Findlay comes as a surprise.'

Fergus grinned.

Meg looked at him. 'Who'd have thought a lassie as fine as Fiona would even look at the creature.'

Jean laughed. 'I wanted to see where you worked, and talk about the kind of things I've been asked for, to see what you can get for me,' she explained.

'That's grand,' Babs replied, and Fergus became a spectator. 'I've one or two new patterns I'd like you to look at. I've only made samples and I was going to send them down with Fergus, but he's that taken up with Fiona, dear knows when he'll be on his travels again, so, I'm right glad you've come. We've got visitors, sister,' she called. 'See if there's not some buttermilk for the ladies, and maybe a drop of something for the men.'

As a figure came from somewhere, Fiona put her hand to her mouth, 'Mrs Lafferty!' she exclaimed.

'It is that, and right glad to see yourself, Fiona McRae,' Mrs Lafferty replied. 'I hope you've kept yourself out of the clutches of that ruffian Maitland. He left me to fend for myself at The Mearns, not a bit of food in the house, and not a penny to buy any either, when he went running after you. It's glad I am to see you're looking a deal better than when we last met.'

While Fergus smiled, Babs stopped the reunion. 'Take her to the back, sister,' she ordered. 'This is a place of work, not a talking shop. And send Davie through while you're at it.'

Fergus wasn't sure why Babs wanted Davie, or how he would join the conversation, but didn't interfere.

'This is the master designer,' Babs introduced, pulling Davie forward. 'As soon as he saw the weaving he couldn't wait to get his hands on it.'

Babs turned to a kist and took out several samples of woven cloth.

Jean clapped her hands, gave a cry of delight, and held the samples up for the others to admire. 'Don't you just see these made into sashes for the ladies and trews for the men at the balls?' she asked no one in particular.

Fiona re-joined them. 'I've never been to a ball, Jean,' she pointed out. 'But if I were going to one, I'd love something like that, over a pale gown, to give it a splash of colour.'

'Never been to a ball!' Jean exclaimed. 'Then you must come to Glasgow for a kind of honeymoon and we'll show you off in style. We'll get something elegant to suit your height, and you'll be the belle, and you can look haughtily at everyone.'

This is getting out of hand, Fergus thought, but was sorry when his scowl stopped Fiona's laughter at the idea.

'Don't you want to show her off, Fergus?' Jean teased.

'I don't want her being gawked at like a side show, Jean,' Fergus replied.

Jean made a face. 'Wait till you see her in a gown, Fergus. She'll look like a dream princess.'

'I've seen her look like a princess hanging clothes on a line,' Fergus answered.

It didn't put Jean off. 'Ask Fiona if she'd like to visit, Fergus. Go on, ask,' Jean encouraged.

Fergus looked at Fiona, not knowing what to expect. His answer was in Fiona's eyes, even before she spoke. 'Our journey through the glens was magical, but I'd like to dance with you like a lady, Fergus.'

Fergus shook his head, but smiled just the same.

Jean jumped up and down, then hugged Fiona. 'We'll go round all the shops and try on all kinds of things and drive the shopkeepers mad,' she confided. 'And we can take Davie …'

'Davie!' Fergus exclaimed.

Jean frowned at him. 'He has a talent, Fergus, and to develop it, he needs to see what other people do. Or didn't you realise he had a talent?'

Fergus nodded. 'I've seen him draw, Jeannie, and he's good at that, but since I've never met an artist, it's just something he's good at, like whistling, or playing the pipes.'

'I think it's time you came to Glasgow as well, Fergus,' Jean insisted. 'But for now, let Babs and I sort out what's what,' she told them, ushering the others outside.

Fiona and Morag started to talk and McNeil went to see about garrons. Tom went with him, leaving Fergus and Hamish together.

Hamish stared at Fergus. 'I'm watching how you treat Fiona, Findlay. If you dinna treat her like she deserves, I'll come after you,' he threatened.

Fergus faced him. 'Let's have this out *now*, Hamish. What do you prefer, dirks, or broadswords, or pistols, or just bare hands.'

Hamish's eyebrows shuttered down till his eyes were slits. 'I'm no match for you like that, but I'll watch and catch you when you're no' expecting. Like you did with Butcher.'

Fergus sighed, his shoulders slumping. 'What was Butcher trying to do to me, Hamish? He fired a pistol in my face, so don't pretend he only wanted to rob me. That man was a killer. I don't know what he was like to begin with, but, by the time the army had finished with him, he enjoyed killing.'

'You didna have to take his life,' Hamish insisted.

'Yes, he did,' McNeil butted in. 'Sooner or later, Butcher would have got *you,* as well as himself, hung, if Fergus hadn't killed him.'

'It was his own swing that deflected my own blade, Hamish,' Fergus said. 'I can't make you believe that, but listen to what McNeil's trying to tell you. McNeil was in the same war, as a sergeant, like Butcher, but he didn't turn to robbing, did he? Did he, Hamish?' Fergus demanded.

Fiona and Morag turned at the raised voices and Hamish glowered and moved off.

'Where are you going, Hamish?' Fiona called.

'To see some friends,' Hamish called back.

Fergus grunted, watching Hamish go. What friends would that be? He wondered. Redcoats, or Maitland?'

As Fergus watched Hamish go, McNeil shook his head and spoke. 'I thought I'd talked some sense into his head,' he said. 'I hope he's not off to stir up to some mischief.

Maybe you should stay here tonight near Fiona, Fergus,' he suggested.

'Aye, I'll do just that,' Fergus answered. 'But there's one thing I want to ask. If we go to Glasgow, would you look after Invercauld for a week or two, McNeil? It'll have to be after the hearing in two weeks' time.'

McNeil hesitated.

'I'll pay you,' Fergus said, and found McNeil's face in his.

McNeil's voice was no more than a hiss, 'If you ever insult me like that again, Findlay, it's not some snot nosed carrot headed bairn you'll be dealing with,' McNeil warned.

Fergus was still shocked when he felt Tom's hand on his shoulder. 'Come on, there's enough trouble to sort out, without you two being at each other's throats.'

Fiona and Morag joined them. 'What's wrong?' they demanded.

Fergus grimaced. 'Och, McNeil said he was a better dancer than me. Maybe you'd both better go with him to Invercauld, where there's a piper and he can practice.'

'I've warned you before about making arrangements for me with men, Fergus Findlay,' Morag reacted.

'I wasn't …' Fergus began.

McNeil was grinning as he said, 'Then I'd better be away by myself, just, before it gets too late. Somebody has to see Gilfillan is tucked up,' and walking off.

'Men!' Morag commented.

Fergus found an earnest Tom beside him. 'I hope you realise what's at stake over this court case, Fergus.'

It brought Fergus back to his troubles.

Tom continued. 'It's not just Kirklea and Fiona married to Maitland they want. They want compensation from you and that could mean all your money and Invercauld as well. Are you prepared to risk that? I could talk to his lawyer about a compromise?'

'I'll give them Invercauld and everything I have, Tom, just to keep Fiona safe. You'll not understand, being from Glasgow, but in the oath I pledged with Babs, I promised more than those living that I'll guard Fiona with my life. That promise ... I'll keep!'

'Then I'll not ask again,' Tom said.

CHAPTER 40

Next morning, it was later than Fergus had hoped before Jean had finished her toilet, organised a picnic, talked to Babs again, freshened up, chosen a calm garron to ride, and they could start on their way to Invercauld.

Despite Fergus's urging, they stopped to pick flowers, to marvel at the view, to tell Fiona how lucky she was, and wonder at how McNeil could leave to go to a place where there were wild animals and even wilder natives.

Half way there, they met McNeil. As they walked and rode with the others for company, for the first time since he had taken Fiona from the church gate, Fergus began to feel that Fiona and he could make a life together free from stress. That feeling made him talkative and he talked excitedly about what they might do at Invercauld; where they might grow corn or barley; where they might build stock pens. Fiona listened but grew quieter as he talked and, trying to raise her mood, Fergus talked more volubly.

He could hear the others talk and laugh now and then; could hear McNeil's firm voice bantering with Jean and wondered at the edge creeping into Morag's voice. Tom was asking questions and paying small compliments to Morag. Against this background, Fiona's silence began to worry him.

'We'll need a cow or two and they'll need to be near the house for milking,' Fergus said.

Fiona made no reply except to nod, and Fergus went on, 'You'll not want the other beasts too near the house and you'll maybe want to have a few chickens.'

Fiona merely nodded again.

'I'll see about getting someone to help in the house,' Fergus said.

'Help in the house?'

'You didn't think you'd be skivying like at Kirklea, Fiona?' Fergus asked.

'I've no desire to slave in a kitchen when there's bens and glens to marvel at, Fergus.'

Fergus laughed. 'Well, the first thing that needs to be sorted out is the house. We'll not need a mansion, but I want a room for ourselves as well as the bairn.'

Fiona frowned, her hand went to her mouth, she looked down and then at Fergus. 'Fergus ...'

'Come on, we'll see the place from the top of this hill,' Fergus announced, running ahead.

Fiona grabbed his arm. 'There is no bairn, Fergus. Babs was mistaken.'

Fergus looked at her, frowning. Fiona returned his stare at first, but her eyes dropped. 'If you feel you'd not want to be wedded to me, I'll understand,' she managed.

Fergus stared and had opened his mouth to speak, when Jean grabbed his arm. 'Come on, we want to see this estate of yours,' she said, pulling him along.

They reached the top of the hill and looked down. 'Where did all these people come from?' Jean asked.

Fergus could see at least five families scattered across the lower part of the farm. His shoulders slumped and he waved his arms in the air and looked up to heaven. 'Gilfillan!' he shouted to the sky.

The others looked at him. 'Let me go and talk to him,' McNeil suggested

'You go, Tom, I've had my fill of squatters. They came here, unasked, then demanded this and that, then accused Davie of murder.' Fergus told him. 'If I go down, I'll slit somebody's throat.' With that, he turned and walked away.

Fergus strode out for some time, then looked up at the sky and the clouds, then around at the far hills across the firth, then at the trees, and started to smile. He was turning back to Fiona when, first Bruce, and then Davie, came out of a clump of trees. Davie waved for him to come, and Fergus walked up to meet him.

Davie led him through some trees and pointed. It took Fergus a few moments to see the Redcoats lying where they could overlook Invercauld with a telescope. When he had seen them, he nodded to Davie and turned back to look for Fiona. He almost missed her.

'What are you sitting there for, Fiona. I thought you'd gone with the rest.'

'I'm not with child,' Fiona said firmly.

'Oh that,' he said, then looked more keenly at her. 'Was that why you were so quiet on the way here?' He shook his head but smiled. 'You weren't with child when I took you from the kirk gate.'

Fiona frowned. 'Then why did you go off after I told you?'

'Because I saw my dream being just frittered away by Gilfillan,' he explained.

He took both her hands. 'I've dreamt of bringing you here for so long, of having you to come home to, of coming in to the smell of your cooking or baking, to sitting with you in the evening. I thought we could manage with just Gilfillan and his wife. She might be glad enough to help in the house but now his whole family's come. At least I take it they are his family. I wanted the place for us, you and me, Fiona, not for a whole herd of Gilfillans, but you didn't seem to be interested.'

Fiona smiled. 'You went too far with your dreaming, Fergus. Your dreams are all what you imagine on your own. They're not shared dreams, Fergus. What you've done is to put me in the place I was in, not just cooking, but ironing and milking cows, and all the other chores that filled my days, for what seemed forever. To me you bring romance, Fergus, not drudgery. If you have a dream for me, let it be in swimming through swollen rivers, and shivering in the sleet until we can find a cave, where we can snuggle together and make love. Oh, I know there are chores to be done, cows to be milked, but I want to do those things with a light heart, Fergus, not because they are part of a day like yesterday.'

Fergus stared at her. 'I wanted you out of the storms, Fiona, safe in a warm house.'

'And where would you be coming home from, Fergus?'

Fergus's eyebrows shot up in surprise. 'From … from about …' he struggled.

Fiona began to laugh. 'While you were talking all the way here, I was seeing myself looking after chickens until I just couldn't take any more, and gave up and died, like my mother. We've a lot to sort out, you and I, Fergus Findlay. Now let us go and join the others for this picnic thing of Jean's.'

Fergus helped her up and they stood for a moment smiling into each other's eyes, before taking hands to walk down to the house.

As they came to the house, a sturdy figure with a Glengarry bonnet above a heavy beard, with a rough cape over its shoulders came through the grass towards them.

'Gilfillan?' Fergus muttered.

'Aye, me, myself!' the man said. He could have been smiling or scowling for all they could see of his face, but his voice was confident and Fergus's hand gripped Fiona's more tightly.

Before Fergus could explode, Fiona asked, 'And how's your wife, Mr Gilfillan.'

'She's as fine as can be expected in the circumstances, m'lady, thank you for the asking,' he said, nodding to Fiona before facing Fergus.

'She'll be the better of the two cows the Redcoats gave you,' Fergus pointed out.

'Aye, she is, but it wasna the Redcoats, it was a man that wasna all that keen to be seen, Findlay. A dark man from about here by the talk of him.'

'Black Duncan,' Fergus muttered.

'Aye, like enough,' Gilfillan answered. 'As well as that, yon carrot headed laddie that came … he seems to ken yon friends of yours, yon McNeil … was telling me the redcoats are watchin' the place, Findlay.'

'I saw that for myself,' Fergus told him. 'But why did he not tell me himself?'

'Because he felt you wouldna believe him. Besides, he wasna concerned about yourself but just the lady here.'

Fergus nodded and Gilfillan rubbed his beard before going on, 'Aye, well, he was also telling me that they've a plan to come first thing in the morning as soon as the lookouts report you're here. I don't know if you want me and mine to put up a bit of a fight. The sojers were feared of the women the other day, and maybe those o' us that are here could chase them away. I doubt it, Findlay, but we can try.'

'What difference is it to you?' Fergus asked.

'We're on your land and you're entitled to expect we'll help when we can.'

Fergus stared at Gilfillan, then shook his head. 'The days when you were called out by a fiery cross, or took up a sword for the landowner, are bye. If you stay here, I'll expect you to work, maybe even ask your wife to help when we move here, but you'll not get yourself, no, nor any of your folk – I take it this new lot are all Gilfillans?'

Gilfillan nodded agreement.

Fergus grunted. 'I'll not have any of their blood on Invercauld. I canna say you're welcome, but you're here, and we'll make the best of it. Thank you for the warning. What happened that day you were helping the redcoats to follow us?'

Gilfillan grinned. At least, teeth showed through his beard. 'I kenned you'd have some kind of a plan, so when that corporal … I'll deal with him one of these days … started to get rough with my wife, shoutin' and the like, I stood it as long as I could to let you get away, then led them away after you. They could have followed the trail themselves without wastin' time wi' me, but I think that corporal enjoyed upsetting my wife, as far on as she is, and it gave you a start. When I saw the lightning and that black stone stickin' out of the heather like a bald head, I nearly laughed. When I told them you'd taken them into the underworld, the captain was mad, but the corporal, for all his show, is a Highlander, and wasna for riskin' the deil takin' him. We'll no' mention this elsewhere for now, but when the redcoats are away, we'll have a fine laugh about it.'

'You ken McNeil was ready to shoot you.'

'It's what I expected you'd be thinkin' of, but you're a Highland man yourself, and I kenned you'd be wanting to see if they took the bait.' Gilfillan's teeth showed through the beard again and he gave a deep chuckle. He looked at his feet for a moment, before raising his gaze and his voice became serious. 'Young Carrot head …'

'His name is Hamish,' Fergus corrected.

'Aye, Hamish, was saying they'll burn the place down.'

Fergus grinned at him. 'Let them, I was for knocking it down and building something a bit more convenient anyway. I hope there's a builder among this family of yours.'

'Aye,' Gilfillan said. 'A builder there is, a cousin of my wife, and plenty to help with the work.'

He turned to Fiona. 'I hope you'll be happy here, Mrs Findlay,' he added, touching his bonnet to her before walking away.

Fergus looked at Fiona. 'What can you do with them?' he asked, shaking his head. Fiona burst out laughing. Fergus grinned and led her to the picnic.

**

The picnic was a success. They were chaffing as they tidied up when they heard the moans of a bagpipe from the Gilfillan camp.

'Maybe you'll get your ball sooner than you expected, Jean,' McNeil commented.

Jean was on her feet immediately. 'Is he playing for anything special?' she asked.

'He's playing to please himself,' Fergus told her. 'It's not a recognised tune.'

The tunes beat increased and Jean looked at Fergus. Before he could answer, McNeil explained, 'Now he's playing a march to get everyone interested. Let's see what he's going to do next.'

By now, a few had come to listen, standing in a kind of half circle in front of the piper.

The pipe tune began to lilt. Jean gave a squeal of delight and looked round.

McNeil rose grinning. 'You'll none of you mind if I go and see if Jeannie can dance as well as she talks?' McNeil asked, but was moving and taking Jean's arm as he spoke.

Fergus looked at Fiona but her attention was on Morag. 'Do you dance, Tom?' Morag asked.

'Not too well, I'm afraid, and this is grass, not a sprung floor, but if you want, we can try a measure ...' Tom answered and took her hand to join the other dancers.

'Well, Fergus?' Fiona asked.

'I don't want to encourage them, Fiona. I suppose they're decent enough but I ...'

'Oh, come on, Fergus, you know how you enjoyed that dance at Kirklea,' Fiona smiled, pulling him to his feet.

The strathspey was already in full swing as they joined the group.

When the piper blew the last notes of the dance, he started the first notes of a reel.

Fergus was just turning to Fiona, when Hamish appeared in front of her.

Fiona laughed. 'I'm sorry, Hamish, but this one is promised to Fergus.'

Hamish glared at Fergus, but let them join the others.

'I hope he'll not be a nuisance,' Fergus said, but his comment was drowned by the wild sound of the reel and, by the time the piper slowed, they were grinning with enjoyment, and too out of breath to say anything.

Fergus and McNeil swapped Fiona and Jean before Hamish could interrupt, and the piper slipped into the gliding notes of a strathspey.

They were joined in the dance circle by Hamish and a young girl, who laughed as she danced, teasing Hamish's occasional stumble over a bit of grass.

After the dance, the piper took a break, Fergus noticed the girl talking animatedly to Hamish. She was insisting on something, now and then glancing in Fiona's direction. Hamish seemed to be objecting, but his complaints grew less noticeable as the girl talked.

***

An old man with a clay pipe upside down in his mouth, came forward, rubbing his Glengarry bonnet round his head as if it was itchy as he drew close. 'I'm hoping you'll not object to me speaking to yourself,' the old man said to Fergus.

'I was brought up to respect my elders and betters,' Fergus answered.

The old man put his pipe in his pocket, spat on the ground, and smiled. 'I may be your elder but I doubt if I'm your better, Fergus Findlay, but I'm glad you've let us bide here.'

'I'll not pretend I'm delighted that you had no other place to go, Mr Gilfillan, and was upset when I found your whole clan come here, but maybe we can find some way to live together. It just wants thinking about.'

'While we are thinking, I was hoping that you'd take a wee drop of our own distillation with myself, and my nephew, Lachlan.'

Fergus looked at the old man for several moments, before nodding agreement.

They talked of nothings for a few moments before Gilfillan left.

'You took your time about accepting his offer,' Fiona said.

'It's not just the dram, Fiona,' Fergus smiled. 'Remember, he first made sure I knew the old rules. He offered an apology, but asked a question at the same time. I've accepted his apology, but told him that he, and all his people, can stay. You'll have them for neighbours until you die, or they leave.'

CHAPTER 41

The Lachlan that Old Gilfillan brought was in his thirties, almost clean-shaven but with dancing eyes and a big smile.

'Try that,' he told Fergus, offering a bottle.

Fergus didn't wipe the top but took a mouthful of the contents, expecting to have his throat burned. It wasn't, and the astonishment on his face made Lachlan laugh.

'What's this? Drinking in secret,' Tom interrupted.

'Taste that, Tom,' Fergus said, handing the bottle over and watching.

Tom sipped. 'Where did you get this?' he asked Lachlan.

'From his own still,' Old Gilfillan answered. 'And you'll be Tom Abernethy all the way from Glasgow,' he added. 'But if you're a friend of Fergus Findlay's, then that is good enough for me.'

Tom laughed, and took another sip of the whisky. 'My father would be glad of some of this, Mr Gilfillan, if Lachlan has enough to sell.'

Lachlan grinned, but the old man drew himself up as far as his stooped figure would allow. 'We'll not be selling to anyone who is our guest, Tom Abernethy. Lachlan will be giving you two bottles for your father. Will you not, Lachlan?'

'We have only this one bit of a bottle, Uncle, the rest is in yon cask to mature, like you said.'

'Och, well, maybe Tom Abernethy will manage to get two empty bottles and we can fill them for his father. It would be a great shame if a man that appreciates good whisky did not get the opportunity to taste a bit of Lachlan's Delight.'

Fergus grinned. 'We'll get two from Ault-na-main.'

Tom became serious. 'Have you registered your still?'

'For why would we be bothering the excise with registering our still?' Old Gilfillan asked.

'Because I'd hate to have it shut down, and Lachlan put in jail. Lachlan's Delight is too good for that. Would it be all right if I saw to the registration of it?'

'Whatever you think yourself, Tom Abernethy. It is just that we would not want the excise men being put to the trouble of coming to inspect it, or anything like that, you understand.'

'It could turn into a healthy business for your family, Mr Gilfillan,' Tom pointed out.

'A healthy business is it! I suppose we must be thinking of the bairns and their future, Mr Abernethy, so, go you ahead and register the still for them.' He turned to his nephew. 'Now, then, Lachlan, we must celebrate this thing. Go you and let your cousin have a nip out of that bottle, and tell him it is time he was blowing his pipes, and not wasting that nice young lady's time talking to her.'

Fergus looked round to see the piper deep in conversation with Jean, or at least deep in listening.

'It's not the piper that'll be wasting Jean's time,' Tom said. 'It's more likely the other way round.'

'Is that your sister, then,' old Gilfillan said. 'She's a fine girl and as light on her feet as a lark.'

He turned to Fergus. 'I see that red headed laddie wants to dance with your wife, Fergus Findlay. I'll speak to him, for he's been talking to our own Lisbeth, and I'll not have him wasting hers, or the lady Fiona's time.'

The pipes started to squawk that the dancing was about to restart. The old man gave a sigh. 'It's right sorry I am that I can not join in, but get yourselves a lassie and enjoy the dancing,' he told Fergus and Tom.

Fergus and Tom moved closer and after another round, the dancers relaxed and stood recovering their breath in puffs.

Fergus and Fiona, standing together, were approached by the bearded Gilfillan and a shortish, very pregnant woman, with dark hair and a pretty face.

'My Rhona wanted to thank you herself, Findlay,' Gilfillan said.

Before Fergus could say anything, Fiona put her hand on Gilfillan's wife's arm. 'How are you,' she asked.

She got a rueful smile in answer. 'I'll be right glad when this bairn decides it wants to see what its father looks like. I'm only worried that when it sees him, it'll want to go back where it came from,' she added.

Fiona looked at the thickly bearded Gilfillan and smiled.

'He's a fine looking man under all that,' Rhona explained.

'Is there anything I can do for you?' Fiona asked.

'Thank you for asking, but I have all the help I need, sometimes more than I want,' Rhona answered.

The Gilfillans left and, as Fergus looked round, he saw McNeil watching a man chase his two small children about. The man was roaring in imitation of some monster, and the children squealing as he chased. McNeil's half smile had a wealth of longing in it, and Fergus wondered if he was remembering Mary Stewart and her two boys on the drove, and regretting not going with them. At that time, McNeil had mentioned he'd never had the chance to have a family.

Dancing on the grass was exhausting and, after another round, the piper slipped into the sad magic of a pibroch. It seemed to draw the spirits from their hiding in the hills, to sit and listen. By the time he had finished, Jean's eyes were moist, and McNeil put an arm round her for comfort as they started back towards Ault-na-main.

Fergus had a last word with Gilfillan. 'We'll go now. I'll make sure those redcoat scouts see us leave so that you'll not be disturbed.'

'Don't be over sure, Findlay. They may not like being up there on the hill, and come down to the house, just to get a dry place to sleep.'

Tom, standing nearby, overheard. 'They might still come, Fergus. This isn't over. Whoever is behind this is too determined to think of stopping, just because they have not yet succeeded. I've asked around, and still can't understand what is really behind it all.'

Fergus scratched his eyebrow. 'I'm sure it's Maitland. It was him that had the people watching along the road. It seems a desperate bit of organising to stop me marrying Fiona, or just to have her charged with breach of promise.'

'They've tried to kill you, or have you put in jail for a long time, more than once, Fergus. If it is Maitland, he's not prepared to wait for this trial, nor to depend on the outcome, so you'd best be on your guard. Have you any idea why the Redcoats are watching Invercauld?'

'Gilfillan tells me the captain will come with all his men when I'm here.'

'To do what?' Tom asked.

Fergus looked at Gilfillan, who shrugged. 'That I don't ken. Maybe to burn the place in the night when Findlay's inside.'

Tom looked worried. 'Kill two birds with one stone, you *and* Fiona, Fergus. I don't like this. I don't like it at all. This is not about you taking Fiona. We need to look deeper. What is there about Invercauld?'

Fergus grinned. 'Lachlan's Delight,' he suggested, but Tom gave no answering grin.

'Don't make light of this Fergus. There's money behind this trouble over Fiona and yourself, and not just money, ruthless money, so the stakes are bigger than we've been thinking.'

Fergus nodded. 'Anyway, let's relax, and go over to Ault-na-main and have dinner together. Hopefully, the Redcoats won't come and upset us.'

Tom frowned. 'I don't think so, Fergus. Legally they've no justification but, then, from what I've heard, that captain doesn't need any legal reason to cause disruption. However, let's not upset the ladies.'

CHAPTER 42

At Ault-na-main, Fergus stood back, letting Meg take over as she greeted them, and showed them into the bar, while she organised for them all to sit at table.

McRae appeared. He served them drinks and went to help Meg with her preparations.

'This life seems to suit your father, Fiona,' Fergus said.

'He worked in a shop before he married my mother,' Fiona explained.

From there, the talk became general, until the table was set and they all sat down.

McRae came though asking for drinks, patted Fiona on the head and leered at Fergus.

It seemed strange to Fergus, but maybe being employed had changed the man.

Fergus, sitting opposite Tom, Morag and McNeil, was amused to see Morag, with her back turned to McNeil, talking to an uneasy Tom.

Tom leant forward to include McNeil. 'That's not a bad piper Gilfillan has,' he commented.

Morag leant forward so that, to see McNeil, Tom had to sit back. But before McNeil count answer, Morag had interrupted. 'He's all right for a country piper, but I doubt if he'd be acceptable in Edinburgh, or even Glasgow,' she said.

Fergus smiled as Tom persisted trying to draw McNeil into the conversation. 'What did you think of him, Neil?'

Morag got in first. 'McNeil thinks a piper should play marching tunes, and dances as if he were on a route march. That's why he prefers to dance with the squatters,' she said. She turned to McNeil. 'Maybe you'll want to go and eat her bannocks tomorrow?' she asked.

'Her bannocks might be as fine as you'd get in a shop in Edinburgh, Morag,' McNeil told her. 'Things like baking are not confined to those who would better themselves.'

The conversation was interrupted by soup. To everyone's surprise, Hamish was helping to serve. Fergus was sure he'd seen a fair haired lassie about but presumed she had other duties.

When they had time for talking, Fergus felt he had to come to Tom's aid. 'What did you think of the dram?' he asked.

'I'm sure father would enjoy it.'

McRae and Davie brought bread and conversation stopped.

It had no chance to restart as Meg came in, dragging McRae by his ear. 'He's sent the serving girl for the ...'

Fergus had just focussed on Meg, when Hamish burst in, waving frantically to McNeil. McNeil frowned but didn't rise.

Hamish's waving became more frantic.

McNeil rose and followed Hamish outside.

Everyone's attention turned back to Meg and McRae.

'He's sent Nancy to tell the Redcoats you're here, Fergus,' Meg said.

Fergus felt Fiona grab his arm and patted her hand, then started to rise. Tom waved him back down. 'You and Fiona are fine, as long as we stick together. We'll all go with you, if needs be.'

'I doubt that captain is averse to using violence,' Fergus told him and took Fiona's arm to take her out.

'It's too late for you to do anything, anyway. I've cooked your goose for you this time, Findlay. The Redcoats will be here in a few minutes to take him away,' McRae declared, joyously.

If Fergus had been closer he'd have wiped the grin that came to McRae's face, very quickly.

Meg stared at him. 'Don't you understand Fiona .loves him?' she asked.

McRae sneered. 'She'll soon see sense and marry Mr Maitland when that no good Findlay is behind bars for good.'

Before Fergus could do anything, the door opened and McNeil leant against it as he staggered back in. Morag rose at the sight of his black eye and swollen cheeks. 'What happened?' she asked.

'It was the sergeant. Someone sent him word you were here, Morag,' McNeil managed. 'And we had a fight over you.'

Morag just stared, the others looked at her.

'You're to go with him, Miss McInnes,' McNeil told her.

'You mean you lost?' Morag asked.

'No, I won.'

Morag looked confused. Fergus began to grin as McNeil continued. 'If he'd won you'd have had to go with Tom,' McNeil told Morag.

'You, you ...' Morag spluttered.

'Keep your hair on, Lassie,' McNeil said, working his mouth and beginning to chew the bread that was puffing his cheeks and rubbing at the charcoal round his eye. 'Now, sit down and enjoy the rest of this grand dinner.'

'And the Redcoats?' Fergus asked.

'Someone sent a message to them. The sergeant got it and came to see if we needed help.'

'So you don't think I'm worth fighting over!' Morag demanded.

'Oh, you're probably worth fighting over when you make up your mind, Morag, but right now, you're wondering if I'm the fine man Babs talked about, or is it Tom, or maybe even the sergeant. It's not about finding the man who'll father your bairns, lassie, it's about finding someone you love. I don't know what Babs was thinking of, putting notions like that in your head.'

Morag's expression changed and McNeil went on, 'Let's face it, Morag, you're fine company, but we're all kind of big brothers to you, and a big brother isn't the one you want to take to bed for a lifetime. Now, get your coat, and I'll see that you're not molested by any fine men on the way back to Invercauld.'

'You're not staying the night?' Jean asked.

Morag put her hands on her hip and addressed McNeil. 'Well, big brother, what are we going to do? I've got a bed at Babs'. But maybe you want to go dancing with Miss Gilfillan, or drinking some of that whisky they make.'

Fergus interrupted. 'I'm not happy about that visit from the sergeant, McNeil. If Fiona doesn't mind, I'll sleep under the trees.'

'You and me both, Fergus,' Fiona said. 'Then there's my bed for McNeil at Babs'.'

'He's not sleeping with me,' Morag put in. 'Big brother or no'.'

'Then I'll sleep under the trees and take you back in the morning.' McNeil told her.

Fergus looked at McRae. McRae's expression was full of hate, but turned to concern as Fiona stepped in front of him. Fergus saw the glint of something in the hand that pressed against her father, but was unprepared for the hissed warning she gave McRae. 'If Fergus goes to prison, or worse, I'll come for you, Father. It's a funeral, not the workhouse, you'll get.'

McRae's eyes were wide with shock, but Fergus's attention was distracted by McNeil talking to Hamish as he cleared up. 'The sergeant was saying you'd been to visit with the lads.'

Hamish blushed at the sudden attention. 'Aye, I have, I miss the army, McNeil. My mother was a good soul but we had nothing and I went about ragged. It all changed when I joined up.'

'So, what's stopping you?'

'Just being, ach, being near proper folk that don't make you feel you're daft, like that captain does.'

McNeil laughed. 'Aye, but there's men like him everywhere, Hamish. That Maitland of yours isn't much different.'

'Would he really put Miss Fiona in jail?'

'And laugh about it,' McNeil added.

***

They gathered in the morning, with the sky clear, and the sun warming.

'Are we all going to Invercauld?' Fergus asked.

Jean shook her head. 'I want to spend the day with Babs and her weaving. I want Davie to stay as well.'

The others raised eyebrows, and Jean became defensive. 'He's a bright lad and I'd like him to learn about weaving and design. You don't need to be able to hear, or talk, for that. There's that much noise in the mills, nobody can hear anyway.'

'And I want to ask some people some questions, here and in Tain,' Tom said.

Fergus smiled as Morag demanded, 'I'm to be denied your company?'

'I'm afraid so,' Tom answered.

'Oh, well, let's be on our way, big brother,' Morag said, taking McNeil's arm.

'What about the whisky, Tom?' Fergus asked. 'Let me go over to Invercauld and get the two bottles Gilfillan promised you before he drinks the lot, or misremembers.'

'I'm coming with you,' Fiona told him.

'The Redcoats …' Fergus began.

'Then they'll take us together, as Tom said. Bring Bruce; he's better than an army.'

'Then get Chestnut and I'll take a garron. We can always make a run for it if necessary.'

Bruce, in front, was the first to catch up with McNeil and Morag and got his ears scratched.

'A big brother would insist I rode,' Morag challenged McNeil.

Fergus dismounted and walked beside McNeil.

Before going over the last rise to Invercauld, they paused to enjoy the view, but the calm feelings created by the view, disappeared with their first view of the farm. There were several fires, from which smoke was billowing, and several women were carrying buckets and pots of steaming water to the sod shelter Gilfillan built lower down.

Fergus found Gilfillan and his father sitting near the main house, smoking pipes. The drinking bottle lay beside the old man. Both stood.

'His wife is having the bairn,' Old Gilfillan told them.

'Then I must go and help,' Morag said.

'Right now, it is more like too many cooks,' the old man told her. 'But go and see for yourself.'

'You're not coming, Fiona?'

'I've no experience of birthing, Morag. I'd only be in the way,' Fiona replied.

'It's taking a while,' Old Gilfillan said, puffing at his clay pipe.

Fergus could see he was worried. 'She's early,' Gilfillan explained.

Morag strode off determinedly.

Fergus and the others sat talking in short sentences. With Old Gilfillan's comment about it taking a while hanging in the air, they were unable to stop glancing in the direction of the shelter.

A long wail from the direction of the shelter made them all sit up, and Fergus exchanged a worried glance with Fiona. The wail grew in volume, seeming to cut into the atmosphere, killing the birdsong, killing the rustle of the wind in the leaves of the birches, killing the breath of their souls.

'The Lord giveth and the Lord taketh away,' Fergus heard Old Gilfillan say.

They all looked at him; the men frowning; Fiona's hand to her mouth. McNeil stood up, his brows glowering his concern. Fergus looked at young Gilfillan, but it was impossible to tell what he was thinking behind the dark mass of his beard.

'She's dead,' old Gilfillan said. 'And by the sound of the keening, the bairn as well.'

Morag came running, wide eyed and shaking, her mouth open in a soundless scream to rush into McNeil's arms where she hid her face in his chest, shaking her head as if trying to shake off some bad dream. She made no sound for some time.

'Oh, God, oh, God,' she said at last, and started to sob. 'The blood, oh God, the blood. And the baby dead. Oh, God,' she managed and began to shake again.

In the end, she started to cry and McNeil began stroking her hair until she seemed to relax a little.

McNeil looked at Fergus and nodded to the bottle. Fergus gave it to him and McNeil eased Morag away from his chest. 'Take some of this, it will ease things,' he told her.

Morag shook her head, but McNeil smiled and insisted.

Morag took a gulp and as the whisky hit her throat, raw with crying, she erupted in gulps and coughs, looking accusingly at McNeil. The coughing subsided, and Morag sat down. McNeil sat in front of her and held her hands.

'It was terrible, Neil,' she told him. 'She was screaming and the women were shouting, trying to get the bairn turned and I don't know what happened but there was blood all over, and the baby lying there dead. They tried, but it was like a rag, Neil, a white rag covered with dark blood. Take me away from here, Neil, take me away. My father is buried on the hill there and so is my mother and now that wee bairn. Don't ask me to have bairns, Neil. Don't ask me to have bairns.'

'Take her to Babs,' Fergus said and was glad when McNeil nodded understanding.

'No, no, to Canada, somewhere far, Neil. This place is cursed.'

'First to Babs. She has medicines for what ails you, lass,' McNeil told her, picking her up and leading her to the garron. He lifted her on to its back and started to lead it away.

Fergus looked at Fiona, who nodded after McNeil. Fergus stood, made his apologies to the old man, shook Gilfillan's hand in sympathy, and led Fiona away to where Chestnut stood.

It was a long, slow, journey, back to Ault-na-main, and the long summer evening was drawing to a close when they got there.

As Fergus helped Fiona dismount, Tom came, 'Didn't go well?' he asked.

Fergus nodded. 'Gilfillan's wife and child died.'

They both watched as McNeil led Morag to Babs.

Fergus looked at Tom, who motioned with his head to move where they could talk privately. 'I think I've covered most things for the trial, Fergus, but you've never said if you met anyone between taking the coach at the kirk, and leaving it behind.'

Fergus looked surprised. 'Aye, we did. Mrs Lafferty. I never expected to see her again, but she turned up here. She's Bab's sister if you want to have a word with her.'

To Fergus's surprise, Tom slapped him on the back, gripped his shoulder and started walking him to Babs' house.

'By the way, I think it would be a good idea to move to Tain,' Tom commented. 'It's too easy to arrange an attack on yourself, or Fiona, out here.'

'Look at Bruce, Tom,' Fergus said. 'There's no threat about here. He's had a good sniff round as we came. He growled at the inn, but that was just McRae. It's a grand night and we'll sleep out, McNeil and me, once Morag's settled.'

As they came to Babs', McNeil came out. 'Babs has given Morag a drink of something to settle her and she's dozing off to sleep. I don't know when she'll get over this. You ken how she kept talking about the father of her bairns being a fine man, well, she said to me just as she was dozing off, "Dinna force me to risk my life to have your child, Neil." She hung on to my arm until I promised.'

'She'll get over it in time, McNeil. Remember you're not the fine man Babs was talking about,' Fergus told him. 'With Tom's permission, we'll take one of these bottles and go sleep under the trees.' He looked at Tom. 'We'll fill it for you again, Tom, dinna worry,' he said, leading McNeil away. 'Go and talk to Mrs Lafferty. You can join us later if you feel like it.'

When Tom joined them, after his talk with Mrs Lafferty, he was in high spirits. 'Did you know her husband was a navigator? Dug half the canals in England, according to what she told me.'

Fergus grinned. 'I didn't have much chance to talk to her. When Fiona insisted on changing, she had her things off, and on, before I had time to even ask for a drink of water.'

Tom smiled and nodded.

CHAPTER 43

As they rode between Tain's sturdy, pale sandstone buildings, dominated by the squarish Tollbooth and Sheriff Court, Tain was in the middle of its morning business. People turned to look at them, some nodding acquaintance to Fergus, others commenting to others on who, and what, his companions might be.

Having settled into accommodation, Jean insisted on exploring the little burgh, and led Fiona into every shop, from fishmongers to haberdashers. Fiona, whose days had, in the past, been filled with chores, was unused to simply browsing, but over the few days before the hearing, she found it relaxing, and learned to chat to the shopkeepers as Jean rummaged.

Fergus tried to relax, but fidgeted, except when they went to the saddlers to have Chestnut's equipment checked.

Tom was busy. He talked to people, getting the feeling of the locals about Fergus, and the poor girl he'd rescued from a forced marriage to 'yon Englishman'. The most voluble were the few farmers and drovers who stopped and shook Fergus's hand.

On the morning of the hearing, as this was only a preliminary hearing designed to test whether Fiona, and later Fergus, had a case to answer, they were spared the indignity of being led through the wrought iron gate to the side entrance reserved for those accused of a crime, and Tom and Jean followed them through the front door of the Sheriff Court.

The court itself was in a large room. A central isle split the wooden benches for the public into left and right sections. At the front, facing the little raised dais for the sheriff, tables served as desks for the lawyer's papers. As Tom made his way to the tables, he noticed the room was already almost full of curious citizens; drovers who had come to give him support against the Englishman; women of the town curious to see this female who was worth abducting, who had stirred such passion in the breasts of two men, that they were prepared to contest the right to have her as their bride. Fergus was nodding to people he knew. Fiona, as Tom had coached, was holding Fergus's arm and smiling as best she could, without making serious eye contact with anyone. That was until she noticed Babs and Mrs Lafferty, when her smile became genuine and, seeing it, other women turned to each other to comment.

They all stood for the sheriff's entrance.

'I hope we'll no' be long,' the sheriff commented as he sat down.

'No, no,' Maitland's lawyer said, smiling ingratiatingly. 'As I'm sure Mr... er ... Mr?'

'Abernethy,' Tom told him.

'... Ah, yes, Abernethy, will agree. This is an open and shut case.'

The sheriff looked at Tom, who stood. 'I'm afraid I disagree, and beg your permission to show that proceeding with this case would be a waste of the court's later time. I'm sure I can convince my learned friend' ... Tom smiled at the other lawyer ... 'that there is enough doubt about the outcome to make it worth considering an alternative solution to a full court case.'

It brought a 'Humph,' from the sheriff and a muttered, 'There's more business than this to do, Mr Abernethy. I hope you'll be brief.'

Tom smiled at the sheriff. 'My intention is to avoid a long court case by offering a possible solution to the present impasse, but I do need a little time, your honour.'

The sheriff gave a loud sigh. 'Then let's get on with it, Wylie,' he said, nodding at Maitland's attorney.

Tom sat as Wylie guided Maitland to a chair beside the sheriff's dais, smiled at him and asked, 'You are betrothed to the young lady called Miss Fiona McRae?'

Maitland glowered at Fergus and frowned at Wylie. 'Of course I'm betrothed to her. She signed a marriage contract. You have it there.'

'She intended to marry you?'

'Yes.'

'Of her own free will?'

'She signed the contract.'

'But the marriage never took place?'

'That's why we're here.' Maitland pointed at Fergus. 'That thief stole her at the chapel.'

Some of the drovers nudged each other and laughed.

BANG! Went the sheriff's gavel. 'Quiet in the court,' the sheriff shouted.

Wylie resumed. 'Did she do this with her father's blessing?'

'Her father was the one who got her to see sense and not waste her life on a worthless tinker like Findlay.'

The drovers grumbles grew louder.

BANG went the gavel again.

'And what happened then?' Wylie asked.

'Findlay took her and I chased after him, but he knew the country better than McRae and me, and he got away.'

Wylie nodded to the sheriff and sat down.

'Mr Abernethy?' the sheriff queried.

Tom rose and walked forward, smiling to the scowling Maitland.

'You maintain that the young lady signed the marriage contract of her own free will – apart from some coercion by her father, that is,' Tom asked.

'Yes.'

'Tell us who Mr McRae's main creditor is, Mr Maitland.'

'I am.'

'And how did that come about?'

'I wanted to save my future bride and her father. I bought up their outstanding debts.'

'Mr McRae's, or Miss McRae's.'

'Both.'

'How much of Miss McRae's?'

'Quite a bit.' Maitland answered confidently.

'Come now, Mr Maitland, ten pounds, ten shillings or ten pence?'

Maitland shifted in his seat. 'I don't remember.'

'Or was it tuppence three farthings?' Tom asked. 'From my researches, just before all this wedding fiasco, Findlay had paid all but that on his way to Glasgow.'

'I don't remember,' Maitland insisted. 'I bought the promissory notes to save my new in-laws.'

Tom turned away, muttering, 'Or possibly just to get Kirklea on the cheap.'

The sheriff leant forward. 'Was that a question, Mr Abernethy?' he asked.

Tom turned back to Maitland. 'I suppose it was,' he said.

Maitland glowered. 'I had no need to buy the debt to acquire Kirklea. Once Fiona and I were married, the farm would be ours, and I would have the management of it. I bought the debt to save my future father-in-law embarrassment.'

'Is that all, Mr Abernethy?' the sheriff asked.

'For the moment, but you can see yourself there are avenues that need to be explored, but to save the court's time, I'll make it all.' Tom smiled.

'Who have we next?' the sheriff asked.

'Miss McRae herself,' Wylie told him.

The spectators craned forward to get a better look at Fiona as she walked forward and, seeing a plainly dressed farm girl, another of Tom's suggestions, started commenting to neighbours.

'This is no' a drying green for gossip,' the sheriff told, with a BANG of his gavel.

Wylie asked about the wedding agreement and Fiona confirmed she'd signed it.

'Why did you sign it?' Wylie asked.

'To keep my father from the workhouse,' Fiona answered.

'Not to become the matron of a big house and have an easier life?'

'No. I'm a farm girl and could earn my own living. It was my father that went on about being sent to the poorhouse.'

'You could have refused.'

'I was only nineteen and my father insisted,' Fiona pointed out.

'Did your father threaten to beat you?' Wylie asked.

'No.'

'Did Mr Maitland?'

'No.'

'Did Mr Maitland behave in any way other than as a gentleman should?'

'No.'

'In fact he saved you from an attacker.'

Fiona looked at Tom, who nodded and smiled. 'Yes,' Fiona answered.

'So, you made a promise and then ran away.'

'I was taken away.'

'By whom?'

'Fergus Findlay,' Fiona said clearly.

Wylie nodded to the sheriff, and Tom smiled as he got to his feet.

'How do you know you signed a marriage contract, Fiona?'

'They told me that was what it was.'

'You didn't read it?'

'I was sick, Mr Abernethy. Even if it had been my own death warrant, I was too tired to read it. They told me Fergus was dead, and I just did as my father told me.'

'But Fergus Findlay is here, Miss McRae,' Tom said, looking round at Fergus.

Fiona nodded. 'They told me he was dead.'

'Were you, or your father, given a copy of this, very important, document?'

'No.'

Tom took the paper from the sheriff's desk and showed it to Fiona. 'This is your signature, though?'

'Yes.'

'Thank you for being so honest, Fiona. Your father must be very proud of you,' Tom said, taking the paper back.

People looked at McRae, who scowled back as he was signalled forward to give evidence.

Wylie smiled at him, but McRae continued to scowl.

'Were you pleased about your daughter marrying Mr Maitland?' Wylie asked.

'I thought it was a very suitable match, Mr Wylie,' McRae answered. 'After all, he saved her from a fate worse than death.'

'But you were pleased anyway?'

'Aye.'

'Did you force her to sign?'

'Never!'

Tom rose as Wylie walked back to his seat.

'Mr McRae,' Tom began. 'You mentioned that Mr Maitland saved your daughter from a fate worse than death. What exactly did you mean?'

'That Duncan Slater tried to have his way with her, but, luckily, Mr Maitland came in time to deal with him.'

Tom rubbed his chin in thought. 'Duncan Slater … Duncan Slater … would that be Black Duncan … would that be the Duncan Slater that guided yourself, and Mr Maitland, to follow Findlay and Fiona?'

'The very same,' McRae agreed.

'Did you know this Black Duncan before the attack?'

'No, I did not.'

'Did Mr Maitland?'

'No, he did not.'

'Did Mr Maitland take him to the sheriff?'

'No, he gave the blackguard a good hiding.'

'And then hired him to guide you both in the chase after Fergus and Fiona?'

'He was the only one Mr Maitland kenned of at the time.'

'You're sure neither you, nor Mr Maitland, knew him before? Didn't arrange for him to accost Fiona, so that Maitland could intervene and save her?'

'That's a damned lie. Mr Maitland is a gentleman. Not a ruffian like that Findlay,' McRae shouted, rising to his feet.

'Sit down, Mr McRae,' Tom said. 'All you have to do is deny that you and Mr Maitland arranged the attack, and we will *all* believe you.'

McRae sat down and Tom turned away. 'It just seems strange that you happily used this blackguard to follow your daughter,' he said, and paused, as if considering what he'd just said, before turning back to McRae. 'I'd have thought you wouldn't want him within a million miles of Fiona again. Didn't it strike you as odd, that the only guide Mr Maitland could find, was the man who'd torn the dress from your daughter as he tried to rape her?'

McRae glared. 'He had to get somebody in a hurry.'

'Hmmm,' Tom answered. 'Let me change the subject,' Tom said. 'Did you know Mr Maitland was buying your IOU's?'

'No.'

'He didn't do it at your request?'

'No, he did it to help us.'

'To help Fiona with tuppence three farthings! Or you with how much, Mr McRae?'

'I don't ken.'

309

'More than the farm was worth?'

'I dinna ken.'

'Enough to send you to debtor's prison?'

'Aye, maybe!'

'So, Mr Maitland saved you from debtor's prison, and paid your daughter's tuppence three farthing bill, and she was somehow so overcome with gratitude that she rushed into signing a marriage contract. Is that it?'

'She did it to save us from the workhouse.'

'Mr Maitland threatened you with the workhouse?'

'Yes, yes, and I could see no way out.'

'Why didn't he just take the farm in settlement of the debt, Mr McRae? Was it because the farm really belonged to Fiona?'

McRae was startled and looked round for some escape.

'Come, Mr McRae,' Tom encouraged. 'Did Mr Maitland want to marry Fiona, or did he really just want the farm. Did he not tell you he didn't care if Fiona was dead, or alive, as long as she was Mrs Maitland?'

'I dinna remember such a thing. Mr Maitland would never say a thing like that.'

'In a trial, you'll be under oath, Mr McRae, and perjury will put you in worse than the workhouse, maybe Australia.'

BANG went the gavel. 'I'd like to remind you this is a hearing, no' a trial, Mr Abernethy. I think you've made your point. Can we get on with things?'

Tom looked at the floor, then raised his head. 'I hope I've given Mr Wylie enough to let him understand that this is not an open and shut case. I'd like to go on and provide him with a possible reason for advising his client to come to an arrangement with Miss McRae and Mr Findlay. As you've realised yourself, this case would drag on, taking up the court's time in cross examination to clear all these anomalies that have now cropped up and, with your permission, I'd like to make a bit of a detour.'

The sheriff glared. 'I'll no' have my court made into a music hall, if that's what you mean to do.'

Tom held up his hand. 'Not at all. I wouldn't dream of it, but please bear with me for maybe fifteen minutes, say half an hour.'

'Half an hour, Abernethy. Half an hour, no more!'

Tom waved to Davie, sitting near the front to come forward.

'He's deaf, your honour,' Tom explained.

The sheriff threw his head back, eyes turned to the ceiling. 'Deaf! What kind o' a witness can a deaf laddie make?' He shook his finger at Tom. 'I've warned you, Abernethy, no music hall tricks.'

'He can't hear, or speak, but he can see and draw, your honour,' Tom explained as he took a slate and a pencil to Davie.

The crowd leant forward, trying to see.

Tom pointed at Maitland and Davie started to scribble.

'He'll not take long,' Tom said.

The sheriff shut his eyes and shook his head. 'Don't ever come back to my court, Abernethy,' he told Tom.

Davie held out the slate to Tom, who took it to the sheriff. The sheriff glanced at it and handed the slate to Wylie. 'So Maitland beat him. Laddies get beaten all the time, Mr Abernethy.'

'Beaten, but not whipped. And for what?' Tom asked, but didn't wait for an answer, before wiping the slate and giving it back to Davie.

Davie scribbled again and offered the slate to Tom, who gave it to the sheriff, who gave it to Wylie.

'So Maitland kicked a dog to death, Abernethy. It disna prove the marriage contract was signed against the lassie's will. She's already said he never threatened to beat hersel'.'

'I'm coming to that,' Tom explained. 'If you'll just write something on the slate, like your name, maybe?'

The sheriff looked as if he might refuse, but after meeting Tom's gaze, and getting no sign of retreat, took the slate and signed and Tom gave it to Davie.

The crowd were now leaning over each other in their attempts to see what Davie was doing.

Davie's head moved and seemed to be following the rises and falls of the sheriff's signature, then he followed the rises and falls with his finger before taking the pencil and working on the slate. He grinned and gave the slate to Tom, who gave it to the sheriff. The sheriff's eyebrows shot up.

'Which is which? 'Tom asked.

'So he can copy my signature,' the sheriff answered.

'To put this in context, what this case is about is that Fiona McRae was pressured into signing a document she was told was a marriage contract. Maybe that's what it was, but she has no copy. Is that the document she signed?' Tom asked, pointing to the contract. 'Maitland swears it is, but can Mr McRae confirm, under oath, that the document we have been shown is the document

Fiona signed, or that someone, like this deaf mute, copied her signature on to another document? I doubt it.'

Tom waved Davie back to his seat and waved to Mrs Lafferty, sat near the back.

Mrs Lafferty shuffled forward.

'What are you doing here?' Maitland shouted.

Mrs Lafferty stopped and glared at Maitland. 'What did you expect me to do? Starve at The Mearns. You left nothing but a few bones and no' enough flour to make a loaf for a mouse, and no money to get any, either,' Mrs Lafferty answered. 'I'm here at my sister's.'

Mrs Lafferty sat down.

'Tell us what happened when Fergus Findlay brought Fiona to the Mearns, Mrs Lafferty?' Tom asked.

'She was in that coach, with yon wedding dress on, but as soon as the coach stopped, she had it off. No' just the dress, but everything underneath as well, ailing and all as she was.'

'You mean, she went away naked with Mr Findlay?'

'No, no, she's a fine lassie, she put on some things, Fergus there, had brought for her. They were laddie's things but they were clean.'

'Why did she do that, Mrs Lafferty?'

'She didna want anything o' his things' ... she pointed at Maitland ... 'to touch her.'

'That doesn't sound as if she was looking forward to being married to Mr Maitland. But that's not what I wanted to ask you about, Mrs Lafferty ...'

'Is this about Lafferty again?''

'It is. It's about your husband.'

'But I've telt ye he was a navigator, dug all they canals.'

'But he was also a miner at one time.'

'Aye, in the mine at Tyndrum. That's what killed him, your honourship,' Mrs Lafferty told the sheriff.

The sheriff banged his gavel and stared at Tom. 'What's this now about canals and mines at Tyndrum. This case is about Breach of Promise to get married, no' workin' in the bowels o' the earth - if you remember - Mr Abernethy.'

'It's as much about Kirklea as it is about marriage as I'll show in a few minutes,' Tom answered, before turning to Mrs Lafferty, as the sheriff looked ready to raise his gavel. 'Tell us about the men who took the rocks from Kirklea, Mrs Lafferty.'

'Oh, that! Well, after Maitland had taken Lafferty on and dragged him all about The Mearns and Kirklea, and dear kens where all, and killed him off with his galavantin',' Mrs Lafferty paused for breath. 'Lafferty was bad wi' that miner's disease from that mine at Tyndrum, but Maitland just walked him till he dropped, lookin' if this was like Tyndrum, or that was like Tyndrum. After Lafferty passed on, men came to the Mearns in the long summer days, when it gets hardly dark, and went sneakin' across to Kirklea. They went late in the day, when decent folks would be thinking about their beds, and came back, sometimes in the mornin', wi' bags o' stones that they gloated on, talkin' about lead and silver, and even gold. I sneaked a look, but damn the bit o' gold did I see. Shiny bits that might have been silver, but deal the bit o' gold, Mr Abernethy.'

'That's fine, Mrs Lafferty,' Tom told her. 'You can go back to your seat.'

Mrs Lafferty puffed her way back to her place beside Babs, and Tom turned to Maitland. 'Maybe you'll be good enough to tell us the name of the mining organisation that wants Kirklea,' he suggested.

'This has nothing to do with the marriage contract, Abernethy,' Maitland shouted.

The sheriff banged his gavel. 'I agree with that, Mr Abernethy. For the last time, will you stick to the point?'

Tom looked abashed. 'Very good, your honour. I think I've shown that if this goes to court there is far more to it than just whether Miss McRae was coerced into signing a document she never read, one that *might* be the same one that Mr Maitland has shown us, but I have in my possession another document that bears on the case.'

Tom went to his place and after a brief shuffle of papers, brought a document to the sheriff.

As the sheriff read it, his brows rose in astonishment. He glowered at Maitland before turning back to Tom. 'Why the devil did you no' show us this to begin with?'

'Because I can't guarantee it is genuine.'

'Genuine or no' it needs explaining,' the sheriff told him before turning to the other lawyer. 'Take a look at this, Wylie,' he ordered.

Wylie rose and came to the sheriff's desk. Wylie read the paper, frowned and gave it to Maitland. Maitland glowered at Tom, and took the paper. As he read, there was a fleeting crease of worry about his eyes, but it was so brief and followed by an angry reddening of his face, that those farther away never saw it, but Tom smiled quietly.

Maitland exploded. 'This is a fraud, another of this man's tricks. I've never been married,' he shouted at the sheriff, and handed the paper back to Wylie.

'That's as may be, Mr Maitland, but it wants investigation,' the sheriff said, taking the paper and comparing it to the marriage contract. 'Is this your signature? It's awful like the one on the contract,' the sheriff went on.

'How can it be? I've never seen the document before,' Maitland shouted. He pointed at Tom. 'He's trying to pass a fraud.'

'He never said it was genuine, Mr Maitland,' the sheriff pointed out. 'And all I'm saying is it warrants investigation, and the only way to find out if it's a fraud is to find out if you are already married, eh?'

Tom stepped forward. 'Might I suggest a compromise? Perhaps Miss McRae would sign over her rights on Kirklea for a signed agreement that Mr Maitland will drop all charges against her and Mr Findlay. In that way, there would be no need for the court to investigate the allegations that Mr Maitland is already married and was planning to commit bigamy, as that paper suggests.'

'I'll not let him away with what he did to me,' Maitland said, pointing at Fergus.

Tom smiled at Maitland. 'No? Well, possibly we must put Kirklea on the open market and notify other mining groups that gold may have been found on the property. That will allow Fiona to pay off her father's debts, and pay the costs of fighting the case Mr Maitland has brought against her and Mr Findlay. I doubt Mr Maitland's mining friends will want to pay for what could become a long and costly case with no more object than to satisfy his pride.'

Maitland's lawyer turned to Maitland and started to talk earnestly, emphasising his points with dramatic thrusts of his hand.

'All right. Get the papers drawn up,' Wylie told the sheriff.

'Not so fast, Mr Wylie. I have an allegation before me that Mr Maitland intended to commit bigamy. This needs thinking on.'

'If the cases against Miss McRae and Findlay are dropped, surely there is no need to waste the court's time with a fraudulent claim that he intended to commit bigamy, your honour?'

'First things first,' the sheriff said. 'Let's see to the transfer of Kirklea, and the dropping of the case, eh?' the sheriff suggested. 'I'll keep this other thing to think about by me, just in case Mr Maitland changes his mind, eh?'

Tom collected his papers and Fergus came to thank him. Maitland tried to leave, but was stopped by the Redcoat captain at the door. As Tom and Fergus watched, the pair started to argue; the captain insistent on something, Maitland shaking his head in denial.

'Don't think this is over, Fergus,' Tom warned. 'Maitland may have agreed to drop the case, but the captain still wants Invercauld. They may be disagreeing just now but, given time, Maitland will support the captain, even if it's just to get even with you. And remember, the threats haven't been just in court. It's not once your life's been at risk, Fergus!'

'I hear what you say, Tom, but I don't mind them attacking me, as long as they leave Fiona alone.'

'It's not to say they won't use Fiona to get to you, Fergus,' Tom warned.

CHAPTER 44

Fergus smiled over Tom's shoulder and Tom turned to find the well fed figure of McRae coming to them.

'How did you find out about that mining?' McRae asked.

'I just talked to Mrs Lafferty,' Tom told him.

'Maitland never mentioned anything about it to me,' McRae said. 'That would have made the price a lot more than I owed, Abernethy. If you'd let me know, Fiona and me could have put it on the market and cleared our debt, and maybe bought a wee place somewhere.'

'And lived on what?' Tom asked.

'Fiona would have found herself a job. Can you no' do something?' McRae asked.

'They're already drawing up the papers to transfer it to Maitland, or Maitland's backers, McRae,' Tom told him.

'Aye, but that's only a bit o' paper, like the marriage contract. You managed the other thing that well, surely you can get round a wee thing like a transfer?'

Tom could hardly keep the sneer from his face. 'No, I'll not even try, McRae.'

'Not even for Fiona's sake?' McRae asked.

Tom laughed. 'Especially for Fiona's sake.'

'You've never been to Invercauld, McRae?' Tom asked.

Fergus intervened. 'Maybe Fiona can bring you across.'

'I have my duties at Ault-na-main, Findlay. They keep me too busy to go visiting drover's hovels.'

Tom laughed, Fergus shrugged and McRae went to where Meg stood waiting.

'We must celebrate, Tom. Let's see what kind of a meal the hotel can lay on,' Fergus suggested.

'It's a pity there's no ball or dancing,' Jean mentioned as she joined them.

'There's a piper at Invercauld,' Tom pointed out.

It made Jean's eyes light. 'Order two coaches, Tom. If McNeil brings Morag and the ponies from Ault-na-main, we can eat and then go in style to Invercauld.'

***

As they gathered at the hotel, Fergus and Fiona stayed close, leaving Jean to bustle everyone to the table, suggesting they all go to Glasgow, where she could show the girls the shops, and then they could all go for a sail in one of the new steamboats.

'There's cattle to drove,' Fergus pointed out.

Jean persisted. 'Then McNeil and you could do as you did before, take them to Wester Ross and collect some more and take the whole lot to Glasgow. Morag and Fiona can come with Tom and me, and meet you at Fort William.'

Fergus looked at Fiona. 'I'll go with Fergus,' she said, smiling. 'I've never seen Wester Ross.'

Fergus answered her smile with one of his own, making their connection intimate.

'You've really taken to this roaming life, haven't you, Fiona?' Jean commented.

'What about Invercauld?' Morag asked.

Fergus laughed. 'There's enough Gilfillans on the place to look after it.'

'You'd trust them not to turn it into a clan gathering?' Tom asked.

'You're just worried they'll drink all the whisky, Tom,' Fergus said. 'The old man will keep them all in order, don't you worry. It may be a wild place, but in these Highlands, a promise is for keeping. '

Morag made a sound, drawing his attention. 'What's wrong, Morag?' Fergus asked, making the others look at her. 'Don't you want to go to Invercauld?'

Morag managed a smile. 'I'm just still upset over that bairn,' she answered. 'And the girl.'

'We'll all be with you, Morag. And Neil will take your arm,' Fergus told her.

Morag looked at McNeil, who smiled and put an arm round her shoulder.

The meal was pleasant and the claret good and the two coaches, filled with Fergus and Fiona, Tom and Jean, McNeil and a nervous Morag, Davie and Bruce, rumbled their way to Invercauld in the evening.

***

They had just disembarked from the coaches, when Fergus saw Old Gilfillan approaching, the stout stick he used as a staff marking his tread. A young woman, no more than a girl, and Hamish, followed him. Hamish's head was lowered and he walked awkwardly.

After the greetings, the old man coughed and stood upright and waved towards the two youngsters. 'Yon ginger headed laddie wants to wed with one of the girls,' he said. 'I've come to ask your permission on her behalf, Findlay.'

Fergus was confused. The others laughed. Fergus pointed to his chest. 'My permission?' he asked.

'Aye, we're on your land and it is only right and proper that you are given the chance to give your blessing.'

'Look, Gilfillan ...' Fergus started, then noticed Hamish lift his head and stare at him angrily, and hesitated.

Fergus felt Fiona's hand on his arm. 'I think it would be the right thing to do,' she smiled.

Fergus turned to her.

'Go on, give your blessing to Hamish and the girl,' she encouraged.

Fergus just stared, feeling bemused.

'I'll come back when you've thought this over,' the old man said.

Fergus jerked upright. 'No, you'll not. The lassie doesn't need my *permission* but she can have my *blessing*, Gilfillan. What's more, I'll say this for Hamish, we've not always seen eye to eye but he's loyal to his friends, beyond reason at times, but loyal. He's talked of joining up again, does she ken that?'

'Aye, she does, but she says she'd rather wander after the Redcoats without a place to call her ain, than want the company of that ginger headed laddie.'

Fergus had no chance to answer before Fiona stepped forward. 'Tell her I know how she feels, Mr Gilfillan. Now, can you get that piper of yours, so that we can all dance to their betrothal?'

Old Gilfillan was about to leave, but turned back and addressed Fergus again. 'Yon Black Duncan's about, Findlay,' he said.

Fergus nodded. 'Thanks for the warning.'

Old Gilfillan frowned, and Fergus wondered what was concerning him. 'There's too many for him as long as you are together, but watch if you, or the lady Fiona, are on the road by yourselves.'

'I'll keep Bruce about, Gilfillan. He has no love for Black Duncan.'

'As you think best, yourself.'

As the old man walked off, Fergus snorted. 'My permission to marry,' he spat out. 'I'm no laird, nor never wanted to be, Fiona.'

'Then maybe your dream is not so far away from my own,' Fiona smiled.

Fergus laughed. 'Maybe you're right, Fiona. Let's go inside and see how the others are getting on, while Gilfillan sorts his piper.'

They got as far as the door, when the squawks of the pipes being charged, brought Jean dragging McNeil from the house.

It was late when they all came back and split to let the women have the house, while the men slept outside.

During the night, it grew cold and the men huddled together. They woke to a grey white world of mist. Fergus could hear someone poking a fire, and then someone coughing awake, possibly Old Gilfillan himself, but where the fire or the cougher were, was impossible to tell. He could make out where the house was but only as a thickening in the mist, a grey shadow.

He roused the others and went inside, where they found Morag had already started a pot for porridge. By the time the porridge had warmed them, the mist had turned to a drifting drizzle, sweeping in banks past the house.

Fergus was about to suggest they should stay for the day, when the bearded Gilfillan pushed open the door.

'Ye'll mind that the Redcoats were watchin'?' Gilfillan asked.

'I thought they'd given up,' Fergus admitted.

'Well' they've no', and Hamish was saying that maybe they've sent word to the captain, telling him you're here, Findlay.'

'The captain,' Tom said. 'What will he do?'

'He'll burn the place,' Gilfillan said. 'At least that's what Hamish thinks.'

Fergus nodded. 'With me in it, if he can. Tom, you and Jean can go direct to Tain. Fiona and I must take to the heather and get there by a round-about road. What about you, McNeil?'

'I'll see you safe away,' McNeil told him, taking his rifle from the thatch. 'Then come back for Morag.' He turned to the younger Gilfillan. 'Can you just keep them kind of busy 'till I get back?'

Gilfillan nodded, whether he was smiling, or glowering, was hidden in his beard.

Fergus saw Tom and Morag away, guided by one of the Gilfillan clan, before mounting a garron, taking Chestnut's reins, and leading Fiona up the hill, and through clumps of gorse. McNeil had followed, presumably to see them safely off, but as they reached a small band of trees, Fergus turned to him.

'Get back to Morag. We'll manage fine ...'

As Mc Neil nodded goodbye, the driving drizzle cleared and Fergus got a glimpse back down the hill.

'Who's that at the house?' he asked.

Before he had finished, McNeil was running.

CHAPTER 45

Morag was clearing and making ready to leave, when Black Duncan broke in through the back door, leering. 'You didn't get what you deserved the last time we met, Lady McInnes, but waiting has given me time to think about what I might enjoy,' he said, but stopped short when Morag turned with a kitchen knife in her hand.

'And I've had time to think about enjoying sticking this in your black heart,' Morag told him.

Duncan rolled his plaid round his forearm, laughing as he tucked the ends in. 'You might be fine on a bit of meat, Morag McInnes, but I've been in more knife fights than you've cut open rabbits. I like my whores to struggle and wriggle a bit, so I'll not do you over much harm until you've been served properly, like any cow.'

As Duncan took a step forward, Morag moved behind the table with the fire behind her.

Duncan didn't bother to try going round the table, he simply turned it over.

As he took a grip of the table, Morag grabbed the pot hanging on its hook over the fire and threw it at Duncan. He dodged it easily and began to move round the overturned table.

McNeil burst in thorough the door and hit Duncan with the butt of his rifle. As Duncan dropped, McNeil turned to Morag. 'Dear God, I thought I'd lost you,' he gasped.

Morag was moving towards him, when they heard the sound of marching feet and shouted commands.

'Come out, come out, Findlay, you can't hide for ever,' a voice called.

Morag followed McNeil out of the front door, to be faced with a troop of Redcoats and a mounted officer.

'What's this? An armed man,' the officer shouted. 'Take his weapon, sergeant.'

The sergeant came to face McNeil. They looked into each other's eyes, a whole unspoken conversation taking place until the sergeant said quietly, 'Better let me take it, he'll shoot you and the girl if you don't.'

'Bring it here, sergeant,' the officer ordered. 'An army rifle, by Jove. A deserter, most like.'

'I have my discharge, Captain. Issued after Waterloo, if you'd care to see it.'

'No, I wouldn't, probably forged anyway. Light the roof, Sergeant.'

'There's someone inside,' Morag protested, pointing at the open door.

'Probably one of his chums, maybe even Findlay,' the officer said, as the sergeant hesitated. 'Hopefully, it's Findlay.'

'You can't burn it down,' Morag shouted. 'It belongs to Fergus Findlay. It's private property.'

The sergeant hesitated again.

'Get on with it man. He's a rebel, a damned Jacobite and the property forfeit. We'll collect those cattle as well.'

'Those are cattle other crofters have brought here for Fergus to drove. They're not his,' Morag shouted.

'We'll take them anyway,' the captain sneered. 'If they want them back they can come and pay for them. Now, what are you waiting for, Sergeant? Get on with it!'

To Morag's horror, the sergeant struck a flint into a tinderbox, blew the tinder into a small flame, from which he lit several torches.

'There's someone inside,' McNeil shouted.

'Light the roof,' the Captain ordered.

Several torches were flung on to the roof and the thatch started to flame and crackle. In what seemed seconds, the roof was a mass of flame; it gave a whump and collapsed as a scream came from under it.

'One less of your damned friends to worry about,' the officer said.

Morag could only stare.

'He might have been a murderer and a womaniser,' Morag shouted. 'But ...' She hesitated as she felt McNeil's hand on her arm.

'His name was Black Duncan and he was some kind of friend of Maitland's,' McNeil told the captain. 'Perhaps you'll let Mr Maitland know you burned him – Sir.'

The captain's face reddened. 'Don't get impertinent with me, whoever you are. If it wasn't that I wanted to get out of this infernal rain, I'd have you thrashed, understand?'

McNeil came to attention. 'Yes, sir. I'll mind my manners in future.'

'Leave someone here in case Findlay's stupid enough to come back, Sergeant. Then follow me,' the officer muttered as he wheeled his horse and rode back along the track.

'Sorry about your rifle,' the sergeant told McNeil.

***

As the rain cleared, Fergus dismounted and was standing beside Fiona's stirrup when Bruce's bark drew Fergus's attention to the sound of hoof beats. Suspecting it was the Redcoat captain coming, Fergus slapped Chestnut's rump to send him into the trees.

Fergus waited until the captain's head appeared over the brow of the hill, before pushing into the copse and going in the opposite direction to Fiona, dragging his own pony's reins behind him.

The captain was soon close. Fergus dodged between the trees, trying to confuse his pursuer but without success.

He could hear the charger's heavy breathing.

As he dodged round a fir, he dragged its long lower branch after him, then released them into the charger's face. The charger shied away and Fergus dropped his pony's reins, letting it stand as an obstruction and raced out of the trees.

'Halloo,' Fergus heard behind him, and looked over his shoulder, to see the captain, sabre drawn, racing across the grass towards him. Fergus ran on towards a ditch that flooding rainwater had cut into the hillside. It looked deep enough to keep him clear of the swinging sabre but he knew he was losing ground.

'Gone away,' the captain shouted, laughing.

Fergus was ten yards from the ditch when he saw Bruce coming at a run. The black dog jumped high on the edge of the charger's vision. Whether the charger was new to its job, or the flying Bruce with his legs spread wide looked like a bear to the charger, Fergus didn't know, but as he tumbled into the ditch, he caught a glimpse of the charger rearing and twisting, throwing the captain out of the saddle. The captain bounced on the edge of the ditch and fell into it, his sabre getting entangled with his legs.

Fergus turned to face the Redcoat, but saw he was struggling with his cloak and sabre as he climbed out of the ditch. As the captain drew his cloak back to free his legs, Fergus saw a red stain spreading over the captain's white breeches at his groin.

The captain looked down, then, in terror, at Fergus. 'Dear God, I'm bleeding to death,' he muttered. He took a few steps forward. 'Help me, help me,' he pleaded, sitting down against the wall of the ditch.

'What is it?' Fergus heard and looked round to see McNeil standing holding the captain's horse.

'He got tangled with his sabre when he fell off, and cut himself in the groin.'

'Help me,' the captain pleaded. 'I don't want to die. It's cold, can you light a fire?'

McNeil returned Fergus's gaze, and shook his head.

'Hold my hand, Mother,' the captain said as he fell back against the ditch wall.

In a few more minutes, he was dead.

Fiona came to the ditch.

'We can't hide this, Neil. Get your rifle from the horse and give it to Fiona,' Fergus told McNeil.

McNeil glanced about to see if there was anyone watching.

'Give it to her,' Fergus insisted.

McNeil took the rifle from the boot on the charger and gave it to Fiona.

'Now we must find the Redcoats and let them have their captain,' Fergus said. 'But first, you must get away from here, Fiona. God knows what will come of this, and it's better you're not involved.'

'I can tell them he was chasing you with his sword out,' Fiona insisted.

'No! Whatever happens, I want you safe. There's no reason to worry about me. Now go, go to Babs if I'm delayed. I'll join you there.'

Fergus and McNeil loaded the captain's corpse on to his charger. The smell of blood upset the animal and it skittered a bit but Fergus calmed it.

Fergus and McNeil walked the nervous charger back to where they estimated the Redcoats would be. They had just started on the downward slope, when three breathless Redcoats came toiling towards them.

'Your captain fell from his horse, cut himself with his sabre and bled to death,' Fergus told them.

'He couldn't have. We were right behind him and saw him chasing someone,' one of the trio shouted. Fergus noticed he had one stripe on his arm.

'Whether he was chasing someone or not, Corporal, he fell off his horse and sliced the artery in his groin, and just bled to death. I've seen it before, in Spain.' McNeil insisted.

'No, he didn't. It was you he was chasing,' the corporal shouted, pointing at Fergus. 'You killed him,' the corporal insisted. 'Take him prisoner,' he ordered the other two.

When they joined the rest of the Redcoats, Fergus found they were herding the batch of unwilling cattle along the road.

'I've arrested this man for murdering the captain,' the corporal told the sergeant.

'He fell off his horse and cut himself with his sword in the groin and bled to death,' Fergus told the sergeant.

The harassed, red-faced sergeant looked at the captain's body, at Fergus, at the corporal, at the unruly cattle. 'Bring him along, Corporal, we'll let the sheriff sort it out,' he ordered.

The corporal grinned and prodded Fergus with his musket. The motion seemed to remind the corporal of McNeil's rifle. 'Where's the rifle,' he demanded.

'The captain must have lost it when he was chasing me through the trees,' Fergus told him.

'You've stolen it, haven't you?' the corporal shouted at McNeil. 'I'll arrest you too, as a thief.'

The sergeant intervened. 'We've enough problems already, Corporal. A lost rifle, that didn't belong to the captain anyway, will just complicate things. Let the man go,' he ordered.

'But, Sarge,' the corporal protested.

'You two,' the sergeant ordered, talking to the corporal's companions, 'help with these damn cows and let that other man go.'

As McNeil stepped away, Fergus called to him. 'Get word to Tom.'

'Move,' the corporal told Fergus, prodding with his musket and Fergus, still leading the charger, moved forward after the cattle.

***

It was growing dark by the time Fergus and his escort reached Tain.

'Dalmighty, what's all this now, Findlay?' the sheriff demanded, standing in his nightshirt at his door and holding a lantern over his head.

'I've arrested this man for murder,' the corporal told him.

'The captain was riding through some trees, fell off his horse ...' Fergus started to explain.

'Shut your mouth,' the corporal ordered, hitting Fergus with the butt of his musket.

'*Stop that*,' the sheriff ordered. 'I'll not have any prisoner of mine misused.'

The corporal looked astounded, but stepped back.

'Now, it seems to me, we have a dead body and that means an inquest.'

'He killed him,' the corporal insisted. 'He should hang.'

Fergus started to protest but the sheriff snapped. 'The inquest will decide how he died, laddie. In the meantime, keep your opinions to yourself. Take the body and Findlay to the jail. I'll be there as soon as I'm dressed.'

***

Under the glowers of the corporal, Fergus waited at the jail until the sheriff came waddling along.

'Put him in the cell,' the sheriff ordered.

'In you get,' the corporal told Fergus prodding hard with the musket. 'You'll dance on the gallows, Highlander,' he laughed.

'You're wearing the King's uniform, corporal,' the sheriff rasped. 'Behave as if you thought it was an honour, or I'll report you for disorderly conduct.'

The corporal scowled and closed the cell door on Fergus.

Fergus was actually relieved to have the cell door between him and the corporal, and was able to smile as the irritated sheriff turned on the corporal. 'Now I'll need to get someone to guard him. What the devil were you thinking of, bringing Fergus Findlay here, corporal?' he complained.

The corporal scowled at the sheriff. 'He's a murderer and needs to be locked up.'

'Findlay! Needs to be locked up! He could have disappeared into the hills any time he wanted this last week, but he hung around because there was a case pending.'

'He could be shot on sight for killing the captain.'

The sheriff sighed.

'We'd best keep you locked up, Findlay, before some buffoon starts taking pot shots at you, eh?', he muttered as he scrabbled in a drawer in a table outside the cell, found a key, tried it in the lock, found it worked, and locked Fergus in.

'Well, you've done your duty, Corporal. You can go and sleep the sleep of the righteous. I'll arrange for a guard.'

'I can stay here. He might try to escape,' the corporal said.

The look on the corporal's face made Fergus worry, but the worry was dispelled when the sheriff answered. 'And you could shoot him in the attempt. No, get you away to your bed. I'll see he's guarded.'

The corporal left and Fergus watched as the sheriff rubbed his chin in thought until they heard a yell, followed by a scuffle and a growl.

'Bruce,' Fergus said.

The sheriff nodded. 'That dog o' yours is the best guard I can give you while I find somebody to sit and make it look as if you're under arrest.'

***

After Fergus take the captain's body away and made her her way back to Ault-na-main on her own.

'Where's Fergus?' Babs asked.

When Fiona had explained, Babs looked serious. 'No good will come of this, I'm thinking, but you never know, sometimes it's the worst that brings the best, lassie, like the rain and the harvest.'

Partly comforted by Babs comments and partly worried by them, Fiona lay awake. A knock on the door and McNeil's voice brought her out to investigate.

'Fergus has been taken to the sheriff and locked up, Fiona. I spoke to the sheriff, who told me he'd done it to make sure the Redcoat corporal didn't shoot Fergus and claim he was escaping. I also had a word with the sergeant of the troop, and he promised he'd keep the corporal in hand. I'll go now and tell Tom.'

From then, Fiona's sleep was disturbed and peopled with dreams, dreams of seeing Fergus but never able to get close to him, dreams of Maitland laughing, dreams of her father rubbing his hands, and she woke unrefreshed.

She spent the day getting angry, and Babs felt the need to add something to Fiona's bowl of broth to allow her to rest. Whatever it had done, Fiona woke next day with the determination to go to the sheriff and arrange a legal wedding between herself and Fergus. In her own mind, they had been made man and wife among the glens and mountains, but that meant nothing in the eyes of the law. She'd have to see him anyway, for the signing of the various papers.

CHAPTER 46

Fiona washed and dressed with care and was almost finished her toilet when Morag came.

'I thought you were taking care of Invercauld?' Fiona asked.

'There's nothing to take care of any more. The house has no roof and the Redcoats took the cattle people had brought for Fergus to drove. Besides, I wanted to ask Babs about McNeil.'

Fiona smiled. 'What does Babs know about McNeil?'

'Well, when we came with Fergus, she told me McNeil would be the father of my bairns, but he keeps talking of going off to Canada. I'm not ready for a baby, Fiona, not yet, not so soon after that girl.'

'What's this I hear of Canada?' Babs asked, coming in from her chores.

'Morag wants to know if she'll have McNeil's bairns here, or in Canada,' Fiona said.

Babs brows gathered. 'I never said McNeil would father her bairns, just that the father would be a fine man. It was her own silly head that jumped to conclusions at the first fine man she met.'

Babs looked at Fiona as she spoke, and Fiona was taken by surprise at the twinkle deep in Bab's glance. Had Babs been more concerned with giving Morag something to take her mind off her troubles than making a prediction? Had Babs been concerned that Morag would throw herself at the first chance of comfort, rather than wait for a decent man?

Babs interrupted Fiona's thoughts. 'I've got things to do, and if you have any sense, the two of you will find something useful to do, instead of making gossip. In fact, I'm in need of an assistant to keep up with that Jean's orders. You could be helping me, Morag McInnes, instead of running about looking for a fine man to have your bairns.'

Fiona intervened. 'I have to go to sign some papers at the sheriff's office, and I was thinking of trying to get him to make my marriage to Fergus legal, Babs.'

Babs cocked her head on one side. 'That's a fine idea, Fiona McRae. Tell that fool I'll put a curse on his cows if he refuses,' she added, cackling.

'It's a fair walk,' Morag pointed out.

'There's chestnut, and Fergus's garrons here, Morag,' Fiona pointed out.

'That horse of yours will attract plenty of attention, Fiona.'

Fiona nodded. 'Maybe we should take the garrons. Even then, it will look odd for two females to ride into Tain on their own.'

At that point, Old Gilfillan walked in.

'Who the devil are you?' Babs demanded.

'I've come to see the laird's lady, not to blether with …' was as far as the old man got, before the astonished women burst out laughing.

Fiona began to feel guilty as the old man drew himself up to his full height. He was still shorter than Fiona, but his stiffening seemed to give him dignity. 'With your permission, Miss Fiona, I'd like to talk, but no' in front of these others,' he said.

'Come outside then, Mr Gilfillan,' Fiona answered.

Outside the old man took off his Glengarry and slapped it against his leg, as if to clear the dust of his journey. 'Miss Fiona,' he began. 'It is not seemly for a lady like yourself to be going about without an attendant and, since our good laird ...'

'You mean Fergus?'

'Aye, just him.'

'I don't know that he'd be too pleased at being called a laird, Mr Gilfillan.'

'Maybe so, but what else am I to call him, Miss Fiona? It is all very well for the younger generation to be free with names but, for myself, I prefer to keep my station.'

Fiona smiled, and the old man began again. 'I know there is that deaf laddie, but I was thinking it would be better to have someone who can hear, since the dog is with the laird himself.'

You want to be my servant? Fiona was about to ask when, seeing the pride in the old man's stance, changed her mind. 'You'd like to offer your services as a retainer. Is that it, Mr Gilfillan?'

The old man smiled. 'Just that, Miss Fiona, a retainer.'

Back inside, Fiona explained to Babs and Morag.

'Dinna belittle him, Fiona McRae,' Babs warned. 'But dinna take it lightly either. He's offered to put his life in your hands as much as he's offered to take yours in his.'

'Then I'd best take him with me to Tain and introduce him to Fergus,' Fiona said.

'If you have a body guard, Fiona, I might just stay here with Babs,' Morag said.

They made a little procession as they wended their way to Tain; Fiona on one of the garrons, the old man walking beside Fiona, Davie walking behind, leading another garron. The old man refused either to ride, or allow Davie to ride, but stepped out smartly, his long staff marking his steps.

'A strange thing has happened, Miss Fiona, something I think you should know about, and maybe tell that Tom Abernethy as well. He's a shrewd man, is that Tom. Yon Hamish loon has stopped talking about the soldiers, even when I asked him to his face what they were about. He wanted to join them, and I'm wondering if he's with them more than he's with yourself, now.'

'Maybe he just has nothing to tell,' Fiona ventured.

'Maybe you are right, but he was thick with that corporal.'

As they got into Tain, the old man took Fiona's pony's rein and led it to Tom's lodgings.

***

Half an hour later, Fiona and Tom were in the Sheriff's office, facing Maitland across the table.

'You've all read the documents,' the sheriff asked.

The others nodded.

The sheriff put his hand on the document on his right. 'This here is the deed of transfer of the farm Kirklea to Mearns Mining. Mr Maitland assures me it is a legal entity, but, as you'll see, he is named as the principal officer.'

The sheriff put his hand on the document on his left. 'This is Mr Maitland's agreement not to proceed with either the breach of promise case against Miss McRae, or the alienation case against Mr Findlay. Are you satisfied?'

he asked, looking first at Maitland, who nodded, then at Tom, who nodded, then at Fiona, who sat forward.

'I'd like it to be added that the promissory notes Mr Maitland has given me are all he has in his possession, no, all, ever one of my father's notes that he has ever acquired.'

'I have other business to attend to and I hardly think ...' Maitland began.

'I insist,' Fiona told the sheriff.

'You'll have to wait for it to be written in,' the sheriff pointed out.

'We'll wait,' Tom answered.

'While we're waiting, perhaps I could talk to you in private about another matter?' Fiona asked the sheriff.

'One thing at a time, lassie. Once this business is complete, and Mr Maitland has rushed off about his other business.'

'Then may I see Fergus?'

'Of course, before you start quoting Habeas Corpus, or anything else, Mr Abernethy, I'm only holding him for his own protection.'

***

As Fiona entered the jail, Fergus rose from his mattress.

'Are you all right? Is there anything I can bring?' Fiona asked.

'No, I'm just waiting until the inquest tomorrow. As far as I know, no one else saw what happened, so the coroner has no option but accept what I say.'

'No other witnesses *as far as you know, Fergus!*' Tom pointed out, making Fiona worry.

'Who else could there be?' Fergus asked.

'Maitland is still about, Fergus,' Tom pointed out. 'Nothing is cut and dried, as long as he's about.'

Fiona put a hand on Tom's arm. 'Old Gilfillan insisted I tell you that Hamish had stopped talking about what the soldiers were doing, Tom. I've no idea why, except that he mentioned Hamish was thick with the corporal.'

It made Tom frown. 'Hamish was thick with Maitland at one time as well, and wanted to join up. I wonder if he saw the captain chase you, Fergus?'

'Surely Hamish would tell the truth?' Fiona put in.

She grew even more concerned when Tom asked. 'Would he really? Maybe the price of joining up is being a witness who saw Fergus kill the captain. How badly does he hate you, Fergus?'

'He tried to kill me, but that was a while ago,' Fergus pointed out. 'I'll not say he's been friendly, but I thought he'd accepted me.'

They were interrupted by the sheriff's clerk.

Back in his office, the sheriff insisted they read the newly prepared document again, before signing.

'Now, all that remains is for Mr Maitland to hand over the promissory notes and we can be finished,' the sheriff told them.

Maitland handed over several papers and Fiona watched as he left.

'Now, what was this other matter,' the sheriff asked.

Fiona looked directly at him. 'I want to legitimise my marriage to Fergus Findlay,' she said clearly.

The sheriff's eyebrows shot up. 'Eh?'

'I want to solemnise the marriage between Fergus Findlay and myself, your honour,' Fiona repeated.

'Well, the man's a prisoner, I ...'

'But not a criminal,' Fiona pointed out. 'Not found guilty of any crime.'

The sheriff rubbed his chin frowning. 'How old are you?' he asked in the end.

'I'm nineteen,' Fiona told him.

'Have you got your father's permission for this?'

'Not yet, but I will,' Fiona answered with more certainty than she felt.

'I'll think on it,' the sheriff told her.

Fiona nodded. 'In the meantime, maybe you'll keep these promissory notes for me?' she asked.

The sheriff looked doubtful.

'I can hardly give them to Fergus while he's in your jail, but you can keep them for him until he's released.'

The sheriff looked at her for several moments before breaking into a grin. 'You and I know Findlay would never stoop to using these to pressure your father into giving permission for you to marry, but your father has another opinion of Findlay maybe?'

Fiona smiled back. 'It's possible,' she said, taking Tom's arm and preparing to leave.

'What about Gilfillan?' Tom asked.

Fiona sobered.

'Best tell Fergus,' Tom suggested.

Fiona stood in front of the bars, unsmiling, and Fergus began to frown. 'Bad news?' he asked.

'It depends on how you look at it, Fergus. Old Gilfillan thinks you're his laird.'

Fergus threw up his hands.

'And I'm your lady and, according to Mr Gilfillan, should have a retainer, at least while you're in jail.'

Fergus just stared.

'He's an old man, Fergus ...' Fiona started, and was surprised by Fergus's reaction.

'Do you know what he's saying, Fiona?'

'That he wants to be a kind of servant.' Fiona answered.

'No, he's offering his unqualified service. If anyone or anything threatens you, he will see it as his duty to kill, or destroy them, or it. He's a traditional Highlander, Fiona, and gives his loyalty without reservation. If you can accept that responsibility, I'll be glad to have him as part of our family.'

'I'd no idea it was so ... so ... desperate, Fergus, or I'd have turned him away.'

'You didn't turn me away.'

'You're my husband, Fergus. And you'd not kill anyone. Not unless they were going to kill us.'

'These are the Highlands, Fiona, where promises and loyalty are given with the understanding that they may have to be honoured in blood. There are no half measures here, neither in love, nor honour, lass.'

'What should I do?' Fiona asked.

To her surprise Fergus laughed. 'He'll make a fine grandfather in the future, if we get him a decent kilt and a plaid. Imagine what Jean will make of him in Glasgow?'

Fiona smiled. 'I love you, Fergus Findlay,' she told him.

* * *

Fergus had settled down, smiling at the thought of Old Gilfillan and Jean, when Bruce rose from his spot near the door and licked the hand of the man the sheriff had put on guard, dozing in the chair. The man was startled but smiled and ruffled Bruce's ears, then turned and rose at a knock to open the door to McNeil and Morag.

Fergus smiled, but there was no answering one from McNeil. 'I've had a letter from Mary's oldest boy,' McNeil explained.

'In Canada?'

'In Canada. It seems Sinclair died on the way across. Mary and the boys kept with the group, and are setting up with them. The trouble is, they can't start a farm because the work of clearing the forest is too heavy for either Mary, or the two boys. She's baking and keeping going. But the lad wondered when I was joining them.'

'So you're both off to Canada?'

'No,' Morag told him. 'He's going to join Mary, and I'll not play gooseberry to that. Babs wants me to be a kind of apprentice to her. Not just for the weaving, but for the healing as well. She seems to think that how I felt over the baby dying was some kind of sign, and I should learn to help save lives. She said once you'd lost one baby, you wanted to love them all. Do you think she lost her own?'

'Babs is not always right,' Fergus cautioned. 'Have a care that you're not being led into something you're not comfortable with. I thought you wanted bairns and a family?'

'It just feels right, Fergus,' Morag told him. 'I don't think I could manage to keep a bairn in me for nine months right now. I'd be terrified I was going to die, and Meg says that affects the bairn. It comes out terrified of being away from its mother.'

'And Canada?' Fergus asked.

'That was my father's dream. In a way, this healing Babs wants to teach me, is just as much going into a wilderness. It's so mysterious.'

McNeil smiled. 'Do what you think is right, Morag. I might not be much of a catch as a husband, but I'm not a bad big brother.'

'I couldn't have asked for a better, Neil McNeil,' Morag smiled.

Fergus turned to McNeil. 'So, Neil, do you wait until I come out after the inquest, or are you off with those beasts from Invercauld to Easter Ross, and meet us at Fort William on our way to Glasgow?'

'The soldiers took the beasts and I have no money to go without you, Fergus,' McNeil pointed out.

'Then I'll give you as many notes as you need, Neil. You're my friend, remember. Oh, come on, we can split the profit if you insist on paying me back. Tell Jean to get loads of Babs' things made up, ready for us going.'

That seemed to satisfy Neil. 'Young Gilfillan tells me he has been on droves in the past but not across to the east and down that way to Fort William. I remember the way you went but some of the places you stopped were off the main track, and I don't know if I could find them.'

'The first from here is just ...'

As they started discussing resting places, Morag left and went to the hotel to talk to Jean.

Having settled the route, McNeil got ready to leave. 'I just feel I'm leaving you at a time you might need me, Fergus.'

'Need you for what?'

'Just for protection. Maitland's still about, and the inquest into the captain's death is in two days.'

'I'm the only witness, Neil. They have to accept what I say.'

'Maitland's still about, Fergus. Don't think he'll not try something, with maybe Hamish, or that corporal.'

'Even if Hamish saw what happened, it would only confirm my own story.'

'If he tells the truth, Fergus. Remember he swore he'd kill you. He's a Highlander, like you and me. An oath's an oath, Fergus. He doesn't have to do it himself. He just has to have a hand in it.'

'You think he's still carries that?'

'He's an odd lad, Fergus. I think he was a fine soldier, but fine soldiers can be loose cannons without the army's authority to tell them what to think.'

CHAPTER 47

Towards evening, Fergus's dozing was interrupted by Tom bursting in. 'Maitland's dead,' he announced. 'The corporal and Hamish were standing talking to him on the edge of town, when Bruce came running, barking and growling. Maitland apparently drew a pistol and Bruce turned tail. Maitland ran after him. The other two heard a shot as they saw Maitland trip. When Maitland didn't get up, they went to see why, and found him dead. His pistol had been fired and they seem to think he must have tripped and the gun went off.'

'Were there powder burns on his body?' Fergus asked.

'He'd shot himself through the mouth,' Tom explained. 'He must have had his mouth wide open, yelling at Bruce.'

'One shot?'

'That's what they heard.'

Fergus grinned. He'd seen shooting like that once before, from a rifle.

***

Late next day, Fiona came to stay in Tain overnight, until the inquest. When she came to the cell, she was hardly able to contain her excitement.

'Fergus, I have my father's consent for us to be married by the sheriff.'

'So he's come round has he?'

'He's still not too fond of you, Fergus, but give him time. He's a new man under Meg. I don't know why he tried to be a farmer.'

'To please your mother, Fiona. Was she bonny?'

'Her smile was like …'

'I know, Fiona. Like yours,' Fergus told her, smiling at her sudden blushes.

'I've had a word with the sheriff,' she said. 'And he's agreed to have a formal marriage ceremony,' she told Fergus. 'Aren't you excited?'

'Of course. Where is your father? I must thank him when I get out of here.'

'He's with the sheriff right now, laying charges against the corporal. You know about Maitland shooting himself?'

Fergus nodded.

'Well, it seems Maitland didn't hand over all the IOU's, and the corporal lifted them from his body after the shooting. He came round to Ault-na-main at darkening, and demanded money from my father. I was there and he had his musket with the bayonet on the end and prodded Father with it. Father didn't have any money to give him, so he turned on me.'

'Threatened you?'

'I won't go into details, Fergus, but then Angus came in.'

'Angus?'

'Angus Gilfillan, our retainer,' Fiona said.

'He tackled the corporal?'

Fiona smiled. 'He saved me from a fate worse than death, as they say. The corporal took his bayonet and was pointing it at me and ordering me to … well … anyway, Angus warned him, but the corporal just laughed, and went for Angus. I don't know what happened really, but Angus hit him on the hand with that staff of his. The corporal dropped the musket and turned on Angus. The next I knew, the corporal was on the ground, and Angus was standing over him with his staff, ready to hit the corporal in the throat. I managed to stop him, and the corporal ran off, not before Angus gave him one or two clouts about the head. I think he broke the corporal's nose. It was bleeding anyway.'

Fergus laughed. 'Old Angus has been dealing with laddies for fifty years, Fiona, and his father, or his grandfather, was maybe at Flodden, and raised him to answer the fiery cross for all we know.'

***

Fergus was preparing for sleep, when Bruce growled, the door to the jail opened, and the sheriff pushed the corporal through.

Bruce stood, back hairs bristling.

'Leave him, Bruce,' Fergus ordered. Bruce looked round at Fergus and grunted, but turned back to watch the corporal.

'Give me the keys,' the sheriff ordered the guard. 'This one's to go in, and the other out. If we left the pair o' them in together, they'd most likely kill each other and save us the trouble of hanging later, but it wouldna look weel, so we'll just do a swap.'

The corporal swore. 'Let me in the cell with him for half an hour,' he demanded.

The sheriff opened the cell door and waved Fergus out. The corporal stepped forward aggressively. Fergus slapped him twice in the face and the corporal stepped back in alarm.

'Get inside before Findlay gets angry,' the sheriff ordered.

Bruce growled, and the corporal stepped into the cell. The sheriff locked him in, before turning to Fergus. 'Your lassie said you were making for Glasgow after the inquest. I'll be glad to see the back o' you this time, Findlay.'

'He'll be in here after the inquest,' the corporal shouted. 'Someone saw him kill the captain.'

***

For the inquest, the big room was half empty, but, coming in with Tom and Fiona and Jean, Fergus could see Hamish among those sitting waiting. He also noticed the Redcoat sergeant in full dress and nodded acquaintance to him.

The sheriff came in.

'This is not a trial, so you'll not need Abernethy taking us wandering half round Scotland, Fergus Findlay. All we have to do is establish how the captain died. I've been informed there was another witness, but we'll take your testimony first.'

'It had been raining ...' Fergus started.

'Dammit, I'm no' interested in the weather, Findlay, just tell me what happened.'

Fergus explained.

'Have you got all that?' the sheriff asked the clerk.

'Aye, yer honour, I have.'

'Then let's hear this other witness. This Hamish ...'

'It's me, sir,' Hamish said, standing.

'Come forward, then, and let's hear what you have to say,' the sheriff ordered. He looked at the clerk. 'I'll tell you when you need to start makin' notes again,' he said, before turning back to Hamish. 'I understand it was you that was with that corporal, when Mr Maitland shot himself?'

348

'That's right, sir,' Hamish answered and Fergus grew concerned.

'And did the corporal take anything from the body? Money or anything?'

'Just a few wee bits of papers, sir.'

'He's in my jail accused of trying to blackmail an old man named McRae,' the sheriff said.

Fergus noted that surprised Hamish.

'You didna ken that?' the sheriff asked.

'No, sir.'

Fergus noticed a wry smile come to the sheriff's lips, and wondered what he was up to.

'Well, it has left the sergeant without a corporal. He needs to get a new one but, unfortunately, there's not one of his privates has any experience, so, he might have to recruit a suitable man, a man that kens the army, if you see what I mean?'

'Yes sir,' Hamish answered, frowning uncertainly.

'Naturally, he'll want somebody that tells the truth,' the sheriff said, making Fergus grin. 'Now tell us what you saw the day the captain died,' the sheriff continued.

Hamish stood still.

'There's no need to be frightened, Hamish, you're no' under oath,' the sheriff encouraged, smiling, but grew serious. 'But if there was a trial, you'd have to tell your story again. Then it would be under oath, and you'd be expected to tell the same story as you're going to tell us now.'

Hamish looked round, glaring at Fergus, then frowning as his gaze flitted past to the sergeant.

'Just the truth,' the sheriff repeated. 'The clerk will write it down for you, then you can have a talk with the sergeant there.'

'I saw the captain chase F … Findlay. The captain had his sword and was wavin' it and shoutin'. Findlay dived into a d … ditch and the captain fell in after him.' Hamish looked at the sergeant, stiffened, and spoke with clarity. 'The ditch was deep and I couldna see what happened in there, but then McNeil came runnin'. They lifted the captain on to his horse and took him to the Redcoats. That's when the corporal arrested him.'

'That was good clear evidence, Hamish,' the sheriff said. 'It seems to me that the captain, who ordered the house at Invercauld to be burned without a warrant, and subsequently tried to kill Findlay, died accidentally, falling from his horse and cutting the artery in his groin.'

The sheriff turned to look in the sergeant's direction. 'The cattle you took from Invercauld under orders from the captain belonged to others. Will you see to having them returned, or must I have them collected?'

The sergeant stood. 'I'll see to it, your honour.'

Epilogue

Jean insisted Fergus and Fiona came with Tom and herself so that Fiona could enjoy the winter season in Glasgow. Fiona insisted she wanted to see to the new house, but promised they would come down for the Spring Ball.

Jean insisted Davie go with her to learn more about weaving and design and Fergus, thinking the new canal would put an end to droving and Davie needed another trade, let him go.

Tom and Jean met McNeil at Fort William and he looked only mildly surprised when told that Maitland was dead, but not surprised that Hamish had been taken into the army as a corporal.

Printed in Great Britain
by Amazon

76835694R00210